G581: Mars

Gliese 581g, Volume 2

Christine D. Shuck

Published by Christine D. Shuck, 2021.

G581: MARS

First edition. February 15, 2021.

ISBN: 978-1393866244

Written by Christine D. Shuck.

Table of Contents

Incident in Philly

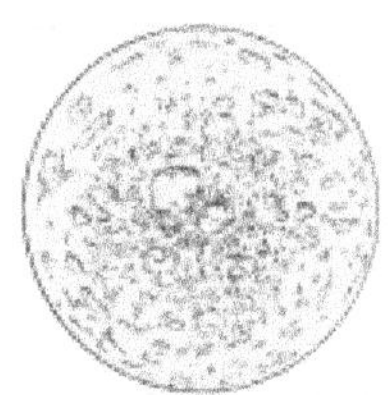

Mars Year 7, Week 18, Day 176
(Earth Date 02.05.2086)

"You can't keep doing this, Selena," Gwen said, her face disapproving. "It will cause problems, big ones, between you and Stan, John, hell, even Toya."

Selena looked away, unable to meet Gwen's eyes. Her friend was trying to help, but she didn't understand, not at all, and Selena chose silence rather than pointless arguing. She had met Gwen during orientation and training, the six-week program that had tested and trained them all on what to expect when they arrived at the red planet. The two had instantly bonded, which was shocking when Selena realized that, apart from the occasional childhood friend, she had had no female friends in over a decade. When was there time, after all? She had gotten pregnant with Toya while she and Stan were still in college. And then there had been the fines, imposed on any unauthorized pregnancies in New York, along with the outrageously expensive rent on their tiny, three-hundred-square-foot efficiency apartment in the massive high rise in Queens. Between both of them working full-time jobs, commuting, Selena trying to take the occasional class in order to get a degree in a few more years, and the additional early-education classes for Toya, there had been no time for friends, no time for much of anything, really.

That had all changed when Stan had sent in the application for Mars citizenship. They had the perfect combination, it seemed, his engineering skills and, inexplicably unless you had met her, Toya. At nearly five years of age, she could already speak five languages fluently, could read and write in three, and had apparently inherited her father's mad engineering skills. Selena had been superfluous, really. Even if she were smarter than the average citizen, she didn't have the off-the-charts I.Q. that her husband, much less her daughter, had. She had felt lucky, resentful, nervous, and intimidated all rolled into one the day she had met Gwen.

Gwen, who had suffered from early childhood cancer and rendered barren by the cancer treatments, had instantly brought Selena into her inner circle. She adored Toya, and Selena felt as if she had suddenly gained a sister, something she had longed for, raised in a family with two brothers, one older and one younger.

Gwen had been in Cryo, along with Stan and Toya, on the long journey from Earth to Mars, whilst Selena had been awake. It was the one way that the Antes family could avoid having to pay a significant fee for the emigration to their new world, since Selena didn't have any of the higher-level skills that would benefit the Mars colony. Instead, she had worked under the Juniper's Maintenance Manager, helped clean, prepare meals, and, in case of illness, was a backup to the ship's Medical Officer. Basically, she was a girl Friday. It wasn't a sexy job, but someone had to do it, and it meant that, once they arrived on the red planet, they would have a full Family Hab, one that comprised nearly four times the space they had in New York, with the potential for more add-ons if they ended up with more children. And on Mars, children were *welcomed,* not discouraged. This was a pleasant departure from the culturally and financially enforced One Child Act that the Reformed United States, Canada, and independent city states Alaska, Texas, and Hawaii had all implemented in recent years to alleviate the burgeoning population explosion.

It wasn't how Selena had envisioned her life going. In college, she had dreamed of a career in the medical field, specifically, the field of life extension, which was on the cusp of ensuring that humans could live forever. It was a field of study fraught with controversy, especially in their currently overpopulated world, which was one reason she wasn't particularly interested in having children, at least not right away. Some part of her had thought it would happen eventually, perhaps in her mid-to-late thirties. Not when she was still in college with years to go until she earned her degree.

But she had met Stan, and one thing had led to another. A few days between prescription refills and, surprise, she was pregnant. It had been Stan who had wanted Toya, arguing that he would hold down three jobs and go to school at the same time if that was what it took for Selena to keep the baby growing inside of her. Selena had agreed, although many times since wished she had gotten those promises in writing. Stan had quickly reneged on them, citing the need to finish his schooling rather than hold down so many jobs. That had meant that *she* ended up dropping out of college, and she had also had to work, right up until she felt labor pains at eight and a half months into her pregnancy. Stan had been smitten with Toya, so much so that Selena often wondered if he loved her half as much as he did their daughter.

All of those feelings, all the sacrifices and struggle, and trying to afford the special classes Stan insisted that Toya needed in order to "fulfill her potential" had weighed on Selena until it felt as if her back would break. The chance at a better life, even if it meant living in domes and never stepping foot outside in the thin, unforgiving Martian atmosphere, had been the only escape she could see to a lifetime of drudgery, of being second, no, third class, and so she had gone along with it.

But in those quiet hours and days of the space flight to Mars, which then stretched into weeks and months, Selena struggled with it. Alone, without her husband or daughter, who were quietly and comfortably snoozing for the six months it took to make the journey while Selena worked at menial shit jobs all so she could earn a more comfortable place for them at their destination. It had grated on her. What about *her* dreams?

Perhaps that was why she had allowed herself the dalliance. Not once had she looked at another man, not once in nearly six years. But John Snelling, who spent his days preparing unique experiments in zero-grav, had taken an interest in her. First, he had asked her when she would work out in the exercise cube, which wasn't a cube so much as a large wheel, not dissimilar from a massive, human-sized hamster wheel. A requirement of one hour per day for every crew member on duty, it had helped belay the effects of the zero-gravity on board the USS Juniper.

Later he had asked her point blank to come back to his bunk with him. The bunks were narrow for one person, nearly impossible for two, but they had made it work, the dark curtains down on all sides, and he had made her scream with pleasure. It was something that had embarrassed her later, knowing any of John's nearest bunkmates could hear them going at it like rabbits. And go after it like rabbits they did, for weeks and weeks, until Mars grew larger in the viewscreen.

Reality set in. She had a husband and a child. This was no time to end a marriage, especially if she didn't want to end up on a return journey, scrubbing the toilets and returning to an even smaller apartment. They made them small, little more than a bed and a strip of floor 60 centimeters wide. Alone.

"We have to stop this," she had told John one day while he hunched over his projects, absorbed in the science. And he had just shrugged and turned back to his experiments.

And a week later, after they had arrived on Mars, she had run into him in the hallway, near an empty set of Habs that were ready for two couples currently planning their commitment ceremonies. He had said nothing, just grabbed her arm and pulled her into an unlocked Hab, locked the door, pushed her up against a wall, and fucked her senseless. When they had finished, he had said nothing, and neither had she. The memory of it, however, had haunted her. It led her to seek Gwen, spilling the details of the affair in a great, gushing flood of guilt. As she watched Gwen's reaction, Selena regretted saying anything about the affair.

Selena felt a sharp betrayal at Gwen's response, defensive too. "I didn't mean for it to happen, Gwen, it just...*did*. And John, well, he does things that Stan would never do." She shook her head. "Stan isn't, he just isn't capable of it. Being with John is raw, animalistic, and being with Stan, well, it's as if he's mechanical, just going through the motions of sex."

She wanted Gwen to understand, even sympathize, but her friend did not waver in her disapproval.

"Selena, this is wrong. This colony," she said as she fluttered her fingers, "is too small for this shit. Whether or not you recognize it, we are living in a life-or-death situation, and we cannot, absolutely *cannot* have a situation where people are at odds with each other. The charter is clear on this."

"The charter?" Selena asked, feeling as if Gwen had just waved a relic like the Constitution of the United States at her. They had lost the original in the nuke and accompanying firestorm that had consumed most of Washington, D.C. during the Second American Civil War. Selena had read through the Mars charter, which had caused her eyes to cross with boredom on more than one occasion. She learned enough to regurgitate the answers back up in a quiz on the subject as part of the application process, and then promptly forgot about it. Legalese, it was, with a bunch of "heretofore" thrown in for good measure. Did anyone actually remember those things?

From the shocked concern on Gwen's face, Selena was looking at someone who definitely had.

"Selena, what you have done is a removable offense. The charter clearly states that they do not tolerate this kind of behavior, that in the event of a divorce, all parties must re-qualify for citizenship. If Stan finds out, *which he will* if you continue this irrational and irresponsible affair, you face being shipped back to Earth, and the accompanying fines could follow your children's children into adulthood...if you could even afford to have any more. End this, Selena, end it now."

She stood up then, hugged Selena, and whispered, "You don't know how lucky you have it, Selena. Stan is wonderful, and Toya is beautiful and so amazingly bright. Don't throw it all away."

If only it could have been that easy. God, she had tried to be good, she really had. And she *had* been good. For months afterward. She thought of that conversation several weeks later as she stared at the parts of a re-breather, parts scattered all over the floor.

"Antonia Legares Antes, what in the world are you doing?" she had asked, her sharp voice snapping Toya out of her focused examination of the re-breather. The contraption was in pieces on the floor, dozens of tiny parts haphazardly rolling about on the floor.

Toya jumped, dropping a gasket. It bounced and disappeared under the bed.

"I was looking at the CO mix, Mama. I think I could torque it so that..."

Selena sighed. "We've talked about this. I specifically asked you to stop disassembling expensive electronics. The microwave still doesn't work properly thanks to your tender mercies."

"Mama, we aren't even using the re-breathers yet," Toya protested. "And this isn't even an electronic."

"And we won't be using it now, will we?" Selena barked in frustration. She strode forward and snatched a piece of re-breather out of Toya's small hand. "What's next, the life support? You take curiosity too far, girl!"

Stan leaned in through the doorway. "Here, here, what's all this?"

"Your daughter has destroyed the re-breather prototype that the Hong Kong Hab has been refining for the Eden Hab."

"I didn't destroy it...I took it apart!" Toya cried, her lower lip trembling. "I can put it back together, I promise."

"Like the microwave?" Selena snapped back.

"I found the extra part. It had rolled under the couch. If you just let me fix it..."

"Enough. You'll probably rewire it wrong and cause the damn thing to explode," Selena interrupted, her lip curling into a sneer.

"Selena, enough." Stan was calm, his voice firm. Selena stared daggers at him.

"I didn't mean to break the microwave," Toya cried, edging away from Selena and running to hide behind Stan.

Stan reached out, a warm hand on her shoulder. "I know you didn't, sweetheart."

"Why must you always take her side?" Selena turned on her husband, her body rigid with anger. "She blew the circuits in the bathroom yesterday right after you suggested she learn more about polarities! Which meant I was late for my shift, and you know Stryker is already riding my ass about those past-due reports on the atmospheric changes!"

Stan backed up and Selena followed, leaving Toya's bedroom behind her. Their fight wasn't the worst they had had. They hid away in their own room, away from Toya, hissing accusations. Stan, who was normally the one who backed down from conflict, cut her to the bone with an offhanded comment about the worth of her work. As if she had wanted to drop out of college and have a child, instead of being pressured and lied to, in order for him to have his precious child. She had stomped out, slamming the door behind her, angered even more when it closed with a quiet snick. What she wouldn't give for a door that slammed properly! On Mars, however, there was no such thing. No cheap, thin doors here. The Habs were built to last decades, if not centuries. Simple in design, unremarkable, and very long-lasting.

Twenty minutes later, at the far end of the Philadelphia Hab, in a supply closet that locked, Selena slowly released the grip her bare legs had on John Snelling's waist. Their breaths came fast, sweat glistening on their bodies.

She let out a sigh. "Thanks, I needed that."

Selena reached for her clothes and John leaned against the shelving and watched her, making no attempt to return to a clothed state.

"What's your hurry?" he asked.

Avoiding his eyes, Selena fastened her bra and reached for her shirt. John's hand closed over hers.

"Hey."

"I have to go. It's time to start dinner and he'll be expecting me back."

John pulled her close, capturing her mouth with his. His tongue explored her mouth and Selena moaned against him. She fought the storm of need that rose to the surface, pushed him away, and met his eyes.

"What are you doing?" she asked, her voice tense.

"It's the end of shift. Come back to my place." He reached out, his thumb tracing her line of her jaw to where her mouth waited.

"Come back to your place? What if someone saw us?"

His other hand slid up her half-open shirt, and his eyes met hers. "And what if they did?"

She should have pulled away.

Then again, I shouldn't even be here now.

His hands moved over her, roaming her skin, possessive. He did it as if it were his right. Stan had never touched her like that.

"Being together violates the Mars Charter, remember?"

"Fuck the charter. They won't toss me out; the director of my department says I'm in like Flynn." He leaned down and took hold of her nipple. A wave of anger washed over her. He was safe, just as Stan and Toya were safe, but if she broke the damn charter, they would ship her back in a heartbeat. Just two more years and she could have had her Bachelor's and entered the Master's program. She pushed him away, but he ignored her and pinned her hands behind her back.

"Come back to my place," he repeated, leaning in close, his mouth exploring her neck. Selena felt a wave of desire crest over her.

"I can't."

"Can't? Or won't?" He pulled away. "I'm tired of screwing you in supply closets and service elevators, Selena. I'm done creeping around."

"I'm married, John."

He pulled his pants up, fastening them without a glance in her direction. "Uh, huh? Okay." He slid back into his shirt. His muscled arms made the tattoo dragon draped down each of them twist and roll as his shoulders straightened.

He turned away and put his hand on the door latch, unlocking it. "You let me know when you grow tired of pretending to be the happily married wife."

"Screw you."

He turned back and smiled at her. "Already did that." The door closed behind him before she could think of a snappy comeback.

Bastard.

The man was infuriating.

Alone in the closet, Selena snarled in frustration. She straightened her shirt and bent down to slip on her socks and shoes. Her fingers slowed.

Toya and Stan are brilliant. Two peas in pod, those two. And me? I'm the asshole who feels stupid and lacking.

She slid down onto the floor and lost herself in memories. Toya had been smart since the beginning. No telegraphic speech for that kid, oh no. Full sentences at eighteen months, reading at two. And the languages. Hell, Stan only counted them when Toya was fluent, but their daughter had a working knowledge of at least twenty now. She had downloaded a Mandarin dictionary onto her tablet last week. No wonder that damned teacher didn't know what to do with her!

And the constant tinkering. Selena closed her eyes.

Why can't I be the bigger person? Why can't I encourage my child and be more selfless?

Toya was brilliant. Selena could remember Stan whispering about her in their darkened room in New York. Whispering so their precocious four-year-old couldn't hear him through the paper-thin walls of their apartment. He had never told Selena that she was brilliant or that she could change the world, but the sun rose and set over Toya. It was because of Stan's genius in engineering that they *had* the opportunity to move to Mars. But the colony board had asked them plenty of details about Toya, enough that Selena was sure her brilliant daughter had been the deciding factor in their application being approved.

Some opportunity. To live and die in these man-made Habs where Mars dust crept into everything.

Sometimes she was sure she could taste the dust, like grit in her food, despite Stan telling her it was just her imagination.

Selena had been ambivalent about the change of scenery. She wasn't much of a walk in the woods or hike up the mountain gal. Selena had grown up within New York, making excursions to the uncrowded beyond a handful of times, usually on school field trips. The trees and grass had made her sneeze. The trip out to Mars had startled her only in her willingness to have an affair. It was as if boarding the ship had changed all the rules and she was free to be reckless, impulsive, and sexy.

Sexy. Stan never made me feel that way.

Sex had been their connector. Animal need, the feel of the hunt, or the one being hunted, had consumed them both. John was single, with no attachments, and he had not indicated that he even wanted attachments.

What was she doing with John, anyway?

Stan's position had garnered them the full twelve hundred feet of living space that most people dreamed of. And here, if they had more children, there were no penalties, zero, and they had additional spokes they could add to the Family Hab to create a room for each child.

"Imagine, Selena, we could make more brilliant babies, a little brother or sister for Toya!" Stan had practically gushed. Wasn't that supposed to be something she would say?

As if he had to do anything more than come in me. I'd be doing all of my work plus that of growing another child.

And they hadn't exactly discussed it, but having a child who was born on Mars meant consigning them to Mars forever. Toya was young enough that she could return. A few rounds of intensive physical therapy and she would be fine. But a fetus developing entirely in one-third gee? That child could never leave this planet. And this planet wouldn't be habitable for centuries. What kind of life was that?

Selena closed her eyes. She was trapped. She had filled out the paperwork right alongside her husband, signing her future away on a hundred different lines, over dozens of pages, without once even having the discussion. Stan was blissfully unaware of her angst. After all, his dream had always been to live here and–with his own high IQ and Toya's brilliant future–he couldn't imagine any other future.

He can't even conceptualize that I might have dreams of my own. But then, really, did I? Did I even have dreams?

It had been such a long time since she had even had a wish independent of the here and now.

I dreamed of having a husband and family. And I got one. I dreamed of having a home with room to breathe, and I got one, even if it is on another planet.

The problem was, she didn't really know what she wanted. All she knew was that it wasn't this life. And now here she was. Selena covered her face with her hands. She could smell John on them. A musky smell. It brought the memory back of the first time she had sought him out on Mars, a full month after their wordless encounter and shortly after a fight with Stan.

Well, not a fight per se, since Stan never really fought. He would simply react in that oh so hurt way of his, which always seems to point to what a fuckup I am.

She had left the Family Hab and instead of turning right to go to the greenhouse, she had turned left, heading for the electrical engineering lab where John worked. He had been there alone and hadn't seemed at all surprised when she marched in, grabbed his hand, and pulled him into the supply closet.

The sex had been phenomenal. Animalistic, raw, almost violent. Sex unlike anything she had ever encountered before.

With John, there was this storm of need. And with Stan? It was more like a pleasant stroll. Something you got used to, something you took for granted. And now John wanted more. This was unexpected yet...exciting.

"Fuck it."

Selena stood up, adjusted her shirt, and left the confines of the supply closet. She knew what she wanted, and she didn't give a damn what anyone thought. The door clicked shut behind her as she headed towards the Singles Hab section.

Hours later, it was the alarms blaring that woke Selena first, with John a close second. They lay tangled together in his sheets, the room's night lighting strips turned from white to red.

ALL HANDS REPORT TO EMERGENCY STATIONS

The colony's artificial intelligence, NARA, was normally a calm, modulated female voice. Combined with the raucous blare of the alarm, however, her neutral tone took on a sharper edge, conveying an additional level of urgency.

Most of the colony remained on a diurnal schedule, with a skeleton crew handling evening tasks and monitoring of the station. For an emergency, however, all colonists responded. Any children were collected and deposited in the education lab section of the Hab, and all able-bodied adults knew their assigned places.

"Christ, we had a drill last week," John griped, reaching for his shirt.

Selena pulled her long hair back and clipped it in place. Something in her gut told her it wasn't a drill. Her feet bare, she wrenched on her shirt and pants and ran for the door.

"Shit, Selena, wait!" John's voice cut off as the door slipped shut behind her. She ignored Bob Levitz and his surprised leer in the hallway as she sped past him and cut to the right, towards the family wing. She didn't get far.

Placed at regular intervals throughout each of the Mars Habs were emergency airlocks. Redundancy on top of redundancy, they served as the last line of protection. If a section of the Hab experienced a malfunction, fire, or emergency that would damage or destroy the rest of the Hab, the emergency airlocks immediately locked.

Selena saw the red light and, skidding to a stop too late, slammed painfully into the closed doors.

"Selena, Christ!" Gwen, part of the medical team, called to her, out of breath from running. "Wait, why you are out here and not..."

"Not what? Not what, Gwen?" Selena reached for the doors. Her fingers scrabbled to reach the override controls as her arms were grabbed from behind. "Let me go!"

Others held her fast. Selena was lifted out of the way as two fully suited figures appeared around the bend, med kits and emergency oxygen equipment in hand. Selena struggled in Gwen's grasp and felt another body join the fray, pushing her down and against the wall.

The suits reached for the keypad, entering the override codes necessary to open the first set of doors. They passed through and the doors slid shut behind them. Seconds later, they moved through the second set and disappeared from view.

"Let me go!"

"Selena, Christ, stop fighting us. They are suited up and going in now. Just stop," Gwen said, her voice steely and hard at the edges.

"What the hell is going on?" John's voice cut through the scuffle.

"The O2 levels hit rock bottom in the southwest spoke of the Family Habs," one of the team barked. "A recovery team is going in now."

Recovery team. Selena screamed wordlessly. She understood what it meant.

More people were arriving, including a second team of medics. Gwen tried to soothe Selena, to calm her down, but Selena squirmed and thrashed, desperate to get through the airlock. She would hold her breath, she knew she could. Just a few hundred feet to reach Stan and Toya and then to return.

A syringe flashed. "Hold her still, damn it." Selena's bare feet scrabbled for purchase against the slick, cold floor of the hallway. The blast of air from the airlock had felt wrong, empty, and a painful throb had begun behind her eyes. She felt the needle slide into her skin.

Toya and Stan need me.

The effects of the sedative were immediate, a warm lassitude spreading through her, and she could feel her body turn to rubber. Her feet were heavy, her arms and legs useless, her mind full of sludge.

Gwen watched her friend go limp, a look of fury spreading across her face. After all this time, Selena hadn't listened after all. She had been screwing John Snelling behind Stan's back. Gentle, kind Stan, who didn't deserve that kind of betrayal. John was standing over Selena, his face twisted with guilt as he looked at her, at Gwen, and then quickly away. Gwen bit back the words of recrimination crawling up her throat and instead said, "You'd better go with her to the infirmary; she's going to need someone there when she wakes up." She turned away before she acted on the impulse to punch the bastard in the face.

The recovery team was just that–they aimed to recover. The sensors told the story all too clearly. The chance that the two spokes had anything but the dead occupying the two Family Habs was false hope.

The recovery team, by a stroke of luck, entered the Antes Family Hab first. And there, at the kitchen table, was the body of Stan Antes, slumped over, a screwdriver on the floor just inches from his limp hand. Toya was just a few feet away, crumpled on her side, turned away from the door.

One man leaned over and checked Stan. His body was already cooling. "He's gone."

His partner Jack knelt by Toya's side and gently turned her on her back. As he did, a re-breather, partially over her mouth, slid off and clattered to the floor. He reached for her. She was limp but still warm, her pulse stuttering, her lips blue.

"Oh shit, she's still alive! I've got a pulse, barely there, but she's alive!" He fitted the emergency oxygen mask over her tiny face and activated it. Toya's face was slack, unmoving, her eyes closed.

"Take her out through the airlock, stat!"

Jack lifted the girl up and raced outside of the Family Hab to the airlock. Seconds later, he had her through both sets of doors and into the arms of a medic.

"When I picked her up, one of the prototype re-breathers fell from her face," he explained as they loaded her onto a gurney and headed for the infirmary. "It wasn't completely covering her mouth, but she had a pulse!"

Moments later, his partner emerged from the airlock. He shook his head. "The rest are dead. I've replaced the malfunctioning sensor and the oxygen levels will be back to normal soon. We have four dead. All three from the Boyers family and Stan Antes."

They would determine later that this tiny advantage, a machine that was only functioning at a fractional capacity at the moment that the O2 levels had fallen to such dangerous levels, was the only thing that had kept the girl from dying with the rest. Just the tiniest amount of air had saved the little girl's life. It wasn't enough to prevent significant brain damage brought on by the oxygen deprivation, but it had been enough to keep her alive.

The investigation took less than a week. A malfunctioning sensor had failed to send error codes on lowered oxygen levels in the Family Habs. This had led to a cascade of errors in which the O2 levels went up and then down precipitously in the evening hours. It was what had caused the headaches in the Antes family, and most likely the Boyers as well, which they would have experienced off and on for weeks.

"What I don't understand is how the daily reports showed these failures, and yet no one noticed them," Myra Stryker asked. As one of the senior colonists on staff, she served as the Investigational Committee's chairperson.

Two of the night techs had immediately confessed. They were new, off the latest shuttle, and therefore at the bottom of the pecking order for optimal shifts. After weeks and then months of smooth sailing, they had become inattentive, and they had not reviewed the evening reports.

The backup sensor had worked intermittently, a tiny failure point in the connection providing correct readings most of the time, but failing more often in the evenings, after dinner, or even later, after most were in bed. Keyed to the environmental system's check that ran at 2200 hours each Monday, Wednesday, and Friday, it flittered off and then on again.

Anyone looking at the board or reading the weekly reports would have seen it. But as with all incidents such as these–and what a lovely understatement it was for the catastrophe they now faced–it was one that follows inattention. The neglect, the departure from scheduled reviews of reports, had spawned from the newness of an affair consummated in the dark corners of the Control Room. They were a skeleton crew of junior techs low on the totem pole whose newness earned them the unpopular shifts. Here they had endured weeks and months of incident-free nights, and with it no small level of boredom.

It had bred no indifference, but a level of presumption, that their tiny, fragile world would continue to perform without hiccup or failure.

And while two techs, bored with the monotony of quiet halls and repetitious reports, had momentarily deserted their posts for a quick bump and grind, two families would forever pay the price.

In retrospect, Selena felt like an idiot for not having reported her headaches, sweating, and occasional confusion. Stan had said nothing about his, although she was sure he must have experienced them, but she remembered Toya out of breath and wheezing the morning before the incident. Textbook symptoms of hypoxia. She had written it off as a play for attention or even an escape from school.

Stan Antes, along with all three members of the Boyers family, were dead. And Toya, a brilliant child with her entire future in front of her, had spent more than a week recovering in the infirmary. Her brain had been permanently damaged. Selena's brilliant daughter was no longer brilliant.

If Gwen was surprised to see Selena in the examination room a few weeks later, she didn't show it. She walked in and made eye contact with Selena briefly. The quick shift to focusing on her tablet sent an obvious message. They weren't friends anymore. Selena felt a stab of hurt but kept her expression neutral. It wouldn't do any good to appeal to the friendship that she and Gwen had shared, not considering how things had turned out.

Gwen was all business, her attention focused on her tablet, her voice professional yet aloof. "Good morning, Selena, what brings you here today?"

Selena struggled to keep her voice even. "I need verification of a pregnancy test."

Gwen raised her eyes from her tablet and stared at Selena. "I see." She set down the tablet and stood silent, her lips compressed in a thin line that Selena had seen when Gwen was most troubled or fighting to maintain her composure. "Well then, you need nothing from me. I'll send in Annie to get the verification you require." She turned to go and said, "Congratulations. I'm sure Stan would have been delighted." Her voice was icy, brittle.

Selena's voice cracked. "It isn't Stan's, Gwen. And you know it. That's why I came here to you. I need an Exception."

A Pregnancy Exception, especially one that would keep a colonist on the planet and ensure that any children born to them were permanent Mars citizens, had been invoked only once before. Selena had broken the colony's charter, but an Exception would keep her on Mars.

Gwen's eyes betrayed her fury, while her voice remained calm. "And is the father of the child prepared to take responsibility?"

"Once a DNA scan verifies paternity, I hope so. If not, well, that's what the Exception is for." Selena's voice quavered only slightly in the face of her former friend's wrath. The only chance she had at a decent life, one that didn't include living out the rest of her life in an efficiency apartment the size of a closet where she could hear her neighbors breathing above, below, and on three sides of her, was in forcing John Snelling's hand. Toya wasn't just damaged, her future had been stripped from her, and if she returned to Earth, it would take time and money for her body to recover from living at this half-gravity, both things that Selena would struggle to provide for her child. Staying on Mars was the best thing for Selena, Toya, and this child growing inside her.

"Fine, well, let's get on with it." Gwen motioned to the exam table.

Selena climbed up and laid back, moving her shirt away from her pants and slipping the waistband of her pants down to expose her tiny pooch. The baby was still tiny, perhaps only a kidney bean in size, but it was her ticket to staying on Mars, something she had not even wanted three months ago. How things had changed!

Gwen removed a device from the cabinet on the far side of the narrow room. "The sensor will enter via a tiny needle into the uterus, test the fetus, and give us a full DNA sample to compare with the records we have for both you and Mr. Snelling. Before we begin, please be aware that this procedure has a .01% chance of causing a miscarriage. Do you consent?"

She said it impersonally, and Selena felt her heart plummet. Of all the people she valued, Gwen, and Gwen's opinion of her, mattered. She was the first woman friend Selena had since adulthood, and the only friend she had here on Mars. Since the incident, the rest of the colony had retreated, and she had rarely seen anyone, except at work. She was a pariah now.

"Yes." She forced it out and did her best to hide the tears welling up in her eyes. Gwen had been clear, and she hadn't listened, and now she had to live with the situation she had caused.

Thirty minutes later, she knocked on John's door in the west singles corridor. He came to the door, his hair tousled. He liked to sleep in on his days off, sometimes until noon. She handed him the scan results.

"Come in." He opened the door wider.

"They have issued me an Exception, so I can stay on Mars. There's nothing for me back on Earth," she said, taking a seat on his bunk.

"Unnecessary," he said, forcing a smile on his face. "I'll marry you and acknowledge the child."

"It's a boy," she pointed out. The genetic details of their future child were clear. "He will have your brown eyes and brown hair and probably be taller than me by his mid-teens. There's also a 78% chance he will be left-handed."

John chuckled. "A boy. I want to call him Leonard, after my dad, maybe Lenny, for short."

"Okay."

She didn't love him, and he didn't love her. That was crystal clear. This would keep them in a Family Hab, the same one where Stan had died. A future here on Mars. It was, after all, the best she could hope for.

John put a hand on her belly and stared at it. "I never planned on being a father. But I'll do the best I can, Selena. For you and for him." He didn't mention Toya, and her heart ached with sadness, a cloud of guilt thick inside her. Toya had been asking for Stan, and she couldn't bear to tell her daughter the truth yet. She was still hoping that Toya would recover, come back from the blank, uncomprehending look she had on her face as she struggled to re-learn how to walk, talk, and more. The memories were still there, but all the foreign languages the girl had known, her keen sense of curiosity and wizardry with mechanical objects, that was all gone too. Possibly forever, her mind damaged beyond repair, thanks to the eleven minutes of little or no oxygen.

It would take six weeks for Toya to learn how to walk again, and another three months before she learned other simple tasks.

By that time, Selena had remarried. Her belly had grown and, while she was still kept at arm's length by most, marrying John had helped return her status to one of quasi-legitimacy. Gwen had insisted on farming out her prenatal care to Annie, obviously unwilling to interact with her until there was no other option.

Selena sat herself down on the couch and patted the cushion next to her. "Toya, it's time to practice reading."

Toya slowly sat down next to her. Every limb in Toya's body looked stiff and miserable. She stared up at Selena, her lip quivering. "It's hard. Why is it so hard, Mama?"

Selena reached out and stroked her daughter's hair. "It will get better, Toya."

Toya stared at Selena's belly, now full and round. "I'm stupid now."

"You aren't stupid."

"The baby is going to be smarter than me."

Selena sighed. "I love you, Toya. Somehow, it's going to get better. I promise."

God help me, somehow, it's easier to love her now that she's simpler.

Selena opened the tablet to *Rebecca the Raccoon Saves the White House.* "Come on, sweetheart, I'll read the page on the left and you read the page on the right."

"Okay, I guess." Toya leaned against her, tucking herself against Selena, something she hadn't done since she was tiny.

"Calvin Coolidge was the 30th President of the United States of America. He and his wife, Grace, and their two sons lived in a large mansion called the White House..."

A Song for Fen

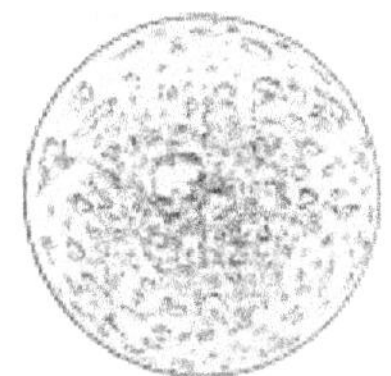

Mars Year 14, Week 17, Day 169
(Earth Date: 02.18.2099)

The Beijing Science Outpost was built to hold more people and would have had more, if it hadn't had been for the ESH virus. Fen sat alone in the Garden Hab; an enormous dome filled with exotic plants that one of the first teams to man the outpost had planted. The elephant ear reached up, its large leaves occasionally releasing a drip of water, sometimes two, as it took in the sunlight and respirated oxygen and some water back into the thick, humid air of the dome.

It was here that she felt most at peace. There was the quiet burble of the small pond, the water aerated and moved by a pump powered by a small solar sensor that tracked the sun in the sky and stored enough energy to continue on at night, long after the sun had disappeared over the horizon.

Each team added something to the space, a continuing, growing, and ever-expanding palette of plants and life. When she had arrived on the Mazu Mars Explorer, she had brought with her a ginger plant to add to the collection of plants that served as a home away from home. It had taken up a significant portion of her weight allowance, but it had been worth it. It was nearly ready to flower now. A flower stalk had shot up during the night and Fen stared at it blankly, her mind in turmoil.

What am I doing? What is wrong with me?

She could hear Bao's words echoing in her head. "If you insist on going to Mars, don't expect me to be here when you return."

He had known her plans for years, had even supported her in word if not in deed, in pursuing her dreams, proud of her accomplishments, and bragged about her to his friends. That was, right up until he realized there would be no one to take care of the house, fix meals, and all the other menial things that most women had stopped handling exclusively for more than a century.

Bao had been different, raised by older parents who had lived in the country, still clutching to the older ways, a way of life that had ended long ago and belonged in the past.

She had left, of course. The opportunity to spend two years on Mars was a lifelong dream, something she had worked hard for, and there had been no messages since, no word from Bao, until the transmission yesterday.

Living with just two others on a small station meant everything was out in the open. There were few secrets. And she had adapted, turning away and giving Chen his privacy when he had received the news that his wife and daughter had died in a car crash, a rare autocar malfunction that had sent them hurtling off a bridge and into a river swollen with rain from the monsoons. It had happened shortly after the three astronauts had landed here on Mars a few months ago.

She had reacted differently when Liu's parents had chided him for not having found and married a girl before flying millions of miles away, their only son, their only child, and their future elder years left to the winds of fate. She had laid a hand on his shoulder, smiled at him, remembering that the others–Bao, Liu's parents–couldn't understand the attraction of leaving Earth behind to go to a desolate planet millions of miles away. His morose expression had vanished, his dark-black eyes grateful for her touch.

And then the news had come of the ESH virus. First, there had been reports of survivors pouring out of Guiyang and waves of infection spreading across the massive country. Later, the broadcasts from Earth had become increasingly grim. The world as they knew it, the one they had left less than a year ago, was a shell of its former self. The news yesterday, that Bao had not survived, nor her parents, nor her sister, or her sister's family, had sent her spinning into grief. And Fen was not sure who she grieved for more, Bao, who she had loved despite his self-centered ways, her parents, or her sister's two young children, aged three and six. There was no one to return to, no one to love, or to love her back, and perhaps that is why she found herself, hazy and thick with grief, knocking gently on Chen's door that night.

Holding each other, both grieving, had led first to a chaste kiss, and then far less chaste groping, before leaping into a frantic lovemaking. A desperate need to connect, physically, with another. Later, in the dark hours of the morning, she had woken, gathered her clothing, and slipped away, back to her own tiny bunk at the far end of the hall.

Now the guilt and recriminations began. Her head and body ached from the emotions swirling inside it. She felt ill. Perhaps it was a bad dream, and she would wake up soon. Knowing that she had slept with another man, immediately after learning her entire family, and her husband, were dead, felt as if she had spit in their faces, their memories.

What am I doing? What is wrong with me?

The door slid open behind her. She didn't look. If it was Chen, she didn't want to face him, to acknowledge what they had done. And if it was Liu, well, she was sure he would see the guilt written all over her face. She and Chen had been quiet last night, barely making any noise at all as they frantically pulled at each other's clothes, tumbling into the narrow bunk. She flushed at the memory. It had been what they both needed at the moment, but now she feared it would put a terrible pressure upon them. They were scientists, astronauts, explorers, and they had no time for such physicality. Especially not now, in this awkward situation. She was the only woman on the mission, after all, and the smallest change, a relationship or otherwise, could put enormous pressure upon them. Stress led to mistakes. And mistakes could be deadly in this harsh, alien world.

Instead of looking up, she stared at the tiny fish darting about in the small pond. That had been Chen's contribution to the garden, five goldfish he had brought on board and cared for on the six-month journey here. The five goldfish hadn't all survived, but the ones who had, bred. Now there were approximately fifteen, give or take a couple. It was hard to count; they darted about so much. The black ones were almost impossible to see; only the orange ones gave themselves away. There were no predators here, though, Fen thought, as she watched the fish rise to the surface, their mouths searching the water for a meal.

She flinched slightly at Chen's hand on her shoulder. He said nothing at first, and she didn't know what to say. His hand was gentle, warm. She couldn't help but remember the night before. He had been a skilled lover.

"About last night," he said, his voice low, "It was something we both needed." Somehow, he knew exactly where her thoughts would go. She felt a wave of misery rise, then flatten out.

She said nothing, not for a long moment. "There is a new fish. It's almost invisible, but that is because it is black and hard to see."

Chen said nothing, and shortly after his hand disappeared from her shoulder and she could hear him retreat, and the door open and close again behind him.

When the door opened a few minutes later, she was sure it was Chen again. Instead, Liu's voice startled her out of her reverie.

"Any new ones?" he asked, his voice milder than Chen's, not the older man's low bass, but more of a tenor. "I saw a black one in there last night, it's tiny, but I think it is hiding near the water lily."

"Yes, it is," Fen responded. She looked up quickly, then turned away from Liu's kind smile. Liu looked far younger than his almost thirty years. He had a face that was kind and happy all the time. Good days, bad days, Liu always looked the same. It was far different from Chen's fierce, troubled face. Even when Chen was in a good mood, his face didn't show it. Instead, Chen often looked as if he had the weight of the world upon him, and his stern scowl was a built-in part of that. Where Liu did nothing but smile, Chen frowned. They were day and night apart.

During training, she had felt Liu's gaze upon her. And then, in the long months aboard the Mazu Mars Explorer, she had noticed him gently flirt with her occasionally. It was subtle; Liu was shy, sweet, and she had been careful not to acknowledge it. There was no need for further complications.

Apparently further complications don't include sleeping with your commander, she thought ruefully to herself. *I have been very foolish.*

She noticed that Liu held his pipa in his hand. The four-stringed lute had been his contribution to their voyage, and he plucked at it daily, usually in the evenings, when they would gather and relax after their evening meal.

Liu had a lovely voice, and he would sing many ancient, traditional Chinese songs while expertly plucking the melody on the pipa, the rich sound grounding the team and relaxing after a long day of work.

"I have written a song," he said, his dark eyes warm, empathetic. "Would you like to hear it?"

Listening meant she didn't have to speak, something she was thankful for, and Fen nodded, grateful to stay silent. He played it, the gentle notes washing over her, her soul soothed by the tune. She felt the weight of loss lighten, just for a moment, as the music spread out over the small Garden Hab, and the sun's rays warmed them both as it crept higher into the sky.

The song ended, the last notes hanging in the air before vanishing. Fen felt the darkness and sorrow close in again. She could feel her misery climb up and wrap itself around her heart, like thick ropes of gloom. What would they do now? What would become of them? Would they die here, alone on this desolate planet with no signs of life, the beauty of Earth millions of miles away? Her eyes filled with tears.

A warm hand on her shoulder and Fen felt Liu settle down on a rock beside her.

"Fen? I heard the transmission." Liu had not been in the room at the time it had first come in. He had been out on an EVA, collecting samples from a small, unnamed crater to the south halfway between Gale Crater and Wien Crater, where the automated drone had found unusual deposits. Liu had been away most of the day, returning late and learning the news from Earth from Chen. "And," he paused, his voice almost at a whisper, "the fate of Guiyang." Fen's heart plummeted again. Her entire family, childhood friends, her teachers, neighbors, everyone she had ever known, the streets she had walked as a child and adolescent, all gone in a fiery ball of heat. She couldn't bear to speak of it. The reality was that something as minuscule as a virus had been so bad, it had meant bombing an entire city to stop the spread.

Her petite, thin frame bowed, misery filling her. Liu's hand stayed on her shoulder, warm, a tiny patch of comfort. They sat there, wordless, as the pond burbled gently, and the hum of the condenser that made sure they all kept on breathing seemed suddenly loud in the space.

Sorrow is a heavy thing. It weighed her down, heavier than the gravity she would feel if she were back on Earth. She felt it pulling at her arms, her legs, her soul. Yes, Bao had been a trial, but she had loved him. How she had hoped for his heart to warm to her upon her return, for them to return to their easy way of love, the lazy mornings, the walks through the gardens in the spring when all the cherry blossoms danced in the air, leaving their delicate floral scent as they fluttered in a gentle pink rain, covering the ground. Fen remembered how Bao had plucked one from her hair, held it to his nose, and breathed in its scent, then leaned forward and sniffed her hair, his lips next to her ear, his breath tickling her as he whispered, "I have always thought that the cherry blossoms in the spring were the most beautiful thing I had ever smelled, until you came along. You are so much better."

A single tear fell from her eyes. It landed with a gentle splat on her black pants, instantly disappearing, gone in a flash. Fen realized how close she was to breaking down here, in front of Liu. In her mind, a voice that sounded very much like her mother's harshly speculated on whether she would end up sleeping with Liu as well. The thought of it all, the loss, their home not being the same, it was all too much.

"I must go," Fen said, abruptly standing, Liu's hand falling away from her shoulder as she stood on wobbly legs and then slipped away before she made another poor decision. She could feel Liu's gaze on her as she hurried out of the Garden Hab, her speed increasing to a trot after the door closed behind her.

Fen slipped into her room, reached for her tablet, and crawled into her bunk. She didn't care what time it was; she was useless for any of the work assigned for the morning. Fen reached for her tablet. The tablet was her lifeline. Fen opened the photos section, paused for a moment, and then opened the folder labeled Shu. Her sister was just two years younger than her, but she had fallen in love in her first year at university and ended up pregnant. Fen had helped Shu get their parents' approval for the marriage, and Shu and Lian now had two darling young ones. Fen adored them both, and they her, jumping and crawling all over her anytime she would visit.

Had been adorable, *had* crawled all over her. Gone now. Nothing but ash and dust.

She reached out and touched her finger to Wei's sweet, innocent face and the video began. "Yima! Yima! Watch me do a somersault!" She rolled effortlessly forward, springing upward afterward with a huge grin. Wei had always been her favorite.

Maybe because I fought for Ba and Mama to accept the marriage and wanted it as much as Shu and Lian did.

Wei had been such a happy baby and had always had a smile for her aunt. Ho had been colicky and cantankerous, but he had shed that, becoming the most handsome and happy boy that Fen had ever seen. It was the only time when she regretted putting off having children until she had finished with her career. By the time she had children, her niece and nephew would already be half-grown.

"Our children won't grow up together," she had said to Shu, her eyes on the children playing in the yard.

Shu had placed her hand on Fen's. "Don't let Bao push you into babies before you are ready. You have always dreamed of going to the stars, of going to Mars; don't put that dream away. It is a worthy pursuit. There will be time for children after you return."

Fen smiled through her tears. Remembering that moment, Shu had always looked up to Fen, always supported her. Bao's ultimatum had occurred on the heels of that discussion, and she had kept Shu's words close to her heart as she stood her ground. It hadn't been easy, taking that firm stance, but Shu had been right, it was a dream she had hoped for, a dream realized when she boarded the Mazu Mars Explorer. It had been the dream of a lifetime. And now? Her smile slipped.

It was one thing to choose to go to an alien world and dedicate three years of your life to exploration, science, and the possibility of turning Mars into a viable second home for humanity, but it was quite another to be stranded here. The ESH virus was highly contagious, lethal, and scarier than Mission Control in Beijing would acknowledge.

Fen's father had often said, "Pay attention not to what they say, but what they *don't* say, for that is where the truth lies bare." As a child, she hadn't understood what he meant, and as an adult, she could not see it any other way. Sometimes she wished she could accept all words at face value, that she could naively believe that the political powers that be were not lying, not withholding information. It would have made her life simpler.

Instead, she took the small admissions, such as the words "we are working on a cure" and recognized that, not only was this virus lethal, it was also uncontrolled. Or worse, the rhetoric at work with the announcement that Mission Control was "working on a safe landing site for their return journey" told her clearly that there was nowhere that was safe, not if you had a blood type other than AB negative blood, that is. Nowhere on Earth remained untouched. Sure, there were pockets of UPs, a term coined by the Americans that referred to Unaffected Persons, those who had somehow managed to avoid exposure to the virus. But the chances that they would be infected wasn't just a possibility, it was a probability. And if she and Liu and Chen returned to Earth, their only choice would be to go to an UP enclave.

The situation was hopeless. Fen closed her eyes, pulled her knees up to her chest, and cried until she ran out of tears.

Beyond the Beyond

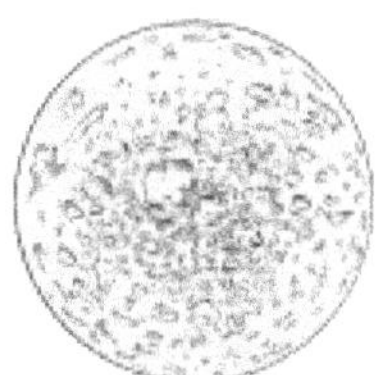

Mars Year 14, Week 24, Day 233
(Earth Date 04.01.2099)

The list of Kuiper Belt Objects, or KBOs, had grown dramatically over the past century of space travel. Long before mankind took their first steps on Mars in 2025, the list of the larger pieces, the planetesimals, had been mapped extensively.

They had mapped them in part to satisfy curiosity, but also to ensure that the larger objects stayed where they belonged: in the Kuiper Belt, far from Earth.

Many of them were so large they were dwarf planets, Pluto among them. Over one hundred and fifty years after its discovery, tiny Pluto fell from its vaunted status as the ninth planet in the solar system. They relegated it to other almost-but-not-quite planets such as Eris, Haumea, Makemake, or Sedna. If Pluto nursed a grudge, it would have only been fair. Named a planet and then having it taken away, it felt as if Pluto had been told it was royalty and then had the scepter wrenched away. Which really didn't seem fair at all.

Among the multitudes, one asteroid, discovered nearly a century earlier, carried the rather boring name of 486958 Arrokoth. In the early part of the 21st century, a few years after its discovery, the New Horizons space probe mapped it, transmitting the data back to Earth. The asteroid was not smooth and round, but a contact binary composed of two lobes, Ultima, which came in at 19 kilometers in diameter, and the smaller Thule, some 14 kilometers in diameter. They were attached at a narrow neck. New Horizons space probe snapped two photos, then carried on its mission, moving further away from Earth.

Ultima Thule was large in the bigger scheme of things. If the entire object were to hit something, a planet, for example, the fallout from such an event would be staggering. The Kuiper Belt Object had existed for a million years, its orbit moving it closer and closer to yet another object too small to draw notice or recognition on the extensive map of Kuiper Belt Objects, yet big enough to matter. Draw one up against the other, and both would lose the round. And as things went, when the impact eventually occurred, it was really only a glancing blow. A mere knock on the edge. What the New Horizons probe had illustrated, however, was just how tenuous Ultima and Thule's codependent relationship truly was. Being joined at the neck, with fractures from other bumps and blows, out here in the darkness of space, had left the asteroid far more fragile than expected. And in a matter of moments, which played out in the silent vacuum of space, the dramatic union of two individual pieces, leftovers from when the system was first formed, Ultima Thule fractured in half. Ultima broke away, fracturing further into multiple pieces that now headed deeper into the Kuiper Belt, looking perhaps for other objects to collect and merge with. Thule, the smaller piece, stayed intact. The thin neck that had held the two parts together for what was but an instant in astronomical terms, yet encompassed the entire history of humanity, fractured into a handful of pieces, rotating and then expanding in opposite directions. But Thule, now the largest piece, moved, with a few fragments inward while the rest followed the remnants of Ultima, not unlike a small child following their older sibling, desperate to be a part of the adventure.

The 14-kilometer chunk of Thule rotated, spinning furiously, still recovering from the impact that had caused the destruction behind it. It knew nothing of the asteroid responsible for wiping out the dinosaurs, yet under the right circumstances, and given the right timing, the asteroid would spell doom for any planet in its path. It continued to move at a steady speed of over 27 kilometers per second, headed, in the broadest of terms, inward, toward the Sun.

An Unavoidable Truth

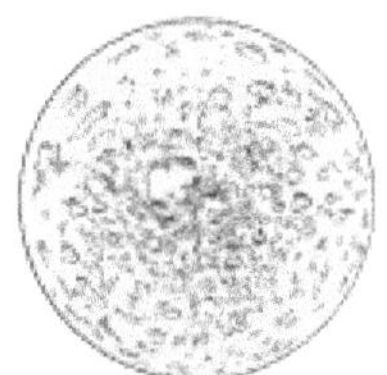

Mars Year 14, Week 30, Day 295
(Earth Date: 06.02.2099)

She had done her best to hide it. Why? If anyone had asked, Fen couldn't have answered. It had just felt wrong, somehow. Proof that she had not been faithful to Bao, proof that she had barely learned the news of his passing, and the rest of her family, before falling into another man's bed.

The nausea had not been bad. At most, it occurred once, first thing in the morning, and was over long before Liu or Chen had emerged from their own bunks. She found that plain rice had helped, or the small rice crackers that had weighed nothing, and which they had in quantities enough to last them for years.

It was her stomach that had finally betrayed the secret she had worked so hard to keep. Liu, who constantly watched her, had noticed first. She had seen his eyes focus on the small bump, the one she had taken such care to hide for as long as possible, and then hold there, before darting up to meet her eyes and then look away. She had seen a flicker of sadness slide across his normally cheery face.

He had said nothing, though, returning to the task at hand and then, uncharacteristically silent, had found duties that took him out of sight of her.

Fen felt a pang of guilt. Liu was a good, sweet man. If she were to have slept with him instead, he would have reacted with delight at the thought of a child, especially here, in the worst of times.

She stopped and daydreamed of how that would have gone. Would he have puffed up with pride, with excitement? Or cried happy tears? Liu was one who pinned his heart on his sleeve, one who loved deeply and obviously. Chen had never sought her out, never said another word about that night of passion that she remained conflicted about. She thought she could feel small flutters now, as if they trapped a butterfly in her womb and it was fluttering its wings trying to escape. She had imagined what it would be like, years from now, to have a child. But not here, not like this.

She heard the squeak of a shoe outside her bunk door, a soft knock, then the sound of receding footsteps. When she opened the door, she saw a large container. Inside of her tiny room, she reviewed the contents of the bottle. A note inside showed that Liu, it could only be him, had painstakingly assembled the correct mix of vitamins she should take to ensure a healthy pregnancy.

Fen's hands shook, fingers tracing the symbols for folic acid, iron, calcium, vitamin D, DHA and iodine. Trust Liu to be so thoughtful, and so kind.

She swallowed the pills with her jasmine tea, which was cold, having sat untouched since this morning. She wondered briefly if Liu would tell Chen. Just as quickly she realized he wouldn't. Liu would keep her secret. With her belly expanding rapidly on her thin frame, it wouldn't be a secret for long.

Chen, lost in his work, hadn't noticed for nearly two more weeks. Fen had avoided him, much as she had avoided even contemplating what raising a baby on Mars would be like. It was too big of a concept to think about, considering they had enough food for perhaps three more years and were hearing nothing from Beijing on when, if ever, they could return. There was also the not knowing, the questions raised about where they would go, how they would avoid becoming infected. These seemed so big, so frightening, that it was little wonder Chen had been oblivious to the signs of her pregnancy.

It was evening, and they assembled for an all-hands announcement from Beijing. Chen announced it over the comm and Fen, her hair damp from her recent sponge bath, let Liu lead the way as she entered the Comm Room. Chen had barely noticed her, but as the announcement began, his eyes wandered over her and Liu, before zeroing in on her belly, which was now pressing against the close-fitting uniform. There his eyes stayed, his mouth working silently, as they learned that much of China was now in the throes of a civil war, the great country breaking apart into several areas of conflict. It was more of what was not said than anything else, the lack of a timeline for return, and the admission that the space center itself, in the Haidian

District of Beijing, was now coming under heavy fire "from a small group of rebels" that left Fen wondering exactly what they would do if they could not return home in a year. Their only option would be to join the Huygens Outpost, although they were over 5,000 kilometers away, a journey that would be impossible to make in even the largest of their ground vehicles without significant modifications.

Chen's gaze, which had now moved from her abdomen to her face, unnerved her. Was he angry? Shocked? Did he wonder if he was the father or if she had been with Liu?

Liu, ever attentive, could not have helped but notice Chen's focus on her. After the transmission had ended, he had put a hand on her shoulder and squeezed it reassuringly before leaving the room. Fen stood rooted to the spot, unsure of how to proceed. In response, the tiny being inside her fluttered again, just a whisper of movement, as if a butterfly danced there, deep inside.

The room was quiet, other than the ever-present fans that kept the oxygen moving, scrubbing the carbon dioxide from the air. The quiet shush-shush was the only noise. Chen's eyes had returned to rest on Fen's stomach, his hands folded behind his back.

He was a statue and so, for the moment, was she.

She thought about Bao in that moment, his dark eyes, his smile, the small scar on his chin from some childhood indiscretion. She thought about the children he had wanted, that he had talked about. Never mind that he had wanted them so she would stay, and stop dreaming of space and distant planets, he had dreamed of a boy and a girl, possibly a third child, a luxury they would have been allowed, thanks to her work with the Chinese National Space Administration.

"Being an astronaut isn't all that you can do in your position," he had pointed out again and again. How he had loved the prestige that came with being married to an astronaut, but not so much the downside, the months away in training, the missions. So good in theory, not so much in practice.

Bao hadn't been perfect, Fen knew that. She remembered how his face had looked once, two years ago, when they were first married and she had been late. She could still see the hope that had shown in his eyes when he pressed the pregnancy test into her hands and they waited for the results.

Standing there, in the tiny room, so many millions of kilometers from home, Fen closed her eyes, wishing she didn't remember the loss that had filled Bao's face when they both read the message "NOT PREGNANT" when it flashed across the screen.

"It is mine." Chen's voice was quiet, but Fen jerked her eyes open. The sound had been loud in the silence between them.

Fen nodded, not trusting her voice at the moment. She looked up, saw his direct gaze, and dropped her eyes to the floor. Fen couldn't bear to look at him and wonder if he was angry, or disgusted, that she had not been on birth control. It had been an impetuous decision; one she hadn't thought twice about until two weeks after their encounter. By then it had been too late for the morning-after pill. She hadn't thought of it anyway, not really. It had been an impossible thing. How often had she and Bao been together with no protection at all? And she had been fine. It was only after that pregnancy scare two years ago that she had even considered using birth control, and then it had been a series of different ones, each affecting her in one detrimental way after the other. Some women could take the pills with no side effects at all, but Fen felt nothing but side effects, from breast swelling and tenderness, to extreme nausea and even headaches.

She had felt better for the first time in two years when she had tossed out the pills on the long trip out to Mars. And it wasn't until the slight nausea hit that she realized it was far too late to go back.

"If you," Chen's voice broke through her thoughts once again, "If you need anything, or require any additional moments of rest, please let me know." His voice was formal, remote. "For now, we will wait to announce this to Mission Control."

"Yes, sir."

Her voice came out as a whisper, and she turned to go. As the door shut behind her, she glanced over her shoulder through the tiny porthole window; Chen had buried his face in his hands, his shoulders shaking. Fen turned and ran, unwilling to see her grim commander's grief. Her feet took her to the only place that could calm her, the Garden Hab.

The sound of water trickling in the pond was a soothing balm. She knelt on the ground next to the water, beside the brilliant blooms of the ginger plant, and felt the tears sliding down her cheeks. Again, her belly fluttered, the tiny fetus moving within her, ecstatic at the space it currently existed within. Soon, all too soon, that space would disappear as he grew.

A boy. She had forgotten to tell him that. The test last week, the one that Liu had also left outside her door, had confirmed that she was carrying a boy. If she had only had her wits about her, she would have told Chen. He deserved to know that she was carrying his son. But in the moment of truth, an unavoidable truth, her voice had failed her.

Fen's tears came faster. Of all the things they had lost, this life should mean hope. But she couldn't find it within her to hope any longer. The world felt dark and full of death, even now with a new life growing inside her, even here, over 200 million kilometers from home. She pressed one hand to her belly, the other to the soil in the garden, and prayed for the child to find peace in this place, as she prayed that she would find happiness again.

The sun had long disappeared from the horizon, and the motion-sensor lights, not sensing any movement, dimmed as well, leaving so little light that Fen could see a dizzying array of stars appear. There were clusters of constellations, so different from the view from Earth, yet familiar all the same as they appeared in the sky above. Fen noticed the slow, bright movement of a satellite circling the planet. It was peaceful here, and she wondered if they would go home, or perhaps travel to the Huygens Outpost if Space Command said they couldn't go home.

She took a deep breath in and let it out slowly. Civil war. Only it wasn't being called that. Typical. Those in power always had to sugar-coat it and give it a pretty name. The closest they had come in the past few months to any raw truth was the admission that they had firebombed her home, along with every family member, friend, and neighbor she had ever grown up with.

Past that, the progression of the disease, this ESH virus, the details were slow in being released. From what she understood, the only ones who survived were those with a particularly rare blood type. None of them had AB negative blood, and thus, they were all at risk if they were to return. Before what appeared to be a coup in Beijing two months ago, they were still discussing a vaccine, but the new group in power weren't saying much past the news that it would be months, if not years, before the crew could return.

They had all signed up for a three-year commitment. Six months to get to Mars, two years on the planet itself, then another six months in space back home. The question now was, would there be any home to return to?

Where I Belong

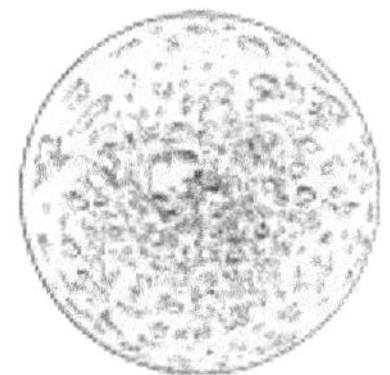

Mars Year 14, Week 31, Day 304
(Earth Date: 06.11.2099)

Chen woke up from the dream with a low cry. He caught it in time, the shout that often came at the end as he watched the autocar skid off of the edge and tumble, spinning, into the Yangtze River and the churning water. It was the same dream, the same agonizing loss.

He stood up and, for a moment, the room spun around him. His infrequent inner ear imbalance had become far more frequent since they had landed on the red planet. Had they been on Earth, the chances of him being disqualified and replaced with far younger, more fit men would have been a given. As it was, only his pull with key men in power had meant that they had chosen him to lead this mission. The thought now, that if he had stayed, the accident that took his beloved wife and daughter from him would likely never have happened, was something he could not shake.

He had been so certain when he kissed his wife Mei and their daughter Li Ma that it would be the last time that he would leave them. It had been bittersweet, knowing he was going on one last mission, fulfilling the dream of a lifetime by spending two years at the Beijing Science Outpost on the red planet, something that only a select few had done. Yet it had been unbearable to imagine what he would miss Li Ma doing as she grew up without him. Her black eyes had filled with tears as they stood near the launch pad, and her lower lip had trembled. Her fine black hair, barely long enough to put into braids, was trying valiantly to escape, some of it slipping from the tight ties to float, tiny errant wisps struggling to not conform, but be free.

"Come back soon, Baba," she had lisped in her tiny voice, and Chen was undone. Tears had run down his face as he kissed his beautiful, perfect girl.

Mei had already been crying, and he kissed the tears from her face and rested his forehead against hers.

"Wo dei ai, be brave for me," he said, his own tears mingling with hers. "When I return, we will try for a little brother or sister for Li Ma, yes?"

"Yes," Mei nodded, her perfect mouth so serious, her lips now curving up into a shaky, yet brave, smile. She reached up and wiped the tears from his face and he closed his eyes, overwhelmed with emotion. This beautiful woman loved him. Why, he could not say. Somehow, she had seen past his stern exterior and reached into his heart. He would go on the mission, and then, when he returned, he would never leave her side again, no matter how long he lived.

The memory of Mei's lips upon his cheeks was so vivid, he swore he could still feel the ghost of them fluttering against his skin.

His cheeks remained dry. There were no more tears to shed for the dead; he was sure that he had run out of tears, run out of love and hope, in the vacuum left by the news of his wife and daughter's deaths. Not even the news of Fen's pregnancy had jogged him from this gray, half-life that he was living. The thought of his seed growing in her was merely a reminder he had lost the two people most important to him. Nothing else compared, nothing else touched him as Mei and Li Ma had.

He had been a bachelor until his early forties. Frankly, women had unnerved him. His prestige as an astronaut for the Chinese National Space Administration had been irresistible to many. He had seen some other, younger men take full advantage of their popularity, bedding the women who flung themselves at them, while Chen had remained resolute and single. Determined to find the right one, there was little to tempt him otherwise. Not that he hadn't indulged in a handful of chance encounters of his own. But they were usually ones easily ended with no expectations on either side.

That was, until Mei had entered his life.

It had been at one of the countless functions his position required he attend, where the rich could rub elbows with celebrities–famous actors and actresses, the sports elite, and, of course, astronauts. It had been a black-tie affair, and he had been squiring a pampered beauty who knew more about makeup and fashion than anything related to science. This affair, like most others, would end with him politely dropping his date at her door and resisting her best efforts to seduce him. It had grown old, and Chen knew the rumors grew that perhaps he preferred the company of men instead of women, but it wasn't true. He was simply more discerning than most. He cared not for clever conversation or the perfect low-cut dress. Instead, he looked for, longed for, the connection of two like-minded souls. He knew too, that when he found it, it would take no effort, no special dance or perfectly phrased lines of introduction, there would just be a simple understanding of completeness, two souls staring at one another and knowing they were perfect for each other.

And just as he nodded mechanically at whatever drivel his date was spouting, Mei had slipped on the slick flagstones and had kept all but one wineglass on the serving platter upright. The full glass of red wine had flown off of the platter, spilling, then bouncing once on the stones before shattering into tiny sharp shards. His white silk dress shirt had quickly soaked, and a few drops had landed on his date's dress, no doubt ruining it.

He had silenced his shrieking hyena of a date with a dark look, then locked eyes with Mei, and fallen completely and totally in love in that instant.

It had caused a stir when he had left the event a few minutes later, ditching his date and instead handing the beautiful Mei, later fired from her position as a server, into a waiting autocar. He had disappeared with her for a long weekend before reappearing, much to everyone's shock, and moving her into his former bachelor pad. They married just six months later.

If his parents had been alive, he doubted that he would have lasted so long as a bachelor. Where his father had insisted that Chen pursue a military career, his mother had been as ambitious as his father with the matrimonial fate of her only child. She had insisted he give her grandchildren, and plenty of them, and her campaign had increased in intensity after he graduated from the naval academy and qualified for the astronaut program. The sudden loss of Chen's father in the 2095 EnviroFirst Riots had stopped her grand plans in their tracks. The environmental group EnviroFirst's demonstration had turned violent, and Chen's father had been in the wrong place at the wrong time when the police fired rubber bullets into the crowd, killing his father instantly as he exited a small shop, dinner in hand, caught in the melee. Chen's mother had never forgiven herself for sending her husband on an errand at just the wrong time, as the protest made its way up the street and to the police barricade.

She had stepped off of the bridge in the middle of a downpour a few weeks later, the river's swollen waters carrying her away in seconds. They had never found her body.

Chen had instead focused on his career, rising with a dizzying swiftness to both military and space command, his fierce intelligence and leadership skills combining with the appropriate political correctness to make him connections in all the areas necessary for advancement. And here he had been until Mei ruined his silk shirt and captured his heart.

Chen took a deep breath in, and let it back out, willing his mind to calm, for the ache he had felt deep inside since hearing of the accident that had ripped his heart and soul from his body to subside enough that he could face another day without them.

Why had he allowed himself to be with Fen? The wrongness of it shook him to the core. In another time or place, Fen was a gem worth keeping. But Chen's eyes only sought Mei. Despite knowing the truth, he yearned, with a hope beyond hope, that the next message from Mission Command would be that they had been wrong, that she was not dead, that it had all been a mistake. That his dreams, the same ones that replayed every night, were a lie. At the end of each dream, he stood there by the side of the bridge and watched the autocar slip, correct, and then slip again, the tires slowly dipping down, the whole of the vehicle sliding until gravity did what gravity does and took the car. Sometimes he saw it in his dreams as tumbling down into the abyss, sometimes crashing against a section of cliff and rocks, and other times revolving in open air, touching nothing until it burst into flames upon impact, immolating his future, his dreams, his love.

He could think of nothing and no one else, no matter what tasks were in front of him, no matter what his mission was. They lay buried without him, alone, waiting for his return.

The wave of dizziness returned, and he sat on his bunk, his mind in turmoil, caught in the past and seeing no actual future. Today was an EVA. The antenna needed adjusting, and he had volunteered for it. It would need to be early, as radar had shown the likelihood of a large dust storm headed their way.

All he wanted to do was see Mei again.

A morbid plan occupied his thoughts as he washed his face, dressed, and joined the others in the small galley and Mess Hall. It remained there as they planned the day, and he put off the EVA until early afternoon.

Liu frowned. "But the dust storm..."

Chen waved his hand dismissively. "We will have plenty of time."

Liu's face still held a frown. Chen turned away from it and focused on Fen. "How are the trials with the groundcover going?"

Fen answered, "The fifth group, which has the highest concentration of seeds collected from the northern regions, they are staying green, despite the overnight temperatures. All that they require is a steady source of water. The carbon dioxide in the atmosphere has sped up their growth by over 30%, exceeding expectations."

Chen nodded. "Good, good. We will continue to seed the western field and monitor. I would like for you to prepare a complete report this afternoon, include samples, images, and a full spectrum analysis of the plant for submission to Mission Control."

Fen looked surprised. "I thought you needed that next week."

"Mission Control has requested the update early," Chen lied glibly.

Fen blinked at him, and then nodded. "Of course, I will have that by 1700 hours."

"Good." Chen turned back to Liu. "I have some other work to attend to; we will plan the EVA for 1400 hours."

"But the storm..." Liu's words, and his objection, died away, as Chen stared at him, saying nothing. The silence was effective, as was the stern look on his face. The younger man stammered, "Yes, Commander, 1400 hours."

Chen had gone back to his bunk, spent hours staring at the photos of his wife and daughter, and of himself in happier moments, before typing a note for Liu and Fen to find.

Seven hours later, as he stood outside, the winds already strong, the feel of the sand and rock scraping at his suit, Chen knew it was time.

"Liu, I will need additional supplies. Please collect the following for me and send it through the tool airlock." He slowly tapped a list into his wrist keyboard and pressed the enter key.

Liu paused. "I will ask Fen to do it, one moment, and..."

"No, she is busy with that report. I don't wish for her to be interrupted; just take off the suit and do it yourself."

The pause was longer this time and Chen could hear the uncertainty in Liu's voice. "Commander, the protocol..."

Chen hardened his voice to steel. "Fong, I wrote the protocol. Do as I have requested, now."

"Yes, Commander." There was silence for several minutes. Chen looked at the approaching cloud. It was a dark brown-red, the color of old blood, and bigger than any he had seen before. This one might last a week, maybe longer.

This place, it was where he belonged now, here in the wasteland, devoid of air or a sustainable atmosphere. It resembled what remained of his heart and soul now that he had lost his beautiful wife and child. Fen would give birth to the child, and she and Liu could raise it. Together they could make it to the Huygens Outpost and live out their lives. The baby would never even need to know who his or her father was.

"Commander, I have placed the tools in the airlock." Liu's voice sounded over the speakers in his suit. "I'll suit back up again."

"Wait, I may need other tools." Chen moved towards the airlock. He needed a little more time.

"Sir, the wind is picking up. The dust storm is..."

"I am aware of the storm, Fong." Chen cut off Liu's protestations. The tools were all there inside of the airlock. If he took them, however, Liu and Fen might need them when it came time to alter the rover. He reached in, certain that he would need at least ten more minutes before the storm would be upon them. "Liu," he said, "I will need additional cable from the cargo bay."

"Sir, that is inaccessible without pressurizing the storage so I can enter it. It will take at least ten minutes. The storm...'

Chen barked, "Fong, do as I say. Now!"

As soon as the younger man disappeared from view, no doubt on his way to find Fen and get help, Chen returned the tools to the small airlock, all except for one, and then he closed it and strode away from the Hab, straight towards the storm. The radio worked for short distances up to a mile. Moments later, he could hear Liu begging him to return, his voice high, strained, before finally, he fetched Fen or notified her via the comm. The wind, though, interfered. By the time their voices faded, Chen had made his way to the northeast edge of the crater. The sand and dirt scoured the clear plastic, and he grew tired of clearing it. It didn't matter, nothing mattered, not anymore. It was time to join Mei and Li Ma. There was nothing left on Earth or Mars, nothing that mattered any longer. His life had ended the day his wife and child had died; his body just hadn't figured it out yet. The edge of the crater was a dark shadow of rock and dirt rising above him. Chen sat down, more at peace than he thought possible. He had left a note in his bunk for Fen and Liu. Chen knew that they would try to come after the storm died down, but by then it would be far too late. The blade from the multi-tool was sharp, but the suit he was wearing resisted tearing, and was, to some extent, self-repairing. He would have to be decisive and quick. Around him, the wind howled and the particles of sand and dirt scoured the faceplate of his suit. He could no longer see the science outpost, no longer hear Liu and Fen's frantic pleas for him to return.

He plunged the knife into his abdomen, twisted, and yanked it hard to one side. Then he pulled it out just as quickly. The pain from the wound was intense, but it only lasted a second. A rush of pressurized air pulled Chen's intestines out through the small hole with a jet of fresh blood. It would have been an agonizing experience, but Chen was already gone, instantly losing consciousness as the air pressure dropped. His body slumped slowly down to the ground, quickly covered with a thick layer of dust as the winds continued to blow.

Back at the outpost, Fen called Chen's name over the comm until her voice became hoarse. After darkness fell, and the dust storm raged on, Liu finally interceded. He had entered Chen's bunk and found the older man's tablet on the small table, the automatic power-saving mode deactivated so that the screen would show his message to whoever entered. He pressed it into Fen's hands and let her read the note as he quietly put away the tools Chen had so easily distracted him with.

"He did this on purpose?" Her voice was a raw whisper.

Liu nodded and waited for her to read the rest.

By now you must have realized the truth. That I am not coming back.

We all must decide on what we hold true, what we want out of this life and beyond.

I realized that my heart and soul were gone. They fell from a cliff into the Three Rivers Gorge five months ago. And with it, my will to continue to live in the face of this terrible future.

Forgive me, Fen, that I leave you now, this child we share growing inside of you. I know that you will raise the baby right, that you will be the mother our child needs. I hope that Liu will stand beside you in this and that together you will travel to Huygens as they remain virus-free.

It is not the future any of us predicted, but it is the one that we must exist within. I only wish that I had the strength to go on, but I do not. Do not look for me. Leave me out there. It is merely a shell, this body. My heart and my soul know the way home. I am where I belong.

Fen collapsed then; her legs no longer able to sustain her. The baby kicked gently inside of her. It felt like a question, a query.

She cried, not out of a love lost, for there had not been that between her and Chen. She cried out of hopelessness, that something as small as a virus had killed everyone she had ever loved and would kill her, this child, and even Liu, should they dare to return. Liu did his best to comfort her, his legs an awkward tangle as he cradled her in his arms on the icy floor of the airlock bay. Finally, Liu lifted her up gently and walked her back to her bunk. He set her on the edge of the bed and slipped away to the Medical Bay for something that would help her relax, something that would not harm the baby. When he returned, she had curled up. Her slight frame looked so fragile there as she continued to sob.

"Here, take these, they will help you sleep." After she had swallowed the pills, he pulled the blanket over her, tucking it in tight as his mother had done for him when he was small.

"What do we do now?" Fen asked. All of her training, all the scenarios, they hadn't included pregnancy, her commander committing suicide, and most of Earth dying from a virus. She hated how her voice sounded, so small, fragile, but she felt lost and frightened.

Liu sat down on the edge of the narrow bunk; his dark eyes full of concern for her. "We let Mission Control know what happened. And then we figure out whether we are better off returning home or going to Huygens Outpost." He shrugged. "We survive. One day at a time."

His words soothed her. Liu reached out and moved a strand of her hair away from her eyes. "Sleep. We will talk about it more in the morning."

Fen felt a heaviness come over her, and her eyelids impossible to keep open. She hadn't eaten dinner, and the sedatives did their work quickly. She slipped into the dark of sleep as Liu watched over her protectively.

The Center Cannot Hold

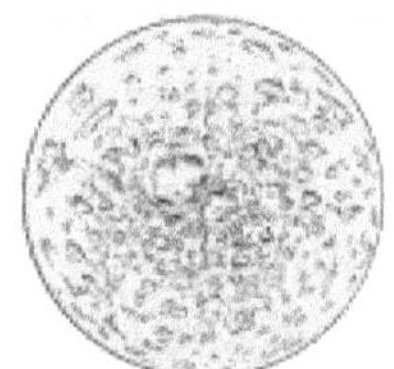

Mars Year 14, Week 36, Day 358
(Earth Date: 08.04.2099)

Ted Danziger was an unrepentant flirt. And here, in the Huygens Outpost, there were plenty of women, and men, to flirt with. He hadn't met all of them yet, not even close, but as the face of ShingDo, the company that had created the atmo generators that were busy pumping PFCs into the atmosphere, Danziger felt that he had more than just an obligation to promote the company, but also to start "positive interpersonal relations" with the colonists. It was a toss-up whether he was more interested in sex or money, or simply could not choose between the two. The income he would earn on this short stint on the red planet was well worth his time, especially since he was having such a damn fine time with a multitude of interpersonal relations while hard at work earning his bonuses.

Eventually, he would head back to Earth, probably on the next ship, whenever that was. The news of the Jupiter Supply Ship being scuttled on the far side of the planet had been rather alarming. But Ted hadn't really considered the implications of it, and he did not follow the news from Earth as closely as the others did.

He had already visited Philadelphia Hab and Hong Kong Hab and was heading for London this morning. Each City Hab had control of one of the small atmo generators. Now that they had been in operation for over a decade, and the environmental measurements had shown a tiny increase in greenhouse gasses, it was time for him to roll out the next phase of the project, a string of atmo generators that would run autonomously, and between them, they would include a new type of clover that could survive sub-zero temps. It was an exciting collaboration, one that was being hailed as "the greening of Mars."

Ted had agreed to come to the red planet for a two-year stint and no more. Living in domes and waiting the minimum three hundred years for the temperatures to level out and another seven hundred years until they had a breathable atmosphere was not his idea of fun. He would leave that to the pioneers, the die-hard colonists who, much like the Pilgrims, gave up all manner of earthly delights in a quest to find and settle a distant land. His boss had promised him a tremendous bonus for three years of his life, and a giant step up the corporate ladder, if he could get the large atmo generators okayed by the political leaders of Mars. It meant billions of dollars in income for ShingDo and a tidy fortune in the commission. Hell, it would be enough of a commission that he could actually choose to never work again. Not that he would, however. He loved the challenge.

He was in it for the money, whereas that ridiculous prude of a woman, Petra Salinger, had markedly different plans from his. She had some insane notion that she could speed up the greenhouse effect and ride out the wait in Cryo. She had even tried to show him the figures that suggested Mars could have a breathable atmosphere in one-tenth of the time previously expected. One hundred years to a breathable atmosphere? It was insane.

He had stared at her slack-jawed when she admitted that she intended on staying on Mars permanently. He shook his head at the idea as he stared out at the harsh, barren landscape. Sure, if the clover took off, then the regolith soil would soon turn green and eventually they would see temperatures rise and water return to liquid state. And while weighing less than half of his weight had made him feel closer to his teen years than his late thirties, living out his life on Mars wasn't something that interested Ted. He was more than satisfied to oversee the deal of a lifetime and then return home to the creature comforts that only Earth could provide.

He rose from the bed carefully, so as not to disturb the two other occupants. They didn't move, both still sound asleep. He slipped on his pants and shirt from the night before and slipped out of the door, his stomach growling for food. He whispered at NARA and asked her the time. The computer whispered back, "It is 0634, Ted. You have a meeting at 0900 hours."

Perfect. He had enough time to visit the Singles Hab assigned to him, shower, eat breakfast, pack his small bag of clothing, and suit up for the short EVA to London City Hab. Why they didn't already have the paths enclosed was beyond him. When he had mentioned it, his guide had given him some excuse about limited resources. It was inconvenient to get inside some damned smelly suit that who knows how many others had used, just to walk a few thousand yards. At the very least, they should have a little golf cart. When he had suggested it, the man had sounded like a broken record when he said, "The rovers are reserved for hauling loads back and forth, and we have limited resources."

Limited resources, limited resources. They always used that tired old excuse! He would be happy to return home. The apartment he lived in was as claustrophobic as the Singles Habs, but that was all going to change when he was back with his tidy commission payable upon successful agreement. He would fill the landscape with the atmo generators and the automated bots, dust his hands free of the red soil, return to Earth, and happily move up the corporate ladder.

His stomach rumbled again, and Ted increased his walk to a brisk pace and headed left instead of straight. Hell, he needed food now, not later. After he had eaten, then he would worry about a shower and a change of clothes. All the clothes looked the same, anyway. He doubted anyone would even care if he looked slightly rumpled.

The Mess Hall was nearly empty, but he shook the chef's hand and clapped him on the shoulder, saying, "Got anything good this morning?" It was a running joke. It was the same damn meal every day, except for once every tenth day, when they did their best to make something special emerge from all the cans and pre-packaged meals. The last tenth day had been some tater tots smothered in gravy. It had been different, that was for sure. There had even been chunks of what he hoped was sausage, but very much doubted. Earth was fond of sending all of their test runs of faux meats for Mars colonists to try out. Considering how disgusting the faux meats usually were, they made a great selling point for accelerating the speed of the greenhouse gas effect, and he used it to its full advantage.

"Just the usual," the man replied, and pointed. "This one or that one today?" Both choices looked unappetizing. The man grinned sadistically. "All the minerals and nutrients...everything a body needs!"

Ted rolled his eyes and grinned in return. "Hell, give me a little of both. And a little extra if you don't mind. I'm starving this morning!"

"You and everyone else these days. I'm going to have to pull out an extra tray."

The server handed him his plate and Ted tried not to smell it as he carried it to a table. Somehow, the aroma, which was far better than the taste, was always a setup for a terrible letdown. He chose a large table that had three others already seated. They ate their meals while scrolling through pictures and text on their tablets. He greeted them all with a smile. None of them were familiar, but then he had only been at Philly Hab for a few days, and there were nearly one hundred colonists in each of the City Habs.

He plastered an affable grin on his face and said, "Hey there, good morning everyone. I'm Ted, Ted Danziger."

They all looked up and responded. He had a gift, and he knew it. Damned if he wasn't going places and he was going to be everyone's friend. It helped sell things, sure, but it also helped sell him. You never knew where or when a connection could help. Ted was always on the lookout for one that would elevate him from where he was now, to where he needed to be. Every face was an opportunity, every person someone who could help him get from here to there. It was an essential lesson his dad had taught him, over and over, as he tripped across the country, Ted under his wing, winning over friends and enemies alike.

He made small talk and learned everyone's specialties, their names, and why they had come to Mars, as he devoured the food in front of him. By the end of the meal, he had a new connection for when he returned to Earth, a woman's brother who was managing a large ad agency and looking for reps who could sign folks on board. He also had the Ident code of the woman, who was single, and they made a date to get a drink when he returned to Philly Hab. Despite the bland taste of the food, he went back for a second helping when his stomach rumbled again. An errant thought stopped him in his tracks.

Could I have that damned virus?

And for a moment the load of food in his guts gave a flip of discomfort.

No, they tested me; they tested everyone, before we got on board Calypso and again when they pulled us out of Cryo. I'm being ridiculous.

He didn't think of it again, no matter what the talk of home became, and damned if the reports weren't grim. Ted remained surprised that, as he moved from Hong Kong Hab to London Hab, then Cairo and Sydney Habs, the vid screens in the Mess Halls streaming constant updates of the ESH virus didn't put him off his feed, as the old saying went. Sure, they were off-putting, graphic, and disconcerting, but his appetite remained as strong as ever.

By the time he had cycled back around to the Philadelphia Hab, he had to ask for a larger suit. He marveled at that. "How in the hell can I possibly gain weight eating this pre-packaged shit?" he had complained to the Airlock Tech. Once again, the fear of infection crossed his mind. Dan checked with NARA, who detected no fever, nothing higher than 98.6. He was fine. He had to be. Nothing else made sense. Viruses made you feel like shit, rundown, tired, and he was none of those.

The first go round of meet and greets through the various City Habs had gone well. Now he would cycle through each of the City Habs in forty-day-long intervals, supposedly to learn as much as he could about each of the Habs' various needs and requirements, which varied, somewhat. As Ted sat in the Mess Hall of the Philly Hab, his stomach still rumbling after he had devoured two large helpings of lunch, he thought about what the next twenty-four months would be like as he waited for the new ship to come and retrieve him. The news from Earth seemed to grow grimmer by the moment, and recently the news had focused on the one variable that seemed to ensure survival, that of a rare blood type.

The news broadcaster was discussing it now, with some high muckety-muck doctor being interviewed and saying, "Right now, we have no idea if this is an anomaly or not, but to date, no infected individuals who carry the blood type AB negative have died from the disease. It requires more testing."

The vid cut back to the broadcaster, who fanned the flames. "Meanwhile, the number of dead in the Reformed United States of America has reached 675 million, leaving a population of less than 25 million people left. They fill our cities with the dead, there are food shortages, rolling blackouts, and widespread reports of looting," the newscaster said, her eyes fever bright.

Ted shook his head. "Nothing sells like blood and death. What was it they used to say? 'If it bleeds, it leads.'" He scraped the last of his food from his plate, his stomach grumbling.

The pretty girl across from him wore a haunted look on her face. "I haven't heard from my family in two weeks now. Not since they shut down news coverage in Texas and enforced quarantine."

Ted reached for her hand and squeezed it. "I'm so sorry. It must worry you sick." He took a leap then, adopting a pained look on his face. "My mother...I haven't heard a peep, she's locked down on the East Coast, in Maine," he lied glibly. Ted barely remembered his mother. She had left him with his dad one weekend and never come back. He had been five or six by then. His dad hadn't been happy when he found himself saddled with a kid, but he had made it work for him, and in the process, he had taught Ted how to ingratiate himself into just about any situation and any bed.

Hours later, as he leaned back against the red brick wall, a fine sheen of sweat on his skin from their exertions, the woman cried, gut-wrenching sobs of distress. Unlike most men, Ted knew just how to finesse a crying woman. His stomach grumbled, a sharp need that was not an acceptable body response to a crying woman. He ignored it and rubbed her back, making soothing sounds while his stomach growled louder.

Christ, I just ate two hours ago!

"NARA, play 20th century instrumental rock music," he asked the computer, and it responded with a stream of music that covered the sounds of his stomach, even if it didn't abate the hunger he felt. "Here," he said to the girl as her tears stopped flowing, "turn on your stomach. What you need is to relax and just breathe, alright?" A massage would take away the sadness and instead re-focus her mind on more basic body needs, especially if he took it slow. He sternly told his stomach to shut up; it was time for round two. After they finished, he'd talk her into a trip to the Mess Hall for a snack before luring her back to his place for round three.

In the middle of a rather vigorous round two, his stomach brought him back to reality with an especially vicious cramping. He stopped in mid-thrust and the girl beneath him, caught in mid-moan, sat up. "What is it?"

Ted felt hot, so hot, and he stood and looked around the tiny, narrow room. "Man, I'm so damned hungry that I can't think of anything else."

The girl stood up and reached for his forehead. "You're burning up, Ted. Like, a serious fever, I think you need to..."

"Get something to eat, I know," he interrupted, reaching for his pants and sliding them on one leg before hopping about, fighting to get the second leg in.

"No," she said, suddenly looking scared, "I think you need to go to the Infirmary. I think you need to get tested for, for..."

Ted waved his hand, partly dismissive, but also with a building sense of fear, and said, "I need to eat, then I'll go to the infirmary." He turned to walk out the door, just his pants on and no shoes. The girl squeaked with alarm and pulled a sheet over her exposed chest as he opened the door wide and walked into the hallway. He strode down the hallway, his stomach in knots, an overwhelming need washing over him. Within a moment, he could hear her bare feet slapping against the floor as she ran after him.

"Ted, please, we need to get you to the Infirmary!"

"Sure, as soon as I get something to eat," he responded, without breaking stride. His finger caught on his pants, and he could feel the flesh split near the nail. He put his finger in his mouth and nibbled, biting the bit of flesh off and swallowing it. Behind him, the girl—what was her name anyway?—had fallen behind. His stomach wrenched again, a gaping emptiness that felt endless in its need for more food. He practically ran the last hundred feet to the Mess Hall, which was dark. Only the beverage and snack food dispensers against the far wall were lit up.

Shit, I forgot to bring tokens.

They had dispensed him several tokens when he first arrived, with the explanation that he would receive more in thirty days. They needed no payment for regular meals, only the special items, the packaged crackers and cookies and caffeinated beverages that kept everyone from growing resentful over the plain, prepackaged foods.

He searched his pockets, the hunger in his stomach pushing him to a frenzy, as he cast about the room, desperate for anything that would stop this awful hunger. His eyes fell on the salt and pepper dispensers. Anything, anything would do. He grabbed a salt dispenser and turned it upside down, fingers scrabbling at the seal. It flew off, and he tipped it into his open mouth and dumped the lot in. His body screamed for more, even as he choked, a plume of salt granules flying out of his mouth. He turned towards the pepper, peeled the seal open, and repeated the gesture. As the pepper slid down his throat, dry and irritated from the mass of salt, he choked again. He needed water, soda, anything. He ran to the wall of dispensers and began pressing the buttons, desperate for something, anything to work. His fingers jabbed at the controls and the screen demanded he insert tokens to pay for the items. He screamed in frustration, more pepper flying out, some of it working its way into his sinuses, where it burned like his face had been lit on fire.

"Ted? Ted, can you hear me?"

The girl was back, and she had company. Two men in uniform, another man behind them. What was her name? Ted stared at them as they slowly advanced. He tried to smile, but his face hurt too much, the pepper burning and burning and his stomach. God, he was starving. "I need more food. Could you get someone to get me more food?" he croaked past the dryness of the salt.

The girl, *Julie, that's her name*, looked scared. "Ted, these men are here to help you. You need to go with them, to the Infirmary."

Ted looked at the three men behind her. The two in uniform were now fanning out to the left and the right. They wore face masks and gloves, and he looked at their hands. No food. He backed away from them, moving backward the three steps it took to hit the wall. The dispensing unit beeped again, no doubt the screen displaying a request for a token.

"I need a token. I just need something to eat. I'm...hungry," he croaked again, his head moving to the left and right, watching the two uniforms approach.

The one on the left reached into his pocket. "I got a token here for you, Ted, but I need you to sit down first, okay?" The other man had pulled a weapon. Ted jumped then, leaping towards Julie, and the man behind her, a wordless scream of hunger issuing from his mouth. There was a blinding pain in his left side and then Ted was on the ground, his body leaden and heavy as the tranquilizer took effect.

As he faded, he heard Julie whisper, "The center cannot hold," as she collapsed in sobs next to him.

At 2300, Ted Danziger, Mars' Patient Zero, went into convulsions and died after he broke both wrists ripping through his restraints in the infirmary and ingested several glass ampules of sedatives to satiate his hunger. The girl, Julie Espinosa, was already in quarantine, the other City Habs notified, and a lockdown initiated. As the doctors traced Danziger's movements since landing and being woken from Cryo, one thing became obvious. Because of the close quarters, everyone on the Huygens Outpost had now been exposed to the ESH virus–either through primary, secondary, or tertiary contact.

Just five days later...

Transmission Packet

HOM to CSC

/BEGIN TRANSMISSION

Huygens Outpost is positive for the ESH virus. All City Habs affected. Lockdown in place. Twenty primary exposures to Patient Zero, Ted Danziger, have already succumbed, and most of us are showing some signs of the illness. We have enacted full quarantine procedures. May God have mercy on our souls.

/END TRANSMISSION

Too Late to Leave Now

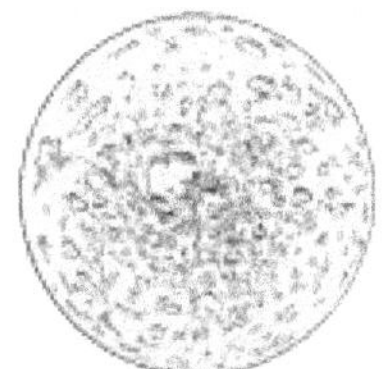

Mars Year 14, Week 37, Day 361
(Earth Date: 08.07.2099)

Since Chen's suicide, the Beijing Science Outpost seemed desolate. Despite his solemn demeanor, Chen's presence had filled the space. Now, in his absence, the halls seemed to echo louder, and the silence itself felt overwhelming. Fen's belly was growing. She caressed her stomach, felt the boy kick. Sometimes, his head would move from one side to the next, and it was fascinating to watch. She had been working so much when Shu was pregnant with Wei and Ho that she hadn't seen the phenomenon, although Shu had called her and told her all about it, excited to share the news.

Fen wished Shu could be here now, beside her. Shu had loved being pregnant, and had wanted more children, lots more, but the cost of a third child would have been prohibitive. Across the world, the various governments took different approaches and stances to the subject of overcrowding, and that of dwindling resources, and the food shortages that followed the overcrowding because of high birth rates.

And while China no longer enforced the One Child legislation that had been so prevalent in the early part of the 21st century, the cultural engineering they had set in place still frowned on couples who produced over two children. Besides, the costs for having over one or two children had become financially impossible thanks to the financial incentives and limitations put in place during the One Child movement that remained decades later.

Fen had imagined she would have just one child, although Bao had pushed her to agree to more. He had pointed to her high status and pointed out how important she was and how the powers that be would turn a blind eye if they were to have more than just one or two children.

The baby inside her kicked again, this time on her bladder, and she stood up and hurried to the restroom, shoving the memory of Bao to the back of her mind. It was nearly time to eat, and Liu had said he had a surprise for her. The way his dark eyes had danced and his mouth had turned up in a bright smile had promised it would be a good one.

She wasn't sure how to respond to him. She could sense his interest, his wish to take this work relationship, even friendship, to something more. It pained her, more because Liu was kind and sweet and thoughtful–everything she could want in a partner. He reminded her of her brother-in-law, Lian. If there were any relationship she could hope for, it was the one that Shu and Lian had shared. She had known that Bao was not the same, not even close, and not the best. Despite this, she had let him woo her, watched as he took credit for her accomplishments, and then did her best to ignore him when he demanded she give up her dreams.

And yet I love him still. He is dead, and Liu is here, but I can't look at him, not that way.

She washed her hands and left the bunk, her feet softly padding through the long hallway to the Mess Hall, a half-smile on her face. Liu's last surprise was a small candy, sweet and sour and splendid to taste after more than a year of packaged meals first on the Mazu and then here at the outpost. Another time he had gathered the small pink berries from the beauty berry plant that grew in the garden and used them to paint a picture of a Martian sunset on the wall of the hallway. The detail of it had captivated her, and she had spent hours staring at it at night when the baby was kicking and she couldn't sleep.

She couldn't help wondering if it had been his parents who had pushed him into astronomy and astrophysics when it was so obvious how much he loved art and music. And not just loved it but was talented as well, talented enough that she could see him performing his music or selling his paintings far more than she could see him performing experiments and traveling to distant planets.

She rounded the corner to the Mess Hall and nearly ran into Liu, grasping at the door frame as she halted abruptly.

"There you are," he said, his face lacking its customary smile. "I was just coming to tell you we received a transmission from Mission Control."

The look on his face said it all. They had been waiting for weeks for an answer to the question of what they should do next, and apparently it had finally arrived. Her heart plummeted.

"They won't allow us back, will they?"

He shook his head. "They say we must go to Huygens. Just as," he gulped and forced the words out, "Just as Chen told us we should. I think that it has gotten worse there."

"How could it get worse?" Fen said, the words slipping from her mouth, before she caught herself and placed one hand over her mouth and shut her eyes. Of course, it could get worse, so much worse.

How she had hoped that they would find a cure. That they would have somewhere safe for them to go. That she could return to Earth, even if it meant not returning home to Guiyang or even Guizhou province.

Liu said nothing, his expressive eyes black pools of misery.

"Well, that's it, then. We go to Huygens. It's achievable, but only if we plot it out carefully," Fen said, choosing her words carefully, reminded by Liu's expression how much her words and moods affected him. His smile didn't return. Something was definitely bothering him.

"Tell me what is wrong."

Liu nodded and began, "Okay, so it's 5,425 kilometers to Huygens in a straight shot. However, the route I plotted out considers the terrain, which added another 900 kilometers onto our journey, which brings us to..."

"Six thousand, three hundred and twenty-five kilometers."

"Right."

"We have enough fuel to make it there, far more, actually, since we don't need it for the Mazu. But it's heavy. And then we will need additional oxygen tanks as well. This slows us down from a top speed of 25 kilometers per hour."

"We also need to factor in terrain, which could slow down our progress as well," Fen added.

He managed a weak smile. "Yes, correct. I estimated that we could count on an average speed of 17 kilometers per hour. We will have approximately twelve hours of sunlight each day, and I don't recommend that we drive at night. There are too many variables, and if we lost control or damaged the vehicle, we would die out there."

Fen nodded in agreement and Liu showed her the numbers on his tablet. "We have to factor in at least a few minutes every few hours to switch places, rest, and more."

"Figure eleven hours per day total at seventeen klicks, equals one hundred eighty-seven per day, or at least thirty-four days' travel." His eyes fell to her burgeoning belly. "In space suits the entire time."

Fen gulped. "I can't fit into a spacesuit, not even if we had..." her lips quivered as she continued, "even if we had Chen's, which we don't."

They had honored his wishes and not retrieved his body. The locater signal built into all the suits showed it was over 3 kilometers from the science station, and neither of them had left the station since it happened.

Liu's fingers danced on his tablet, and Fen leaned over to see the schematic better. "We could part up the module to the west, add an environmental unit onto it, a small airlock, and power it with the fuel from MOXIE, and solar collectors for when we stop at night." He frowned. "The extra weight calculations mean that it would take us closer to forty days, and only I could drive. You would stay inside the module. It's that or we wait for, well..." He broke eye contact and stared at the ground.

Fen felt a stab of guilt. The evening before, she had reacted badly when Liu mentioned the baby. She had snapped at him, told him she didn't wish to speak of it, and he had immediately shut down, his excitement dulling. He had mentioned in training how much his parents had wanted a grandchild. Even if she wasn't excited, he was, just as excited as if it were *his* child she was carrying. He had even taken the extra uniforms in storage and begun making tiny shifts that would cover the baby. He had engineered them with additional folds, so they would grow with the child.

It was that, along with his humming as he had sewn, that had driven her to the edge the previous evening. When he had asked what she had thought of for names, that was when she had snapped. It hadn't been fair, and it hadn't been right, but part of her wished she didn't have to accept the truth of it. That she could remain ignorant, ignore the child moving inside her, and believe that any day the message would come that her family had escaped the firebombing, that they were one of the groups of Unaffected Persons and that Mission Control had a plan for them to join an established enclave and be safe. She wanted to hold on to that fantasy, because reality, well, let's just say that reality felt like an endless night had descended upon them.

She changed the subject. "You promised me a surprise."

Liu looked up, his mouth curving into an excited smile. "I did." He reached out and took her hand. "Come, come, I'll show you."

The meal waiting at the table was the standard fare and Fen cocked her head, waiting for the grand reveal. Liu just grinned wider, before shrugging and saying, "It's actually for after dinner."

His excitement was obvious, and as soon as they finished, he reached into one of the cupboards and pulled out a cellophane-wrapped bag. It was flat and said POPCORN in large letters on the side. Fen eyed it. "What is it?"

Liu practically danced in place. "An American treat! I found it while going through the food-storage area. You remember Kim Yee? He was a huge fan of America and always talking about..."

"Jujubes!" Fen said at the same time as Liu. "I remember!"

Liu laughed with delight. "He said the only thing that beat Jujubes was popcorn and *The Three Stooges*."

Fen cocked her head. "I thought you didn't learn English."

Liu waved a dismissive hand. "It's comedy. I don't need to understand the words. I'll bet I can figure it out without it." He ran over to the wall and opened up the microwave built into it. While the popcorn popped, he shoved the chairs together, forming a couch, and added blankets. "Dim the lights, Fen. I set up the projector earlier."

Fen settled herself on the chairs awkwardly, the baby having changed her center of gravity as he grew. The timer for the popcorn sounded, and the popping subsided to an occasional odd pop. When Liu opened the microwave, the smell of it was intense, a buttery odor that suffused the air. Liu grinned as he brought the steaming bag over to Fen, his smile expanding as he pulled a battered box of Jujubes from his pocket.

Fen laughed, the sound of it startling her. How long had it been since she laughed? Since she had smiled? Liu handed her the box of candy and gingerly opened the bag of popcorn. He sniffed it and laughed with delight. "It smells good, don't you think?"

Fen nodded. Her smile was still there, and somehow, despite everything, it felt good to smile again. Liu punched the buttons on the remote and scrolled through the choices, landing on *The Three Stooges* episodes. Fen pointed at the picture next to one episode. "Are they dressed as women?"

Liu shrugged and read the title, "Wee Wee Monsieur?"

"It means little sir," Fen translated after a quick search on his tablet. "Although it may be a play on words. The French word oui is pronounced wee, but it means yes, not little. Perhaps the title means 'yes, yes sir.'"

Liu looked at her, a curious expression on his face. Fen hadn't sat this close to him before, side by side like this. He looked so young, but he was also handsome in a boyish sort of way. How had she not noticed that before?

"I didn't know you spoke other languages besides Mandarin and English."

Fen blushed, "I don't. Not really. I just..." she shrugged. "I like words."

"Will you teach me English?" Liu asked. "I must know when we end up at Huygens." His face became reflective, and Fen could see his ignorance troubled him.

She put her hand on his. "Yes."

They sat for a moment in silence, imagining what it would be like to leave here, to go to Huygens and find themselves surrounded by strangers. Fen broke the silence, squeezing Liu's hand, and said, "Play the Wee Wee Monsieur." She reached into the bag and took out a single kernel of popcorn and ate it gingerly. The flavor differed from rice. The salt and the butter combined to make it a tasty, exotic treat. She handed Liu the box of candy and sat back as the ancient show played out in black and white.

By the end, Fen's sides ached from laughing so much. Liu grinned at her. "That was even funnier than I had hoped for!"

He had been right; a grasp of the English language was unnecessary for such slapstick comedy. She smiled at him. "Thank you, Liu, for this." She swept a hand out to include the now half-full bag of popped corn, and the empty box of candy. "This was wonderful."

His expression changed, and the smile slipped only for a moment. "You have been so sad."

Fen nodded, her throat closing with emotion. "I know."

They were silent, each lost in their own thoughts, and neither brave enough to share them. Liu broke the silence first. "There's more; should we watch another one?"

Fen opened her mouth to say yes only to hear a chime from the Control Room. It was odd; they had received a message just two hours before, and it was unusual for Mission Control to have much more to say in a day. Fen's heart beat faster, her anxiety resurfacing.

Without a word, they both stood up and headed to the Control Room. Fen was the one to reach out and play the message. It was a short one, and after it, they both stood in silence. The baby rolled and kicked in Fen's belly, as if he could sense the dire news. Fen's face was numb, her mind in turmoil.

Liu slowly reached out and raised her chin, waiting for her to open her eyes and meet his. "Fen, it will be alright."

"We are going to die here," she said, her body shaking.

Liu took her in his arms and pulled her close. "I won't let that happen. We will find a way."

Fen's mind spun in circles. The message from Mission Control had been devastating. Huygens Outpost had fallen to the ESH virus. Their last safe refuge was no longer safe at all. The Mazu spaceship could leave Mars, but not while Fen was pregnant, and not with an infant. They were trapped here, for *years*.

"It's too late to leave now," she said, her voice faint.

"We will find a way. I promise." Liu's voice remained firm, reassuring.

Fen didn't resist when Liu led her back to the Mess Hall, arranged more blankets and, after a trip to one of the bunkrooms, leaving her in a shocked silence, returned with soft cushions and pillows. He arranged them thoughtfully before he gently led her to sit down and pressed a small pill in her hand. Fen swallowed it mechanically, then laid down, her heart and mind too overwhelmed to say anything as he tucked himself in next to her.

Liu dimmed the lights and leaned close to her. "Fen, I won't let anything bad happen to you. I promise this. I'll find a way for us to survive."

Fen said nothing. Instead, she tucked her head into his arm, resting a cheek on his chest. He smelled good and his body's warmth was soothing. The pill pulled a thick cover of exhaustion over her and she sighed, her eyelids heavy. In the darkness, just as she was dozing off, Liu whispered, "I love you. I always have."

We Are Who We Are

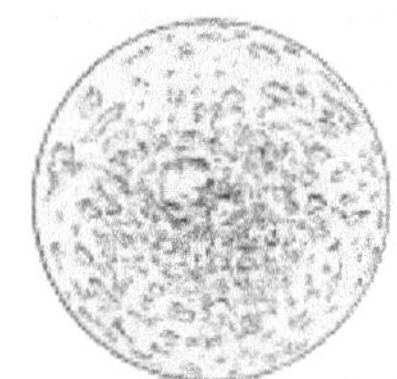

Mars Year 14, Week 38, Day 376
(Earth Date: 08.22.2099)

Nix covered Denali's face and wished, if only for a moment, that he believed in God. It seemed as if it would come as solace now. He had hoped that the older man would make it, but the virus had taken him just like the others. It had only been delayed, after all, by his isolation from the others, and his late exposure. He hadn't been immune after all.

Fuck.

And now, here they were. Or rather, here Nix was. Alone.

Together he and Denali had moved the bodies as they fell. One by one, then in clusters, Hong Kong Hab had fallen to the ESH virus. So small, it seemed insignificant, yet so virulent it had reached across millions of miles to bring death upon everyone it touched. The space stations had gone silent, then Ptolemy Lunar Colony, and now the other Habs of the Huygens Outpost.

Nix felt a bitterness spread through him. Trapped on a planet he had never wanted to be on. And everyone, everyone who had mattered, who had insisted on his being marooned here, were likely dead. What he had done to get here; did it even matter anymore?

Trust Denali to die at the opposite end of the Hab from where they had been taking the bodies. Nix stared at the hallway that led to the nearest airlock and considered taking Denali's body there, but if he left Hong Kong Hab, he really didn't want to have to walk past the body of his dead friend. And this airlock would be the one he left out of. It seemed to make sense, to go to the Philadelphia Hab after this. Staying here, where he had seen so many of his friends and neighbors die, it would haunt him. He was better off leaving.

First things first. He needed to get the older man out of the far airlock. This meant putting him on the tarp they had used to pull the bodies out one by one. It was just a hell of a lot harder to use when there was only one person pulling it.

His lower back had barely recovered from clearing the west side of the Hab, where the Family Habs were located. The moment he bent down and pulled on Denali's body, the lower muscles of his back seized, contracting in an agonizing twist that took his breath away.

"Shit," he gasped, "Den, you are one heavy sonuvabitch." He released his hold on the man's shirt and his left hand explored the hard knot of muscle. He could feel it ripple and tremble as it seized. It had never been the same after the police had slammed a hard rubber truncheon into his lower back during the EnviroFirst protests in Beijing. He remembered how it had felt: first a shockwave of pain, not unlike being electrocuted, as the pain receptors overloaded in his back, and the numbness that had spread through his legs. He had collapsed on the ground, unable to walk, which had likely saved his life and meant he hadn't rotted in prison, or been executed, along with the leaders of the movement.

Nix rocked back on his heels and tried to breathe through the pain in his back. After he had sat there for a few minutes, he knelt by Denali's body again and tried instead to roll him onto the tarp. This worked, and the man was now on his stomach, his head lolling to one side. Nix caught his breath, and then immediately regretted it. Den's last meal had been chili, and it was making itself known. The last gasp of a digestive system caught processing food into shit. Nix's back continued to seize, and he did his best not to breathe through his nose as Denali's intestines emptied themselves.

"Thanks, man, I..." Nix leaned back against the wall of the corridor and laughed. "Of all the shitty places to end up, here I am, with my last friend on this shitty damn planet. And you have to smell of piss and shit, Den. Christ." He continued to laugh, but somehow it turned into a nightmare of tears and anger. This turned to an overwhelming rush of endorphins, which overrode the pain in his back. He grabbed the paracord tied to the opposite sides of the tarp and pulled, moving down the hall, headed for the farthest airlock on the southeast side. He was going to get Denali outside of the Hab, now, and then go get drunk. He had found a large stash of alcohol when clearing up the mess in Food Storage a few weeks ago. Don Spillman had likely been the one who put it all there. The Spillman family had come in with Nix, some two years past, and the concoction they dubbed Mars Hooch would knock him three sheets to the wind.

Maybe, for just a little while, I'll be able to forget what a fuck-up I am.

Even with the burst of adrenaline, he was shaking with pain by the end of the long journey, pulling his friend to the airlock, then suiting up and dragging him outside to join the others.

Nix stripped off his clothes as soon as he was safely inside and had shimmied out of the suit. He walked, naked, all the way back to his small room in the singles quarters and showered, pushing the reset button every three minutes, until his finger ached from pushing it, the skin on his back was red from the heat, and his fingers and toes pruned.

His back was still seizing. It felt as if a tiny being were running its hands up and down his back now, the other muscles of his back joining into the fray. He reached for a small container of Nocdon and shook out two small white pills. He dry-swallowed them, then reached for the bottle of Mars Hooch and uncorked it.

"Pretty sure I'm not supposed to take the Noc and drink hard alcohol, but fuck it, the doc's dead, just like everyone else." His words were loud in this small space. Before Denali had died, they had talked about moving into one of the Family Habs. But hell, every one of them was a reminder of someone. There weren't any of them that Nix and Denali didn't know, not even the newer ones. Two years in a confined space meant that every one of them had faces, names, personalities, a *history*. It was bad enough walking down the corridors, existing in the public spaces they had shared with so many others, but then to go into their Habs? Where they had lived and breathed and slept? It had been too much. Both men had stuck to their own Singles Habs. And until yesterday, they had been certain they were the last of the settlement. Two things had changed that perception: the sight of one, possibly two people in Philly Hab and Denali showing signs of ESH.

Nix took another large gulp from the bottle and let the warmth spread through him. It was a bit of liquid fire that ran from his mouth, down his throat and esophagus, and into his stomach.

Denali had been so damned sure he didn't have the virus that Nix had finally believed him, despite the reports from the space stations and Earth being so sure that it linked the virus to blood type. Frigging AB negative blood...for once it had turned into a positive to have it. He remembered the car accident when he was small, the pain and the bright lights of the ambulance and a hospital whisking him along while his father, a nasty cut on his head, told the doctors his son had AB negative blood as they ran down the hallway, bright lights zipping past overhead.

Mom hadn't made it. He barely remembered her. It was more the memories of her smile, or a smell of a woman's body that usually triggered the half-memories.

"They got it wrong, man," Denali had said, his dark-brown skin the color of mahogany, his teeth perfectly white. "I got me A-positive blood and I'm telling you; I feel *great*."

And his friend had seemed fine, or at least said he was, until the virus turned on inside of him. Nix winced at the memory and took another swig. The fire spread down to his groin, his legs, and now arms, dulling them into lassitude as the pain meds did their work as well.

Nix pulled on pants. His door was wide open, as if that mattered. There was no one here to see him. No kids to shock if they were to see him half-dressed or full Monty, no women to leer at, not that he did much leering. No one. He was completely and totally alone. He contemplated going to the Philadelphia Hab. The shortcuts, through the Eden Hab, were not complete. And then there was the promise of Eden sitting there, ready and waiting to become crops and forest and garden. He didn't even know how to make it happen now. He was a goddamn farmer with a fancy degree, after all. Dad had called him an enviro-hippy with delusions of grandeur. And, as he tipped the bottle once more to his lips, he thought of his other names and labels. Some would call him a bio-terrorist. A murderer to others. Nix closed his eyes and tipped the bottle back, the alcohol harsh on his tongue. Each gulp burned its way down.

The room already seemed warmer, the edges blurring.

Nix thought about what had brought him here, wishing for the thousandth time he had made a different choice. Had it been the sex? Brigid had been amazing in the sack. So much so, that he had followed her thousands of miles to a foreign land to fight for the environment through protests that had quickly developed into violence.

"Sometimes it takes a violent act for people to wake up to the reality of the violence we do every day to Mother Earth," Brigid had said.

Or had he really bought into the dream that, if they just stopped the corporations that were pumping contaminants into the air, soil, and water, that they could bring their world back from the brink?

It had all been a misguided pipe dream. And he had been the stupid asshole to go along with it. They had separated him from the others, kept him in the dark, with no one answering his questions. Nix had known that something was being done behind the scenes. Nothing else would explain how he had ended up moved from the Chinese prison to a transport plane and now isolation in an American prison.

And when Dad had shown up, in his tailored suit and his vintage Bugatti watch, Nix had known that whatever his dad said to do, his one and only chance to avoid spending the rest of his life in prison, or possibly the death penalty, was to go along with it. It had meant leaving behind the verdant world he loved and coming to a place devoid of life, of greenery or breathable air outside of the pressurized domes. He had committed himself to living out the rest of his life in bubbles, staring at a barren landscape, and doomed to remember the world he had lost.

"It keeps you out of a life sentence, possibly worse," Dad had said. "With your degree in ethnobotany and my connections, you can be part of the Eden project." His lip had curled then, and he had smiled in a way that Nix knew wasn't a smile at all. "You can grow your flowers and play farmer, or you can face charges of eco-terrorism, and face a life sentence," he had said when Nix had opened his mouth to speak. "I will remind you, however, that this falls under the Condaga Agreement, and with it, the charge of terrorism of any kind can be a death sentence."

This had shut Nix up, and good. He hadn't been ready to die.

Isaac Nix had leaned in close. "Michael, take the deal, and you will go into Cryo within forty-eight hours and be shipped out on the next flight with the Jupiter Supply Ship. You can use your skills and passions to make a life there for yourself." And Nix had looked into his father's eyes and saw compassion there for just an instant, before the billionaire entrepreneur returned to his natural state: cold, dispassionate, and highly effective at saving his only child's life.

Nix had taken the deal. He had signed his life away, blindly, with Dad's vintage Aurora Diamante fountain pen, and handed it back, his sight blurring with emotion. His father had stood then, reached out, and uncharacteristically pulled Nix into a tight embrace.

"Be well, my son."

Nix had forced the words out past the lump in his throat. "Thank you, Dad."

It had been the last time either had spoken to each other.

He had entered Cryo on Earth and woken up eight months later on Mars. That had been over two years ago.

A year ago, a transmission had come through. Isaac Nix had died of a stroke, a catastrophic one, from all accounts. Brain dead before he hit the floor, his body had finally figured out reality two days later. His long-time assistant had notified him of all this, and the missive had included a brief message from Isaac to his son.

Dear Michael-

If you are receiving this, well, you know how the saying goes.

Michael, I'm leaving everything to charities. I know you won't care–the money never really mattered to you–and I understand you better in your absence than I ever did when you were here.

When you went after the ethnobotany degree, instead of following me into law or business, I will admit to being disappointed. However, I have come to re-evaluate those feelings. Now, in your absence, so far away from me, I recognize that we are who we are, and that you were true to those feelings and deserving of my respect. I read all the reports from the incident; I recognize now that you had done nothing wrong, and nothing worthy of being labeled an eco-terrorist. That fate rests squarely on the young woman you were with, Brigid Teraby. I wish that I could bring you back to Earth, but they have apprised me that, should you return, your fate would be that of a prison cell, no matter your innocence. After all, it became an international incident, and the Chinese government is not a forgiving sort. In case you were unaware, they executed Brigid as a terrorist under the codicils put forth in the Condaga Agreement in a Chinese prison the month after you left on the Jupiter Supply Ship.

Forgive me, son, for not understanding you better, for belittling your choice in occupation and giving you the impression that I thought less of you than I should.

Apart from your mother, there is no one I have cared for more. Be well, my son. Find happiness and fulfillment wherever you can.

Your father,

Isaac

The executor, a long-time business friend of his father, had included a short note informing Nix that his dad had saved his life by paying one hundred million Ameros to a judge who had commuted his sentence to a life on Mars and then promptly retired to a remote South American island in the Pacific, far from the Reformed United States of America's reach. Nix gaped at the revelation. Apparently, enough money *could* buy you a new life.

Nix had seen the wisdom in his father's words and had focused all of his energy on seeing that Eden Hab would become a functional part of the Martian landscape as soon as possible. It was the only thing that had kept him sane in this place of barren views and endless red dust.

And now, he would likely die here, in this desolate place, with nothing but prepackaged MREs to feed him for the rest of his life. He would be trapped forever on a planet that didn't give a damn about whether he lived or died, and which would kill him in seconds were he to venture outside without a suit.

The Eden project, the one thing he had been so damned keen on and had been looking forward to seeing brought online in the next two months, was on hold as well. He knew nothing about how to set up the solar arrays, much less understanding the HVAC requirements of such a vast space. And without Eden Hab, what could he do past a simple hydroponics setup?

He needed more people for Eden Hab to become a reality. Hell, he needed more people for himself. The silence, the absence of others, it was devastating.

He took another swig of the hooch and watched the room swim out of focus, his eyelids heavy from the NocDon and booze mix. The hooch had to be at least 50 proof.

Nix's thoughts strayed to Denali's insistence that he saw movement in the Philly Hab some days past. Each of the Habs was far enough away that you needed binoculars to see anything much from the large windows. Add in the dark-grey shielding that helped protect against the radiation, and looking out to see any signs of life from another Hab was an exercise in frustration. Could Denali have been right? Or were hallucinations another aspect of this mysterious ESH virus? Nix rubbed his face with his free hand. It felt rubbery, not like skin, and his thoughts were slowing. A thick sludge was forming in his brain. He stood up slowly, the room swimming around him. "Fuck this place," his words slurred. "I'm going to Philly in the morning," Nix announced to the empty room. He took a piss in the toilet and then staggered back to his bunk, collapsing on it heavily, his mind already descending into a drugged sleep.

Baoying

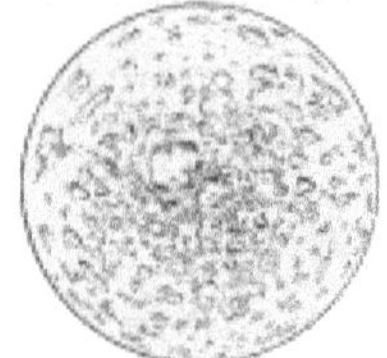

Mars Year 14, Week 39, Day 387
(Earth Date: 09.02.2099)

In the month since the movie night, and the terrible news that Huygens Outpost, their one last refuge, was no longer safe, it felt as if Liu and Fen's relationship had changed. They did not return to their own bunks. All the bunks were narrow affairs built for one. At first, they had simply bunked in the Mess Hall and that had worked well enough. Liu's brainstorm a week later saw him moving their two singles cots into the Garden Hab. He placed them on a large, flat rock next to the burbling pond. With the stars lighting the sky above at night, and the quiet gurgle of the water, it brought a rare smile to Fen's face.

It was beautiful there, in the Garden Hab, and Liu noticed that Fen responded well to it, her mood improving as she chose to spend most hours of the day, and her evenings, within it. She added seeds, expanding the plantings further into the regolith that served as the base for most of the expansive Hab. They had moved the remainders of their food scraps into a large compost heap, which Liu turned each day. Countless plants now thrived in the alien soil, and Fen's face had grown rounder as her pregnancy wore on, her belly pushing out sharply on her thin frame.

It had taken a while for her to process her disappointment, learning that their only place of refuge had vanished. There were still times when he caught her staring off into the distance, a haunted expression on her face.

He loved her. More than anything. It was a strange thing, really. They had slept next to each other, hugged, but never anything more. Despite this, he knew, without a doubt, that Fen was the only woman he could ever want. That she was so sad, in mourning still for the family she had lost, even her husband, made him want to protect her until his dying breath. He wondered if she realized that he would give his life for hers, and even for the child that grew inside her. Liu thought of Chen. How could he have chosen death, when a new life with his blood running through its veins was on the way? And yet, Liu understood it. If he lost Fen, he would feel the same way. Perhaps Chen's will to live had ended that fateful day that his wife and child had perished. If Fen were to die, he wondered if he would want the same. Would he wish to die with her?

They often spent a day without saying much more than "Good morning" and "Good night" but in some ways, Liu was happier than he had ever been. The unknown of their future was frightening, yes, but he focused on the here and now, and dreamed of the near future when they would become three. It would be soon, only eight weeks, possibly less.

Fen feared the impending childbirth. And who could blame her? Liu had studied basic first aid, with an emphasis on oxygen deprivation, decompression sickness, et cetera. They both had. These were things they were most likely to encounter on a mission to another world, not childbirth. They had a video library that rivaled most libraries back on Earth, and he spent several days combing through a multitude of documentaries and educational videos on the subject. By then, Fen had been more receptive to talking about the baby growing in her, and the corners of her mouth had twitched up into a half-smile as he regaled her with the information he had gleaned.

He had further calmed her fears by cataloging every food item in the station and determined that they had the equivalent of nearly five Earth years' worth of food. Mission Control had included redundancies upon redundancies. When it came to food, Mission Control had ensured that every member of the station had enough food for over four Earth years. They had only been on Mars for eight months, and nearly four of them had been without Chen.

And that was if they only ate the pre-packaged meals. Growing rice would require more space and variation in the growing environment than they currently had, but Mission Control had included plenty of other seeds. Liu estimated that they could continue to live on the crops they grew for months, if not years, and together they had worked the compost into the regolith, improving the quality of the soil enough to withstand a gentle soil rotation of soybeans, leafy greens, and more. The tiny heads of bok choy were almost ready to harvest, and Liu remembered his mother's baby bok choy with mushroom sauce. Just thinking about it made his mouth water, followed by a wave of sorrow.

There had been no news of his parents' fate. The chaos on Earth continued, and with it, an answer of sorts. They were likely dead, but Liu held onto hope. As the weeks had flown by, with just the two of them, alone so far from Earth, he found that he couldn't let go of the impossible wish that his parents had escaped the deadly virus. As he watched Fen's belly grow, the baby inside had become his just as much as it was hers. He knew the reality, but it mattered not. It was a baby, a little boy, and he smiled at the thought of holding him soon. It also made his thoughts turn to fantasies of returning home, Fen's hand in his, their son in his arms, placing the child in Liu's mother's arms. How she would weep tears of joy! It was something he kept close, this dream, despite knowing that his future would likely never include stepping foot on Earth again.

He did his best to fill each day with plenty of activities, whether it was cleaning the red dust that invaded their living spaces despite their lack of EVAs or use of the airlock, or maintenance, of which there were always filters to clean, systems to check, and reports to review. He had taken it upon himself to troubleshoot what they would need in terms of infant care. Fen knew she would have to breastfeed, and he had juggled the vitamins to ensure she had the additional nutrients she needed for a healthy pregnancy and researched appropriate nutrient levels for nursing women.

Fen had insisted that she did not want anyone knowing of her pregnancy. She would not meet his eyes when she asked, "Please say nothing about...this," her hands briefly resting on her abdomen. "Please."

He tried asking her why, but she would only shake her head. It saddened him, but he respected her wishes and said nothing. After all, what could Mission Control do, really? That is, if Mission Control, or the Chinese government, even still existed. They were now communicating with the fourth director in the same number of months. The details of what exactly was happening in their homeland were not totally clear, and Liu found himself increasingly detached from whatever was unfolding in China and on Earth. Their future–his, Fen's, and the baby's–was here, millions of miles away. The baby was developing in Mars' gravity, not Earth's. He would have significant health issues if he returned. Unrealistic dreams of returning to Earth aside, as far as Liu was concerned, Mars was their home now.

Liu removed the filter and examined it carefully. It was amazing to him how even in the tightest closed system designed, the red Mars dust still got in. He frowned, and wondered if he should double-check the seals and gaskets throughout the station, one room at a time. The dust was getting in somehow, unless it was a leftover from the last EVA, when Chen... Liu shut his eyes, trying not to remember the look on Fen's face as she had called Chen's name over and over. The dust storm had lasted for nearly a week and it had felt like retribution. For what, he could not imagine. He hadn't stopped Chen, but really, who could have? Chen had timed it so well, waiting until the storm was almost upon them before sending Liu to the opposite end of the outpost on a fool's errand. Liu paused, lost in the memory of that day, the small hose of the vacuum in one hand, the filter in the other. He might have stood there for several seconds or even minutes, reviewing the options he wished he had thought of, including donning a suit and going after Chen, when Fen's cry over his Comm shook him from his reverie. He came back to present in an instant.

"Liu! Liu!" her voice sounded pained, fearful.

Liu dropped the vacuum and filter, turned, and bolted from the room, his heart hammering in his chest.

He found her in the Garden Hab, crouching in an empty section where they had discussed planting cabbage seeds, or possibly some eggplant. One hand was on her belly, the other hand buried in regolith. She rocked back and forth, her face white with terror.

"Is it...is it the baby?"

"Yes," she whimpered, her face contorted in agony. He could see the wet soil at her feet. "My water has broken."

The baby was coming early, almost two full months by Liu's calculations. He fought panic, then remembered the videos and placed a calming hand on her back. "Shh, it will be alright."

Everything he read suggested that first children took their time, that the labors were long, and that Fen might have hours upon hours of labor ahead of her. This was sudden and intense. Or was it?

"When did this start?" Liu asked, as he gently raised her to a standing position.

Fen's face was wet with tears. "This morning."

"Why didn't you tell me?"

A contraction hit her as she shrugged, and she gasped at the pain. "I thought, oh, I thought they would go away!" The last words came out as a whimper and she buried her face in his neck. "It hurts."

He wrapped his arm around her and picked her up. She was so light, a small woman already and, thanks to Mars' gravity, weighed no more than a child would on Earth. He carried her easily. "I know it does." He fumbled at the garden door, then eased his way through it and down the hall to the infirmary, where he placed her gently on the table and turned to pull out the tray of supplies that he had assembled weeks ago.

Despite her reticence to speak about things such as baby names, she had clarified that she did not want an epidural. Which, if Liu were to be completely honest, was something that relieved him deeply. It had terrified him he might injure her. A simple misstep could cause permanent paralysis, and an epidural was simply too far above his basic first aid and emergency medicine training.

She groaned, her face contorted with pain, and he stared at the built-in clock on the wall. "I need to time your contractions."

Fen cried out, "Two...minutes."

Liu gaped at her. "Between the contractions?"

Fen was shivering. "I need... I need..." What she needed was something to throw up into. But her words came too late and instead ended up all over Liu. He looked down at his arms, dripping, and stifled the urge to return the favor. His stomach was now flipping around the breakfast he had eaten as if he were back on the launchpad, about to blast off into space.

"I am sorry, Liu!" she cried, horror and embarrassment warring for control.

"It's, oh, hold on a moment." He dashed away to the small sink and did what he could to wash his arms and hands off before returning to her side.

"The contractions seem to have increased in duration. Do you feel any need to push?" Liu asked, trying to stay calm for Fen. All the videos he had watched had prepared him, but reality was, well, terrifying.

Fen nodded, tears tracking from her eyes. "There's a lot of pressure."

"Alright, well, I think you need to try pushing during the next..."

Fen's face crumpled in the onslaught of the next contraction.

"You can do this, Fen, you can."

The lunch hour came and went, and Liu barely noticed. His focus was on Fen, his entire being dedicated to walking her through the birth. And less than two hours after he had first heard her call for him, the tiny baby slid out, gray and limp, as first his head and then his shoulders cleared the birth canal and Liu eased him out of Fen and stared at him, a frown on his face.

"He's not..." Fen cried, "He's not breathing. It is Baoying! I have sinned, and this is the retribution for my sins." She fell back on the table, moaning in her misery.

Liu blinked. The baby was so tiny, so limp in his hands. Perfectly formed, a boy, just as the tests had promised. Liu felt as if he should do something, and then it hit him. He reached into the limp mouth, cleared the airway, sticking his finger partly down the baby's throat, and gave him a light smack on his back. "Breathe!" he yelled, and the baby made a mewling sound, a wet half-cough, and then cried, a thin wail of discomfort and shock. The sound reminded him of a tiny kitten. It was also the most beautiful sound Liu had ever heard. He burst into tears, holding the baby close to his body, reaching for a warm sheet to wrap him in.

Liu couldn't take his eyes off of the tiny creature. He picked up a warm, clean cloth and wiped the baby off, clearing away the white paste and the blood that coated him and had kept him warm inside of Fen's womb. Liu marveled at the tiny toes, so perfectly articulated, and the tiny little fingernails and toenails that wiggled and opened and closed. He was perfect.

Liu reveled at the love he felt for this baby, one he shared no blood ties with, one who, despite his tiny size and the earliness of his arrival, seemed healthy, if not happy. His little face screwed up with distress, no doubt shocked at the bright world they had thrust him into.

"Hello, Little One," Liu whispered to the baby. "Fen, he's absolutely perfect. It isn't Baoying, not at all! He just needed help with his first breath!"

He turned back to her and met her eyes. She stared; her eyes fixed, unmoving in her preternaturally pale skin. Liu's own eyes widened in horror as he looked down the length of her and saw the mass of blood now staining the sheets of the exam table. So much blood. Too much blood.

"Fen?" The baby had slowly relaxed as Liu cleaned him. Now he cried, a thin wail of loss, as if he sensed the soul of his mother lift away and leave him orphaned.

"Fen!" Liu howled, placing the baby in a drawer he had lined with cloths, and ignored the baby's shrieks as he tore through the medical equipment, searching for epinephrine, for the paddles, for anything that would stop the gouts of blood draining from the woman he loved.

It was too late. In a hospital, with staff who knew what they were doing, her chances of survival could have been different. But here? Alone on this distant planet with barely any medical knowledge to speak of, Liu hated himself for not being able to save her.

The baby, nestled in the lined drawer, cried inconsolably, and Liu sobbed with him.

He buried her the next day, digging deep into the regolith, and planted the seeds of an Osmanthus on her grave, with the baby snoozing in a wrap nearby.

Liu's head ached from the tears he had cried. How had he never expected this? Why had he not prepared better?

The infant made a snuffling sound, and Liu felt a rush of resentment toward the tiny creature who had partially been to blame. His birth had caused the hemorrhage and then cost Liu the love of his life. He reached for the child, anger rushing through him, before he paused.

Look at what you have lost, Little One. Your father and your mother, before you ever drew breath.

"It isn't your fault. I know this. Forgive me." He picked the boy up gently and stared into his eyes. "I must name you then." The baby stared back, his face serious, a small bubble of drool at the corner of his rosebud lips.

"I will call you Huan, for I am pleased to be your father." The baby's gaze did not waver, and Liu kissed his little boy's forehead and tucked him in close. He couldn't have imagined this outcome in a thousand years. Yet here he was, here Huan was. Alone. Just the two of them, on a barren red planet. What in the world was he going to do?

Trip to Sydney

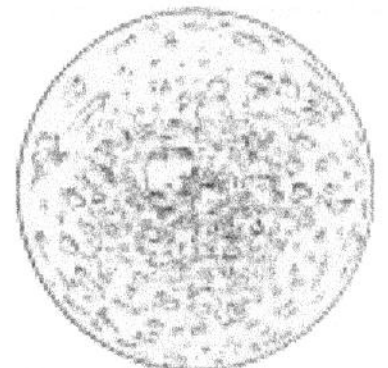

Mars Year 14, Week 43, Day 424
(Earth Date: 10.09.2099)

Nix was still asleep when he heard the front door of his Hab chime. He had stayed up late working with the spreadsheets, and he tried to focus his bleary vision on the display from the NARA unit near the bed. The chime repeated, clearer now that he was at least half-awake. He groaned. It had to be Lenny. Nix had been in Philadelphia Hab a while now, long enough to notice that the kid was an early bird, his sleep/wake cycle nearly the opposite of Nix's own. Lenny seemed to fall asleep shortly after sundown and he had woken Nix up damn near every morning before rays of the distant sun lit up the thin Mars atmosphere.

Nix had set up in a Family Hab near Toya and Lenny's, marveling at the luxury of the extra space. After over two years of living in the tiny Singles Hab in Hong Kong Hab, it was a guilty pleasure to have more than quadruple the space. He could reach his arms out and not touch the opposite walls. It felt wrong, somehow, to have an extra two bedrooms, but he was adjusting. He had removed the bedding from one, added lights, and the two totes on the floor included nutrients and amended Mars soil. The amendments smelled disgusting, so he kept the door closed. This did not eliminate it, however, and he wrinkled his nose as he passed by it, shuffling over to the front door of the Hab. It chimed a third time, as Nix opened the door and glared at Lenny.

"What?"

The boy stared at Nix, apprehension on his face. "I just, uh, did I wake you up, Nix?"

Nix gave him a pained look. For such a smart kid, Lenny could also be remarkably obtuse. "Nah, Kid, I always look like I just woke up and rolled out of bed." He was wearing pajama pants, and he was pretty sure his hair was sticking up. It was getting shaggy. How long had it been since he got it cut? He preferred it buzzed short and after nearly two months of chaos, it was now long enough that he could feel the curls forming. He winced at the memory of the kids at school calling him Curly-locks after a popular vid with a bear detective that bumbled his way through investigations while obsessing over his curly fur. The little fuckers. He hated that show. As soon as he had a say, he had gotten his hair buzz cut and kept it that way.

The boy winced and looked embarrassed. "I'm sorry, Nix. I was up, had breakfast, and was thinking about the other Habs and wondering if we could go on an EVA, check out each of the City Habs, and see if there are any others. You know, besides us, I mean..."

Nix walked away from the boy, the door hanging open. Whatever else was on Lenny's mind would likely require Nix to ingest coffee, copious amounts of it. He turned, yawning and stretching as he did, and walked toward the tiny kitchen in the Hab. Lenny stood in the doorway for a moment, staring, obviously unsure of what to do, and then he finally followed. He slid into a seat, watching Nix as he filled the instant water heater, turned it on, and began preparing a mug.

After a moment of silence, the boy asked, "I, uh, I could come back later. If you wanted to sleep more."

Nix cocked his head to one side and stared at Lenny, eyebrows raised. "It's a little too late for that, Kid. Just give me a moment to get my head on straight, drink some of this crap they call coffee, and then you can talk all you want about EVAs and more. Okay?"

"Okay." The boy grinned. "I just think that getting out there and finding out who we have left and being able to get a solid count on supplies and..."

His words petered out as Nix held up a finger and gave the boy a stern glare. "Just...*stop*. Five minutes to wake the hell up with no words. None. Can you do that, Lenny?"

The boy opened his mouth, then shut it again, and nodded.

The small water heater burbled, showing it was at temperature, and Nix reached over and poured it into his cup. The coffee smelled far better than it tasted. He would never, ever get used to freeze-dried instant shit. Damn the millions of miles and the need for every single thing to be lightweight. Earth had decided the matter based on a few ounces' differential, and Nix had to pay the price. He could barely stand to call it coffee. It was one of those things he missed, desperately, and had even dreamed of. He hoped that, with the proper environmental controls and lighting, he could grow coffee plants here on Mars. But that was a dream on hold. Until they could get the connections established to Eden Hab, along with the proper atmosphere and growing conditions, he would have to make do with the freeze-dried crap.

He sipped the boiling hot concoction slowly, eyes closed, fully aware that Lenny was nearly squirming with impatience to continue along the train of thought that had obviously been burbling inside him for the past few hours.

Nix wasn't looking forward to another EVA. Not at all.

After working through his spreadsheets and counting the amount of food stores they had left, Nix was less worried about running out of food or water, and more about the fact that he might never get laid again. Considering he had a grand total of one woman to choose from, and she was brain-damaged, inwardly Nix grimaced. Toya was beautiful, no question about that. Now that Nix had made sure she stopped eating so much crap and locked down the food stores, she had instead turned to walking circuits around the outer ring of the Philadelphia Hab, trying all the doors, looking no doubt for treats she could scavenge. He suppressed a smile. She was out of luck. He had already gone through each of the Family Habs and individual units, clearing the rest of the bodies and returning all the food and drink items to the central Food Storage next to Philadelphia Hab's Mess Hall.

Undeterred, Toya did it every day, as if the situation would magically change.

The exercise and reduced intake of junk food had already helped slim her down and, combined with her natural good looks, well, he couldn't help but notice. Noticing her, however, was as far as it was going to go. Her body was that of a young woman, sure. But her mind, well, thanks to the hypoxic event some thirteen years ago, her mind was so damaged that she was little more than a child. And Nix wasn't in the habit of having intercourse with children.

Frankly, the idea of it made him ill. It was getting harder to be around her. His body reacted to a pretty girl even as his mind screamed that she was off limits.

Lenny squirmed in his seat, obviously itching to talk. Nix stifled a grin, took another languid sip of the coffee, winced at its taste, and then relented. "What do you have on your mind, Kid?"

The boy perked up. "I've been wondering what specialized supplies might be at the Sydney Hab and other City Habs. There was this workshop there at Sydney, where they were working on improving the solar array, and there were also plans to install more of the atmo generators. All kinds of supplies are there, and I thought..."

Nix held up a hand. No amount of freeze-dried crap in the world could help him keep up with this kid and his endless enthusiasm. "Cut to the chase, Kid."

Lenny sat up straighter. "I think we need to do an EVA of Sydney Hab, and the other Habs. We need to see if there are any survivors and make a list of every single item that we can use to survive on Mars until Earth can send more people." He paused, frowning. "You do think they will send more colonists, don't you? I mean, if they don't..." His words hung in the air and he looked at Nix as if he knew the answers to it all.

Nix sipped the coffee, saying nothing. He wasn't exactly looking forward to seeing more dead bodies, but Lenny had a point. They needed a full picture, something they didn't have here in Philadelphia Hab. From what he could tell, the food supplies could last them indefinitely, even after he factored in the increased usage for the first forty-five days after the ESH virus spread through the colony. Not to mention that the last shipment had brought the artificial wombs. It had also brought an A.R.C. similar to the one sent to Zarmina's World last year with the colony ship Calypso. The Moon colony, Huygens, and the space stations had all received copies as part of the standard protocols put in place after the Human Diversity Act passed less than a month before Calypso left the solar system.

This virus had proven the scientists' point that humanity could no longer remain just on Earth. Despite all precautions, it had even made it here, over 34 million miles away. And just like on Earth, it had proved deadly. Except that Huygens Colony didn't have billions or even millions. Earth might not have the wherewithal to launch a mission to them. It was something no one had ever considered, a virus that made a mockery of the coronavirus strains which had ravaged the world's population in a series of five waves over, what, eighty years ago? Nix wondered what the people living through the 2020s lockdowns would think of ESH.

He realized Lenny was waiting, expecting an answer. Or maybe permission. He was a kid, after all. And despite being some kind of wunderkind who could run circles around Nix–hell, he could run circles around most of the population of pre-ESH Huygens Outpost–the boy was used to deferring to adults. Nix was struck suddenly with the realization that they would need to use those artificial wombs for more than just livestock if they ever hoped to do something other than grow old and die alone on Mars.

Really, what were the chances that Earth was going to come along and save them? For Toya and Lenny, especially Lenny, who had been born on the red planet, Mars was home. It wasn't something they needed rescuing from. Nix had known when he came here that he had a choice of returning to Earth. It would have meant spending the rest of his life in a prison cell, but that was the choice he had made. At those moments when he missed Earth the most, he would think too of the life he would have if he returned. He had decided his fate already. And sure, the ESH virus had set Earth, the space stations, and the Moon and Mars colonies on their ear. But really, what could he do? This was his reality. He could work with it or rail against it, but it didn't honestly matter either way. He was stuck, so he might as well make the best of it.

Lenny shifted, uncomfortable at the long silence. "So, what do you think?"

Nix sipped the instant coffee. Now that it had cooled slightly, it tasted even worse than it did steaming hot. He pursed his lips in disgust, turned, and tossed the remnants down the sink and watched as it disappeared down the pipe that would lead, eventually, to the compost. It was time to focus on what they could do–create a life here for themselves–and damned if that wasn't what he was going to do.

"I think this coffee sucks donkey balls."

Lenny blinked at him, his forehead furrowed, perplexed.

"In answer to your question, though. Yeah, I think it's time we did a full evaluation of the other Habs. Hell, we need to reduce or eliminate the heating and lighting in them in order to conserve resources. And yes, we absolutely need to clear out the bodies. Eventually, we will need to figure out how to move forward with getting Eden Hab online and producing crops, along with some meat." He stared at the boy. "You up for helping me clear the bodies, Kid? It ain't going to smell pretty in most of 'em."

Lenny sat a little straighter. "Yeah, Nix, I can handle it."

Whether the kid could, remained to be seen. As it was, Nix wasn't sure he was up for it himself. It was, after all, what drove him to leave the Hong Kong Hab. He had cleared the bodies of those he didn't know well, but seeing some women he had been close to, and the kids. He shook his head at the memory. Dealing with those bodies had sent him tilting over the edge. At least when Denali had been alive, Nix had someone else to share the burden. But when he'd died, hell, Nix had suited up and made tracks, desperate to find others, fearing he was all alone on this alien planet. Instead, he'd found Toya and Lenny. Finding more people was still possible. He hoped they would find others, anyone else. That would mean they weren't alone, just the three of them, on this entire planet. For that, he would deal with the gruesome task of disposing of bodies, especially if it meant moving forward and making a future for themselves on Mars.

Lenny still had a questioning look on his face. Nix thought of everything, the chaos on Earth, and so much more, before he answered the boy. "And yeah, Lenny. Earth will send more colonists in time. The virus has proven how very fragile humanity's existence can be. It's just a matter of time."

Nothing but the Dead

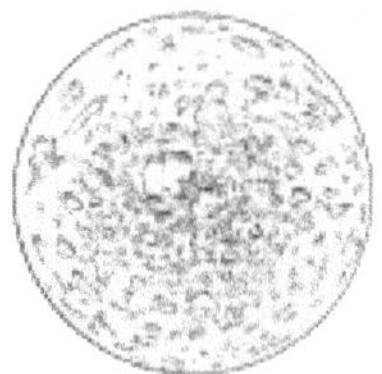

Mars Year 14, Week 43, Day 425
(Earth Date: 10.10.2099)

The sandstorm outside had darkened the sky so much that the Hab's hallway lights had turned on automatically, despite it being almost noon. It came, stayed for a few days, and then moved on, destined to scour some other part of the desolate planet.

Not that Petra Salinger knew or particularly cared. Her leg felt hot, and it ached. The wound was seeping yellow pus and around it the swelling spread, the skin red, hot to the touch, and angry red streaks spread away from the wound. She had marked the edges of it on the second or third day, but now the swelling had spread behind the fading blue lines of the marker.

She moaned and tried to shift, the touch of the blanket on her skin too much to bear. Even a cool, moist cloth was too much. It felt oppressive, heavy, and, despite its softness under her fingers, scratchy.

She couldn't even get to the bathroom now. The last time she had tried she had tripped, bumped her leg on the wall, and a blast of pain had seized her as she collapsed to the floor. She had passed out, waking up on the icy concrete floor, her leg pulsing a drumbeat of agony with every heartbeat, a streak of red and yellow pus dried in a trail down her thigh. It had taken a long time to find the strength to stand back up and make her way to bed. She cursed her luck, her stupidity, and felt a wave of nausea wash over her. It wasn't as if she had anything in her stomach now, anyway. It had been days, maybe more than a week, since she had eaten.

If Father could see her now. When she closed her eyes, she could see his look of disapproval, of barely disguised contempt. "Perhaps your mother named you far more accurately than anyone could have known. Petra means stone, after all. And as far as I can see, that's all you have in that head of yours...rocks."

He had said that after her grade in chemistry had slipped from A-plus to A-minus. Then he had left the apartment for a week without a word. By then she was used to it. Used to being alone, used to being disliked and frowned upon, and used to being unwanted and unloved.

Petra winced, not at the pain of the wound, but at the memory of his voice, the image of his face in front of hers. She had always fallen short of his expectations, never smart enough or good enough, and if she ever questioned it, if she ever attempted to rewrite the reality of who she was, she had so many memories to remind her otherwise.

Her dreams blended with hallucinations as she lay there, edging closer and closer to death. Moments of clarity were becoming infrequent as the infection slowly expanded along her leg. And in only those moments, those tiny infractions of sanity, did Petra fear what was coming.

Death.

She had seen it twice before it struck Huygens and Sydney Hab. Petra had been unlucky enough to watch both of her parents die. First her mother, when Petra was barely three and then her father, just two months before she left on the mission to colonize Mars.

Losing her mother at such a young age had marked her. As she lay there, waves of pain throbbing from the infected leg, Petra remembered overhearing a school therapist try to talk to her father. She had been an amiable woman, plump, with soft, floral-printed shirts and a seemingly unending supply of denim skirts. Petra had met her for the first time at the elite primary school in which her father had enrolled her.

By then Petra had learned not to cry, not about anything. Father hated crying more than anything, and he would quickly move to silence her when her lip began to quiver.

"There's no use in crying. The dead won't come back to life, your life won't magically improve, and no one, especially me, cares to hear you wailing like a banshee. Especially over a hopeless addict who preferred getting high over being a proper mother."

After several altercations on the playground led to the office sending her to the school counselor, the woman had called Father in for a one-on-one meeting. Father glared at Petra as he came in and pointed to a chair near the office door and said, "Sit there." And then he had gone inside of Miss Hicks' office and shut the door behind him. A mere gesture, for the walls were far too thin to obscure the conversation. Petra had leaned against the wall, just to be sure. She needn't have bothered. Every word came through loud and clear.

"Thank you for coming, Mr. Salinger, I'm glad to meet..."

"Yes, yes, Miss Hicks, if we could dispose with the pleasantries, I have a client meeting in half an hour."

Miss Hicks had sounded surprised, taken aback by his brisk manner. "Oh, well, of course. I, well, I wanted to talk to you about Petra and see if she is receiving any counseling services."

"No." Father's voice dripped with disapproval and Petra winced, despite the wall separating them. "Why?"

"Well, I..." Miss Hicks' voice faltered for a moment and then recovered. "I mean, considering she lost her mother at such a young age and the incidents here at school..."

Father interrupted her again. "Incidents? More fighting?"

"Well, no, not since last month, but..."

Petra could hear her father's chair knock against the wall as he stood up. "I thought you had a good reason for me to come in, Miss Hicks, but I see that you do not. I really must not be late for my meeting."

"But, Mr. Salinger, Petra is obviously suffering from the loss of her mother," Miss Hicks said, her voice rising. "She has significant feelings of loss and even abandonment that she needs help to work through. Without the proper guidance..."

"Spare me the sanctimonious lecture, Miss Hicks. Petra's mother was a drug addict and mentally deficient. She left Petra for me to raise and I'll be damned if I'm going to mollycoddle the girl. That's what her mother's parents did to her. Her mother raised her to be weak and foolish and maudlin. I'll not put up with that kind of behavior from Petra. I have a hard enough time getting her to focus on her schooling."

Miss Hicks had grown enough of a backbone that she shouted at Father in return, "Mr. Salinger, she's barely six years old! Few children her age have seen such loss. She needs..."

"She needs a firm hand, Miss Hicks," Father said dismissively. "The school already has my permission to discipline her as you see fit, or simply send a note home and I will see to it."

And with that, the door had opened, and Father had exited. Petra had seen Miss Hicks' mouth hanging open in shock as Father had grabbed Petra's elbow and pulled her off-balance. He forced her out the door as she held onto her coat and lunchbox, all at a half-run to keep up with his pace as he strode down the hall. Miss Hicks' face had said it all–a combination of horror and outrage before Petra lost sight of her. Outside of the school entrance, Father had dropped her arm and said, "I'll be late for my meeting. Go straight home." Then he had walked away, leaving her six-year-old self to walk the fifteen city blocks home alone.

When he finally died, it was years after Petra had graduated high school and college. She had sat there in the hospital and watched him slip into a coma after a series of heart attacks. Petra had watched as his breathing became irregular, and finally stopped altogether. There had been no reason to stay, he hadn't even asked for her, but she had come anyway.

Petra tried to roll onto her other side then, and the pain erupted in a fiery roar at her pathetic movements. She moved again and felt the hot agony wash over her, a single tear tracking down her cheek. She was stupid, so stupid. What had she thought she was going to do, cut through the secured door to the food supplies with the reciprocating saw? The door, already dented and battered, had held against four dozen sick, virus-ridden souls determined to get something, anything to eat. The drive to do so seemed unbearable, unstoppable, and she had watched everyone else in Sydney Hab succumb to it. Why hadn't she? She had searched through every one of the transmission packets from Earth, long after the first massive sandstorm two weeks or more ago that had cut off all communication with Earth, to discover that answer. And in one of the last ones, there had been a clue.

Her rare blood type was AB negative. The reports of those who were contracting and yet surviving the ESH virus were all AB negative blood types, like her. The information had been vague, full of questions rather than answers. Somehow, even though she likely had the virus, it simply did not turn on in those with AB negative blood. At the end of forty-five days of incubation, she hadn't been consumed with hunger. Well, at least nothing more than was normal. By then, there was little food left.

And that was the problem, the thing that would likely cost Petra her life. The locked steel door to Food Storage remained unaffected, even when she used a reciprocating saw. It had bucked in her hands, and she had felt it slip, just for a moment, but a moment was enough. The saw had dug into her upper leg, cutting through skin and the meat of her thigh as if it were butter, before it had jumped out of her hands completely and landed on the floor, its motor growling before it rattled to a stop.

"Stupid Petra, so stupid." Her lips shaped the words, but no sound came out.

Miss Hicks had been the one source of comfort Petra had as a child. She had sought Petra out, showing her a world of emotions and kindness that simply did not exist outside of the confines of her small school office. It hadn't been enough, not nearly enough, but it had been all that Petra had. The memory of Miss Hicks became a shining light that Petra held onto now, here, millions of miles from Earth, surrounded by the dead.

Outside, the wind hadn't howled so much as it scratched. Flecks of the hard Martian soil scraped along the walls of the Hab. Petra's eyes fluttered open. She couldn't see much outside of the open door. A patch of hallway, lights glowing bright, and sun had replaced the darkness of the sandstorm. She wondered, with a fevered detachment, how long it would take her to die. Surely not long, a day, maybe two. Her thoughts ran in circles, occasionally veering into hallucinations, a fever dream memory of life that should have been but so obviously wasn't.

"This isn't how it is supposed to end." Her words sounded as dry and rough as the dust storm outside the Hab. And, as if he hadn't died, Father had to add his two cents.

"As if you deserved something better."

She could even see his lip curl in disgust. This close to death, reality and dream were the same, looping about each other in a Gordian knot until it was impossible for her to unravel them. And perhaps that is why, a few breaths, or possibly even a few days later, she thought nothing of the voices that interrupted her fevered dreaming.

"There's nothing here but the dead, Lenny." A man's voice. It sounded as if he was down by Corridor B, which led to the Supply Rooms and Mess Hall.

"We should just check anyway," a far more youthful voice said, moving closer. "Hey Nix, there's blood here."

"Careful, Kid, don't just go running off. If someone's still got the virus here, they will not be at their most sensible. Wait for me to catch up. We gotta stick together."

And then the younger voice, so close. "Oh shit, Nix, look!"

Petra forced her eyes open, desperate to focus on the blurry vision filling the open doorway of her Singles Hab. Two figures, one tall, one short. She opened her mouth to speak, but everything was so dry, so parched, and all she managed was a weak, incomprehensible sound. Not a groan, nor a whimper, more of a rasping sigh.

"Hang on, ma'am," the boy said, his hand on her arm, "we need to get you to Medical Bay." His words intersected with an agonizing wave of pain as arms enclosed and lifted her, her swollen and infected leg knocking against the uninjured one. And with the pain, she managed a short, aborted scream before the black curtain of unconsciousness swallowed everything.

Time slipped and rolled and moved. So did everything else around her. They occupied flashes of moments, pain, dark, light, and the two faces she eventually came to recognize. A man by her side, his dark hair disheveled, repeated sharp jabs at her arm. "Damn it, the veins are impossible to find, she's too dehydrated."

Or later, the room darkened, an IV bag of fluid steadily dripping into her arm. A dark-haired boy curled up on a nearby chair asleep, his tablet, the screen dark, slipping from his fingers.

It could have been hours, but it felt more like days. Moments punctuated by agony as the man, what did he say his name was, Dix, Nix? –he cleaned the wound on her leg, wincing at her groans of pain. Finally, after a long time, she opened her eyes and saw Nix in a chair, intent on the tablet in his hand, his finger flicking through the pages.

He was handsome, in a rugged sort of way. Not the cultivated, clean look that her father had, with his tailored suits and expensive watches. More of a day laborer kind of look, even a reformed bad boy, but definitely a man who worked with his body and his hands, not in an office, issuing commands.

She cleared her throat, and he glanced up, a smile appearing on his face. "You're awake. How are you feeling?"

Petra didn't respond for a moment, taking stock instead of her current situation. She had a hospital gown on, and nothing else. And from what her nose was telling her, she direly needed a shower. Her leg ached slightly, but it didn't feel hot anymore. No doubt she had received antibiotics through the IV, along with fluids. Petra felt weak all over, and she was starving. She opened her mouth, but her stomach beat her to the punch, loudly growling its complaints. She flushed red, feeling the heat spread across her face.

Nix's smile grew to a wide grin. "Well, that's a good sign." He reached over and took her hand in a powerful grip. "I'm Nix, by the way."

"Petra."

"Yes, I know. We found your info in the Hab's directory."

Petra scanned the room for evidence of the boy. "Where is he? The boy, I mean?"

"Lenny? He had to head back to the Philadelphia Hab. Once you are up to it, we can head back there and join Lenny and his sister."

Petra blinked, taking it in. "Two kids? Are they your kids?"

Nix laughed. "No, I've never been the family type. Toya, Lenny's sister, is an adult, well, age-wise she's grown up, but..." He made a motion with his hand. "She's not all there. Oxygen deprivation event in the Hab when she was young. Lenny's brilliant, and I imagine Toya had been as well, once." He shrugged. "Now, she's a bit of a handful. We couldn't leave her alone for long, so Lenny headed on back there."

"Is Philadelphia Hab in better shape?" Petra asked, thinking of the corpses scattered throughout the Sydney Hab, mainly clustered in the Mess Hall, where they had desperately tried to access the Food Storage section and failed thanks to Manny, who had locked himself inside and never come back out.

Nix had stood, walked to a nearby cabinet, and pulled out a container of juice. It was the first orange juice container she had seen for weeks, and she could practically taste the thick citrus flavor on her tongue. Her stomach growled again. Nix stuck the straw into the container and gently wrapped her fingers around it. Her arm shook as she brought the straw to her lips.

"I guess you could say it is. They tossed a lot of folks out of the airlock when it got bad. And they locked the Food Storage down, like yours was, so most of the food stores are intact. Yours had a body in it, so we had to take care of that."

Petra nodded, intent on sucking the orange juice into her mouth. Her mouth felt withered and dry and the orange juice, despite being pasteurized and robbed of its fresher flavors, was an explosion of taste in her mouth. She sighed then, swallowing mouthful after mouthful of its tart sweetness. The straw stuttered along the bottom of the container, complaining as she cleared it of every remaining drop.

"How did you get in?" Petra asked, thinking of her foolish attempt, which had nearly cost her life.

"I'm the Food Supply Manager for the base. I have all the codes." Nix grinned. "It came in handy."

"But Manny changed the codes on the Food Storage here, and then we couldn't get in." Petra frowned and shook the container; it was empty and her stomach was ready for more.

Nix tapped his temple. "Manny and I had both read this old science fiction book, *The Hitchhikers Guide to the Galaxy*. The answer to the ultimate question of life, the universe, and everything, is 42. Or in this case, 424242." Nix grinned, for a second, before it faded. "Anyway, he must have reprogrammed it and then locked himself inside." He looked away; his lips tight in a grimace. "I took care of the rest of the bodies, including Manny's."

Petra's stomach growled again, loudly, and Nix shook his head as if he could physically shake out the memories in it, and smiled at her again before asking, "So, would you like a breakfast burrito?"

Petra couldn't help but smile back. The breakfast burritos had been among the least favored breakfasts a mere month ago. Made on Earth, flash frozen, and transported on the last supply ship they had seen land before everything went to hell, the burritos had been a terrible choice. They tasted greasy, flavorless, and the faux NearBacon had been nothing like bacon in taste, texture, or appearance. Despite these incontrovertible facts, after days of scavenging from the barren cupboards of the dead inhabitants of the

Sydney Hab, a breakfast burrito sounded absolutely wonderful. Her mouth watered, and Petra managed a rare smile. "Yes, please."

Babysitter

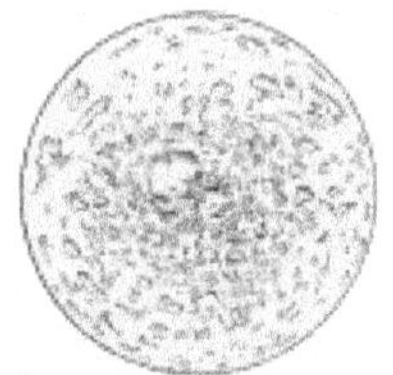

Mars Year 14, Week 44, Day 430
(Earth Date: 10.15.2099)

Petra opened her eyes to see a very different figure in the chair near her bed. Instead of Nix's tall frame, or the boy, Lenny, a young woman now slouched in the seat. Her attention appeared wholly absorbed by a tablet she held in one hand. She was young, late teens or early twenties at most. A simple rubber band contained her dark hair, disheveled and overgrown, in a ponytail at the base of her neck. Her cheeks were a ruddy pink, perhaps from a touch of rosacea. Overall, she was attractive, and Petra instantly disliked her. Her face and eyes looked vaguely familiar, but Petra was fairly certain she hadn't seen her before.

Had Nix found her at one of the other Habs? Perhaps at the Cairo Hab? Or London, even? She was loath to ask, to even speak with this young woman. She didn't need a pretty girl gobbling up all the attention, not now. It had been bad enough in a Hab filled with people, having the good-looking men ignore her and focus instead on the attractive ones, the ones who smiled pretty and flattered their stupid male egos. And Petra, with her plain looks and boyishly flat chest remained ignored, passed over. If there was anything good to come out of all this death and misery, it was that the virus had leveled the playing field; hell, it had obliterated it.

Nix had said there was only him, and a boy and girl left of the once-bustling population of Mars colonists. He had fed her one of those terrible breakfast burritos, and she had reveled in the greasy, heavy taste of it, intoxicated by an attractive man's focus solely on her. It had felt like some biblical Adam and Eve story, and she couldn't help but envision her and Nix becoming a couple. Hell, he had even gotten her to smile, and he had no idea how rare that was.

Petra knocked out her two front teeth when she hit a rock and flew off her bicycle at ten. The inconvenience of it, and the unexpected expense, had angered her father. Since they had been adult teeth and had shattered, Petra had required implants. Jerome Salinger had stared at the dentist, pointed to the cheapest option, and grudgingly paid for the pain medicine at the front desk.

"They look ridiculous," he had said later. "If I were you, I'd keep my mouth closed and never smile." He had smiled at her, his bright white teeth, uniform and perfect, gleaming. Her new teeth had looked odd, a bright shade of white that didn't look natural and contrasted with her other teeth in a jarring way. She had taken his advice and stopped smiling entirely. It wasn't that hard. There was little to smile about. Between living with a man who despised her, missing a mother she barely remembered, and being far too smart for her classmates, Petra didn't have many moments that required a smile.

Nix was attractive, in a very non-cerebral sort of way. Her classmates in high school and college would have tittered and giggled over such a man. As much as Petra wanted to like the cerebral type, there was some kind of primal attraction to someone who looked like Nix. She had wondered, more than once, if it were an instinctual response, a basic primal edict built into a woman's psyche, similar to the perfect woman's body measurements built into men's—one that said, "This one will protect you from lions and bears and give you strong, healthy children."

Petra was so lost in her musings she missed it when the girl glanced up.

"Hey, you woke up. Finally. I've been sitting here forever."

The young woman's eyes rolled up in her head as she stretched and flopped in the chair. Her tone, which sounded petulant and self-indulgent, surprised Petra. After all, Petra was the one who was injured. This female, this challenger to Petra's position as the only likely woman in Nix's immediate future, was acting as if *she* were being put out.

Petra's lip curled in anger and resentment for a half second until the realization hit her, a lightning bolt of clarity lighting up her future. This had to be the brain-damaged girl Nix had mentioned, the older sister of Lenny, the boy who had found her. She almost smiled as delirious joy flooded through her. Her position as the biblical Eve of Huygens Outpost was intact.

She would easily outstrip any base physical attraction that this creature held over Nix, because she was nothing more than a feeble-minded child stuck in a young woman's body. This girl was no match for Petra's intelligence; her future as progenitor of a score of Mars-born children was secure. *If* that was what she wanted.

Petra thought of what that would be like, bearing children and chasing the little brats around, changing their nappies and cleaning up puke. Now that she thought about it, it didn't sound attractive at all, miniature versions of this creature sitting in her room, irrational, whining, and clingy. Perhaps being the proverbial Eve to Nix's Adam would be more fun in practice than in reality.

"I'm guessing you are Toya?" Petra asked, twisting the corners of her mouth up in what she hoped was a pleasant smile.

"Yup. I've been sitting here for hours, waiting for you to wake up. Nix said he needed me to babysit you." Another dramatic eye roll accompanied the words.

"I see." Petra clamped down on the surge of annoyance. Nix expected this feeble-minded creature to babysit her? More likely it was the other way around. "And where are Nix and Lenny right now?"

Toya shrugged. "I dunno."

"They didn't tell you where they were going?"

Toya looked pensive for a moment. "Um, I think so? But I was watching a movie, so I forget what Lenny said."

Petra could feel fiery anger rising. It began in her belly and roiled through her. She had an idiot for company, and where was Nix? Not here, obviously. She pushed herself upright and noticed a bandage where the IV had been. She pulled aside the covers and looked at her leg. It looked relatively normal; the wound was healing around a long line of irregular stitches. One end of the healing wound looked better than the other and, from the stitches, she would guess that whoever had done them, it had been his first time. By the end of the wound, they had improved in appearance, but she would still have a scar. Would he hold it against her? Perhaps he would feel guilty for not having known how to stitch it properly. She could work with that.

She saw that she was in a hospital gown, nothing else. The smell hit her then, body odor and sick built up over days of lying in a hospital bed. And before that, on the floor of her Singles Hab. God, she stunk! Her leg ached and then, as she slid off the bed slowly, putting pressure on it, it throbbed in time with her pulse. It hurt like hell, but damned if she was going to lie here one moment longer than necessary. She needed a shower.

Along one side of the room she could see the bathroom. It was little more than a box with a toilet, sink, and shower all packed into a corner of the room, but it would get her clean. She couldn't stand the thought of smelling. It reminded her of Father wrinkling his nose at her when she had tried out for track in high school. It had been the one thing that she was good at, that the other girls actually respected her for, and her legs had stretched over the brown and green rubber track, feet flying as she flew past the others. They might not have liked her, or asked her to come with them to their after-school hangouts, but at least they had known she was the fastest. Father seemed less than impressed after the first track meet. He had insisted on opening all the car windows, letting in an icy breeze, and watched her shiver in the thin fabric of her runner's outfit.

"You smell. From now on, be sure to bathe before leaving school. This stench is likely going to stay in my car for days."

And she had, even if it meant her wet hair froze stiff in the brutal cold of winter. After a few more pointed comments on the lack of thinking necessary in athletes and him wrinkling his nose even after she had bathed, she had dropped out of track. Petra had hoped it would make him proud of her. Instead, it had generated the opposite response, and she had joined a chess club and other, more cerebral after-school activities. It hadn't seemed to jostle his opinion of her, but at least he wasn't telling her she stunk at every opportunity.

Her need to be odor-free had resulted in a near-obsessive fixation on daily bathing, something the rules discouraged when she arrived at Huygens Outpost. It had caused no small amount of friction with her and Environmental Services. Now she could use whatever amount of water she wanted whenever she wanted. Jennings, head of Environmental Services, had been one of the first to die from the virus. Ever since, she had taken showers daily, sometimes twice daily, hitting the three-minute reset button over and over until her skin was red from the heat and free of any dirt, perceived or otherwise. That was, until her leg injury. At first, it had just ached, but later, some infection had gotten in, despite her good hygiene, and when the fever and chills had set in, her ability to move, much less stand, had fallen away.

As soon as her feet hit the floor, there was a jolt of discomfort in her injured leg. She was thinner than normal, and her hands and legs shook as she took one hitching step at a time, thankful for once that the room was small enough that she could put her left hand out and reach the wall. It helped steady her as she made her way slowly across to the tiny bathroom and closed the door. There was just enough room in the small space for a tiny sink, toilet, and the small shower. She turned on the water and sighed in relief as the hot water ran over her body, instantly soothing. Petra leaned against the wall, resting her leg by taking all the weight on her other foot and feeling the near-scalding heat run across the stitches and bruised skin on her upper leg.

She was lucky to be alive, lucky the boy and Nix had found her, and she closed her eyes and let the water run over her body, the fingers of her free hand working through her thin hair, before reaching for the shampoo dispenser built into the shower unit. The sensor dispensed a dollop of the 3-in-1 shampoo and body wash into her hand, and she almost groaned in relief as she felt the built-up grease and dirt wash away. No matter how well the colony screened for particulate matter, the Mars dust got in, creating a mostly invisible layer of grit that she could feel on her skin, in her hair. A set of three beeps from the unit warned that her expected water usage was almost at an end. Petra pushed the reset button, smiling. She wouldn't have Jennings in her face ever again trying to tell her to be more responsible with her water usage. A few minutes later it beeped again, and she pressed the button. After the fifth press of the reset button, she had finally gotten her fill and reached for the controls to shut off the water. Her entire body felt invigorated, clean, and she felt better than she had in weeks.

The cooler air outside of the shower unit was refreshing. The steam had built up, coming in clouds of vapor around her, fogging the small mirror on the opposite wall. Outside of the thin door she could hear voices and Petra realized she had only a towel, no clothing, save the filthy, stinking hospital gown to return to. As she stood there, wrapped in the towel, trying to sort out what to do, a soft knock came on the door and the boy's voice. "Ma'am? I brought you some clothes from your room."

Petra opened the door and Lenny thrust them at her, looking away as he shoved them into her hands and quickly scampered away.

"Thank you."

He had brought her the drawstring pants and shirt, a pair of underwear and a bra. He had even remembered socks. She toweled herself dry, sitting awkwardly on the toilet so she could slowly slide her injured leg in first, then wrestle the rest of the outfit on. The socks, however, eluded her. She just couldn't seem to bend her injured leg enough to wrestle her foot close enough. It would have to wait. She smiled again. Perhaps she would ask for Nix to help her.

As if on cue, she heard his deeper voice, asking Toya for an update on her, and she opened the door, socks in hand.

Nix smiled at her. "You're up! That's great. How are you feeling?"

She smiled, her lips curving up of their own accord in response to his. "Better, now that I've had a shower. I just," she waved the socks in her hand, "can't seem to get these on."

She limped over to the chair, not wanting to return to the bed. She gave a tight-lipped smile at Toya, who stared back at her, obviously not getting the clue to get up and move. Nix cleared his throat and said, "Toya, could you please find another set of sheets for the bed?"

The girl said nothing, just rolled her eyes and stood up grudgingly, giving a dramatic sigh before leaving the room. Petra nodded her thanks to Nix, and sat down in the warmed seat, then bent slowly to put on the socks. Despite the heated floors of the Hab, her feet were always cold.

Nix bent down and took a sock from her hand. "Here, let me help with that." He slid the sock on her foot and squeezed it reassuringly. "How are you feeling?"

"Much better, thank you." How could she turn this around and make it easy for him to see her as someone desirable? "Did you stitch my leg up?"

"I did." His mouth widened into a sheepish smile. "I apologize...it was my first time doing that."

"You saved my life."

Nix shrugged. "I can't take all the credit. It was Lenny who figured it might be sepsis. If it hadn't been for the boy wonder, you might not have made it. He's a smart kid." He stood up, turned away from her, and cleared the bed. "Toya will be back with fresh sheets in a moment, but rest some more. The antibiotics seem to have done the trick, but we don't want to rush things. When you can walk longer distances, we can do an EVA back to Philadelphia Hab."

Petra nodded. "Okay, sure. But why Philadelphia Hab?"

Nix shrugged. "I don't know about you, but I wasn't as familiar with the folks there. I was stationed in the Hong Kong Hab and, honestly, I had a hard time, what with knowing so many friends who died there. It just seemed, easier, to go to a different Hab."

Petra nodded, pasting what she hoped was a slightly haunted, sad look on her face. "I know exactly what you mean."

Nix nodded and patted her hand. It lingered there for a moment, a touch from one person to another, and she closed her eyes, reveling in its warmth. When she opened them, Nix was staring at her with sympathy. He was kind. She could work with that.

"Anyway, Philadelphia Hab could be a new start for you...fewer memories of who you have lost."

She nodded, cultivating a suitably pensive, solemn look. She couldn't give a damn about any of the other inhabitants of Sydney Hab. They were all miserable excuses for human beings. She felt a small twinge when she considered the children, but there had only been a handful of them. Really, who was there to mourn? The men who had interested her had gone for the more attractive women, or women who weren't a challenge to their overly high opinions of themselves. It seemed that if you went to Mars, you had more brains than sense. Petra fell into that category. Her only failure had been that she thought the men here might be different, that they might appreciate an intelligent woman over the illusory and fleeting benefit of beauty. But even here, the nerds and eggheads still chose looks over brains. It had been a maddening experience, one that had caused her to wonder, over and over, whether she had made the right decision coming here to this barren planet.

A lifetime of research was ahead of her, for sure, but it would be a lonely one, until the ESH virus leveled the playing field. Petra felt the corners of her mouth tug upwards. Go to Philadelphia Hab? Sure, why not? She had the advantage of being the only woman on the planet. That stupid, feeble-minded girl didn't count. And Petra couldn't help but feel that fate had just hit the big reset button.

For the first time in her life, she would be desirable, wanted, and, best yet, in control.

"That makes sense, Nix." She gave him a rare smile, suddenly not caring whether her front two teeth matched the rest. "I'm in."

The words had barely left her mouth when Toya came in, a pile of sheets in her hands, trailing another that had become unfolded behind her. "Lenny says he has found more people!"

They Haunt Me

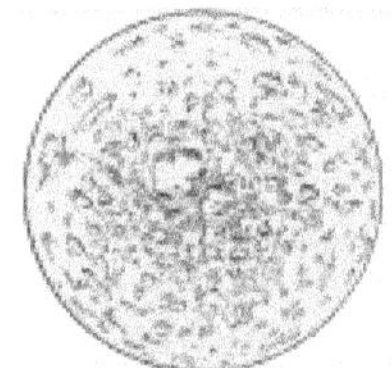

Mars Year 14, Week 44, Day 430
(Earth Date: 10.15.2099)

Each of the five Habs existed independently from the others. And, as their names indicated, they were based on key cities across the globe back on Earth.

World Geographic, who had funded Calypso's journey to Gliese 581g, also had a heavy hand in creating Huygens Outpost. The board of directors had intended for it to have an international focus. The designs had taken years to perfect, but each of the Habs–Philadelphia, Hong Kong, London, Cairo, and Sydney–sat in a ringed shape, 300 meters between them. In the middle of the ring was an enormous dome, Eden Hab, a space intended to connect the City Habs together and serve as a common space. Larger than all the Habs put together, it would serve as a place of both community and as the agricultural center of Huygens Outpost.

The first settlers had rolled out Huygens Outpost in strategic phases. Phase One, begun nearly twenty years ago, had included the first Hab, where the communications array and space hangar now stood. The important work of creating the massive atmo generators that pumped ammonia and CFCs into the thin Mars atmosphere had begun over eighteen years ago. The generators, built to last for hundreds of years, worked endlessly to create the greenhouse gas effect that would be a necessary component for a habitable atmosphere on Mars.

Phase Two had included the City Habs, constructed one after the other, beginning with Philadelphia, then Hong Kong, London, Cairo, and finally Sydney. There had been hiccups, errors in design that had required improvement in each of the City Habs. This delayed Phase Three, the construction and design of the massive Eden Hab. Eden Hab would bring

Huygens Outpost to a self-sustaining reality, capable of turning the barren Mars soil into a substrate in which plants could grow and they could also raise farm animals.

Phase Four would also have meant a ring of smaller Eden modules in an outer ring next to each of the City Habs, creating a paradise of different habitats meant to mimic Earth's rainforests, deserts, and more. In these, the colonists could grow coffee beans in subtropical conditions, and olive trees in more Mediterranean climates, each Eden a little different from the next. It was a way of re-making Earth inside the Habs, while they waited for Mars to become a habitable space, some fifty generations from now.

Phase Five would have been stepping out into the Mars atmosphere for the first time, first with re-breathers and protective equipment, and later unassisted, the Mars atmosphere capable of sustaining human life.

It had been the opportunity of a lifetime for James Fulk to stand at the beginning of it all, and later, to see his creation in action. He had been part of the team that designed Huygens Outpost, the youngest architect on the team. Everyone else had been older, far older. After he had helped work everything out, the schematics and details intricately laid out and the funding approved, James had gone on to other projects. He had worked on the vast undersea colony based on the Shimizu Corporation's dreams of Ocean Spirals, one that had created a mesmerizing space to live and work for nearly 2,000 people in the Taiwan Sea. He had even lived on another ocean spiral, Roma Nueva, for a year in the Mediterranean shortly after its completion. He had loved watching the denizens of the deep move past the enormous plastiglass windows.

Despite moving on to other projects, his thoughts returned over and over to the Huygens Outpost and the City Habs. He had joined the team working on the expansion of the lunar colony on the Moon and stayed for a short time in it as well, before applying for a permanent residency at the Mars colony. He had arrived with the latest batch of colonists, just in time to see it all come apart at the seams.

Eden Hab was newly installed when the ESH virus hit, bringing progress to a standstill. And James had watched as each of the colonists, new and old, fell to the virus. Despite his work creating habitats for humans, James would likely have been far happier alone in a cabin in the middle of nowhere. He dreamed of quiet solitude, something he wasn't able to find, no matter where he went. The London Hab had been bustling, and loud, and despite staying in a Singles Hab, claustrophobic in its size, it was preferable to joining his neighbors. He had been hard at work creating the plans for a four-person exploratory outpost, one where he could live and not feel as if he were shoulder to elbow with the other colonists. It would have been far from Huygens Crater. Noctis Labyrinthus, at the far end of Valles Marineris, was nearly half a world away on the far side of Mars. The earliest explorations of Noctis Labyrinthus discovered a significant amount of hematite, a necessary component for the radiation shielding in the thin atmosphere. As well, the opaline silica discovered there was well-suited for opal jewelry back on Earth.

And then ESH happened, and James locked himself in his bunk and waited for the end to come. When it didn't, he emerged, shaking with hunger, the food supplies he had hoarded having run out nearly three days earlier. There was nothing left but the bodies. It wasn't loud any longer. There wasn't the ever-present press of humanity on all sides either. It had taken him days of struggling with the bodies while the smell inside of London Hab intensified. He had adjusted the temperature throughout the Hab to 0 degrees Celsius, except for his own Hab. This had stopped the advance of the decay on the bodies and he had cleared the entire Hab over fifteen days, dragging bodies and stacking them like cordwood in each of the airlocks, before donning a suit and dragging them out, one by one.

And now he was alone. More alone than he had ever imagined, or even really wanted. It was one thing to wish he were alone, away from everyone. It was another to see them dead, their faces contorted with pain, eyes staring, stomachs distended. Was there anyone left at all? Or was he completely and utterly alone, the last human left on a planet that would never be inhabitable, at least, not in his lifetime? Would he die here, his body slowly decaying, only bones left to show evidence of his pathetic existence in a near future when humans once again returned to the red planet?

James had considered suiting up and walking to each of the City Habs to check.

He had headed to the suit room next to the airlock, but somehow, as his hand had fallen once again on the suit, one he had used so many times when emptying London Hab of its dearly departed, he had stopped. It had been enough to drag them out, he didn't want to walk past them. Not yet. As it was, the stench, real or imagined, still filled his nostrils. It would be a long time before he could bear the thought of walking past them. Especially the children.

James had never wanted children, not really. From the outside looking in, they seemed loud and overly needy. Had he ever been like that? The thought was rather off-putting. Despite this, seeing their tiny bodies, having carried them outside with the rest, it had brought home to him the true horror of this virus. Each of them had bloated stomachs, having ingested God knows what before they had died, and likely in excruciating pain. Even the most obnoxious, whiny brat hadn't deserved that kind of death. Their bodies were so light when he picked them up and moved them outside. He had moved them first. It had been easier, but it had also seemed wrong to cover them with the heavier corpses of the adults. He had set them to one side, gently, their tiny bodies side by side, so alone on the rocky Mars ground. Already there was a thick layer of dust settling upon them.

Why had he survived? It was something that woke him up at night, gasping, sweating, his clothing damp and clinging to him. He didn't have an answer, and that, more than anything, troubled him.

James didn't know enough about the virus, hell, he hadn't even followed the coverage of it when he was there on the Moon. Earth had been a distant concern, despite the regular arrivals and departures of lunar colonists and supply ships. How could he not have realized it would touch them there on the Moon or, later, millions of miles away on Mars?

There had been no genuine concerns upon arriving at the red planet. Sure, they had warned the colonists even before the Juniper Supply Ship had arrived that the ESH virus had infected the crew. The crew had perished during the voyage, but the people in Cryo had been in Cryo the entire trip, and they had passed all temperature checks before boarding. The colonists had taken every precaution, and they scuttled the Jupiter supply ship in a fiery explosion on the far side of the planet.

Despite this, the ESH virus had already been among them, and now hundreds were dead. Perhaps, after a lifetime of seeking solitude and quiet in the throngs of city-dwellers on Earth, or the bustle of new Ocean Spiral cities off the coast of Japan, and even the crowded lunar colony and growing

Cairo Hab—perhaps he had gotten his wish. If so, it was in a way he never would have dreamed of in his wildest nightmares. He was finally alone. But at what cost? And as the days wore on, each not much different from the last, he couldn't help but think that this was all a horrible, horrible nightmare, one that he might never wake from.

James had a sliver of a view of the Hong Kong Hab to the northwest, and Cairo Hab to the southwest. Before they had installed Eden Hab, the view of the other City Habs had been unobstructed, but now they were difficult to view, the large dome distorting any clear view.

He had found that the central Control Room, with its own miniature communications array and banks of screens that showed active cameras, was a place where he could, in a limited sense, search for survivors in either the Hong Kong Hab or the Cairo Hab, since they were within the line of sight. Eden Hab obstructed the view of the rest.

After days of viewing the Hong Kong Hab, during the day and especially at night, when the automatic lights would turn on in response to any movement, James concluded that there were no survivors within the Hab. The Cairo Hab occasionally showed flickers of light at night. Someone was tripping the sensors and that meant that there was at least one survivor, possibly more. Did they have the virus? Were they sick and dying? He felt conflicted. Should he stay in London Hab, or find other survivors? One part of him wanted to suit up, do the EVA and go find out, and the other part of him was sick with dread. What if they had the virus? What if it hadn't finished with them yet? Could he stand watching them suffer and die?

When the first cases had begun, it had been horrifying. One in particular had haunted him and contributed to most of his nightmares. She had been young and slender, a medical technician. He couldn't remember her name now. When the ESH virus fully turned on, it was unstoppable and starkly terrifying. She had stopped there in line at the cafeteria. No matter that there was a line of people behind her, she had just stopped for long enough to scream this wordless sound of despair before she launched herself forward over the plastiglass barrier that protected the food and servers from contaminants. She had scrabbled up and over the plastiglass, landing in a tub of mashed potatoes, digging her hands into hot gravy, tears streaming down her face as she lifted the steaming tub of food up and tilted it into her mouth. Hot gravy had flown in all directions. One of the cafeteria workers had flinched as a large splash of it reddened her arm, burning it.

As the woman had died on the floor moments later, her body seizing and thrashing, there had been pandemonium. James had just sat there, frozen in place at his table, eyes riveted on the woman. The scene had felt impossible, surreal, as he sat there, his fork suspended halfway to his mouth. It had been shortly after this that he had found himself carried on a wave of hungry, panicked colonists, through a narrow door and into the Food Storage area. Like the others, he had grabbed handfuls of MREs, shoving them into a half-ripped box and fled back to his singles unit, closing and locking the door behind him. He hadn't answered the door, no matter who had hammered at it, until the sounds of the other London Hab inhabitants had ceased. When he had run out of food, he waited as long as he could, shaking with hunger, only to find he was alone.

Did he really want to see that again? What if whoever was there in the Cairo Hab was on the verge of death? What if they were out of food? He had seen things, bite marks, even chunks of flesh missing, on some bodies of his London Hab neighbors. The ESH virus created a hunger that took all reason from a person. Would whoever it was still alive in Cairo turn on him?

He watched the screens, turning all available cameras so that they pointed towards Cairo Hab. He moved a heap of blankets into the room, stocking it with everything he could need, and spent the next five days watching the screens, intent on learning if the survivors in Cairo were sick or healthy. It became an obsession. He would sleep for an hour, maybe three, then return to watching the camera feeds. Several cameras had ceased transmitting shortly after the dust storm from a few weeks earlier and needed repair, but many were still functioning, some nine in all. There was someone over there. He would catch glimpses of a figure, mainly at night, walking the outer spoke of the City Hab, triggering the motion-sensitive, energy-conserving lights. Occasionally he switched over to the camera feeds that focused on Hong Kong Hab, just to check. Nothing but darkness. No one remained there. Or if they did, there was no movement on the side facing London Hab. James continued to check infrequently, but his focus remained on the movements of a person, or persons, in Cairo Hab. His eyes were red and burned after countless hours of watching the screens for any signs of life.

An outpost-wide communications system had also been on the brink of implementation just as the virus hit, sending all of their plans into chaos. James' friend Dolan had been consulting on the project. In the weeks since the virus hit, James had wished, plenty of times, that they had already had it. It had been the same concept as the one used by the crew of Calypso. The comm link badges would attach easily to the uniform. They would have routed the communications through NARA. Why the colony hadn't already had them was beyond James' understanding or pay grade. If only the virus had hit a few weeks later, after the planned rollout of the new comms.

He shook his head, frustrated at his lack of options, as he stared at the monitors. The lights had flickered on, yet again, for the third time in an hour, and he watched a figure walk through the outer corridor of the Cairo Hab. Whoever it was over there, they moved fast, as if agitated. James tried to count the number of days it had been since everything had gone to hell. Could this person still be sick? Or was he, or she, all alone there, a survivor like him?

"I have to at least try." His voice, gravelly from disuse, sounded overly loud in the space. James lay down, instructed NARA to dim the lights, and closed his eyes. He needed sleep first. James hadn't slept much at all, so desperate to watch the monitors, to find any signs of life but his own. He closed his eyes and fell deeply asleep in minutes, his mind temporarily at peace with the decision to go to Cairo Hab in the morning. He would find his answers.

As the dark abyss of sleep took him, James fell into a dream, the same one he had experienced nearly every night since the virus had brought the Huygens Outpost to its knees.

James stood on the edge of the Huygens Crater, no suit, his breaths coming in frosty puffs as he inhaled the thin, cold air of Mars. Beside him was a woman he was sure he had seen before, but for the life of him, could not place. Their backs were to the colony—he knew this without looking—and before him, the rim of the crater plunged deeply down, the walls flaring at the top, the rocky soil not as barren as he would have imagined, but with odd flecks of green vegetative life appearing in patches that were expanding slowly, gently covering what had been barren, reddish soil and rock. The woman turned to him. "Do you miss them? All of those people?"

He shrugged, wishing he had a different answer to give, knowing somehow that he was less for not feeling the loss of the others more keenly. "I don't know."

And, as she had in every dream before, something he remembered intuitively, a conscious dreaming and memory of the other dreams, an awareness he carried with him, night after night, she said, "They haunt me."

She jumped then, plunging straight down, falling into the abyss, her body turning, tumbling, and bouncing. Limbs snapped, splotches of blood appeared on the larger rocks, until her body finally came to rest, a mere speck, a hundred feet below.

James woke with a shout, sweating, trembling. Despite feeling as if he had just fallen asleep, he could see the dim rays of sun lighting up the outside terrain through the monitors. It had felt like minutes but had to have been hours.

A thick cord of exhaustion ran through him. He didn't feel rested at all, but it was time to suit up and see who was occupying Cairo Hab. He was about to find out just who it was that was over there.

What is Real?

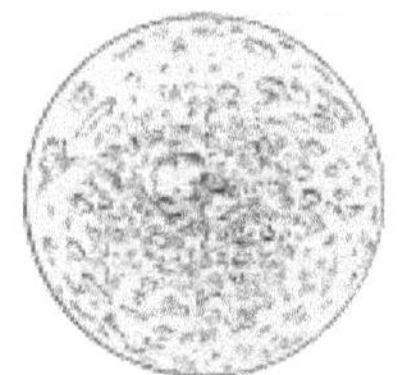

Mars Year 14, Week 44, Day 431
(Earth Date: 10.16.2099)

James would have to shower first. He had realized as he reached for his clothes that they stunk, as did he. How long had it been? Days? A week? He walked back to his Singles Hab and slipped into the tiny room and its claustrophobia-inducing private bath. There was an entire Hab worth of living spaces to choose from, but he couldn't bring himself to take something larger. He had entered every one of them, seen belongings, art, and more that had made the spaces unique, individual, and personal. And despite the anxiety he had felt with the press of so many around him, their deaths had not removed their presence from his mind. Moving into one of the now-vacant spaces, it would have been too much, a constant reminder that he had lived when others had not.

A couple of weeks ago, he had entered the Spinnets' Family Hab looking for the gourmet Earl Grey tea that Allen Spinnet had brought with him as part of his personal weight limit. Allen, having learned that James enjoyed the tea, had given him a tiny bag of the prized tea as a welcome gift upon his arrival. The gifting to new arrivals was a custom begun when the original crew received Mars' first wave of official colonists. And the custom had been continued with each new incoming group. From refined opals collected from a trip to Noctis Labyrinthus at the west end of the Valles Marineris to the tiny fossils found in an outcropping of deposits near the northern edge of Terra Sabaea. Later incoming colonists, when learning of the tradition, had brought their own small gifts to their new neighbors. It was a tradition that helped build bonds and friendships as veteran colonists learned about the new arrivals and vice versa.

James had enjoyed every precious sip, savoring the firm notes of bergamot. It hadn't been with the shelf-stable milk, that was reserved for the children, or at least it had been. But still it had reminded him of home.

The memory of sipping each precious cup, rationed out carefully by re-using the tea leaves twice, sipping the ever-thinning flavors, and savoring the dwindling supply, had driven him to Allen's Family Hab in search of the tea. He had found it easily, a large bag of loose-leaf tea sealed tightly and in the back of a shallow cabinet in the kitchen. On the counter, a baby-sized fistful in a sealed plastic jar. He had held both in his hands for a moment, then stopped.

It hadn't felt right. Not at all. Despite the knowledge that they were dead, and no longer needed such things, he left the Spinnets' Family Hab with just the tiny amount of tea that was in the jar. Long gone now, he thought of it as he hit the button on the shower, twice, then a third time, feeling the water run over him until his skin was red from the heat, scrubbed and squeaky clean from top to bottom.

After he dressed in a standard jumpsuit, he slowly maneuvered his way into the suit for the EVA. His stomach growled, but he was too nervous to eat or even indulge in the standard black tea available by the boxful in the cafeteria. James wasn't sure if it was the thought of seeing all of the dead, or the EVA itself, which he hated. It didn't matter, though; he was committed. He had to know if he was all alone.

As he passed through the airlock and out onto the bleak Martian soil, the light of the sun wheeling its way up in the sky felt weak. He moved past the stacks of the dead, noting only that the dust had thickened, thankfully blotting out features and details, something he was quite thankful for. As he passed the last of them, he let out a lungful of stale air, surprised to realize he had been holding it in until then.

The thousand-yard walk to the Cairo Hab felt like forever as he trudged along in the heavy suit, dust kicking up and coating the legs of his suit in a coating of rust red. It was insidious, this dust, and found its way into everything, requiring constant monitoring of equipment and regular cleaning. It felt like a fine grit that coated every surface, even the food. But he was, most likely, simply imagining things.

The sun felt as if it had already moved higher in the sky as James arrived at the Cairo Hab's northeastern airlock. There were a few bodies outside of it, but not nearly as many as he would have expected. Perhaps they were at one of the other airlocks.

Each City Hab had four large airlocks, allowing for access from the City Habs on each side. Then there was the "inner" airlock that connected to the unfinished Eden Hab and an "outer" airlock that would eventually connect with the future individualized nature Habs designed to mimic a particular temperate zone from Earth. London's would have been filled with sheep, ducks, and crops such as barley, sugar beets, potatoes, and greens. Cairo's would have included figs, flax, pomegranate, citrus trees, and there had been discussions about cultivating a small herd of goats before the virus had descended upon the outpost.

The hope had been to recreate Earth's agricultural zones, while becoming more self-sufficient over the decades to come.

James reached the airlock and hesitated. He didn't have to do this; he could go back. He had everything he needed there at London Hab–all the food, water, and air he needed to live out his life. Eventually the nightmares would go away, they had to, and then it would be just him, master of his own destiny, the last man on Mars. His hand froze in midair, while his mind ground its gears, trying to imagine what might wait behind these doors. James had the upper-level access codes, thanks to being a part of the design team. All he needed to do was enter it on the keypad. He didn't know the people inside, not like he had known his fellow Londoners. He could go into the Habs, take what he needed, and not feel the nagging guilt and horror he did in his own Hab. Stealing from dead people you didn't know somehow felt easier than stealing from those you had known. James raised his hand, entered the code, and waited as the lights whirled inside, a distant alarm sounding, and the outer doors of the airlock opened to him.

A few moments later, he was inside, through the inner airlock and on the inside of the Cairo Hab. Here the hangar was large, open, and free of any visible bodies. After checking the readings on his suit, a precaution to make sure that the air inside the Hab was still breathable, he pulled off the helmet and instantly gagged. The smell of death was unmistakable. Sweet like fruit gone bad, cloying, and rank. A mixture of shit, rotting fruit, and more. James felt relieved that he had eaten nothing substantial. Despite this, his stomach roiled and threatened to empty itself on the vast floor of the entry bay.

"Get a grip, Fulk," he murmured to himself, and then concentrated on shedding the rest of the suit while trying not to breathe through his nose. It confused him. He was sure that he had seen someone alive in here. How could they stand it, the smell? Hell, by now there had to be putrescine. The human body, composed mainly of water, became a gross mess as it decomposed. He knew that firsthand; it had taken weeks before the air filters had cleared the last of the smells from the London Hab. And that was even with his precaution of taking the entire Hab down to the temperature of a refrigerator while he slowly cleared the bodies from the Hab. It had slowed the decomposition down, allowing him to remove them before the process was too far along.

Whoever was here, they had not had the wherewithal to do the same. The Cairo Hab, with its dozens of dead bodies, would be uninhabitable for months, or longer, if the dead stayed. And the smell! He gagged again, his hand to his mouth. How could anyone still alive stand it?

James hesitated at the door that separated the entry bay and hangar attached to this airlock from the rest of the Hab and wondered again if this was a good idea. He was here though, he reasoned, might as well get on with it.

The scene that greeted him was reminiscent of London Hab, only far messier and reeking of death. His stomach roiled again as he walked through the hallways, past corpses, and into the cafeteria, where most of the dead had congregated. After all, when you have a virus that compels you to eat and eat until your stomach bursts open, the primary source of food is where you want to be.

His steps sounded loud as he moved along the corridor away from the cafeteria and its scores of bodies. He had counted roughly thirty, maybe forty, inside. They had been dead a long time. He could see the black putrescine puddled out around the heaps of dead. Without flies, the decomposition process was taking longer. It was something he had noticed within his own City Hab. It had removed the disgusting creepy crawlies from the equation, but did nothing about the fact that when humans die, all the liquid has to go somewhere. A human body is composed of 60% water and flesh and, once death stopped the heart from pumping, it broke down quickly.

James shook his head, his stomach continuing to roil. How could anyone stand to exist around all of this death? Had it been a child that had survived? Someone too weak to remove the bodies? And what would he do if it was a child? He blinked, trying to process the thought, imagining a small child crying, alone, surrounded by the dead. It would explain a lot, the infrequent glimpses of movement, the radio silence, and the bodies strewn about Cairo Hab, rotting where they lay. His stomach did an extra flip at the thought of how in the hell he would deal with a child. The youngest of three, James had essentially been an only child, his brother and sister both nearly twenty years older than him, long gone from the house when he arrived. Neither had ever married or had children, and they had rarely visited. It had just been him and Mom after Father died when he was ten. He had spent most of his childhood either with his nose buried in a book or hiding out in his room when Mom invited her friends, all retirees with grown grandchildren, for a round of pinochle.

James continued to walk down the long corridors, passing bodies contorted and rotting, the silence of the dead Hab haunting him. If it wasn't for the realization that a child had to be alone in here, possibly hurt, or starving, surrounded by the dead, he would have turned around and fled back to the London Hab, and left Cairo to decompose all on its own.

He had to search strategically. After all, a kid left alone with the dead would be traumatized. James' focus moved to the Family Habs. He would look there first. He began with the first Hab and entered the override codes for the doors, seeing one horrifying tableau of death after another. Then he went room by room, individual Hab by individual Hab, until he had exhausted the entire Family Hab section. There was nothing, and no one. Had the kid left the Family Habs and gone elsewhere? A supply closet or classroom, by chance? He broadened his search, calling out intermittently, and finally headed over to the Singles Habs. Could the child have hidden out here? As he entered the outer ring of the section, he heard a sound, more of a murmur or whisper really, and immediately stopped, listening intently. It was definitely coming from one of the Singles Habs. James walked quietly to an open door on the left, following the rhythmic murmuring. It was there that he found a young man with dark, curly hair that sprayed out wildly from his head. He was unkempt, disheveled, and rail-thin. The younger man knelt on a small rug, his forehead touching the fibers and murmuring the words of what had to be a prayer. His shoulder blades jutted sharply through the fabric of his shirt, which otherwise hung off of him loosely, looking as if it were several sizes too large on his frame.

James didn't know whether to speak or to walk away and allow the man to continue to pray. Instead, he found himself frozen in place, watching him as he prayed.

"Iyyaka na'budu wa-iyyaka nasta'een," the man uttered. "Ihdina alssirata almustaqueem."

It didn't feel right to stand there, staring at him and saying nothing. It felt as if he were witnessing a private moment, the communing of this man with his God. James cleared his throat. "I, uh..."

The young man froze, the prayer forgotten, his head raising from the prayer mat, and staring wide-eyed at this stranger in his doorway.

"Are, are you dead?" he asked, his brown eyes round with fear. "Are you the dead come to haunt me?"

James blinked. "No, um, no. I'm from, I'm from London Hab. I was all alone there, and I saw you, well, I saw someone walking and came to see if there were any survivors." He paused, looking down the hallway. "Is there anyone else, or is it just you?"

The young man blinked hard, tears forming in his eyes. "L-L-London Hab? You, you are...you are real?"

"What is real?" James said, a flood of emotion stealing over him. Reality was awful. He wished the ESH virus had stayed on Earth. He wished he had died with the rest. That it was all a nightmare that he could wake up from. "I'm James. James Fulk. I haven't seen another living soul in over four weeks." He stepped forward and held out a hand. "I'm happy to have found someone else."

The young man rose from his mat, stood, and instead of shaking James' hand, took it within his own. His olive skin was warm, and he clasped James' hand between the two of his for just a moment before wrapping his arms around the older man in a tight hug, shaking with emotion.

James fought the urge to jump away, to shove this stranger from him. Instead, he reached his arms around the younger man and held him as the man's body shook with emotion, and with tears. James could feel the tears wetting his shirt as the thin young man clutched at James like a man drowning.

He would learn later, amongst more rounds of sobbing, that Abdul Hammadi was twenty-six years old. A devout Muslim, he had watched his lover and partner of five years, an engineer he had emigrated to Mars with, die in the first wave. Abdul was adrift, so haunted by those who had died that he could not deal with moving their bodies out of the Hab. James, in a rare moment of Zen-like calm, continued to hold the younger man as he sobbed out the story of loss.

One thing was for sure, though. From what he understood from Abdul's wandering confession of pain, sorrow, and loss–they weren't alone. Apparently, Abdul had seen movement a few days ago in the Sydney Hab. There were more survivors, and it was time to find them.

Once Abdul had calmed, apologizing profusely, and asked for a few moments to complete his prayers, James doubled back, and began clearing the bodies from the corridor that led to the opposite airlock, the one closest to the Sydney Hab. Here he could see signs of the chaos that must have unfolded in the Cairo Hab. Some bodies showed wounds. In one case, James noticed a sharp, long kitchen knife buried almost to the hilt in the chest of a younger woman. He shuddered and pulled her out of sight, through an open doorway. Abdul looked fragile, haunted, and James worried that the younger man would fall apart at the sight of the dead. As it was, James could tell by the way Abdul's bones were jutting out that he hadn't eaten in days. Cairo Hab was toast. Later he could return and clean it as he had London Hab, but for now, he needed to get Abdul out of it and away to a place that was hopefully in better shape. On his way back to Abdul's small Singles Hab, he stopped by the Control Center and turned down the temps Hab-wide, just as he had for London Hab in the early days, when the bodies decomposed faster than he could get them out.

He returned as Abdul was zipping a large rucksack closed, his prayer rug already rolled and tucked neatly under his arm.

He gave James a small, almost shy smile, his mouth quivering. "It is cold." It didn't take long to realize just how cold Mars could be without the environmental generator working constantly. Yet another reminder they were on a planet where they were not welcome.

James nodded. "I turned the heat down. It will help with, well, it will help, um, preserve things."

Abdul winced, staring at the ground. "I should have done something, anything really. I tried, I did, but I just, I just couldn't." The shame bled through, and James looked away, reminded of the first days after he emerged from his Hab to find himself utterly alone, surrounded by death.

He put his hand on Abdul's shoulder, felt the bone jutting through the shirt again, and saw how traumatized the younger man was.

"Don't blame yourself. It does no good, believe me. Let's get out of here. We'll go to Sydney Hab and find others. We should get going. I had a good look to the west, and I think there might be another sandstorm brewing. Time to get going, yeah?"

Abdul nodded; his brown eyes fixed on James.

"Are you going to be alright walking over to the Sydney Hab?" James asked, no small amount of unease running through him. Abdul was not okay, not mentally or physically. The question was, would he be better off out of this place of death? Or would they be walking into more of it? "I could go ahead of you and scout it out. We could always head back to London if it was, you know..."

He didn't want to use the words "full of bodies" or anything else that might set Abdul off. He could see in the younger man's eyes that his very sanity was at risk if he stayed where he was, but despite it only being a few thousand feet, he worried about risking both of their lives if Abdul panicked. They built Huygens Outpost at the edge of the Huygens Crater, a hole in the ground that was over 467 kilometers in diameter and nearly 25 kilometers deep. There was a sharp decline from the edge rim just 2.75 kilometers away from the outpost. If the younger man lost his marbles, ran the wrong way, and slipped, he would end up dead.

Abdul's warm brown eyes searched James before giving him a faltering smile. It held for just a moment before fading once more. "Please, don't leave me here. If Sydney is...if it is bad like here, then it is better to be with someone else than alone here." He reached out and clasped James' arm. "I can do this, as long as I have someone with me."

He looked vulnerable, afraid, but James could also see that Abdul's mental state was improving with each moment that passed. They had trained everyone for EVAs. Monthly EVA practice drills were mandatory for everyone, even the children. As they suited up at the airlock closest to Sydney Hab, James watched as Abdul finished his preparations, sliding into the suit with care. His shaking had subsided.

James was also thankful that Cairo Hab had removed what bodies it had before everything went to hell, placing them out of the southern airlock which faced the crater's edge. He wished he had thought of that when dealing with the bodies in the London Hab. Not having to walk by them would have been far better on his own emotional well-being. In the distance, he could see low piles of the dead clustered at the southeast airlock facing Cairo. He would be better off leading Abdul further, to the southwest airlock, which he hoped would be corpse-free.

He listened carefully to the short-range transmitter that connected him and Abdul. It was sensitive and he could hear the younger man's breathing, which would help warn him if Abdul panicked.

"Okay, we are all set. You ready?" His voice echoed inside of the helmet, and Abdul nodded, giving him a shaky thumbs up. "We're going to skirt around the nearest entrance and head for the southwest airlock at Sydney Hab. It looks a little more...well, it's clear of obstacles."

Abdul's breaths were clear and regular. "Thank you, James."

The inner airlock opened, they walked through, and closed it behind them. James gave a thumbs-up to Abdul as the outer airlock opened and they walked out into the sunlight. It was midday, and the sky was clear, and the sun now hung high overhead. James could feel the gentle warmth of it, even through the thick plastiglass of the helmets. It was warm enough, in fact, that by the time they reached their destination, James could feel beads of sweat running down his back and across his forehead. The EVA had been without incident, thanks to his decision to skirt the airlock with the bodies stacked outside. The southwest airlock was free of corpses, and James felt a smile tug at his lips as they passed through the outer airlock and through into the large bay. A young boy on the cusp of adolescence was waiting there for them, his eyes round with surprise and excitement.

The boy grinned as James removed his helmet. "Welcome to Sydney Hab!"

What to do with the Dead

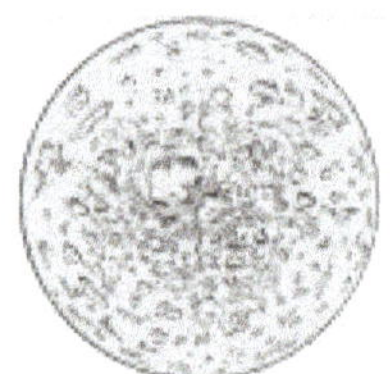

Mars Year 14, Week 45, Day 446
(Earth Date: 10.31.2099)

James looked around the room and wondered why he had ever agreed to the meeting this morning. The lot of them, Nix, Petra, Abdul, and even Lenny and Toya sat together in the Mess Hall. They had finished breakfast and now it was time for their first official Mars survivors planning meeting.

He was unnerved when Nix ushered the siblings into the room and turned to Lenny, nodding at the boy with encouragement. The kid was a genius, James had to admit that, but that didn't mean he knew what was best for the survivors, no matter how smart he was. And what the boy had suggested was grotesque. Horrid, really, no matter how you looked at it. And of all the days to suggest it. He couldn't help wondering if the veil between life and death was as thin here, on Mars, as it was on Earth. Somehow, the idea of All Hallow's Eve, of celebrating death, seemed crass, especially on the heels of the ESH virus. But this idea of Lenny's was far worse.

He fought to keep his voice even. "So, you are actually suggesting we use our former friends, family, and neighbors as *compost*?" The tone of his voice came out sharper than he would have liked and Lenny squirmed uneasily in response, looking at the tablet in front of him, instead of at James, before he answered.

"The founders proposed it early in the colony's history; there was the oxygen failure twelve years ago..." He faltered, looking sideways at his sister. "They laid the deceased to rest in a section where Eden Hab now stands."

James couldn't keep the condescension from his voice. "I doubt the colony founders envisioned a time when we would plant crops on their remains." He looked at Petra and Nix for support, avoiding locking eyes with Abdul. He could hear the younger man's leg juddering under the table, his body already rocking rhythmically. It had been two weeks, and Abdul still looked haunted.

The younger man was less skeletal, his ribcage and shoulder blades no longer prominent through his clothing, but he was far from recovered. It had taken James and Nix the better part of a week to clear the rest of Sydney Hab and Cairo Hab of the dead, but now the City Habs were clear, the bodies of their former friends and co-workers stacked outside of the airlocks, already half-covered by the slow drifts of Martian sand and dust. Until today, James had assumed that it was simply triage, and that they might use an earthmover to create a large mass grave for all the dead.

What Lenny was suggesting sounded absolutely horrific. Petra looked slightly green, but Nix stared back at James, unblinking. He was obviously all in on this whole grotesque plan.

James couldn't believe they were actually considering it. If they used the dead for compost, planted food crops on top, and then actually ate the fresh vegetables and fruits, wouldn't that be akin to eating their dead? The thought of it made his stomach roil. Across from him, Abdul rocked even harder, muttering some prayer under his breath in Arabic. Petra noticed it now. She turned and stared at Abdul with naked curiosity. James had had limited interactions with the woman in the past two weeks. He could see that her focus was on Michael Nix and he noticed how her face changed when Nix was around. She was a plain woman, her hair thin and lifeless. Her tongue was a sharp one. He was disgusted by her responses to Toya, the retarded girl.

It is brain damage, Fulk. The girl isn't retarded.

He had his own demons to fight in this arena, but he knew that Toya's affliction was oxygen deprivation-induced. He remembered the incident when it had happened, and the inquiry that had taken place more than a decade after he had worked with the team who designed the Huygens Outpost. In some way, he felt responsible for Toya's injuries. Although he could not remember every last detail, there had been concerns about keeping the costs down on some sections of the Hab design. Had the oxygen sensors been one of those details sacrificed for the almighty bottom line? Had he been complicit? It had been more than twenty years, and he had been the youngest member of the team, but the idea of it haunted him.

He had interacted with Toya in a limited manner. He just marshaled patience and lowered his expectations of the girl. Besides, Nix and Lenny were the ones who dealt with her most. They seemed to have a better handle on it. Petra was transparent in her disdain for the girl. She saw no purpose for Toya, none. James watched now as the same look of disgust that Petra wore when dealing with Toya turned towards Abdul. It was an untenable situation. Abdul had been through a great trauma. They all had. But Abdul had lost his lover, and with that loss, and the subsequent weeks of isolation, surrounded by the dead, his grip on sanity was a tenuous one. He needed caring for. He needed kindness and patience, not the disgust and disparagement so obvious on Petra's face. She continued to stare at the young man as he rocked, forward and back, faster and faster.

James reached across the table and clasped Abdul's hands where they lay on the table. Before he reached over, Abdul had been wringing them, his fingers constantly in motion, his rocking more and more severe. James' touch seemed to calm him, though, and his fingers stilled beneath James' hand, the rocking slowing to an occasional nervous twitch.

Lenny spoke, "The cardinal rule of space travel: let nothing go to waste. In order to survive and thrive, we must use every source of nutrient available to us. The next delivery from the Jupiter Supply Ship would have carried the final raw nutrients and fertilizers we needed to transform the Mars soil into something worthy of growing crops in. Without it, we have to make do, and create our own soil." He took a breath, then continued, "Nix has inventoried all the food supplies and we have enough in MREs to last the rest of our lives, it's true. But is that what we want? To eat out of packages forever?"

The boy shrugged. "I know there is a way to replenish our numbers in time. Once the virus has run its course, or there is a vaccine, we will see more colonists. We can request more as well. And you always have the option of returning to Earth once Earth has sorted itself out and sent a supply ship."

The boy paused, and James realized for the first time that for Lenny and Toya, there was no going back. Not really. They had grown up on Mars. Lenny had been born here, and his thin, lanky frame was taller than his sister already, and promised to rival Nix's 185-centimeter height. Toya was tall as well.

The consensus before the ESH virus had ravaged the colony was that children born and raised on Mars would end up an average of 5, possibly as much as 12 centimeters taller than their Earth-born parents. If they ever returned to Earth, Lenny and Toya would likely spend the rest of their lives in powered walkers, their bones aching from a gravity more than twice what they were used to.

"There is a future here on Mars," Lenny continued, "One that we must make ourselves out of the materials available to us. The bodies will help enrich the soil. We need that, rather desperately, for any long-term success."

James hated the idea, but the kid was right. Lenny was approaching the future in a no-nonsense way. They were ignoring a resource, one that was, as Lenny pointed out, desperately needed.

He reached up and rubbed his eyes, lifted his cup of rapidly cooling coffee to his lips, and sipped. Nix was right, the freeze-dried instant coffee was disgusting. He made a note to go back to London Hab soon and get that special Earl Grey tea from the Spinnets' Hab. "Fine. Fine. I'm in."

Lenny's face stretched into a victorious grin for a few quick seconds before it disappeared into a far more nervous state. "There's just one more thing. And you will not like it."

The next day, as he and Nix struggled with the logjam of bodies at one of the airlock doors, James thought about the discussion. Lenny had been right; he hadn't liked what the kid said next. He still didn't. Even if it had made sense, even if it needed doing.

When Lenny pointed out the cardinal rule of space travel, James had remembered a concept that was put to use in the Lunar Colony, that of using human urine to help make concrete. It had disgusted folks. But the reality of limited water and the need to waste nothing and reuse everything had quickly changed their minds.

By the time they established the Martian colony, it was so accepted that people didn't even question it. The facilities installed from the get-go, and all the City Habs, had seen their concrete bases formed by human urine mixed with regolith and substrate in order to make a concrete capable of standing for centuries.

Their former friends and fellow colonists' bodies would help the poor Martian soil turn into a rich loam capable of growing the plants they would need in the years ahead, but not if their clothing remained. The artificial fabrics resisted the natural process of decay. This meant that everybody, every person they had known, worked with, squabbled with, or loved, would have to be stripped down to the skin, then laid into the trenches. Abdul and Petra were already digging them with the newly 3D printed shovels in Eden Hab. A morbid and disturbing job, but one that needed doing.

They had connected one of the five passageways, the one that traveled from Philadelphia Hab to Eden. They had also re-routed the environmental power grid to Eden from the four now unused City Habs and it was slowly heating to 12 degrees Celsius, cooler than what they would need for anything but the cold-weather crops like kale, spinach, and other high-nutrient greens, but a workable temperature for beginning the first crops that Eden Hab would produce. Eventually, the plans were to raise the ambient temperatures to a range of 20 degrees Celsius at night and up to 26 degrees Celsius at midday. To do so, they would need to recreate the effect the atmo generators were doing a far slower job of outside of the domed Habs. They couldn't wait one thousand years for Eden Hab to become habitable. It would have to be a wee bit sooner than that.

The off-gassing from the bodies rotting in the soil would help, as would the ton of freeze-dried human shit the colony had been collecting over the past fifteen years in anticipation of this step forward. The seminal science-fiction novel of a scientist left behind by his crew in a sandstorm on the red planet, *The Martian*, written early in the century, hadn't been so far off after all. The movie version had gone into great detail about how the principal character, Mark Watney, fights to survive, alone, without enough food. It turned out that shit, even the human variety, makes great compost. The book became mandatory for incoming colonists.

James' face wrinkled in disgust at the thought of it all. Creating a new world had sounded rather sexy when he was still on Earth, and even when training for the mission on the Moon. Reality was far smellier. It was also visually off-putting as he mechanically snipped through the corpse's shirt, the man's eyes still unnerving in their open, sunken, and desiccated state. The man looked familiar, and James couldn't help wondering if they had met or interacted. This work was exhausting, physically and mentally. It was worse when you knew the person. Although now that the bodies had been outside, in the thin, airless Martian atmosphere, they had lost a good deal of their fluids, resulting in them barely resembling the people they had been. This had been of some benefit, however. They were now far easier to handle and carry. James flipped the corpse over and cut the shirt and pants off with the sharp scissors he had found in the medical bay and adapted to use while in the spacesuit. They were sharp as hell, so they still had to be careful. It wouldn't do to cut the outside layer of their suits and compromise the suit, no matter how many spare suits they had.

It was all hands on deck for the project, but that didn't mean all of them out on EVAs dealing with the corpses. The pinch-faced woman, Petra, was still recovering from her leg injury and could not kneel, stand, or drag the corpses while in a suit.

And Abdul of course, well, he couldn't handle any of it past digging into the soil there in Eden Hab and creating the troughs where they would bury the bodies. After he completed that task, he had assumed a role in preparing meals for all of them. This he had excelled at, including a stint in baking, which he swore up and down he had never done before. The last shipment from the Jupiter Supply Ship had included over 450 kilos of flour, which he now dug into. Meant for special occasions, they now had enough baking supplies to last them for years. Abdul plowed into it with zeal, finding a sense of peace in the simple task of creating flatbreads, fresh and warm, and serving it with a delicious hummus he had created from the cans of chickpeas originally intended for soup. Filling a role that was both necessary and innovative had raised Abdul's spirits and James had watched as the younger man's face relaxed and the nervous rocking vanished.

Lenny lacked the strength to move the corpses, even in their lighter state, but he worked together with his sister, Toya, who would flip the corpses over while he cut the fabric away. Together, they would drag the corpses back in through the airlock of the Eden Hab, and into position. Lenny tired quicker than James and Nix, however, and Toya had the attention span of a gnat, which made her taking part in the work difficult to near impossible after more than an hour or two.

This meant that the bulk of this gruesome job fell to Nix and James. They moved methodically between the City Habs, loading the bodies onto the small short-range, solar-powered cars, an improvised sled of sorts attached behind it. And on it went, day in and day out, until the faces no longer looked like faces, just cordwood, blurred features, stiff arms, legs, flat breasts. It was awful, but it was necessary. Their former friends, lovers, enemies, and supervisors would become one with Mars and eventually feed them. It was what had to be for them to do more than just survive. They needed more than that. They needed to thrive on this hostile planet.

Closer to Normal

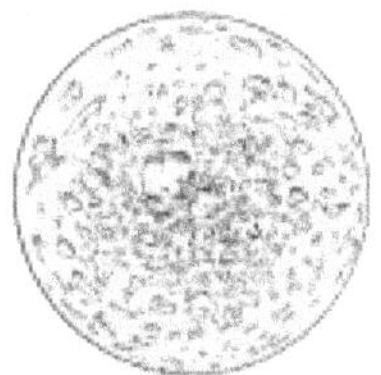

Mars Year 14, Week 46, Day 451
(Earth Date: 11.05.2099)

Despite James ensuring he wouldn't have to deal with the bodies, Abdul still shook, and rocked back and forth, as he worked in Eden Hab. Just the thought of what the others were having to do was enough to send him to the edge of the abyss, and it seemed his body was trying to do everything possible to cope.

His hands shook. They ached from gripping the shovel. He wasn't wearing a pressure suit, only a re-breather since they had turned the environmental controls on the week before. Eden Hab was now at an acceptable pressure, the air almost breathable, and the furnaces had warmed it to a cool 10 degrees Celsius. Still, it had been chilly, at least for the first twenty minutes, until he could feel beads of sweat trickling down as he shoveled. It had been uncomfortable, some of it pooling inside of the re-breather, while the rest of the sweat found its way down to his collar and the small of his back. Petra had been digging just six meters away, silent, except for the occasional grunt. She was still limping, the injury on her leg mostly healed, but Abdul could see that it still bothered her.

The re-breather was necessary equipment for at least another Mars week. At the end of the ten days, James and Lenny's calculations showed they would finally breathe unaided. The mask pulled at his hair, chafed the sides of his face, and he had struggled with the desire to rip it off of his face. He left it on, though; he would pass out in seconds without it. Instead, he kept digging, shovelful after shovelful, a trench slowly widening and deepening in response to his efforts.

As he dug, he tried to think of something, anything, that would cover and replace the images in his mind of what the others were doing. The thought of them having to handle every single body, and worse, remove their clothing, had sent him straight back to his days alone in Cairo Hab. The smell of the corpses that littered the Hab came back to haunt him. Sightless, staring eyes. Removing their clothing seemed even more of an affront to Allah, to the dead themselves. But the boy, Lenny, he had pointed out that their clothing was a mix of artificial fibers that would not degrade, so they had to go. His stomach flip-flopped and he murmured the prayer for the dead as he dug. "O God, forgive our living and our dead, those who are present among us and those who are absent, our young and our old, our males and our females. O God, whoever You keep alive, keep him alive in Islam, and whoever You cause to die, cause him to die with faith."

Petra, now even farther away, stopped and stared at him. "Pray all that you like, Abdul, but the dead stay dead and we still live. Prayer changes nothing."

Abdul didn't like the woman. She was thin, plain-looking, but those were merely superficial attributes. As it was, Petra lacked something that all the others had: a heart. He wondered what her life had been like, how bereft her childhood must have been to be so cold, so unloving, and, truly, unlovable. He thought of Gerard, and how kind he had been. The Couples Hab they shared had been filled with love, happiness. They had even discussed adopting a child via a surrogate. Abdul had been against it at first; later though, the thought of a small child's hand in his, being called Daddy, that had appealed to him on some very basic level. He had told Gerard "yes" and they had approached a lesbian couple just down the hallway from them. The four of them had been deep in discussions about the idea when the ESH virus had turned their world on its ear.

Had it really only been two months since Gerard had woken Abdul up in the middle of the night, complaining of a hunger that no amount of food could satisfy? Hours later, he had died in the infirmary. It had been pandemonium, chaos with the doctors and nurses, all three shifts on duty, running back and forth, tending to the multiple surges in patients. How had the virus spread? Especially with all the precautions the colonists had taken. Abdul still had no idea. He had walked out of the infirmary and checked into a Singles Hab, leaving every personal belonging, every shred of the life that he and Gerard had shared, behind him. The clothes on his back, the prayer rug, and his well-worn copy of the Koran his only possessions. And that is where James had found him those three weeks later, twenty pounds lighter and desperate for human contact.

NARA chimed an alert on his personal commlink. Adding the commlinks and connecting them to NARA had been one of the first things James did after they moved to the Philadelphia Hab. Abdul had warmed to it quickly. He had set reminders for Fajr at dawn, Zhuhr when the sun was highest overhead, Asr just before their evening meal, Maghrib when the last rays of sun had set in a glowing blue haze at the horizon, and finally Isha'a before he closed his eyes for the night. NARA continued to send his notifications faithfully.

His body and arms aching, he broadcast to the others, "I will stop now. I must attend to a personal matter before preparing our evening meal."

Petra gave a derisive snort and muttered, "Your god is a lie."

Abdul felt his anger rise, then fall just as quickly. She couldn't understand, and for that he pitied her. Where he had some level of solace, she obviously did not. He nodded in her direction and said, "Dinner will be in one hour," before he strode away. Half an hour later, having slipped on the pressure suit, exited Eden Hab, and walked through the open, unfinished passageway to Philly Hab, he stood in the shower of the Family Hab he shared with James and pressed the button for the third time. The water washed over him, melting the tension from his limbs. The water at the bottom of the shower turned rust red as he rinsed his hair free of the Martian dirt, leaning into the hard needle spray, his eyes closed. He wished he could stay here forever, watching the swirl of water eddy into the drain, disappearing from view. He knew where it went–from the gray water collectors through a series of filters that removed impurities, added a small amount of nutrients, and re-issued the water through the pipes that fed into the showers, the sinks after a lengthy cleaning process.

As he knelt on the prayer rug, his body clean, his hair damp from the shower, Abdul closed his eyes and focused on the first sajdah. It was in moments such as this that he felt peace. Other than that, or when he was kneading flour while trying a new recipe, reality felt like a nightmare he might never wake from. He moved through the motions, standing, kneeling in turns, the words of the prayer a balm to his soul, a respite from the horrors he had seen, a reassurance that life was not only illness and death and loss, but something more.

After Abdul completed his prayers, he prepared the evening meal. It was something he had not done since he was a young boy visiting his grandmother. Gerard had been little for cooking and Abdul had been so busy with his work, that it made sense to take their meals in the Mess Hall with the others. They would take a few moments to eat and share their day with friends before returning to their Couples Hab. Occasionally, Gerard had fixed something for breakfast on their days off, and they had nibbled at it in bed, their bodies molded together.

Since he had come to Philadelphia Hab, Abdul found the act of collecting the recipes and planning the meals to be deeply rewarding, as if the food was a gift, or an act of love. He had discovered an old cookbook, *The Joy of Cooking*, by an American woman, written in the middle part of the 20th century. At the preface of the ebook was a quote by her that read, "Cooking is like love. It should be entered with abandon or not at all."

Somehow those words had moved him, and he found the act of creating food to be almost an art, one that was transitory, yet gave happiness to others. It gave happiness to Abdul as well. It was not unlike prayer. It calmed him and focused his intent and will.

He had settled into the routine of fixing the evening meal every day. In return, dinner had become a time to review what they had gotten done, to look at their progress, and even share ideas about what they needed next.

Living in a three-bedroom Family Hab with James had just...happened. He had been in such a dark place when James appeared at the door of the Singles Hab there in Cairo. It seemed that James had sensed how adrift Abdul had felt. He had said nothing, not really, he had simply taken charge, and they had settled down in a Hab that still had pictures of the family who had been here before. James had quietly cleared the space, removing the belongings of the dead without a word.

Abdul considered this a gesture of deep kindness. James had done what Abdul could not bring himself to do, and for that Abdul was deeply grateful. It had needed doing, but he hadn't had the strength. James had what Abdul did not, a will to live that superseded the ghosts of yesterday. And his actions had an immediate soothing effect on Abdul. He no longer needed the sleep meds that James had found and dispensed, one pill at a time, in the evening.

Abdul was grateful for this as well. How had James known? Or had he just suspected? A bottle full of those pills would have given him the end he would have preferred in the wake of losing Gerard, of losing everyone he had known. Allah might never have forgiven it, but prayers only went so far, and he would have had an end to the torment. To go to sleep and never wake up. Allah alone knew how often he had dreamed of doing just that.

James was a good man. Abdul remained in the dark as to the older man's sexual orientation. James had a kindness that superseded sexual attraction, and for this reason, and possibly even that James needed someone to care for, here they were.

Abdul sat on the couch and watched the sun disappear. The gradients of blue were brilliant and beautiful, and he thought of how different it was from the pinks and reds of Earth's sunsets. The door to the Hab opened and James walked in carrying a large plant that looked exactly like one that thrived in Abdul's grandmother's garden back on Earth. Judda had kept it lush and thriving, despite the dry desert air. Abdul remembered how the temperature would drop under the shade of the date palms, the hot air mitigated by a forest of green. How he had loved to sit outside with Judda, sipping some of her mint or rose lemonade like only she could make and indulging in heaping spoonful's of shaabiyat. Judda had understood him like no one else in his family had. He suspected that she knew, even back then, of his proclivities, and unlike his stern, traditional father, she had accepted and loved him. Papa had wanted him to be the boy he had waited for through the births of five daughters in a row. Papa, who had loved him but frowned at Abdul's effeminate ways. It was Judda who had been his refuge.

"I found this and thought you might like it for your room or even here in the living room near the window. Nix said it is a tropical hibiscus," James said, as he struggled to hold the plant. The tips brushed the ceiling of the Hab, and only part of James peeked out from behind it.

Abdul felt his mouth stretch into a smile, and he rose to his feet to take the plant from James. "It reminds me of my childhood and my Judda. She had a beautiful garden filled with many plants. Thank you, James."

The older man looked away, nodded, and added, "You seem better these days. The cooking and all that is nice; everyone appreciates it." He pointed to the plant. "It wasn't me, really. Nix mentioned this plant grows well in the Middle East and so, well, I figured you might like it." He shrugged and then turned to see the last rays of the sun disappear from the horizon. "I, uh..." He paused as Abdul's alarm for evening prayer chimed. "I'll leave you to it, then."

Gerard had been a lot like James. He had always excused himself, given Abdul space and privacy to conduct his prayers. Abdul unrolled the prayer rug in his room and completed the evening prayers, his body moving from one position to the next, in the same way that countless Muslims had done before him. When Abdul had finished, he opened his door. James was there on the small couch, the vid remote in his hand. He looked up and met Abdul's shy smile with a warm one in return.

"Shall we continue?" he asked Abdul. They had been making their way through the 1950s television files and they were both fascinated by *The Twilight Zone* series that they had delved into a few days before. "The next episode title is The Lonely."

Abdul grinned and nodded, slipping onto the opposite side of the couch, just a cushion away. Abdul stole a look in James' direction.

"I think we could swing three, maybe four episodes, and then we can sleep in late tomorrow, yeah?" James asked.

Abdul simply nodded. If there was one thing that James was not, it was a night owl. He would likely make it through most of the second episode before nodding off. That evening, however, James held out longer, and he didn't say a word when Abdul's body slowly closed the distance between them. Just ten minutes into the third episode, his head nestled against James' shoulder, Abdul fell deeply asleep.

Deep Space

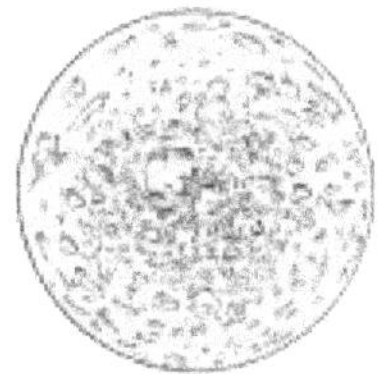

Mars Year 15, Week 47, Day 464
(Earth Date: 11.18.2099)

"What in all the moons of Jupiter are you?" Liu muttered; his eyes locked on the blurry image he viewed from the giant telescope. He stared at it until his eyes watered and his head began to ache. It crept up, wrapping tendrils of pain around his eyeball, then straight into a sheath that surrounded his head. He backed away from the telescope, rubbed his eyes, and wondered if he would ever sleep the night through again. It had been over two Mars weeks since the baby's birth, and Liu felt as if the twenty days had been a century. He looked down at Huan's soft, downy head as the baby whined in his sleep, his tiny face scrunching up.

Do babies dream? Liu wondered. *And if they did, what did they dream of?*

There couldn't be much to dream about. No actual life experiences yet, unless the newborn had brought with him dreams from a life before.

He had found several books written for expectant mothers, and as he yawned, his jawbone popping, he thought of the advice to sleep when the baby did.

Perhaps that was best, after all. Huan was intolerant of anything but constant close contact, and Liu had taken a sheet, folded it, and then wrapped it around Huan and his own torso. The wrap secured the baby against him and kept his tiny body close to Liu's chest. In an instant, Huan had stopped crying, content to rest his head against Liu, and thankfully went to sleep.

Liu yawned again. Huan wouldn't need a feeding for another hour or two, so he might as well try to get some sleep as well, whether it was prime viewing on the mystery object or not. He stood up and Huan whined again, his tiny eyes tracking back and forth under the paper-thin eyelids.

"Dream of good things, Little One," Liu whispered, one hand rubbing against the baby's back as he ambled towards the Garden Hab, where he and Fen had slept before Huan was born. He had set up the pillows and cushions and slept partially upright, on an incline. Huan slept best that way, still on his chest, and these days, everything revolved around what would keep this tiny creature happy and serene–from his bodily needs to sleep.

It took barely a moment. He was so bone-achingly tired that sleep took him once he lay down and closed his eyes. A deep sleep, blissfully free of dreams...or the nightmares that had tormented him since Fen's death. The first days had been awful, with Huan crying constantly, shrieks of fury that clearly demanded to know where his mother was and why she had abandoned him to this inept and useless male.

Figuring out what to use for formula had been the first challenge. It was one thing that Liu and Fen had depended upon, taken for granted even. Fen would breastfeed the baby, eliminating the need to scramble for any cobbled-together type of formula. Pregnancy and childbirth were not in the plan when Mission Control had selected the foods. Following Fen's death, Liu had sat, frozen with grief, unmoving, until Huan's hungry cries had forced him into action. He faced two challenges. He had to create a nutrient mix that would give Huan what he needed nutritionally. But it also had to be something he would willingly drink. The other problem, that of a bottle, was quickly solved, thanks to the 3D printer, which quickly churned out the necessary pieces.

The bottle had been easy, but the formula had been far more difficult. He had combined water and powdered coconut milk with a protein and vitamin slurry. Huan had rejected it, shrieking furiously, the redness spreading from his face to the rest of his body in one large flush of misery and anger. Liu had tried everything, weeping, his head pounding, certain that he was a failure in everything, and that Huan would die if he didn't somehow convince him to eat.

Worse, he had lost weight, something that terrified Liu. He had read that it was normal for babies to lose weight after birth, but Huan was only 1.8 kilograms. Losing even 1/10 of a kilogram seemed to be far too much for an already fragile, orphaned newborn.

Liu had carried Huan through the outpost in a daze, jiggling the baby as he stumbled through, heating a meal for himself. He pushed the food, tasteless as it was in his exhausted state, into his own mouth. As he ate while jiggling the baby, Huan had screamed in his ear, red-faced, miserable. It wasn't until Liu had placed a bite of pumpkin pancake in his mouth that he realized exactly what Huan needed. The baby needed the formula to be *sweet*!

"That is what you need!" Liu dropped his chopsticks and stood up, filled with purpose. He added 10 milliliters of palm syrup to the formula, shook it, resealed the container, and placed it in Yuan's mouth, which was in mid-shriek at the moment, and it cut off abruptly. Moments later, the baby began drinking the homemade coconut milk vitamin slurry, and less than fifteen minutes after that, he had consumed half of the bottle.

Liu's moment of victory was short-lived. It took more reviews of the infant care handbook before he realized that babies required burping. By the time Liu had read that, Huan was at full shriek again. He patted the child, over and over, walking, patting, and finally, when a large burp arrived, so did an overflow of warm, foul-smelling sick. It was a mere fraction of what Huan had ingested, however, and Liu counted it a win. The tiny baby, exhausted from hunger and distress, fell asleep immediately. He had slept for nearly four hours and Liu had slept right alongside him, a hand on the infant's tiny chest, monitoring every breath the baby took. Sometimes he still did, waking from a dead sleep, certain this tiny child would have stopped breathing.

What followed those initial two days of despair, fear, and endless wailing was a pattern of sorts. Once he had figured out that Huan preferred being held close, they had settled into a schedule that was completely infant-centric. Wake up to Huan's cries, change his diaper, feed him, burp him, change him again, wrap him back against his chest, sleep, and repeat. Day in, day out. When Liu could smell himself and needed a bath, he did it with Huan crying on the floor next to the shower, his tiny hands opening and closing, searching for comfort, for the warmth and heartbeat of his parent.

Liu lay there, propped up on the cushions, his eyes coming open slowly, hearing Huan's tiny breaths, the baby slowly coming to consciousness. The dawn light was stealing over the horizon, and he watched Huan's eyes open and look up at him. Liu realized then, in this quiet place, that Huan had never even seen his mother, and that she had never held him. Had she died thinking he was dead? In those seconds when Huan was not breathing, when Liu's attention was solely on him, had they passed each other? Two souls, one a life barely begun finding air filling his lungs, the other slipping away as the blood drained from her body. How many times in the past twenty days had his thoughts fallen back to those moments? If he had only turned back to her, he would have seen the blood, and done...

What would you have done, Liu? What? Stopped the bleeding, how?

The guilt warred with the facts, the simple facts. He could never have stopped the hemorrhaging, not with the minimal training he had received. He was an astronomer, a navigator, and in his heart of hearts, an artist and musician. There was nothing he could have done. He knew it, yet still he mourned.

He looked at Huan, with his dark eyes and soft, black hair and tiny, delicate mouth. Liu leaned over and sniffed the baby's head, and the delicate smell sent a wave of joy and love rushing through him. Who was it who said that babies smell just right, so that parents don't eat them? His lips curved up into a smile and he couldn't help but laugh at the thought of it.

"Good morning, Huan," he said, and the baby snuffled and blinked at him, then fit his fist in his mouth and whined softly. "You are hungry. I will feed you, and then I will show you someone very special. Would you like that?"

Huan didn't answer; he just stared at Liu with those dark eyes and mouthed at his fist some more.

After he handled changing Huan's cloths and fed and burped him, swallowing his own meal along the way, he wrapped the baby up against him one more time. He collected his paints from his bunk and a soft pencil, walked down the hall, and stood outside of the Garden Hab for a moment as he studied the opposite wall. "I think that it should be right here, so we see it when we get up in the morning and also right before we go to sleep at night. What do you think, Little One?"

He looked down and noticed that the baby had already fallen asleep. Not surprising; his belly was full, and he was in his favorite place. Liu kissed the top of his head, picked up his pencil, and, after studying the wall for a moment, sketched an outline.

He managed the rough sketch before his own exhaustion caught up with him.

"Sleep when the baby sleeps, Liu." He said it out loud, but quietly–he did not wish to wake Huan–and made his way back to the cushions, slipping into sleep immediately.

The next three days were much the same: sleep, wake, eat, burp, work for a little while on the mural, and then sleep. Once when Huan was restless and cranky, unwilling to sleep, he retrieved his pipa and played a gentle lullaby for Huan, Liu's voice and the soft music lulling the baby to sleep. He was gaining weight and looking less thin. For what little Liu knew of babies, he seemed to grow well. He found that, at night, if he unwrapped him from his chest and placed him in the crook of his arm, Liu could sleep on his side, Huan content within the circle of warmth. Huan remained inconsolable when set down for even a moment or two during the day, preferring to rest against Liu's chest, or occasionally in a pack on Liu's back.

And despite the sleep deprivation, the incessant needs, and the furious shrieks that Huan emitted when his needs were not met immediately, Liu was smitten. Never had another human being needed him so much. And he knew as well, that Huan's need for him kept him sane, not insane for lack of someone to speak to.

There had been another change, likely another coup, and new voices sent orders now. They battered the comm, over and over, with their demands, their questions, and empty threats.

Liu ignored them. He stopped going into the Control Room entirely, content to spend his days with Huan, catering to the newborn's every need, and putting the finishing touches on the mural. The past week had been a blur outside the windows of the station. A massive sandstorm bearing down on Gale crater had stirred up sand, rocks even, and the howl of winds had been audible, they were so strong.

He carried on, ignoring the storm, and did so while maintaining a steady stream of words, chatter really, occasionally interrupted by an impromptu song. He had sketched her face, captured that wistful longing that Fen had often had. It was the one that had told him she was unhappy, deeply so, and that she did not know how to change it. Perhaps she had not even considered that she could.

He thought of her husband Bao, dead along with so many others. He had seen how Bao enjoyed the status her position had conferred on him, and how he used it to his advantage and enjoyed it, until the reality of the downside had presented itself to him. Then he had demanded she stop. Liu shook his head in disgust; Bao had been a social climber, a user, and Fen had deserved better. She had deserved a partner who would cherish her, not her position. The colors of paints he chose, a tiny spot of pale pink there, brought Fen back to life, if only here, in the hallway, in a mural. Huan deserved more than just an image of her. Liu had added Huan to the picture, carefully detailing the baby's features that were so like Fen, and yet had tiny bits of Chen in them as well. In the mural, Fen was smiling down at Huan, and he was looking up at her with a serious expression.

As he finished the details of Fen and Huan, Liu frowned. There was something missing. He added a landscape behind them. Not of Earth, but of Mars, for Mars was their home, and Huan's birthplace, now.

It looked rocky and desolate. Which didn't matter at all. It was home now.

"Someday, you will look out and up into the sky, Little One, and you will see Earth, Phobos, and Deimos, all at once," he whispered as his brush illuminated each bright point in the sky above Fen's profile. "This is your home."

Huan cooed, his tiny fist in his mouth, a small smack of the lips as he gummed his fist, his little eyes staring unfocused at the mural on the wall. Liu smiled at the baby. The love he had felt for Fen had not faded with her death, but merely transferred to Huan. Each day, he loved the child more and more. Could love be limitless? Could it suffuse every part of him, right down to his toes? Sometimes it felt overwhelming, as did the baby's needs.

He stepped back, paintbrush in hand, and stared at the sky, at the glowing points of light that showed the path of the moons, and of Earth, so clearly. And in the back of his mind, something felt...wrong. He stood there unmoving, and Huan kicked out restlessly, his contented gurgles turning to something else as the baby picked up on Liu's change of mood.

Liu stood there, staring at the points of light, and his heart pounded. The paintbrush slipped from his hand and clattered to the floor.

The blurry image he had been studying, he had to study it more. He needed to know exactly what it was, and hopefully, what it wasn't. Oh God, let it not be that.

Huan sensed his mood and let out a wail, his tiny hands becoming weapons that alternated between grabbing at Liu's hair, now long enough to place in a ponytail, and pummeling randomly on his chest. Liu turned his focus back to caring for the baby and fought to control his anxiety. *I can do nothing until the storm passes.* And this was true. The sandstorm obscured any view of the sky. Instead, he turned towards the Mess Hall and jiggled Huan and sang to him, calming him, until he could prepare a bottle.

It took over fifteen days for the storm to pass, and the sky above to clear enough for Liu to turn his telescope once more towards the blurry image in the sky. He licked his dry lips, focused on the trajectory, and took measurements. Each night, after Huan had settled in to sleep, his tiny belly full of the formula, his wraps clean and dry, his body warm and relaxed against Liu's back, Liu would study the object, noting the location and estimating speed, trajectory, and more. It had come from the Kuiper Belt, but the shape was no longer recognizable of that known as Ultima Thule.

Nearly thirty days passed as he studied it, charted it, and performed calculations each night, his fears growing until he was certain. He double, triple checked, then he checked it again, from the very beginning. No matter how many times he factored it, checked it, and tried to disprove it, the facts remained the same. This object, some 14 kilometers in diameter, was on a collision course with Earth.

It was only then that he reached out to Mission Control, sending a message through the coded channel as instructed for highly sensitive subjects such as this. There was no reply. None. No matter the time of day, or night, no matter how often he sent the message. He finally switched to the public channel. What could they do to him, after all? Punish him from millions of miles away? Mars was near its apogee, nearly 380 million kilometers from Earth. Liu realized then that he didn't give a damn if he was breaking Mission Control's rules or committing treason. The entire planet was in trouble and he had to warn them.

Turkey Faux Pas

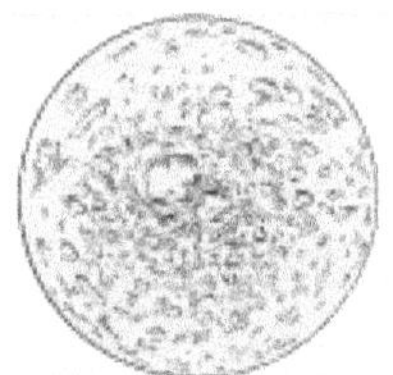

Mars Year 14, Week 48, Day 472
(Earth Date: 11.26.2099)

There was silence at the table, save for the occasional scrape of utensil against plate. The turkey, however, remained as it was, the gelatin from the package it had come in forming a thick film around the edges. Abdul had simply removed it from the wrapper and set it on a large plate.

Nix exchanged glances with James and Lenny, stifled a grin, and attacked the green beans and stuffing with glee. The small hydroponics that he had completed before they had found Petra, James and Abdul had yielded the first harvest of string beans. Tasting them, lightly steamed before being pan fried with butter and garlic, was heaven. He didn't care about the pies, or the catastrophe of the faux-turkey congealed lump in the middle of the table, just the green beans.

He stole a glance at Toya's plate. She had a mountain of mashed potatoes and gravy, a fair-sized heap of stuffing, and she was poking at the congealed turkey with an unenthusiastic expression.

Nix thought about how that must have been, the family dynamic within the Antes/Snelling household. Constant fights, to be sure. As Lenny had explained it, his mother had never forgiven herself for the affair, for her first husband's death, and of the tremendous damage that Toya's brain had suffered. It had resulted, unfortunately, in the girl being allowed anything she wanted. This until she was a child in an adult's body and with little or no sense of control.

When Nix had entered the mix, just two months ago, Toya was petulant, overweight, and borderline abusive towards her brother, Lenny. Thankfully, in some odd way, she seemed to look up to Nix, or at the very least, wanted him to approve of her. He had taken the lead in dealing with her misbehaviors.

Now, however, as they all sat around the table, eating what was a very thoughtful gesture on Abdul's part towards the American custom of an annual Thanksgiving dinner, Toya looked ready to rebel. She pushed the faux turkey around with her fork and was opening her mouth to speak when James spoke up, his mouth twitching with amusement as he pressed a fork into the quivering, gelatinous monstrosity at the center of his plate.

"I'm correct in thinking that this is, erm, turkey, is it?" He looked at Nix for confirmation, then turned back to Abdul. "Turkey, right. I'm thinking it needed a bit of nuking, first."

Abdul's face reddened with embarrassment.

"I thought the gel, that it was, what do you call it, Jell-O?" His lips protruded as he tried the unfamiliar word on for size. "And that I should serve it cold." His face fell, his voice falling to a whisper. He looked so disappointed that Nix felt relieved that James had said it and not him. Abdul was sensitive, sometimes moody, and James handled Abdul best, with a mix of kindness and affection that Nix found surprising.

Abdul had, after all, spent a week talking about the dinner and planning for it. He had even decorated their table in the Mess Hall with 3D printed turkeys and another random shape that looked vaguely like a Pilgrim's hat, except for the color, which was a bright pink. His idea had been for them to celebrate some holidays that were important to all of them, with the appropriate matching foods and drinks. They had started with Nisfu Sha'ban, on October 29th. Abdul had described it as a time when the fortunes of individuals for the coming year are made known and Allah may forgive sinners. He had made halwa, an exotic-tasting sweet. He also prepared zarda, a sweet rice dish. His brown eyes were troubled, but his halting voice had spoken of hope, the wish for not just their survival, but good fortune in the year ahead. He had uttered a prayer, and when James had asked what it meant, he had repeated it in English.

"O Allah, make me better than what they think of me, and forgive me for what they do not know about me, and do not take me to account for what they say about me."

He had plans for other special days, so many of them that it appeared they would celebrate many Earth holidays and holy days regularly.

Toya, in an uncharacteristic show of solidarity, took a large bite. "I dunno, it's kind of good cold, even if it is a turkey faux pas." She giggled then, the side of her cheek bulging, and suddenly it was contagious, a wave that began as a few chuckles and ended up as deep-belly chortles.

Abdul, who had looked stricken with disappointment and embarrassment, finally joined in. Petra, in an uncharacteristic show of kindness, had reached across the table and taken his hand, the edges of her normally grim, tight-lipped resting bitch face, twitching. She squeezed Abdul's hand, her sour expression melting into a bemused, closed-mouth grin. Abdul looked over at her, surprise on his face.

Nix turned his gaze back to Toya, who was grinning now, mouth barely closed over the bite of cold turkey. The girl was an enigma. There were moments when the brilliant brain that had once been would appear, if only for a second. The intense curiosity, even the vocabulary, was still there. But it was intermittent, almost as if it were wading through a pyroclastic flow of mud and downed trees, the path between thought and action obscured and flooded with debris. He wondered, and not for the first time, what she would have been like, had she not endured the hypoxic event? Who would she have become? What would her brilliant mind have achieved?

Lenny gave Nix plenty of clues about how much Toya had lost in the freak accident. And from what the kid said, his sister had shown capabilities that far outstripped his own when she was only half his age.

Nix looked at each of them sitting together at the table. He was probably the least of all of them, in terms of intelligence and brainpower. James had helped design the Huygens Outpost in his early twenties. Petra had been part of a team dedicated to terraforming Mars. Abdul was a geologist and astrobiologist, intent on studying the microscopic forms of life they had found on the red planet. Lenny had amazing potential. The kid could literally do just about anything he set his mind to in engineering and mathematics. And then there was Toya. It felt as if she remained frozen in place, a six-year-old in an adult's body. And yet, despite this, he could see the threads of brilliance. They were there, locked up, not gone, desperate for a path out to functionality.

She chewed the mouthful, swallowed, and turned towards Nix. "Hey, Nix, you said you were going to get the artificial wombs going, right?"

He blinked, what a non sequitur. "Uh, yes?"

She nodded and smiled. "I know what I want first."

"First?" The other day she had sat quietly as he discussed the artificial wombs with James and Abdul. She had been sorting the MREs they had brought over from a trip to Sydney Hab the week before. He hadn't even realized she was listening. Nix had been trying to decide between starting a batch of chicken embryos or possibly a couple of goats. The more complex the lifeform, the more problematic the outcome. The artificial wombs were still difficult to use, and Nix barely understood the process. It was one of their pain points, that none of the survivors had worked with the artificial wombs, and it was a desperately needed skill.

Abdul had been in favor of the chickens, pointing out that the hens could lay nearly an egg a day upon maturity. They had all had quite enough of the powdered eggs, and Abdul wanted to try his hand at baking a cake. His last attempt, using the powdered eggs, had been a dense, rather dry disaster that Nix and the others had tried to eat out of politeness.

Nix had wanted the goat so they could form a chain of biodiversity, including goat shit. Lately all of his plans seemed to include some kind of shit, the human variety or otherwise. Lenny had been right about adding the bodies to Eden Hab, and once they had completed that, they had added the loads of stored feces. After almost two decades of human habitation on Mars, there was plenty of it. The place reeked, but he was seeing the changes occur right before his eyes. Now they just had to wait for the shit to do its work and the smell to subside.

Petra's help in the environmental aspect had been invaluable. She was the one who had suggested speeding up the process by rerouting several of the solar arrays that were already powering the City Habs. Considering no one was living in them, the fixes had meant that the two farthest Habs, London and Cairo, were now dark. The contents of the Habs were mainly still there, save for the food stores, which Abdul had enlisted Toya's help in organizing. Considering the girl's love of food, it had been a simple choice. Nix had said nothing about the additional bags of chips and cookies he had noticed when rounding up the garbage for their new compost heap. All the empty bags were biodegradable, a forethought that the planners had thought of, thankfully. Corn-based, they would disintegrate into dirt within a year or two at the most.

"I want a raccoon. A female, please."

Nix stared, open-mouthed.

"A what?" He gaped at her in surprise.

"A raccoon. They will help with the bio, bio..." She stopped, frowning over the word, before enunciating it slowly. "Biodiversity."

Lenny had devoured the mashed potatoes and gravy and had a fork full of green beans held in his hand. He cocked his head to one side. "Huh, I thought you always wanted a cat."

"I only wanted a cat because Mom said I couldn't have a raccoon." Toya shoved another forkful of food in her mouth. "But then I realized, Mom couldn't tell me 'no' anymore, so I want a raccoon."

Lenny shrugged. "A raccoon, then. You know, Calvin Coolidge, the 30th President of the United States, he had a raccoon."

Toya rolled her eyes at him. "Duh. Everyone knows that, Lenny."

James blinked. "Really? I didn't. I truly had no idea Americans kept raccoons as pets."

Lenny stuffed the green beans in his mouth, chewed, and managed a muffled, "They don't. The President and his wife got the raccoon while they were in the White House. She was supposed to be the main course at Thanksgiving dinner, but they kept her as a pet. My mom used to read *Rebecca the Raccoon Saves the White House*, and it was all about her life. Do you remember that book, Toya?"

Toya nodded. "That was the first book I ever read by myself. Mom said I had trouble operating the pages of the tablet but that I was correcting her words when she read it."

Lenny nodded, a cheerful smile on his face. "Same here. I always loved the part where Rebecca caught a burglar and chased him around the Oval Office until the First Lady woke up and knocked the guy over the head with the candlestick."

Abdul's face looked horrified. "Wait, Americans *eat* raccoons? Aren't raccoons those cute little masked bandit creatures? Like the one from *Guardians of the Galaxy*? The um..."

"Trash pandas. They're called trash pandas," Nix added, shaking his head in disgust. "They're vermin. Do you have any idea how much trouble they can get into?"

Toya straightened her spine and gave Nix a look that he could only interpret as indignation. "Raccoons are very smart, smarter than dogs or cats."

"Hence my objection."

She glared at him. Nix grinned; Toya was cute when she was mad.

"I fear I am lost," Abdul muttered, pushing a piece of cold turkey around on his plate, a look of revulsion marching across his face. "So, are raccoons pets, food, or vermin?"

"All of the above, really." Lenny shrugged. "I guess it all depends on your point of view."

Toya giggled then. "Lenny, do you remember the jokes in the back of the book?" Her eyes lit up. "My favorite one was the man in the movie theater."

Lenny snickered. "I remember that one." He closed his eyes for a moment, then recited, "A man in a movie theater notices what looks like a raccoon sitting next to him. 'Are you a raccoon?' asked the man, surprised. 'Yes,' replies the raccoon. 'What are you doing at the movies?' The raccoon replied, 'Well, I liked the book.'"

The room erupted with laughter at the corny joke.

Nix watched them all laugh. They were completely different–from their backgrounds to their beliefs, even their hopes and dreams. They hadn't even known each other before the ESH outbreak. And now, here they all were, sharing a meal, laughing, and moving from just holding it together, to learning enough about each other to work together effectively, and hopefully, to that of creating a future for themselves on this planet.

They weren't perfect. Hell, when he looked at them, he grouped them into the simplest of descriptors–a dumb jock with a green thumb, a scary smart boy and his brain-damaged sister, a plain woman with serious daddy issues, a Brit who hid his kindness to others behind a dry, biting wit, and a homosexual Muslim turned kitchen wizard.

They had survived so much in the past few months. What would the rest of the year, and the year beyond that, bring?

The Road Ahead

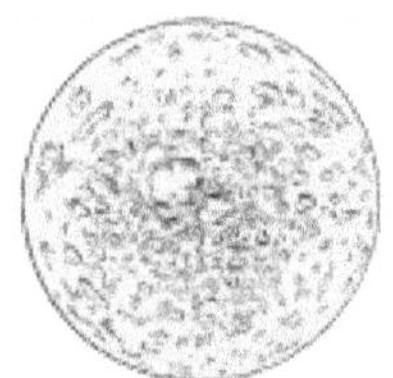

Mars Year 14, Week 51, Day 502
(Earth Date: 12.26.2099)

The delectable smells coming from the Mess Hall made their way to Eden Hab long before Abdul's message announcing dinner did. By the time James and Lenny arrived in the large room for the meal, Toya was already seated at the table and ladling soup into a bowl.

Abdul smiled at James, his brown eyes warm, his smile coming easier these days. "Happy Kwanzaa! Sit, sit!" He looked up to the corner of the room. "NARA, announce, "It's dinner time!"

Lenny raised his eyebrows at James, mouthing, "Kwanzaa?" before shrugging and sliding into a seat. The table had several large serving bowls, as well as a plate of squares of yellow bread stacked on it.

At least once a week, Abdul prepared a special meal. This was one he had kept under wraps, not saying anything about it to the others, except for James, however, since he had requested it one evening when he sat with Abdul in the living area of the Family Hab that they shared.

Living in the same Hab as Abdul just made sense, James reasoned, and he hadn't felt the need to change it. The younger man had needed reassurance, company, and they had made the living situation work. Each slept in his own room, and Abdul had asked nothing of James, except for occasionally nestling against him in the shared space as they talked or watched the vidscreen.

James didn't particularly care what the others thought of the arrangement, although he imagined that they likely assumed he and Abdul had a romantic or sexual relationship, which they didn't, at least not yet. In some ways, oddly, it felt more intimate than some sexual partnerships he had

had with women over the years. He found that he looked forward to the evenings when it was just the two of them.

Abdul's eyes sparkled with happiness. "There is chicken and sausage gumbo, mashed sweet potatoes, black-eyed peas, and corn bread."

Toya shrugged and, a bowl of steaming gumbo in front of her, was lifting a spoonful to her lips when Abdul laid a hand on her shoulder. "Perhaps wait for the others?" he asked gently.

"Oh," she said as she set the spoon back in the bowl and leaned back, a small sigh of frustration escaping her lips.

Petra arrived a moment later, eyes flashing as she marched into the room, her shoulders set, a tight expression on her closed mouth. Nix was right behind her, and his eyes rolled as he sniffed the mouth-watering aromas coming from the steaming dishes of food before them.

As the two sat, Toya asked plaintively, "Now can I eat?"

Abdul's hand on her shoulder stopped the next attempt at eating, the spoon suspended in air, the thick broth steaming.

Abdul cleared his throat, and the others joined James in waiting for him to speak. "Happy Kwanzaa, everyone."

Nix barked out a laugh. "You do know that Kwanzaa is an African cultural holiday, right?"

Abdul's smile slipped slightly, then returned. "Yes, of course. But I chose this for our meal because today is the twenty-sixth of December on Earth and the beginning of seven days of celebration that center around principles that are essential to our future: unity, self-determination, collective work and responsibility, cooperative economics, purpose, creativity, and faith." He pointed towards each of them in turn and continued, "We have the opportunity to create a future for ourselves based on our unique abilities and talents, and together we can create a community out of the ashes, one that will find a way to eventually contact Earth, continue to build our home here on Mars, and live a life of purpose. I thought that this holiday embodied those hopes perfectly."

There was a moment of silence as they took Abdul's words in. Then Toya sighed loudly, her spoon still suspended in midair, waiting for the go ahead. Abdul patted her shoulder and said, "Fine, fine, eat!"

They dug in, passing the large bowls around the table until each of their plates were full. James looked over and saw that Abdul's plate held only the sweet potatoes and cornbread. The younger man was thoughtful and kind; he was willing to prepare and serve others the haram foods he himself was unable to eat. James had asked him about it early on when Abdul had prepared an American-style breakfast of eggs, bacon, and waffles. The bacon, being pork, had been haram, and James had realized that it was not allowed by the Quran to even *touch* the bacon.

Abdul had smiled in answer to James' query. "I use gloves." He had shrugged and continued, "My imam was progressive in his interpretations."

After the bowls had been passed around, their plates and bowls full, there was silence, except for the sound of chewing. Finally, Petra leaned back, her eyes shrewd, her bowl of gumbo scraped clean.

"So?"

"So... what?" James responded as her eyes met his.

She rolled her eyes. "Cut to the chase, James, I can see you have done your homework and Abdul has fixed a meal evocative of whatever plans you have in mind, so why bother beating around the bush? What's next?"

She had nailed it, and him. When he had seen the list of holidays Abdul had posted, along with their meanings and more, James had asked for his help in preparing a meal that would serve as a graceful beginning for the conversation that he knew they all needed to have. Petra didn't waste time. And for that matter, considering the IQ levels of most of the people in the room, neither should he.

"Fair enough." He set his spoon down, nodding to Petra. "Direct as always, Salinger." He stood up and walked over to a table that held his tablet and a small projector. "NARA, please dim the lights and link the projector to my tablet." NARA complied, and the room's lights dimmed, until they were all cast in the gloom.

A few finger taps later and the projector cast a beam of light on a nearby wall, his presentation clear and concise, in black letters that now appeared a foot in height on the white wall.

"As everyone knows, I was on the team that designed the Huygens Outpost." An image of the original habitat, now the very much altered communications array and receiving ship hangar, along with a lone

Philadelphia Hab, with the ghostly outlines of the other five Habs, Eden Hab, and the corresponding city-specific Garden Habs, all appeared on the schematic.

"Phase One was the establishment of the first semi-permanent habitat, now home to the communications array and space hangar. And then Phase Two was the construction and populating of the five City Habs. Phase Three, that of erecting and completing Eden Hab, was nearly complete when the ESH virus hit."

The image metamorphosed, running quickly through the laying of the concrete, made of the stores of human urine and Mars regolith, to the assembly of the dome, a nearly transparent, relatively new, engineered two-inch thick glass that allowed the sunlight through while maintaining just the right protection against the damaging radiation that the thin Mars atmosphere could not provide. There was a string of solar panels along half of the base of the Hab, and there the fast parade of images halted.

"Phase Three was to include fully pressurized passages which would lead from each of the City Habs to that of Eden Hab. It also included the solar array we put in place to provide the heat, environmental controls, and more to Eden Hab." Again the images rolled through, a phantom hand placing the rest of the solar panels into place, then attaching each of the passageways from the City Habs one by one.

"And we would have finished Phase Three with a two-prong approach: first, the production of a certain amount of farmland, which would produce basic crops as well as a grassland to support other domesticated farm animals. Second, would be the utilization of the artificial wombs to create the first generations of chickens, goats, and more, eventually creating a self-sustaining population of meat animals for consumption." A section of Eden Hab zoomed in from above, showing chickens pecking at the ground and goats munching on grass.

"The ESH virus actually accelerated some of that plan, since the engineers would have been limited by how much we could amend the soil, even with the biomass that had been accumulated over the years.

"We now have the grassland well in hand. In a few more months, it will be enough to provide for a handful of small ruminants, as well as a beginning flock of ten chickens. We need to finish the passageway from Philly Hab to

Eden, which will allow us easy access to the space that will become our hope for the future."

A list appeared on the wall. It began with the title Post-Virus Reassessment of Goals and included a bulleted list.

- Complete access to Eden Hab and make habitable
- Begin farming Eden Hab
- Utilize artificial wombs to produce chickens and goats
- Connect Eden to all other City Habs via the passageways
- Rebuild Huygens population

He cleared his throat and continued, "Eden Hab must be our first priority. We have plenty of MREs, enough to last years, but the plan was, and still should be, to push forward and make the settlement as self-sustaining as possible. To this end, the five of us must do the work of ensuring we are ready for more colonists once Earth recovers enough to revive the Mars settlement program on their end."

Petra stared at him, her thin lips forming a moue of surprise. "You actually want to stay here, after all this? What if there is no one left on Earth? No one capable, or particularly interested, in coming to this planet that is centuries away from being habitable?"

James cocked his head. "Would you return to Earth if you had the chance, Petra? Or would you stay?"

Her eyes darted to the others, and one thin hand smoothed down her hair in a nervous gesture. "Well, I would stay. I mean, I *wanted* to come here, but..."

"We all chose to come here," James replied gently, "with the exception of Toya and Lenny, that is."

Lenny shrugged. "And Earth would be impossible for Toya and I to even visit, so I for one have never really wanted to go there." He threw his hands up. "I mean, don't get me wrong, it *looks* nice, but I wouldn't be able to enjoy it. It would feel awful, all that gravity, so why go? Better to focus on a life here on Mars."

Nix nodded. "I can handle the EVAs to the other City Habs to collect supplies we will need, and you can give me lists of what to look for while I'm there." He pointed to Toya and said, "You can help me with that."

Toya crossed her arms across her chest and leaned back in her chair, a petulant look spreading across her face. She had been going back and forth with Nix over her request for a baby raccoon. They were equally stubborn, her with her insistence on having one, and him telling her that raccoon were vermin.

Nix added, "Fine, I'll get you your damned trash panda, alright?"

"Really?"

"Yeah." He waved dismissively. "I found the embryos, although I have zero idea what Earth was thinking when they included the damn things in the A.R.C."

James stifled a grin. Toya had not let go of the idea of having a pet raccoon and had been talking about it daily. Nix was quite obviously over it and worn down from hearing Toya repeat her demand over and over. The A.R.C., which stood for Advanced Reconstructive Colony, had been sent to Mars four years ago, when the dream of sending the Calypso to Gliese 581g had become a real mission. The Moon had received one as well. A.R.C. contained more than just the basic human genome. In fact, it contained more than two hundred thousand human embryos from around the globe. A.R.C. had also contained every domesticated animal, along with thousands of common wildlife from around the world. Nothing too deadly, mind you–they had decided against the venomous snakes, for example–but plenty of odd creatures that one would question the need for, including, apparently, raccoons.

Toya sat up straighter, rocking the chair back and forth with excitement. "How soon? How soon?"

"Sixty-five days in the artificial wombs and then another four weeks of intensive care with feedings every two hours." Nix growled in response; his disapproval obvious. "You'll be lucky if the damn thing lives and you will be useless for anything else while caring for it."

"It'll live," was Toya's cheery response, "I'll make sure of it."

"Yeah, well, meanwhile, you got two plus months of working every day with me to get the other Habs assessed and stripped of any necessary items."

Toya merely grinned and bounced some more.

Petra, who had been uncharacteristically silent at the far end of the table, said, "I have some research I need to do on potentially accelerating the terraforming process." She sniffed. "I'll want to present my findings at some point in the future."

James nodded and said, "If you could work with Lenny on increasing the efficiency of the solar panels, we could really use your help on that as well."

Petra made a derisive snort. "Right, that should be fun." Despite Lenny's help on a medley of mechanical and mathematical problems, she still considered him a child, and therefore annoying.

James stifled a flash of annoyance. He looked at Nix, catching the remnants of the glare he had leveled at Petra. Somehow, they had to get along, all of them, if they wanted this to work. Petra was a difficult one, and James had recognized that from the get-go. Nix was just catching on.

James turned once more to Lenny and said, "Now, you have some mechanical expertise, as I remember. Seems I remember you had a robot you were working on the other day. Automatons could help us with the construction of the passageways and lessen our need for so much EVA time. Follow that path, and see where it leads you."

Lenny's eyes shone with excitement. "I'll do that, oh wow, yeah." He reached for his pad, opened what looked like a CAD program, and began making notes, fully absorbed in the task at hand.

James returned to the list on the wall. "I'm going to work with you, Nix, on trying to get a handle on the artificial womb technology." He smiled apologetically. "I studied it for a very short time and I'm far from experienced, but I hope we can get the operation of it worked out. Our future depends on it."

Nix nodded, and he looked relieved. "I'd appreciate that. I'm out of my depth when it comes to that. Animal husbandry, crops...those I can do, but the artificial wombs are above my pay grade." He pointed to Lenny and said, "You might be able to help with that too, Kid."

James watched as the boy sat up straighter and nodded. "Sure, Nix."

James added, "I'll also reach out to Earth and see if we can get a definitive timeline on a batch of new colonists. I'll be taking suggestions from everyone on exactly *who* we need to get out here and *what* specialties are needed most."

A few questions back and forth, and they broke up, Toya staying behind to help Abdul clean up, and the rest to their Habs to begin working on the plan. Somehow, they would do more than just survive. Somehow, they would rebuild Huygens Outpost and move forward on this alien planet. And someday, generations from now, their children's children would walk outside of the domes and breathe the air on Mars. They were committed.

Bandit Burrito

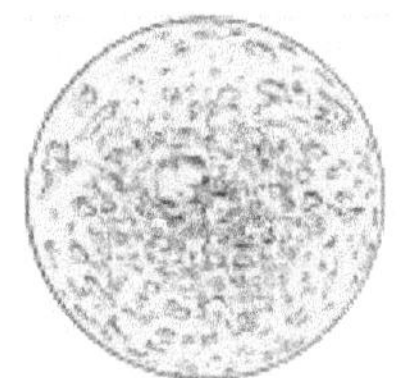

Mars Year 14, Week 62, Day 612
(Earth Date: 04.15.2100)

Nix wasn't sure what had woken him, only that he was awake, suddenly, in the heavy darkness of night. He looked over; the clock proclaimed that it was 0300. Nix lay there, wondering why in the hell he was awake. Seconds later, he realized what had woken him. There were noises coming from the kitchenette outside of his bedroom door.

Sleep-addled, Nix wondered who it could be. He heard a cabinet open, then close. Who in the hell would be in his kitchen in the middle of the night? There were whispers as well, as if whoever was out there was not alone.

What the hell?

Nix rolled out of bed, reaching for a pair of pants, fumbling to put one leg through and then the other, hitching them up. He didn't bother with a shirt. Nix felt for the door handle in the deep gloom, twisting it silently, doing his best to not make a sound as he opened the door and crossed the threshold into the combination living space and kitchenette.

A small light over the tiny stovetop in the kitchenette showed a small, dark figure standing on the countertop, the top half of its body head-deep in an open cabinet. Beside the cabinet, the water blasted at full volume, pouring into the sink. On the countertop and area surrounding, Burrito had left waterlogged chips everywhere. She spied him then and churred happily before she popped a potato chip into her mouth. The raccoon sat back on her haunches and munched on a chip.

"Goddamnit, Burrito! You get out of here, right now!"

She responded with a cheerful churring. Nix, annoyed as hell over being woken up, marched over to her.

The raccoon had found a bag of potato chips that Nix had been eating the day before. She had apparently wanted a midnight snack. The door to his Hab stood open, the light from the hallway spilling inside. Burrito reached out and petted Nix's hair as he picked her up, churring and clicking happily.

She had been tiny when they removed her from the artificial womb, smaller than the first two they had tried, and Nix had been sure she would die too. How Toya had cried over their tiny, lifeless bodies, and he had been reticent to try again. Toya had begged, though, and they had two more embryos left. Lenny had tinkered with the artificial wombs, adjusting temperature, fluid levels, and more, and they had tried again. Burrito had been so tiny, so impossibly fragile. A thin layer of downy fur had covered her tiny body, her eyes still closed. Toya had diligently fed her, one drop at a time at first, keeping Burrito nestled against her so that the tiny creature would have warmth and a heartbeat close to her, just as she had with the first two.

It had been a surprise to Nix when Burrito had survived, and thrived, even as Toya walked around in a haze, worthless for any work that didn't include holding a raccoon kit.

By six weeks, Burrito had been over nine inches long, fat, sleek, and curious. By the time she was eight weeks old, she would warn Toya and the others with a trill they learned to recognize well. It meant she was about to evacuate her bowels. They learned it well after a few bouts of soiled clothing, and Bandit learned too, using the litter box much as a cat would. Her furry back end often hung over the edge of the box and she would crap outside of the area covered in litter.

At four months, Burrito was half the size she would be full-grown, and she had become a complete pain in the ass. She was smart as a whip and would get into anything and everything with a regularity that was maddening. And for reasons that Nix could not understand, Burrito was particularly interested in him.

He sighed as her small, dexterous hands explored his hair. She sniffed him, groomed him with her hands, and then bit his ear gently, warbling and chittering. She was nocturnal, thus fully awake, and ready to interact with him.

"Burrito, you are a righteous pain in the ass." The raccoon chittered softly in response, her sharp claws running through his short hair. "Come on, let's get you back to Toya."

Toya and Lenny's Hab was just down the hall, the door standing open just as Nix's had been. He knocked anyway, but the rest of the Hab was dark. Toya's room stood open, and he could see her still form on the bed. She roused at the sound of Burrito chittering and blearily raised her head. "What? Nix?"

"Burrito came for a midnight snack," he told her softly, and her head flopped back on her pillow. Nix wondered if she had even heard him. Toya barely moved when Nix placed Burrito by her side. Adventure over, Burrito curled up in the crook of Toya's arm and she curled her body around her pet, her breathing deepening.

Nix stood there for a moment, watching as Burrito nestled into Toya, churring quietly in contentment, and his mind, still half-asleep, suddenly realized how creepy it would look if anyone else saw him standing there.

Creep. You are standing in a girl's bedroom watching her sleep.

Nix shook his head and slipped out of the room, closing Toya's door behind him. He was about to leave when he noticed Lenny's light was on and his door partially open. He knocked on the door lightly and Lenny, absorbed in some kind of range rover he was building in the CAD program on his tablet, looked up, a smile spreading over his face when he laid eyes on Nix.

"Hey, Nix, I was just working on the new automated vehicle we will need for supplying the array, and..." He stopped, frowned, and asked, "Wait, it's still dark out, what are you doing up?" He looked at the digital display. "It's 0330."

Nix yawned. "Yeah, El Bandido Burrito came over for a chip snack at my place."

Lenny snickered. "Oh man, sorry about that." His mind, still obviously deep in the project in front of him, took a moment to process the information. He blinked, and set down the gear set in his hands. "Wait, she got out of Toya's room *and* out of our Hab, and then all the way into yours?"

"Yeah," Nix said as he stifled another yawn, "I put her back in with Toya and I'm guessing she's all adventured out for the night. Goddamn trash panda. She had the water pouring at full tilt and was washing the chips and making a shit sandwich out of my kitchen. I should clean it, but the hell with it, I'm going back to bed now."

Lenny laughed again, shaking his head. "You warned us they were smart, but I had no idea she could manipulate doorknobs."

Nix shrugged as he turned to go. "Well, now you know." What he didn't say was how much he liked the little raccoon. She was adorable, truly, something he had not expected. "I'm going back to bed. I plan on sleeping in," he said over his shoulder.

"Don't forget Petra's called an all hands meeting at nine a.m.," Lenny called out.

Nix swore under his breath, then paused, asking, "What about you, Kid? Don't you need your beauty sleep? Have you been up all night, or what?"

Lenny turned and shrugged. "I get my best work done at night. Besides, Petra lumps me in with Toya. She thinks we're both stupid kids and she won't expect me to do much more than go along with whatever you guys say."

Nix stifled a grin. The kid was smarter than any of them, including Petra, who was a genius in her own right. Lenny had sure sussed out Petra, though. Her biggest shortcoming was assuming she was the only one with brains. It didn't serve her well, and it often caused friction with the others.

Nix ignored NARA's gentle reminder at a quarter past eight. This led to several rounds of automated wake-up calls, and finally a harsh clanging fifteen minutes later. Nix groaned and stretched as NARA continued to blast sound at him.

"Christ on a crutch. NARA, stop, please."

"My apologies, Michael, but I have been instructed to continue until you are standing upright in order to ensure you are properly awake," NARA responded gently before resuming the loud alarm clock clang that sounded in sets of three spaced apart by two seconds of silence. It was impossible to ignore.

Nix rubbed his eyes, stood up, and immediately the clamor ceased.

NARA's dulcet tones continued, "Thank you for waking, Michael. Please be aware that any return to the horizontal state will cause the alarm to reset and resume until you are vertical once more. They require your presence for the all hands meeting at 0900."

Nix growled, "Let me guess, Petra did an administrator override, didn't she?"

"That is correct."

Nix nodded, then ambled over to the nearest sensor. "NARA, open up the camera function, please." He waited until the computer verified that the camera was currently on before he bent over and dropped his pants. "Send that to Petra, with my compliments." He grinned. "A full moon is just what she has coming to her."

And with that small revenge, he sauntered out to the kitchenette, sighed, and got to work cleaning up the mess that Burrito the Bandido had created in the middle of the night. Soggy masses of chips were everywhere, sticking to his feet as he swept them off of the counter onto the floor and then pressed the button for the auto-vac to clean it all up.

He downed two cups of coffee. When the auto-vac slammed into his bare foot as it wound its way through the Hab, bruising his toe, Nix swore. He hobbled into the second bedroom that was serving as a tropical rainforest with several coffee plants. He kept the door closed, so that the thick and humid air would not escape. Here he had dozens of plants that were at home in the thick, steamy jungles of Earth–ferns, dwarf bananas, orchids, and more. There was even a prized coffee tree in the corner. He had converted every inch of space. Plants hung on the walls from the ceiling, and there was barely room to walk because of the large numbers occupying the floor.

Once they had figured out a way to reproduce the rainforest in one of the city-level Garden Habs they had planned, he could move these plants into it. For now, however, they would stay here, in his Hab, where he could monitor them.

Currently, they had planted a second round of cool-weather crops in Eden Hab. Recently, they had planted the first trees on Mars, a line of trees best suited toward a Mediterranean climate. The temperatures inside of Eden Hab were slowly rising, thanks to Petra and Lenny's adjustments on the solar array which pumped heat into the dome. The olive trees would take a long time, but they had also planted almond trees, mulberry, loquat, fig, and pomegranate. Lenny and Toya were obsessed with them, likely because neither had seen trees before.

When they had first begun, the carbon dioxide levels that were beneficial to the plants were also too high for humans to breathe for any length of time. The first few months, they had had to work with re-breathers. Now, however, the oxygen levels had risen high enough that they no longer needed them.

They had walled a six-foot-high section of land off, and it contained kale, lettuces, and broccoli. The walls would prevent the farm animals from devouring the human crops. There was already a vast swath of grass and clover growing to feed the three goats currently developing in the artificial wombs. Two females, one male, with more embryos to grow later. And among it all were six hens and one rooster that wandered loose through the Hab, pecking at the grass and clover, and adding their own nutrients to the soil. They had recently begun laying eggs, and Abdul had celebrated by baking a three-layer cake.

He was considering a third cup of coffee, having found a flavorful dark roast in Cairo Hab, when NARA chimed, "The all-hands meeting will begin in fifteen minutes; please be aware that your presence is required."

Christ on a crutch, he had a laundry list of priorities, and sure as anything, Petra would have more for him. Nix carefully added the thick, soupy coffee grounds to one plant and turned to leave, closing the door firmly behind him. He loved that it was a thick, humid feel in the room, but was thankful he didn't have to endure it throughout the rest of the Hab. Nix had spent nearly two years of his early twenties in Costa Rica. The moist, sticky heat had been unrelenting.

As he walked down the hallway, Lenny and Toya's door opened and Toya led the way, Burrito perched on her shoulder, chittering away. Lenny followed behind, looking beat.

"Morning!" Toya caroled, the picture of perkiness. Nix looked over at Lenny and the boy rolled his eyes in response. Toya was the quintessential morning person, something he envied and hated all at the same time. Lenny shared Nix's sentiments. At just two months past his thirteenth birthday, Earth time that is, Nix noticed the boy's sleep patterns change. These days, Lenny was up most nights and asleep, given the chance, all morning and sometimes as late as mid-afternoon. Whereas before, Lenny had been up at the crack of dawn, now his sleep/wake cycle had done an abrupt shift.

Nix remembered when it had happened to him. It was as if adolescence and puberty affected teenagers on the most basic level.

Unfortunately for Nix and Lenny, Petra fell into the early-morning riser camp. This led to morning all hands meetings and plenty of yawning from the kid as he struggled to stay awake.

Something has to give, Nix thought to himself, because Lenny's contributions were far more valuable than Petra realized.

Petra was ready and waiting, complete with the meeting notes that appeared, with a cheerful chime that announced their presence on each of their tablets.

Nix scanned it as he walked and groaned, "Great, she's got it color-coded, with red for all the delayed projects. Wanna guess who has those projects?" He turned his tablet towards Toya and Lenny as they walked. The items he and Lenny were in charge of were in a bold red.

Lenny pursed his lips in disgust. "I'm working my ass off to get those automated construction drones completed."

"Buck up, Kid. You'll figure it out." Nix punched Lenny lightly on the arm. "You are a goddamn wunderkind, after all."

Lenny scowled back. "Nice word usage, Nix, but right now, I just want to sleep."

Nix laughed and let the kid's bad mood roll off of him. It looked as though Lenny had pulled an all-nighter. No wonder he was cranky.

Abdul's face lit up when the three of them rounded the corner. The smell of scrambled eggs and toast almost masked the odor of the NearBacon. It had delighted Abdul to try it since it wasn't technically meat. After nearly a year of effort, however, the only thing that had made the vat-created monstrosity taste half-decent was the hot sauce, and lots of it. Nix noted that Abdul had refilled the hot sauce container recently. It sat waiting near his spot at the table.

Petra nodded to each of them as they sat down, fingers tapping with impatience. Nix could see she had already eaten, her empty plate now pushed to the middle of the large table. They had slept together over half a dozen times now. Each time at her place, not his, and each time she had asked him to stay, and he had skillfully avoided it. What they had was sexual, nothing more.

After all, Petra was technically the only woman available. Toya was beautiful, but the whole brain damage thing had him as uncomfortable as hell. And things had built up long enough that sex with Petra felt like more of an act of desperation rather than something meaningful. She wanted it to be more than that, of that he was sure. Petra might not have said it out loud, but her intent was clear. She wanted to claim him as hers, but that was more commitment than he was ready to make, no matter how blue his balls got. As he sat there at the table, smothering the NearBacon and eggs in enough Tabasco that he couldn't taste much else beyond the spicy hotness, he tried to not think about how long it had been and how giving himself a hand just wasn't the same as being with a woman, no matter how off-putting and obnoxious she was.

James sat in his usual spot next to Petra, and Abdul was next to him, as usual. That James and Abdul had paired up was obvious to everyone except possibly James, who seemed completely oblivious to the looks of adoration that Abdul sent his way.

"Ugh, this is gross." Toya picked at the piece of NearBacon and made a face.

"Try it with hot sauce," Nix suggested, and Toya shrugged and reached for the container of Tabasco sauce. She copied his liberal application of it and then handed it to Lenny, who applied a few drops of it to his faux meat.

Petra appeared unimpressed. "If you could finish with breakfast, we could get on with the meeting." Her tone was bitchy, her face mirroring her words.

Nix felt a wave of irritation surge through him. As if they didn't have all the time in the world, years and years ahead of them for all the projects they could dream up and not much else. They were stuck here until Earth decided whether to send more colonists or a ship to rescue them. Neither of which, according to James, was likely to happen anytime soon. The man had spent months discussing it with a half dozen people back on Earth. Things were bad there, even now, after the deaths had dropped off significantly. It seemed Earth was too busy planning new cities and salvaging from the remains of the old to bother with a colony that was millions of kilometers away.

Meanwhile, Petra was driven, that was for sure. Nix wasn't sure if that was a bad thing. They needed people like her, even if she rubbed him and the others the wrong way.

Nix suppressed laughter as both Lenny and Toya reached for their water cups while fanning their mouths. He caught Petra glaring at them. If looks could kill, the siblings would be dead on the floor. When she noticed him watching, however, her expression changed, and the look of loathing that had flashed across her face seconds ago disappeared. He already knew how little she thought of Toya, but Lenny being included in her glare had been a surprise. His gut churned. He hated conflict and kept the peace when others would egg a situation on, even to violence. Was Petra feeling challenged by Lenny? Or by Lenny's intelligence? The kid didn't flaunt it, but he also didn't hide it. Lenny shouldn't need to keep quiet or dumb it down for anyone.

"As I was saying," Petra continued, the room growing quiet in response, "I have sent an alternative plan of action to your tablets. It's something to consider, and carefully, because it could mean the difference between living out our lives breathing canned air, or actually walking out onto the surface of Mars and having a breathable atmosphere."

On cue, Nix's tablet chimed for a second time that morning, as did Lenny's, James' and Abdul's. Toya, her cheeks glistening with sweat and still fanning her mouth, stared at her tablet and looked up with a frown. "Mine didn't ding. Why didn't mine ding?"

Petra ignored her, a half-smile on her thin lips. She nodded at Nix. "Go on, read it."

Nix opened the document, scanned it, and gaped at Petra. "You want us to go into Cryo?"

"Mm, hm." Her smile widened, but her lips, as always, remained closed, hiding her mismatched teeth.

James gasped audibly as he read the outline on his tablet, "For one hundred years? Are you insane?"

"Petra, my tablet didn't ding," Toya repeated. Petra continued to ignore her.

Petra's eyes flashed, and Nix noticed how her body vibrated with excitement. Petra played it cool most of the time, but this idea was something she believed in and wanted to happen. "Why not? What have we got to lose?"

The rest of them sat slack-jawed in shock.

Abdul spoke first, "This is assuming the equipment would be reliable that long. Petra, we don't know if the Hab itself could survive one hundred years, much less one thousand."

"We wouldn't stay here. We could build a new, functional station in the lava tubes," she answered. "I detailed it on the third page." She leaned forward. "Why do you think they brought me here? I had no intention of living out the rest of my days breathing canned air and drilling for potential disaster scenarios in a 25-kilo spacesuit every damned month. I still don't."

James stared at her. "No one ever said anything about going into Cryo for a hundred years, and sure as hell we would have heard about it."

Petra ripped off her Ident tag and removed it from its protective sleeve. "It was need to know, James, and, well, as the saying goes," she smirked, "you didn't need to know."

Her Ident card looked normal, until she turned it over, revealing the cardinal red Level 5 security clearance. "We were planning on announcing it at the beginning of next year, after we had conducted a few tests on the long-term reliability of the equipment. Calypso's crew were the perfect experiment. We were waiting until we heard from Calypso's crew after they dropped from light speed and began the deceleration process of their journey. As for the long-term aspect, it would have been on a strictly volunteer basis; the powers that be knew there would never be a consensus on it. And they planned on a skeleton crew to monitor and maintain, after all. But for those who had made the commitment to Mars, those who had no family or friends or ties that would pull at them, they would be the first humans to truly *live* on Mars." Her eyes glowed with a fevered excitement that Nix had never seen before. "What would you do to be the first human to breathe Martian air without the need of a spacesuit or even a re-breather?"

The Case for Cryo

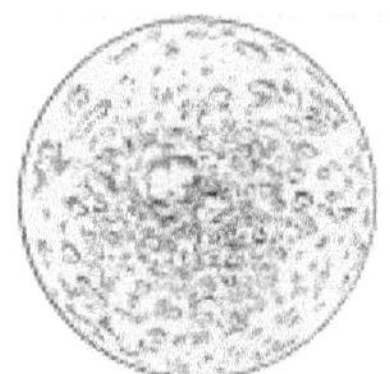

Mars Year 14, Week 62, Day 612
(Earth Date: 04.15.2100)

Nix spoke first. "Are you completely insane? We are centuries away from a breathable atmosphere on Mars."

Petra turned; her gaze openly disdainful. Her lips thinned into a hard line.

Toya, still frowning at her tablet, had leaned closer to Nix to see what his screen read.

Lenny's fingers flew and a second later, Toya's tablet chimed, showing it had received the document. Petra rolled her eyes at this. "Why bother? She can't understand it."

Toya glared at Petra. "Can too." She frowned, and her lips shaped each word clearly, yet silently. She leaned closer to Nix and whispered, "What's c-r-y-o-g-e-n-i-c h-i-b-e-r-n-a-t-i-o-n spell?"

Petra snarled at the room, "Christ, is this an edition of *Romper Room*? Does the village idiot need a recess?"

Lenny fixed a hostile glare in Petra's direction. "She has just as much right to be here as you do, Petra." His voice trembled, whether from anger or fear, James couldn't tell. Lenny struck James as a polite young man, and he had been polite, but Petra's open hostility towards Toya had raised the boy's hackles. And with good reason.

Petra smiled at him patronizingly. "Well, of course she does, Junior. Now if you don't mind, the adults are talking now."

Lenny stared at her, mouth open in shock.

James could feel the tension in the room ratchet up. "Stop it, Petra." He desperately wanted to understand the information she had sent to him and the others. The idea of it was intriguing. The acrimony her words were causing, however, was not helping. He turned back to the tablet. "Let me see if I understand what you are saying on Section Two of this plan. You want to aim the nukes currently stored on Phobos at the far side of the planet in order to cause a chain reaction which would push the greenhouse gas effect into overdrive. It looks as if you are estimating a ninety-five-year timeline."

"As little as ninety-five years, yes." Petra nodded, her cheek muscle twitching, her mouth still set in a thin line. From the fiery flash in her eyes, she didn't like being corrected by him. "One hundred and fifty at the longest."

"For an atmosphere that won't require pressure suits and could support re-breather masks?"

"Yes, precisely."

Abdul chimed in then, "And you think we could essentially sleep through the entire process by going into Cryo?"

"Yes." She smiled then, looking quite pleased with herself.

Nix shook his head. "Too much could go wrong, even in the lava tubes."

"We can build in redundancies," Petra snapped back, "Create several backups and install robotic handlers programmed to wake us in case of a crisis." She glared at Nix, and James wondered how much it had to do with the man disagreeing with Petra, or how much it had to do with the fact that he was not as interested in Petra as she would have wished. And if truth be told, whether Nix would admit it, far more interested in Toya.

"And depend on robots to keep us alive?" Nix snorted, "No thanks."

Petra leveled a look at Nix that looked positively lethal. "I wouldn't expect you to keep up, Nix, but you really should know when to let your betters discuss the details."

Oh, Christ, now she's done it.

James found himself on his feet in the half second before Nix opened his mouth. "And we're done here. Petra, enough. You've proposed your idea and we will adjourn until tomorrow to allow for time to read the entire proposal and reconvene then."

Whatever Nix had been about to say, he closed his mouth, his face reddening. He stood up abruptly, the chair falling behind him, grabbed his tablet, and walked away, his stride long, ground-eating. Lenny and Toya followed, leaving Abdul and James alone in the room with Petra.

James shook his head. Damned if she didn't have a talent for pissing people off.

Petra's mouth was open in shock and anger, her eyes flashing. "We aren't finished."

"Oh, I think we are," James responded with a tight smile. "You really need to work on your interpersonal skills."

Abdul, normally the peacemaker, gave a quiet cough that sounded suspiciously like a laugh as he followed on Toya and Lenny's heels. James trailed behind, leaving Petra and her sullen superiority to sit, alone, in the room.

The next day, they assembled in the morning, just as they had the day before. Petra still looked angry, but also determined, and the smile on her lips appeared forced and false.

"Good morning, everyone."

There was a scattering of responses as they dug into their plates, eyes fixed on their food. James wondered how today would go. He had read over Petra's plan and found it more than interesting. The case for Cryo, and for the chance at a breathable, livable world as opposed to living in tin cans with a view, was a fantastic dream. But he had to side with Nix. Robots were excellent for a variety of things, but he wasn't ready to trust them with his life, at least not for a hundred years or more.

"In reviewing the proposal, I sent all of you yesterday, I made one change that I think you will find appealing." Petra's voice was even and calm, and surprised James. Somehow, he had expected her to go on the attack, but she wasn't.

"I believe that we should request a new infusion of colonists," Petra continued, "At least one hundred more colonists along with a full A.R.C. of viable embryos that we could use at a later time, perhaps at the end of the one hundred years, to create a diverse population base on Mars." Her fingers danced across her tablet, and seconds later there was a chorus of notifications, including Toya's.

James bent his head to focus on the new document, his eyes scanning over the proposed changes. There was silence in the room as the others did the same, their food temporarily forgotten.

Abdul was the first to speak. "Very interesting. How much power would we need to accommodate the extra number of people in Cryo?"

"You find that in Section Eight," Petra answered, and then continued, "As you can see, the plan now incorporates a skeleton crew of five individuals who would serve five-year shifts at a time. We would need a wide range of talents in the one hundred colonists, but all the skeleton crew staff would need to have the capabilities as listed in Section Four, and of course pass all the psychological profiles that we did upon being accepted to the Mars mission."

The psychological profiles had included extensive personality tests that gauged everything from how one handled working under pressure, to how someone responded to isolation and close quarters. For every individual who had applied to come to Mars, they had denied at least one hundred or more. The mission to Gliese 581g had been modeled on the Mars parameters.

"And you think we will get enough takers?" Nix asked, his expression tight and his words clipped. He looked as if he were still angry over Petra's comment on his intelligence, and James couldn't blame him. Petra made it difficult for all of them.

"I do." Petra allowed herself a small smile. "There are approximately fourteen million people left on Earth. Of that number, there are perhaps half a million, likely less, of Unaffected Persons. They could conceivably send those individuals to Gliese 581g soon if a vaccine to the ESH virus continues to elude them. But as for the rest, those who are ESH-positive like us, well, I imagine there are still plenty of those who would like to make the commitment to Mars."

She tapped her screen. "We need to keep our numbers low in order to have Cryo be an option. The power drain will be significant, but it is still doable. The ESH virus was, ironically, a godsend. It culled our population to a low enough level that we can push the atmosphere formation into overdrive and ride it out in Cryo."

Nix looked disgusted. "A godsend? Christ, Petra, you just can't help yourself, can you?"

Lenny's voice was quiet as he piped up, "It was a poor choice of words, but she's correct. We never could have dreamed of doing this with the colony at full capacity. As it is, if we ask and get one hundred new colonists, we will need them to bring more solar panels than we currently have in order to power the Cryo units."

Petra added, "Yes, you saw that in Section Four, right?"

The boy didn't look at her, but his head nodded. "Yup, saw it."

James sat back, his fingers templed in front of him as he thought about it. The idea of it was...exciting. He found his heart rate speed up at the thought of stepping out into a world with an atmosphere, with breathable air, and remembered the vintage exhibit back at the Mars Dreams expo on Earth. It had included a display created way back in 2016, one that showed the future terraforming of Mars. It had progressed through large panels over one thousand years to show a view of Mars that was verdant, albeit on the colder side, compared to places like Norway or Finland, really, and more than habitable.

"What spaceships could they use now that they have scuttled the Jupiter?" Abdul asked, "Do we even know?"

The Jupiter Supply Ship had been relatively new. It had handled all the Mars missions for the past six years and constructed in space on the Gan De space station. When the ESH virus hit the crew, Huygens Outpost had watched it come in on autopilot, its crew already dead inside. They thought they had taken every precaution to avoid contamination. With the Jupiter scuttled on the far side of the planet, Huygens Outpost lacked any space-worthy ship.

Petra's fingers flew over her tablet again. "I've been looking into it. There are a small fleet of ships in various stages of construction, a multitude of them on Earth and at least two were in progress on the Gan De space station. The European Union had one, as did the South American Co-Op. China had two in the works, one that was a larger colony ship that they were planning for the mission to Kepler in 2102, and a smaller supply ship that would supplant the Mazu if it required repairs."

"Wait, the Chinese were also planning a mission for Kepler?" James raised his eyebrows. "I didn't know that."

Petra nodded. "And then the Serenity Deep Explorer, which the Reformed United States of America was planning for Kepler for 2103. I'm guessing the Chinese wanted a jump on the RUSA for once."

"So, there's plenty to choose from," Abdul interjected.

"Well, possibly." Petra lifted her shoulders in a small shrug. "I need to find out how close any of these are to completion. And then there is the question of what shape the ship's corresponding government is in. China is in full meltdown from the sounds of it, and the South Am Co-Op is fracturing, as you have likely been aware of from recent news reports."

James sighed; he could feel a headache coming on. Just thinking about Earth dissolving into infighting in the wake of such unimaginable loss was difficult. Weren't over ten billion dead enough? Did they really need to be fighting now?

"And you are proposing that we put feelers out and see which government is the most stable and how close they are to being complete with a ship that will meet our needs?" Lenny asked.

"Exactly."

"I disagree." Abdul's voice was soft. It went unheard by everyone except Lenny until he repeated himself, louder this time, "I disagree."

Petra stared at him. "With what part?"

"All of it. At least, for right now," Abdul responded, his brown eyes matching hers and then turning to each of the occupants of the room. "Earth is in pieces. They aren't capable of maintaining a steady government, much less working on ships with thoughts to the future. Let them bury their dead. Let them figure out who is going to run what. Give them time. We need it as well. It's been, what, less than an Earth year? We are still struggling with our own infrastructure; one an infusion of colonists would undermine."

"Huh, well I didn't see that coming," Lenny said, his face thoughtful.

Abdul leaned forward. "Look, I'm not saying we put this off forever, but we have work to do here first, work we have every capability of completing before we bring in new lives that depend on us and the systems here with their lives. I'm not saying no to Cryo, I'm saying not yet." He spread out his hands and continued, "We just got Eden Hab online. We still have the passageway connections to Cairo, London, and Sydney Habs to complete. We also have to re-route power, manufacture and install solar cells, and so much more. Let's continue to focus on that and let's revisit this case for Cryo in another thirty weeks once we have harvested our first round of warm-weather crops and have a clear idea of where we are going with this.

"We need to fully understand what kind of impact those nukes might have on the far side of the planet. We can't forget, those nukes could affect the Beijing Science Outpost. We need to plan for them to move, or for our ground zero targets to change, in order to keep them safe."

Petra stared at Abdul, her mouth open, stuck between shock and incredulity. "Of all the people..."

Abdul held up his hands. "I'm not saying no, I'm saying not now."

"He's got a point, Petra. We might be rushing things by implementing your Cryo project now," Nix added, reflective. "We have time, after all, so let's do this right."

Toya spoke up then, "I vote waiting until we have the crops in. And more goats and chickens."

James watched as Petra glared at her and said nothing. It was obvious how Petra felt about the girl.

Petra turned to James, a desperate look in her eyes. And James wrestled with it. On one hand, it was an amazing plan, one that really looked as if it could work. On the other, it felt rushed. He wondered why she was so emphatic that it had to happen now. There was so much work, and so many changes, that would need doing before they could welcome the crew of fifty that Petra was describing. He went with his gut.

"This is important, game-changing. It seriously is," James began. "The idea of being able to see a green Mars, that in itself is staggering. But, Petra, the others are right. We need to have a solid framework first. We need to get to where we are self-sufficient and growing enough of our crops so that we don't need to depend on Earth in the decades to come. I suggest we revisit this in a year. It will allow us to have some significant progress under our belt."

"An *Earth* half year? Or a Martian half-year?" Petra asked, her lips thin, her jaw set.

"Preferably a Martian year, but I'm willing to revisit in an Earth year. What do you think?" he asked the rest of the room and they all nodded in agreement, except for Petra, who was now shaking with anger.

Petra stared at him and then tracked the room, landing on James first, then Nix, Lenny, and finally Toya. "You are all idiots." She stood up and walked out of the room.

Getting to Know You

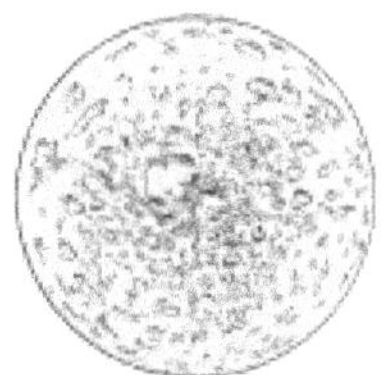

Mars Year 14, Week 62, Day 617
(Earth Date: 04.20.2100)

Petra stretched back on the bed, a half-smile on her lips as Nix turned away, pulled his clothes back on, and slipped on his deck shoes. He avoided eye contact. Somehow, after the deed, he always wished he had never come. Later, he would tell himself it couldn't happen again. That lasted until Petra got him alone and found some excuse to touch him, run her fingers down his spine. His body reacted to her, the basic animalistic side, and he was growing to hate it, especially because it felt like he was being stalked and manipulated by her.

He knew she wanted him to stay. It hung there in the air between them, unspoken, but an expectation all the same. He waited for it. She would ask eventually; she couldn't help herself.

"Got a hot date with the feeb?" she asked, a note of acid in her voice.

He didn't bother answering. What was the point, anyway? A wave of irritation in her choice of words followed swiftly with one of self-loathing. Why did he keep coming back to her, this plain woman with a sharp tongue and zero heart? Sure, the sex was great, if only she didn't have to open her mouth and ruin it afterward.

His voice was steady. The last thing he wanted to do was show her how angry her words made him.

"I'm going to go for a run now."

He reached for his tablet. It was where he had left it, on the edge of the small table that extruded from the wall of the Hab, a picture of efficiency and maximized space. Petra's hand closed on his wrist. Her fingernails were claws that dug into his skin, sharp, demanding. He could feel the scratches she had left on his back as she had moaned in ecstasy just moments before. One stung, and he was pretty sure she had drawn blood.

He tried to pull away, but her grip dug in tight.

"What?" he said, staring into her eyes. His pants tightened, and immediately a wave of revulsion washed over him. Why did his body have to respond to her, of all people?

Not that there was a plethora of women to choose from. Petra was the only choice he had in sexual partners. Thinking about Toya that way, it felt...*wrong*. Every time he did think of Toya, he felt a wave of shame that delivered him to Petra's door, the last place he should be.

"Look at me," Petra replied.

"I am looking at you," Nix answered, trying to pull his wrist from her grasp.

Her eyes narrowed, even as a coy smile did its best to brighten her plain features.

"Look at my *body*," she said, trying to pull him closer to her. A pink tongue poked from her lips in what he could only assume was an attempt to be alluring. It fell flat.

"I have to go, Petra."

Her coy look vanished, replaced with her familiar sneer. Between the two expressions had been a flash of anger. Nix had spent enough time with Petra Salinger to see it and mark it for what it was.

"Really? So, what, you screw me, and then it's back to hanging with your favorite feeb? What do you see in that retarded disaster of a girl, anyway? I'm surprised they didn't feed her out of the airlock way back then. It's not as if she'll ever be right in the head. It's a drain on finite resources. What does the colony charter say about that, anyway?"

Nix held back the rush of anger he felt at Petra's cruel words.

"Let it go."

She snorted. "Really, Nix, I'm wondering if you are screwing her too." She tilted her head, her eyes searching his, a snide smile touching her lips. "How is she? Does she work up an appetite for Choco-Snax afterwards? Do you give her extra for, you know, a trip in through the back door? I mean, really, I guess you could knock her up if you wanted to. After all, she's good for breeding and all that; it isn't as if any kids she had would be feebs like..."

He slapped her. Her head snapped away, his hand making a sharp crack against her skin before he even realized his hand was in motion.

Her hold on his wrist went slack in shock, nails no longer digging into his wrist. Nix pulled away, backed up, and wheeled towards the door.

It took less than three strides to make it out of the bedroom. He stole a quick glance back at her as he did.

Petra sat on the bed, her legs curled up under her, shoulders curving forward as she held a hand to her flushed, red cheek. She didn't look at him. Instead, she stared at the wall, outrage and hurt warring for control of her face.

Nix tried to think of what to say, but he couldn't bring himself to apologize to the woman he had been banging daily for the past two weeks. Really, what was there to say? He pulled the door closed behind him and strode down the corridor, blind with anger over Petra's snipes and yet horrified at his own response. He had *never* hit a woman. Well, at least not until now.

What a hateful woman she is. Why the hell did I ever get involved with her?

His steps were long, especially in the lower Martian gravity, and Nix soon found himself at an easy, loping run. It was this running that had become both a distraction and reassurance. The Hong Kong Hab was just under one kilometer in circumference if he stuck to the outer ring. It was the same for all the Habs and, until they could continue work on the Eden Hab, the connecting center spoke that would provide a green forest-like destination for all the Habs, it was the closest he could get to a routine that exercised his body and quieted his mind.

He made one pass through before he allowed himself to think of Petra again.

Enough is enough. I'd be better off taking myself in hand than getting intimate with that viper.

He grimaced as he passed the hall that led to her sleeping quarters. There was no sign of her, thankfully. Petra wasn't the sort to enjoy running. This meant that the soonest he would have to endure her presence was tomorrow morning's team meeting at 1000 hours. That would be all too soon, in his estimation.

The second lap around the Hab slipped by just as quickly, and Nix could feel his breathing settling into a rhythm. It was in the third lap that he heard the light footfalls and breathing behind him. He glanced over his shoulder and Toya grinned at him, her shorter legs pumping fast on the thick, rubberized walkway.

"Hey there, Nix."

"Hey, Toya."

He slowed down, and they ran side by side, saying nothing for two more laps before Nix veered off towards the Eden Hab. Toya followed. They both slowed, Toya panting as they approached the membrane that separated the Philadelphia Hab from a long tunnel that ran into the darkness of the Martian night. The lights were automatic, motion-sensing, like the rest of the facility. They glowed to life in advance, providing a warm, yellow light above and at the edges along the bottom of the rounded sides of the tunnel, a sharp contrast to the blackness outside of the Hab. A soft whir blew a breeze of air over them. They were walking now, but the heaters took a moment to kick in and the air was frigid inside of the tunnel. Once darkness fell, so did the outside temps, plunging from a balmy 18 degrees Celsius, to minus 100 degrees Celsius. No matter how much insulation they added, the tunnels became ice cold at night. The Habs themselves had massive heaters, along with redundancies in case of failures. A night on Mars could be deadly, after all.

Toya shivered as they slipped through. "Brr."

The tunnel was wide enough to accommodate small machinery, and Nix and Toya had more than enough room to run side by side.

Nix grinned at her. "Yeah, tell me about it. Come on, let's get to the other side. It'll be warmer there." They began to run again, feet pounding a rhythm on the plasticrete under their feet.

A few hundred meters later, they slipped through another membrane into the vast, open dome that was Eden Hab. Situated in the center of Huygens Outpost, Eden Hab was truly massive, nearly three football fields in diameter, and the top of the dome was over 45 meters tall. It would serve as a natural space and house the crops that the colony would need in the years ahead. Even if they did act on Petra's plan, it might still be centuries before there was a breathable atmosphere on Mars. Eden Hab was intended to be the first of multiple temperate zones that would serve humans in the years leading up to a fully terraformed Mars.

But everything was up in the air. The reports from Earth remained grim, and there was no talk of sending a supply ship, or possibly new colonists, in the next year. They were in good shape in the nutrition department. It was human companionship, and the future of the outpost that was an issue. After Petra had called them idiots and stalked out of the meeting, they had voted to table the case for Cryo until at least half of an Earth year had passed. Abdul had been right. They needed to stabilize themselves here on Huygens Outpost first, otherwise they would find themselves in the same shape as Earth's governments currently were, albeit on a smaller scale.

Nix thought of Petra's cruel words as they warmed themselves in the vast open space, littered with various clumps of new plant life and boxes of seeds waiting to be planted. Toya didn't *look* damaged. She had pulled her black hair back in a slightly misshapen, off to one side, ponytail. Her cheeks were a bright pink, not just from the run but also from rosacea. It gave them a ruddy appearance, as if she had spent the day on a mountaintop in the wind. Somehow, that was always Nix's go-to image of her, a young woman with windblown hair and ruddy cheeks, outside and carefree.

It wasn't the reality. The last time Toya had stood out in the wind, she had been a small child on Earth.

Toya's appearance had improved in the seven Earth months since he had first met her and Lenny. She had been slightly overweight, with greasy hair and a sprinkling of teenage acne covering her skin. Her extra weight and acne had resulted from poor eating in the aftermath of the ESH virus. With no one left to tell her no, she had binged on snack foods and sweets. That had changed with Nix's arrival, and Lenny had looked visibly relieved when Nix had taken control of the situation. It hadn't been easy, and Toya had responded as any spoiled, indulged child might. Eventually, with Nix's enforcement of the rules, and Abdul's mad skills in the kitchen, Toya had thrived. The pounds had melted off even before Nix talked her into running with him regularly.

She smiled then, a flash of bright white teeth, her breath now slowing from the run to where she could easily talk. "You looked mad when I first saw you running."

Lenny had been working with her, teaching her to search faces for verbal cues. The Lion's Mane and Cordyceps mushroom supplements seemed to help as well. Toya called them her "brain pills" and consumed them eagerly. They might not heal the damage that the hypoxia had done to her brain, but she had shown significant progress in all areas–from learning new skills to better self-care.

"Sorry, Toya, I wasn't mad at you. Just had some dumb look on my face, I guess."

"Okay."

She accepted this explanation and turned to look at a tester plot Nix had set up a few days before. Seeds were sprouting and a small carpet of green seedlings had appeared. A cheerful grin appeared on her face.

"It looks all green now, Nix. I think more popped up since this morning."

They edged closer, and he nodded. "Yup, it's looking nice and thick, good to see." He refrained from calling her "Kid" like he did Lenny. Even though her mind was that of a child's, Toya was nineteen and fully in the throes of the realization that she was no longer a child. And she was embracing her new status as an adult. Petra had exacerbated the situation, of course, manipulating the girl by alternately telling her she was an adult while also pointing out the areas where others were controlling her–by limiting what she ate or telling her what to do each day. It had caused problems, but then again, that was what Petra excelled at, creating problems that would then walk and talk all on their own.

There had been fights, mainly over food. Junk food was dwindling fast, and Nix suspected that Petra had moved a few boxes out of the stores to whereabouts unknown. He wouldn't put it past her to find a way to sabotage his and Lenny's work in helping Toya become more active and less fixated on food.

"Can we plant the carrots next?" Toya asked, running her fingers over the packets of seeds in one open box. "I like this one. It's a yellow carrot, Nix. I didn't know carrots could be yellow."

He grinned. "Yup, they even come in purple and red."

She looked up at him, her eyes intent on his face. "You're teasing me, aren't you?"

He shook his head. "Look here, in the box's bottom. Even white ones."

She grabbed the packets from his hand, a look of delight on her face. "I want to plant them all!"

"Okay, we'll plant a little from each variety."

She stood up. "Now?"

"Toya, it's nearly ten, time for bed and all that."

Her lips pursed and turned down at the edges into a frown. "You always say 'no.' Petra says it's because you think I'm a baby."

Nix thought of Petra and felt his anger rise. Why the hell did that woman have to be so petty? So manipulative?

"You know what?" He stopped and let his anger go, turned it into something else. "Hell with it, let's plant them now."

"Yeah?" Toya smiled again, and Nix could see her for what she was, a person with hopes and dreams just like his. And really, what was so different? A few less-functioning cognitive skills differentiated her from a normal human being. Lenny said that his mom had told him that Toya had survived where the others had died, thanks to her incredible engineering abilities.

He grinned back at her and tilted his head. "Come on, let's plant them over in the west quadrant. I was prepping the ground for it last week. It should be perfect."

It was less than an hour later when Lenny found them hard at work, placing the labels at neatly spaced intervals over the planted ground. He didn't ask why they were planting crops well past sundown. The boy was brilliant in his own right, but also gentle and patient with his older sister. He wheedled Toya away with the promise of a story and one-quarter of a chocolate bar before bed, if only she would take a quick shower. Nix watched them go, Toya still towering over her brother, despite his recent growth spurt, her clothes damp with sweat and covered in dirt.

His thoughts strayed back to Petra, and he sighed then, regretting the day they had ever brought her back to Philadelphia Hab. The woman was a harpy, not to mention malicious and vindictive. How much more peaceful it had been with only Toya and Lenny.

The smell of the earth on his hands, combined with the gentle breeze of warmed air from the fans, enticed him to settle down against the soft bags of organic matter destined to feed the crops they were planting and close his eyes. It was here in Eden Hab that Nix felt closest to the Earth he had left behind. Soon the Hab would see the trees rise and stretch towards the barrier. They could add birds, beneficial insects, and more. It would be, as its name implied, a place dedicated to nature, and as close to verdant beauty they had all left behind. As he lay there, unmoving, the auto-lights dimmed, and the darkness closed in. Far above the translucent dome, he could see a vast array of stars, along with Mars' moon, Phobos. Near the horizon, he could see the bright blue light that was Earth and below that, also equally bright, Venus.

There was no returning to Earth. There was no one left, no family or friends left alive. Even if he missed the forests, mountains, and rivers of Earth, it wasn't enough for him to flee this barren red planet. Besides, Toya and Lenny could never leave. To return would mean a lifetime spent in wheelchairs and fighting a gravity their bodies were unused to. The past one-third Mars year had shown Nix that a family was more than just parents and children. And Lenny and Toya were family now. So were Abdul and James, for that matter.

But it was Toya and Lenny that Nix felt closest to. Lenny was this fascinating mix of brilliance and awkward pre-adolescence, and Toya, well, Toya made him smile. He didn't think of her like he did Lenny. Lenny was almost like having an impossibly intelligent son that he could only partially understand. But Toya, sometimes, hell, most of the time, the girl unsettled him. He liked her. Her needs were simple, but she could also be sweet in her own way, and she was pretty. That was the unsettling part. He knew it was. It felt like it wasn't right for him to like her, to find her attractive, and yet he did. Nix sighed; he didn't know what the hell to do about that either. Perhaps that was what had propelled him in Petra's direction. Simple biological needs had a way of pushing their way to the front. And after food and shelter, well, the need to reproduce, or at least practice at reproducing, was a natural drive. What wasn't acceptable was his interest in Toya, who possessed a woman's body but also the mind of a child. It was hard too, knowing she had once been more, should have been more, and lost it in a stupid accident. Nix wrestled with his attraction. What was wrong with him, anyway? He had no answers, no simple solution, and the thought of the two women in his life was in his mind as exhaustion washed over him and took him deep into a dream of a future Eden Hab, replete with so much plant and animal life within its sheltering dome, that the stars could no longer be seen at night.

The next morning, after a quick coffee and protein bar in the Mess Hall, where he avoided eye contact with Petra, Nix found himself drawn towards Lenny and Toya's Hab.

He gave a knock and then walked in. Lenny was hunched over the corpse of a robot.

"Hey, Lenny, gotcha some of that Ovaltine you like." He looked around and realized Toya had to be in the shower. A yodel from the closed door confirmed it.

Lenny looked up from his project. "Hm?" He spied the three mugs balanced on the tray and grinned. "Thanks, Nix!"

Nix handed it to him, and Lenny took a sip before setting it down and falling back into his obsessive focus at the moment.

"Getting to know you, getting to know all about you. Getting to like you, getting to hope you like me," Toya sang slightly off-key, the steam escaping in puffs beneath the bathroom door.

"That's a new one," Nix said, a bemused expression on his face.

"Oscillator, damned if it isn't the oscillator and this frigging coupling link," Lenny muttered, then frowned. "What?"

"The song," Nix answered, and when Lenny looked confused, Nix clarified, "Toya, she's singing a song I haven't heard before."

Lenny set down the part he was working with, turned toward the bathroom, and listened for a moment as Toya belted out, "Putting it my way, but nicely. You are precisely, my cup of tea!"

He shrugged. "Oh yeah," he said, picking the part up again, "It's from *The King and I*, this musical set in the early 20th century. My mom used to watch musicals with Toya all the time. She thought it would help improve or even repair her language center. And of course, I watched them too, when I was little." He focused back on the task at hand. "Hand me the torque wrench, would you?"

Nix stared at the mess of tools on the bench and pointed. "Um, do you mean this one?"

Lenny groaned. "The red and black one, there on the left. Damn, Nix, even Toya knows what a torque wrench is!"

Nix growled, “Gee thanks, Kid.”

From the bathroom, Toya had segued into something that sounded vaguely like a mix of Latin and English. “Onusday, it blows! Duoday, don’t you know! Triadday, learn from a threesome, Quattroday, isn’t three enough? Quinqueday, don’t we all love kinky? Sexday, what were we talking bout before? Septumday, it’s time to use your nose! Octoday, will this week never end? Novemday, just say no today? Decemday, and finally we’re done!”

Lenny snickered at the look on Nix’s face. “They tried naming the days of the week, all ten of them, in Latin, like just about everything else is on this planet. It, uh, didn’t go so well. The older kids made it into a rhyme and the story goes that the first time a founder heard their kindergartner sing it, they dropped the idea like a hot rock.”

Nix shook his head. “No doubt.” He laughed. “Trust a teenager to come up with something catchy like that.”

“Yeah, by the time the song had circulated, with more risqué amendments added, the Council gave up on trying to get everyone to use days of the week and just settled on the day of the year,” Lenny mused, frowning as he rotated a piece of hardware in his hands. “It seems silly to me. Why bother with days of the week, anyhow? There are sixty-eight weeks in our year and that last short week is a holiday for everyone.”

“Yes, I noticed that when Year Fourteen ended.” Nix sat down on the couch. Toya was recycling some Disney-Pixar tunes from the last decade, and he swallowed a smile. The steam from the shower was escaping underneath the door. “It was one hell of a party.”

“I was too young to join in the fun,” Lenny said wistfully, “And now, well, there isn’t much to party over.” He stopped tinkering and stared at Nix. “No offense, Nix, but why are you here right now?”

“Tiring of me, Kid?” Nix laughed.

Lenny grabbed the mug of Ovaltine and sat down on the couch across from him. He stared at the bathroom door and shook his head. “She takes showers for so long we’ve got mold spots on the ceiling.” He turned back to Nix, stared at him, and said, “Nix, are you going to keep banging Petra or are you going to choose Toya?”

Nix, who had made the mistake of sucking in a mouthful of the hot Ovaltine, choked and sprayed some of it out. "Mother Mary!" He shook his head and wiped down his shirt.

Lenny just stared at him, a slightly bemused expression on his face. "I mean, look, it's up to you. But just tell me, so I can help steer Toya in the opposite direction. She likes you, Nix, and if Petra is more your style, then..."

"God, no." Nix spit the words out, still mopping the Ovaltine off of his shirt. "Damn, Kid, is it that obvious?"

Lenny shrugged. "I dunno. I just know that Petra has been eyeing you like you were a sexy block of man cheese..." He stopped, frowning. "That sounded better in my head. Anyway, since she came to in the Sydney infirmary, she's had her sights set on you. And Toya, well, Toya never listened to anyone the way she listens to you."

"So, what, you want me to be with her so she stays in line?" It was Nix's turn to ask the shitty questions. And Lenny's eyes flew open in shock.

"No! I just don't want to see her get hurt."

"Yeah, well." Nix kicked at the low table between them. "Neither do I."

"You do like her!"

"This is feeling more and more like high school, Kid. Can we stop with the twenty questions now?" Nix growled, practically squirming.

"You think it's wrong, or perverted, or something," Lenny observed calmly, "But you don't know her like I do. She might be brain-damaged, but she's not a kid, Nix. She's an adult. And she knows what she wants." He stole a glance at the bathroom door. The water had stopped, and they could both hear Toya humming away. Lenny leaned close and lowered his voice. "All I'm saying is, if you like her, let her know it. And if you're going to keep bumping uglies with Salinger, then be honest and tell Toya that. She deserves to know."

"Shit, Lenny, are you sure you're only twelve?" Nix felt as if he'd just talked to a cute girl's dad, just without the threats of maiming if said girl were disappointed. Toya, with impeccable timing, walked out of the bathroom just then, wrapped in a towel, a fogbank of steam gushing from the tiny room. She stopped in mid-song when she saw him, blushed, and scampered to her room, slamming the door behind her. He heard Burrito hiss in surprise, no doubt wakened suddenly by the noise.

"See what I mean?" Lenny asked, eyebrows raised. He smiled crookedly at Nix.

"I gotta go." Nix felt an overwhelming urge to run. "Yeah. I'll, uh, I'll catch you later, Lenny." He stood up and headed for the door, suddenly desperate to run the long halls of the Hab and not deal with anyone.

Tensions Rise

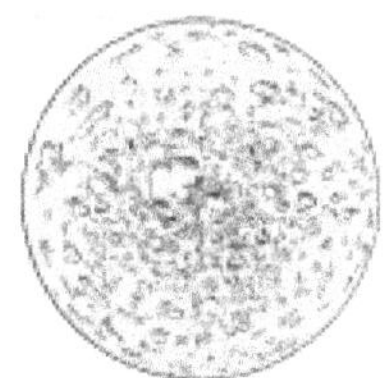

Mars Year 14, Week 63, Day 627
(Earth Date: 04.30.2100)

Their regular tenth-day meeting started off rocky and went straight downhill.

"It is a simple solution with maximum return. I really don't see what everyone's objection to it is." Petra was not taking the news of the Cryo proposal being tabled well. It hadn't been a half Earth year and she was already back on it.

"These nukes you want to drop," Lenny said, his voice sounding thin, strained, "have you considered what they would do to the planet itself?"

Petra glared at him. "The planet is a ball of red dust and rock right now. Hell, nuking it would be an improvement."

Nix watched her face closely. She was angry, far angrier than he had ever seen her. He knew that last night's incident had plenty to do with that.

Lenny frowned. "It's an untested theory that the nukes could produce a chain reaction that would end up creating a sped-up greenhouse effect. And what about the Beijing Science Outpost? They could be within the explosion radius. What if this affects them?"

Petra shrugged and glanced away from the boy. "They're dead anyway, and their government is in ruins. Some damn civil war, from the sound of it," she scoffed. "As if the ESH virus wasn't enough, now the slant-eyes are fracturing into city states like they were before Genghis Khan showed up. As for the team at the Beijing Science Outpost, they have at most another four hundred days of supplies and then it is slow starvation after that."

"We have more than enough to spare, if they run out of food," Abdul objected, his handsome face paling at the thought of the Chinese scientists' fate.

Petra waved her hand dismissively. "The chances they have AB negative blood is so minuscule as to be nonexistent. And if any of us contact them, they'll be dead in forty-five days. There's what, three crew members there at most? It's not enough for a breeding population. Not to mention that they've been radio silent for months now."

"We don't have a breeding population ourselves," James said. "We can't lay down nukes on Mars without taking them into account. It isn't right. Mars is an international property, which means multiple countries have rights. We can't just make that decision without a consensus of all of the occupants, along with Earth's agreement as well. Which they haven't given!"

Abdul nodded. "We have other issues to deal with before we consider bringing out weapons like that. It is a discussion we must have with the future colonists of this planet. The newly formed TUPG is discussing whether to send colonists within the next two or four years. We should wait for them to arrive before unleashing any nukes. To decide that, especially with innocent lives in the balance, is immoral."

"Oh, please," Petra said, and rolled her eyes, "Please spare me any lectures on morality, or is homosexuality suddenly okay with dear Allah?"

James' face reddened and his eyes flashed with an uncharacteristic anger. The Brit had remained unruffled through many horrors, but Petra seemed to bring the worst out in everyone. Abdul's brown skin paled. He bit his lip and stared at the ground.

"That's uncalled for, Petra," Nix said. The woman was never subtle, but calling the two men out was over the line. What he didn't expect was how ready Petra was for a fight.

"Really, Michael? When everyone here is ignoring the fact that you lust after a child in a woman's body?" She cocked her head to one side, her eyes wide with pretend shock. "Hm, does that qualify you as a pedophile? Or just a pervert?"

Nix gritted his teeth and didn't respond. She glared at him, her cheeks red, and a snarl on her lips.

This definitely had the taste of last night's interaction. Nix had tried to avoid her, had avoided her for days on end, but Petra was persistent. When she had cornered him in Food Storage, he had done his best to put her off. She had damn well thrown herself at him, and he hadn't known how to push her away without being a complete ass. His body, however, had surprised them both.

After avoiding her for days, her libido had taken over. She had moved quickly from a warm hand on his hip and lips nibbling on his ear to pushing him against the shelving, before shoving her hand down his pants. That had been Nix's problem, and one that Petra had taken full advantage of. His body always betrayed him.

At least it had until last night. Her long fingers had stroked, rubbed, and her free hand had squeezed his ass–and nothing, nothing had happened. His body had stopped responding entirely to her, and he had been as surprised as she. Her face had alternated between confusion and anger as she tried anything that she could to convince his body to respond to her.

It had been Nix who had finally pushed her away last night, saying, "Stop Petra, just stop."

And now, sitting here today, she was doing her best to air all the dirty laundry. He stood up. "This meeting is over, Petra. We will revisit this later, as we all agreed to late last year." The others followed his movement. No one wanted to be near her right then.

Petra turned crimson. "We are not done here, Nix, not by a long shot." The others were already leaving. Abdul was first through the door, with James following closely behind. Lenny had stood up, looking from Nix to Petra, obviously unsure what to do. He stood there, rooted to the spot for a moment, then skittered towards the hallway.

Nix was thankful that Toya had slept in and not had to see it all go down. She didn't need to hear Petra's hurtful words, and he doubted that Petra would have held back at all in her current state.

Petra's jaw clenched. "We need to talk," she hissed as Lenny disappeared down the corridor.

Nix blinked; Petra's version of talking usually involved vigorous sex. "I really don't think there is anything to talk about, Petra." He stared down at her, watching her pulse jump in her neck.

He could see a flurry of emotions chase themselves across her face. Fury and hurt. He could see now exactly what she had wanted from him. She had wanted far more than just the occasional fun in the sheets. She had wanted a relationship. Nix tried to mask the revulsion he felt at the thought of being with this woman.

Damned if you didn't screw the pooch on this whole situation, Nix.

"Petra, you and me, we are not going to do this anymore. Whatever it was, it's over. I need you to hear that and accept it."

She stood. "You are seriously going to choose a retard over me? What the hell is wrong with you, Nix? Are you so insecure that you prefer the company of the feeble-minded over someone who might have a few more IQ points than you?"

Every time she used those hurtful words, Nix felt his blood pressure spike. He struggled to contain his anger and keep his voice level. "Think what you like, Petra. You make a habit of labeling others, after all. Perhaps you should consider what some of your own labels might be."

Her eyes narrowed. "Oh, let me guess, I'm a bitch. I'm not nice enough. I'm not pretty enough." She said it all in an angry, singsong voice, one that betrayed the river of hurt. She never talked about it–they hadn't had that kind of relationship–but it was obvious she had issues. Part of him wondered what had happened to her; most of him, however, simply did not care.

Her voice changed again, turned hard. "So sorry I'm not a pretty girl who thinks you are the cherry on my chocolate sundae." She pouted then, an obvious affect. "Are you sure you don't want to keep me on the side so you can come by and fuck a real girl every so often, instead of the vacant-eyed little girl who wants you to be her daddy?"

He walked away then. There was no point in saying anything more, and if he stayed, he would likely slap her again.

"This conversation isn't over, Michael! Don't you dare walk away from me!" Petra shouted at his back.

He kept walking. The farther he walked, the deeper his strides. Nix wasn't sure when the walk turned into a jog, then finally into a run, but he found the long windows of the outside hallway spoke of the Hab flash by. He had nearly completed one circuit of Philly when the spoke that led to Eden Hab beckoned him. He turned and continued the ground-eating strides that would take him further and further from the bitter-faced snipe he had made the mistake of getting involved with.

The air was warmer now that the bitter cold of night had given way to the warm sunlight. He passed through the second airlock on the far side of the spoke and slowed as his feet hit the rich humus of regolith and compost.

He could see their lone goat in the distance, grazing on clover, which had been one of the first fields Nix had sown. Clover was easy, and a nitrogen fixer, so it would be excellent for future crops that needed more nitrogen-rich soil to grow effectively in.

Here, with the world turning green around him, he could at least relax a little, surrounded by life, watching as it burst forth from the ground. He seethed over Petra's words. These days, the sight of her, hell, her voice, was like nails on a blackboard.

I caused this. I was the one who got involved with her. Should have kept my dick in my pants.

He paced along the edge of the Hab, striding faster, and finally broke into a run again. There was something about the act of pushing himself physically, until all he could do was focus on breathing and moving, to help the anger melt away. As he followed the edge of the massive dome, he passed the stumps of spokes that led to the Hong Kong, London, and Cairo Habs. Eventually, all the spokes would be finished, and they could move about the entire Huygens Outpost using the long passageways that connected Eden with each of the City Habs. Eden had been intended as the central meeting space of all the City Habs, but it wasn't necessary right now, not with just six survivors. So far, they had only connected the spokes for the Philadelphia and Sydney Habs.

His breaths were regular, deep, as his feet cut through the soft humus. It was harder running in the dirt than it was in the hallways of Philly, but there was more room here and he didn't run the risk of encountering Petra or anyone except for Toya. His anger burned away, and his thoughts turned to focusing on how he would suggest they build a running track along the inside circumference of Eden Hab. It was a perfect place for people to use for exercise and there was plenty of room. He was so engrossed in it and what materials he would need that he didn't notice her until he was almost on top of her.

Toya grinned at him and then grimaced as her shoes dug into the regolith and she struggled to keep up. Nix slowed his pace, and she quickly advanced, settling into a rhythm by his side. Toya said nothing, and all that Nix could hear was their breaths and the sound of their feet hitting the dirt. They did an entire circuit, then half again, before Toya slowed, and Nix slowed to match her pace. They were close to the Cairo Hab spoke when together they slowed to a fast walk and then finally stopped.

"Whew! It's harder running without a pathway," Toya said, gasping.

"Yeah," Nix said, struggling to slow his pulse, "I'm thinking we should build one around the entire circumference of Eden Hab. It would make it easier to run and once Earth sends more colonists; we won't be running them over in the hallways."

He grinned at Toya, and she giggled.

"When are they going to send people here, Nix?"

He shrugged. "Got me. It's not like Earth has an overpopulation problem now, but I imagine that there are still some who want to live on Mars." He glanced at her, tilted his head, and said, "Maybe a cute guy your age?"

Toya frowned as she shook her head and averted her eyes.

"No?" he probed gently.

She shrugged and drug her left foot through the regolith, scattering smaller pebbles that still lay on the surface. "What about you?"

"What about me, what?" he asked.

"Are you hoping for a cute girl your age? Or are you into Petra?" She had lowered her voice, nearly whispering, as if saying the words was painful.

And just like that, what he said next came just as easily as the running had been, the hours they had spent planting together, or even sharing meals. He caught her eyes. "Nah, I know a cute girl already and she sure as hell isn't Petra."

He watched as her fearful expression changed and fell away. She smiled and blushed.

"Really?"

"Yeah, really."

She broke eye contact, stared at the ground, and kicked at the pebbles. "I'm not...I'm not smart."

"Hell, Toya, neither am I. Does it matter?"

"Not to me."

"Yeah, well, not to me, either." He reached for her shoulders and gave her a little shake. "What's in your heart matters more. It's why I can't be with Petra; she doesn't seem to possess one." He said it wryly, and Toya snorted in response. "I like you, Antonia Legares Antes. I don't think you're stupid, or lacking, or, or, or whatever that pathetic excuse of a woman told you."

She stared up at him then, a smile on her lip., "I like you too, Michael Isaiah Nix." She raised up on her tiptoes and kissed him.

I Can Fix You

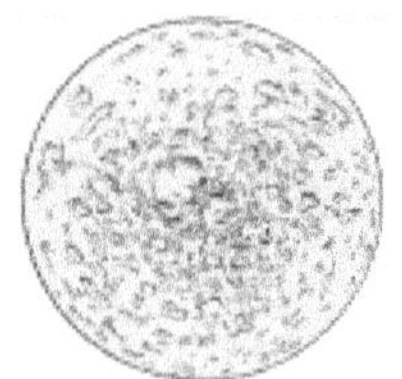

Mars Year 14, Week 65, Day 646
(Earth Date: 05.19.2100)

"The problem isn't technology or supplies," Lenny said in exasperation, "It's people."

The meeting had started off on a grim note, with word that the artificial womb had failed yet again. Only one had been built prior to the outbreak, and it had been hellish to work with.

Of the creatures produced, only one goat, three chickens, and one raccoon had survived. This befuddled James and Nix.

"Funny, that's exactly what I've been saying," Petra pointed out. "With that crew of one hundred new colonists, we could specify *who* we wanted based on our needs. Now that you can't make the artificial wombs work, suddenly you want more people. Funny how that works out."

Lenny watched Nix's face turn red as Petra stared at him and the others smugly.

"It isn't just more people that we need, but certain ones," Lenny continued. "When Calypso was being staffed, they called for tens of tens to join the crew. Brilliant polymaths, capable of multiple specialties. We need more of those. We are all intelligent..."

"Yes, well, *most* of us are," Petra cut in as she stared at Toya. Toya, however, was deeply involved with wrestling her pen from Burrito and didn't notice.

Lenny refused to take the bait. "But we have our specialties. And the artificial womb's specialty is one that none of us have." He ran his fingers through his hair. It was time to cut it again. "If only..."

Lenny looked up, his eyes growing wide. He stood up, his chair clattering to the floor behind him. "I have to go."

He turned and fled from the Mess Hall, his mind awhirl with possibilities he couldn't voice, not yet at least, not until he did some further research. As he left, he heard Petra mutter something under her breath.

Lenny didn't give a rat's ass about what the pinch-faced woman thought of him. His mind was too busy with the answer, one that had been staring him in the face all along. He just needed to dig into the research he had run across in Sydney Hab and see if the prototypes were there and run some experiments first. Once he had done that, he could talk to the group again.

"NARA," he said out loud as he walked down the hall towards the junction that connected to the Family Hab units, "Please raise the environmental controls in Sydney Hab to habitable levels."

NARA's calm voice responded, "Environmental oxygen and heat turned on. Please allow zero-point-five standard hours for it to come to temperature and proper oxygen mix before proceeding into Sydney Hab."

Nix had successfully campaigned for the reduction in power because of the other City Habs not being in use. Although they currently *had* the power, Nix had pointed out that it would help create redundancy in the machinery and allow them to reroute power to Eden Hab, which took a significant amount of power now that it was running at full capacity.

It wouldn't take long for the chill to raise to eighteen degrees or to pipe the oxygen mix in at full strength. Lenny could go now, but he would need a re-breather until the oxygen levels stabilized. He grabbed the re-breather, sent a note to Toya's tablet to let her know he wouldn't be back for several hours, and grabbed a small rucksack. He had hours of fact-checking and research ahead of him, and he paused in the kitchen and grabbed an MRE of chicken cacciatore in case he got hungry. The food stores were still there, but he wanted something nearby so he didn't have to leave. He added a couple of bags of chips and a squeeze bottle of soda and shoved it all into a rucksack.

By the time he made it through the spoke to Eden, then down through the equally long Sydney spoke, the heat and air were functioning and the temperature had risen to 10 degrees Celsius, chilly, but not too cold to work. Lenny passed through the airlocks and into the Sydney Hab, his feet echoing through the empty passageways, carrying him by memory to the Family Hab section.

They had given Jack Durham a Family Hab, despite him not having any children, or even a partner. It was either that or sacrifice half of their laboratory space and add a living space to it.

The old man had been brilliant, and Lenny had been looking forward to his internship, something his mom had arranged shortly before the virus hit the colony. Mom had fought hard for the colony's movers and shakers to accept Lenny, and so had his dad. Just like Toya, he had encountered plenty of difficulty at school. Part of it was the memory of Toya, who had left her mark before the oxygen-deprivation incident. Then there was his own innate curiosity, which seemed to serve him poorly in the structured educational model. It had relieved him when Mom had told him she was going to teach him at home. That had lasted about half of a Mars year, and by the time he was two and a half Mars years, or seven Earth years, Selena had outsourced his education to mentors willing to spend an hour or two every few days answering his endless questions. Jack Durham had resisted Selena's every effort for nearly two Mars years until she had thought to bring Lenny along with her.

"Touch nothing," the old man had snarled at Lenny, and let the two in through the door of his Family Hab. He had taken the smaller of the rooms for a bedroom and turned the master bedroom into a laboratory that spilled out into what should have been the living room. Instead of a couch, there were microscopes, workbenches, and more. He had turned every single wall into whiteboards, covered with sketches and notes, some extending to the ceiling above.

Lenny had nodded, fixed his hands behind his back so that the old man could see he was behaving himself, and walked over to a detailed mathematical equation, studying it with curiosity.

Just as Jack was telling Selena rather irritably that he wasn't taking on any interns since the last one had destroyed nearly a year of research by accidentally tossing out the trash, Lenny interrupted.

"Excuse me, Mr. Durham, but this equation here, I believe it is incorrect."

The old man raised his eyebrows in astonishment, stood up, and walked over. "Show me."

Lenny unclenched his hands from behind his back and pointed with the left. "Here, and over there, you applied the Langcroft Theorem, but you didn't do the same down here. Without it applied in all three locations..."

Jack held up a hand. "Yes, yes, but if you see here, the calculation requires a standard equivalent."

Lenny shook his head. "But not when the first section ends in a constant, according to Dawes' theory of advanced relativity."

The old man gaped at him. "You've read that?"

"Yes, sir. It turned all of my previous calculations on their ear but helped resolve the disparities between Einstein's work and the practicalities of physics on a microscopic level," Lenny answered, hope rising that perhaps the old man would reconsider his previous seemingly stone-hard resistance against mentoring him.

Durham had turned to Selena and asked, "Did you teach him all that?"

Selena smiled ruefully and shook her head. "I couldn't even keep up with the discussion, frankly. Lenny needs a mentor like you, Mr. Durham. He has no place in the local colony school, even in the advanced program where he is waiting on students nearly twice his age to catch up. He's read your three books, and he could be here on your schedule, whenever you have time for him," she said, pressing for a positive response.

Durham returned to staring at Lenny. "Three books, huh? That's funny; they have published only two."

"You already uploaded the third to the colony website," Lenny answered. "It was your work on nanites with an emphasis on repair that had me the most interested. It particularly impressed me to see the tech you used to engineer the recovery and upcycling of the Pacific trash vortex and the six other gyres in the other oceans. The pictures of the floating city that the nanites formed were simply amazing. Have they completed studying the structure enough to allow for settlement yet?"

The old man straightened, clearing his throat. "Shame they didn't approve the project before half of the whales had gone extinct thanks to the plastics damaging their food chain and ecosystem," he growled.

"Yes, sir. That was sad to read about." Lenny had mourned the loss of the blue whale, the great white shark, and a host of other large ocean creatures. It didn't seem fair that now that Earth's oceans were cleaner than they had been in two centuries, those giants were no longer there to experience it. "I was happy to read that a group of Southern right whales have been located recently, though."

"You have read my research, I can see that, but what exactly would you do with nanites, young man?"

"The applications are endless, Sir." Lenny hadn't been ready to blurt it out, not right there in front of Mom. And Jack Durham had sensed that.

The man's eyes had narrowed, and he had looked over at Lenny's mother. "Mrs. Snelling, if you might be so kind as to procure a small list of supplies for me while I speak to your boy here, I will have a better idea if this is a good fit or not."

Lenny had gaped as his mother nodded and left the Hab with a short list of items to request from Food Storage. Mom didn't kowtow to anyone, but Lenny could see the old man was important enough to send Mom on an errand that would get her out of the Hab long enough to have a discussion.

As soon as the door closed behind his mom, Jack Durham had turned towards Lenny, his blue eyes piercing. "This is about your sister, isn't it?"

"Yes, sir." There had been no point in beating around the bush. After all, Jack's third book had introduced the possibility of the application of nanites to repair damaged organs and even the brain.

"You know I'm years away from trials, and that's on the organs, not something as complicated, or as easily traumatized, as the brain."

"Yes, sir."

The old man had regarded him steadily. "How old are you, anyway?"

"Twelve Earth years, sir."

"Born here, weren't you?"

"Yes, sir."

The old man nodded and said nothing, just examined him. Lenny stood up straighter, although that felt equally strange since the old man was short, shorter than his mother, and far shorter than Lenny. By the time Selena had returned with the requested foodstuffs, Jack Durham stood with Lenny in front of a different equation, the old man waving a marker around as Lenny scribbled in an open blank spot on the wall.

Mom had looked panicked when Durham spun on his heel and ordered her and Lenny out. It was only when the door was closing and Lenny heard the old man shout, “Come back in a month. I’ll be ready for you then. Twice a week, mind you!” that Mom’s look of concern had turned into a shocked grin.

“He wants you back? I was sure he was furious with you!”

“He was,” Lenny had assured her. “I corrected his math a second time. But yeah, he said he wanted me back. He’s working on a theory right now, and says when he’s done, he wants me to come by twice per ten-day.”

“I can’t believe it!” She had hugged him with excitement, one that he had returned with enthusiasm. Mom’s persistence had paid off. He was going to figure out how to fix Toya’s brain damage, heck, he was going to reverse it.

And three weeks later, the ESH virus was running loose, uncontained, throughout the colony. Jack Durham had been one of the first to die. And with the old man, Lenny’s hopes for helping Toya had died as well. He hadn’t even thought of Durham until that moment there in the Mess Hall. They needed certain people, ones that could take really complicated problems and find solutions. From everything he had heard about his sister, she was exactly the person they needed.

Just as Calypso’s crew had required “tens of tens”–Toya had been that. In the absence of more colonists from Earth, they had a finite number of people to work with. Toya had possessed the capability to create (or deconstruct) complex machinery before her accident. The ability wasn’t *gone* necessarily, more that it was currently inaccessible. That was what Jack had explained to Lenny while they waited for Lenny’s mom to return.

“Your sister, and all of her formidable talents, are still there, Leonard. It is only the path to those talents that remains obscured. Find the path, retrieve the genius,” the old man had said. And Lenny had been so excited by the thought that he had nearly spilled the beans and shared his dreams with Mom. The words had been on his tongue, but he had kept his mouth shut. Mom didn’t need any disappointments. Not after all the reminders, day in and day out, by the other colonists who still shunned her. If the nanites couldn’t be developed, then who was he to give her false hope?

When he had heard the old man had died, it had felt like someone had slammed a door in his face. Toya would never get better, never be the person she should have been. It wasn’t until he was sitting there, thinking about the people they needed, those who were more like Toya, that he realized he had never given himself enough credit. He had seen several errors in Jack's logic, so was it possible that he could carry on in place of Durham? The man was a genius, sure, but so was he. What was he waiting for?

The hallways lit up as Lenny made his way unerringly to Jack's Hab. There was a black X marked on it, and Lenny paused. Had Jack died inside?

He stood there, frozen in place. He and Toya had been lucky, there hadn't been that many bodies left behind to deal with. Surely, they would have disposed of the body. So why the X? Each City Hab had handled things differently, and Philly Hab didn't have markings on the doors. He paused a moment more, shifted the rucksack from one shoulder to the other, before taking a deep breath, opening the door, and walking in.

There wasn't a body, not even a telltale stain or foul smell. He heaved a sigh of relief and a notification beep sounded. NARA units were located in all the Habs, and she was equipped with face and voice recognition. This helped eliminate crime and it also enabled a person to receive notifications wherever they went. Toya was likely trying to find him, or Nix, thanks to his abrupt departure from the meeting this morning.

"NARA, do I have notifications?" he asked as he set his rucksack down onto a countertop cluttered with parts and dug for his tablet.

"Leonard Snelling, you have a video message from Jack Durham."

Lenny dropped the tablet in surprise. "I do? I mean, NARA, please play video message."

The screen in the living area was part of the wall. Equations covered it, but when the screen activated, they vanished, and Lenny could see Jack's face.

"Leonard, I don't have a lot of time. You and your sister both have AB negative blood, according to your medical records, your chances are good that you will live through this. If so, there's a handful of others, tops, in the colony. Hopefully you get this and can do with it what I couldn't." His face crinkled into a lopsided smile. "I know you can make it work."

Lenny sat down in the nearest chair; his eyes glued to the screen.

"I figured out I had ESH a while back, and I kept putting this message off, hoping things would change, that I'd manage to work out the kinks with the nanites, maybe get them to help me out. But the equations were off, just like you pointed out. Damn, but I hate being shown up by a boy one-sixth my age. I changed those equations, and that added a fifth level of order that didn't seem possible before." He stopped talking, grabbed something from off-screen, and shoved a wad of something into his mouth.

"I ran out of food last night and I don't want them shoving me out of an airlock yet, not when I've got important research to do." He chewed then, swallowing with difficulty, sweat running down his face. "Now look, you need to fine-tune the off switch, along with ordering the nanites to expel themselves through the digestive tract." He paused again, laughed, and said, "It's a hell of a lot easier to crap 'em out than any other means of expulsion. And for God's sake, complete a couple of test runs on animals first...don't go Joseph Mengele on me, you hear?"

He reached for something else off-screen and crammed it into his mouth, sweating profusely now. As soon as he could, he continued, "You'll find all the files under my name and the passcode below the newest equation in red on the far wall." He managed a sideways grin. "I'm sorry we didn't get to work together side by side, Leonard. You strike me as someone I would have enjoyed working with. Keep at it, Son, and good luck to you and your sister."

The screen went black and the equations on the wall returned. Lenny could see the passcode from here; it sounded familiar, but he couldn't place it. He powered on his tablet, accessed the colony's mainframe, and typed:

Username: jackdurham11172021

Password - T1thereisnofateT2!

Lenny pressed the Enter key, and the screen flashed. "Welcome, Jack, it has been 372 days since your last login."

The lists of folders stretched through hundreds of pages according to the info at the bottom, but it was the very first folder listed, with the title, "Leonard - Start Here" that stood out to him. He wanted to cry, scream even. The old man had kept working, right up to the end, and he had left it all, all of it, for Lenny to find. How could he have waited this long to even *think* of the old man? He selected the folder and clicked the download button. The screen flashed, and he sat down and watched the progress bar crawl along the bottom of the screen. It was terabytes of data and, with it, a hope was growing. He could fix Toya, he could. Lenny was sure of it. He'd start with a chicken, maybe the goat, hell, even Burrito. He'd find something, anything, to test these theories out on, and then he would bring Toya back.

He had never seen her be anything other than the Toya he knew. Mom had told him stories, whispering them when his sister couldn't hear, while she was away at school. Mom had never forgiven herself for what happened to Toya and to Toya's dad, even though, if she had been there, she would have been dead too and he would have never been born. Still, he remembered seeing Mom's face as she remembered back to how Toya had been, the intense curiosity, the love of language, and so much more. Lenny was smart, but he was pretty sure Toya had been even smarter. And right now, her smart was just what they all desperately needed.

"I can fix you, Toya," he murmured, as the screen flashed with schematics, diagrams, equations, and pages upon pages of text. "I *will* fix you."

Just a Pinch

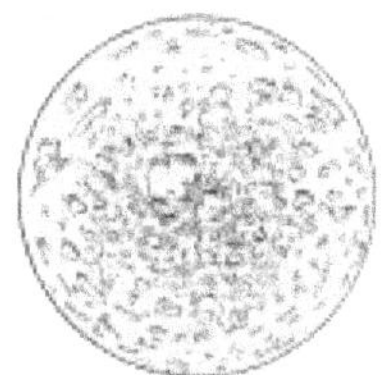

Mars Year 14, Week 67, Day 664
(Earth Date: 06.06.2100)

Lenny studied the data that Jack had left him. There were several points where the old man had left personal notes, pointing out how Lenny's suggestion of reworking the equations had helped him move forward. He had even created several prototypes of nanites on a molecular level, and Lenny's head hurt from taking in all the details. It had been a full Martian week, possibly longer, and Nix's appearance at the door of Durham's Hab startled Lenny. He had fallen asleep in a recliner, his tablet still in his hands, and woke to Nix standing over him.

"Kid, what in the hell are you up to over here?" Nix looked around the cluttered room. "I had to get NARA to tell me where you had gone to. The project you were working on with Abdul is sitting there, unfinished, I've got Petra working on the grid to keep power to here, Philly, and Eden Habs, which means she is bitchier than normal since she can't focus on that new atmo generator she's obsessed over, and now I've got an emergency over at Eden." He tossed up his hands. "Who the hell was Jack Durham, anyway, and why are you here? Tell me this isn't some damn existential teenage crisis, because, frankly, I haven't got time for it right now."

Lenny sat up, rubbing his eyes. They burned. He had seen the sun come up before sleep had finally taken him. "Sorry, Nix. I've been, uh, well, it's research."

Nix grumbled under his breath and turned away to the small kitchen. "Christ, there isn't open space anywhere. You make this mess?"

"Um, kinda. Jack was messy too, but I just was busy, and..." He watched blearily as Nix cleared a space and opened several cabinet doors, surveyed their meager contents, threw up his hands, and headed for the door.

"Well, shit. Kid, you need sustenance." He turned back towards Lenny, looked him up and down, and said, "And a shower, clean clothes, and a pot of coffee." He stopped and frowned, his nose wrinkling. "Come to think of it, I'll go scrounge through Food Storage, you take a shower. You stink something awful there, Lenny."

Lenny would have laughed off Nix's words, but he noticed a rank odor and realized it was coming from him. How long had it been since he showered, anyway? Two days? Three? He didn't argue, just shrugged and headed towards the small bathroom, holding his breath as he stripped off his clothes. They smelled sour.

Half an hour later, a towel twisted around his middle and his hair still dripping, Lenny walked out into the living area, skirting a pile of parts and a large 3D printer, before wedging himself into the one free chair at the table.

A plate of eggs and sausage patties, along with a huge mug of steaming liquid, was waiting for him. Nix, busy clearing the dishes and trash from the kitchen, flapped a hand at him. "Eat something, damn it. Fill your gullet with that shit they call coffee and then tell me what the hell you have been doing for nearly two ten-days. Toya has been nagging me to come find you, Petra is being her normal bitchy self, and James is too busy taking care of Abdul after he got food poisoning yesterday to help. I've also got a sick goat and no working artificial wombs to replace her if she croaks."

Lenny stopped mid-chew. "I've been here *two weeks*? What day is it?"

Nix tossed the last meal tray into the compost and glared at him. "Seriously? It's Day 664." He slammed the compost door shut and pressed the button. "You left the meeting and never came back."

Lenny winced and swallowed the mouthful of food. "Sorry, Nix. Seriously. I lost track of time."

Nix looked up from his rapid cleaning, frowned, and said, "It must have been important then. What's got you ass-deep in research, Kid? Knowing you, it has got to be good."

Lenny stared at the eggs. They were fresh from the hens; nowhere else had he seen such a bright-orange yolk. "I'm not sure I'm ready to discuss it."

He looked up at Nix. The older man stood there; his brow furrowed. He set down the cloth he had been using to wipe off the counter and walked over, cleared a chair of its stack of servos and a stack of diodes, and sat down across from Lenny.

"And now you have my attention." He crossed his arms over his chest, then held up one hand off to the side. "You left a meeting without a word, abandoned a project you have been working on for nearly a year, and came here, to Sydney Hab." He ticked off the points with one hand, a finger for each one. "I looked up Jack Durham while you were in the shower, by the way. He headed the team that cleaned up Earth's oceans a few years back and created a floating city of plastic through the use of nanites. Lately, just before the virus spread through the Outpost, he was researching possible applications for atmospheric changes to Mars using nanites." He stopped for a moment; three fingers extended. "He was also working on a rather interesting project, one in which nanites would have potential uses in organ regeneration and repair." He stared at Lenny. "So, why don't you tell me where you are in your studies and how soon we can attempt human trials?"

Lenny gaped at him. "You figured that all out while I was in the shower?"

Nix rubbed his chin. A stubble of hair was growing there. "I know you want to fix your sister, Lenny." The man had a haunted look on his face. "I love her, you know? Just the way she is. I don't care if she's brain-damaged or not, she's got a heart that, well..." Nix stared at a spot on the table, reached out, rubbed at it. "I just love her. And I know you have been wanting to fix her brain damage and I'm in favor, no matter what happens between us as a result, but just say it out loud, Kid. Be honest with me."

Lenny blinked. "You know she loves you too, right, Nix? That won't change if, no, *when*, the damage is repaired."

Nix smiled at Lenny broadly, but it looked forced. "Of course, I know that, Kid. Look, just tell me how far you've gotten."

Lenny frowned. "I will in a minute, but you said the goat's sick...what's going on?"

Nix's face fell. "She got into something she shouldn't have. Oleander."

"That flower that Abdul was so in love with?" Lenny asked, his mouth falling open.

Nix's expression was rueful. "The same. She broke out of her pen and ate a ton. Turns out it causes breathing issues, what looks like colic, and likely irreversible damage to the heart." He shook his head. "After all the care we took to keep her healthy these past three months, I think she's going to die."

Lenny tilted his head, thinking hard. "I think I can help, and it could double as our first animal trial for the same nanites that could fix Toya."

Hope stole over Nix's face. "You're that close to trials?"

Lenny shrugged. "It wasn't me; it was Jack. And yes, I think I am."

Nix slapped the table. "Well, hell, what do you need to do to fix Bessie? When can you start?"

Lenny laughed. "I thought you named her Curry. Isn't Bessie the name for a cow?"

Nix rolled his eyes. "Your sister insisted on Bessie." He stood up.

"Speaking of, Toya's with Bessie now. She's plenty upset because she was the one who forgot to latch the gate and that's how the damn goat got into the oleander." He rubbed his forehead. "She alternates between being spitting mad at Abdul for asking for the damn plant and furious with herself for not being more careful."

Lenny shoveled the last of the food in his mouth and sipped the scalding-hot drink. He wasn't sure if it was coffee or just very strong tea, but whatever it was, Nix had undoubtedly made sure it had plenty of caffeine in it. "Give me an hour to tweak the instructions and create the commands. I've got a sample of nanites ready and waiting."

"I hope the damn goat has that long," Nix said and headed for the door. "See you in Eden in one hour."

Lenny watched him go, took a few more sips, and felt the caffeine surge through him. It made him jittery, but damned if he wasn't awake now, and with all of two hours, maybe three, of sleep. He reached for his tablet and dug deep into the program, altering the base commands to accommodate for the goat and included the kill switch, before heading towards Eden, the small tube of nanites next to his tablet in the rucksack.

When Lenny arrived, the goat was on its side, gasping for air. She groaned mournfully as she sucked in air and twitched on the ground of Eden Hab. The red soil stained her black and tan hide.

Toya had been crying, and Nix looked grim.

Please let me have been in time.

It was the perfect opportunity, far better than risking the life of Burrito, because if she died, Toya would never forgive him. Besides, there was nothing wrong with Burrito, so the chances of measuring any changes wrought by the nanites would be difficult. Same for the chickens. He hurried over and crouched by the goat's side as she moaned in distress. He reached for the vial and a syringe.

"I'll inject the nanites. They have already been programmed for Bessie's vitals. Just a pinch now, Bessie." The goat didn't seem to notice the needle sliding in as she continued to pant and groan.

"How long will it take?" Nix asked, one hand on the goat, the other rubbing Toya on the back soothingly.

Lenny shrugged. "That I don't know." He opened up the tablet and watched the screen flow with information. The nanites, each of the thousands of microscopic machines with their own job to do, were surging through the goat. "First, they will assess the situation. I'm getting readings now of her various organ functions, along with comparative averages, what they should be at versus what they currently are. Once that occurs, if the nanites need any additional intervention from us, I'll get a message requesting a particular injection; otherwise, they go to work."

"How small are they?" Nix asked, fascinated.

"Inside of each nanite are a thousand smaller ones, the level of microbes. But they are all on a kill switch, which really isn't a kill switch per se, more of a 'time to evacuate the host' kind of thing."

Nix frowned and asked, "What does that mean?"

Lenny grinned. "It means that I'll need you to collect Bessie's poop."

"What?"

Toya giggled then. Her face dissolved into mirth. "Poop! They're in the poop!"

"Well, they will be," Lenny added, struggling not to laugh with Toya. Was he imagining it, or was Bessie already breathing better? "They run through their assignments, and when the identified affected organs are within 80% of their functional capacity, then the nanites automatically enter the digestive system and, well, nature runs its course. They should head for the intestinal tract, and the RFID transmitters will allow me to track their progress." He stared at the tablet in his hand. "Right now, there are groups centered in the heart and the lungs, and there's another smaller group already heading for the intestines."

The goat had stopped groaning.

"Christ, they are quick," Nix commented, still petting the goat. He was staring at the creature, transfixed at the noticeable progress. "How in the hell can they do that?"

Lenny shrugged. "Imagine all of our medical knowledge downloaded into a computer that operates on the molecular level. Jack's work, it would have changed the way we practice medicine."

Nix stared at him. "You did this, Lenny, not Jack Durham."

"I simply put into practice the theories he had been closing in on. I looked at it with a fresh set of eyes, sure..." Lenny hitched his shoulders, uncomfortable with Nix's praise. "...a few tweaks here and there." He glanced up at Nix and continued, "We all stand on the shoulders of giants, Nix. Without the work that has gone before, none of this would have been possible."

"Damned if I don't know that, Kid–we're sitting on the surface of Mars, after all. But don't sell yourself short." He glanced down. "She's breathing better, isn't she? It isn't just dreaming on my part."

Toya nodded. "She stopped making those awful sounds." She looked up. "Lenny, what else can the nanites fix?" Her voice was wistful, as if she was afraid to ask.

Lenny felt a surge of fear. What if he was wrong? What if the nanites couldn't repair the damage? He looked away, focusing on his screen. The nanites continued to move through the goat and he was watching the creature's organs regain functionality. The heart had been at just 45% efficiency a few minutes ago, and now, now it was at 62% and rising, the numbers continuing to tick upwards.

His fingers ran across the keypad.

"What are you doing now?" Nix asked, his voice loud in the silence. The goat was no longer groaning; instead, Bessie was silent. Her sides rose and fell with regularity, her breathing smooth.

"Adjusting the kill switch levels to 90% from 80%," Lenny answered. "I was being overly cautious, and I want to make sure she's almost fully recovered before the nanites head for the exit."

“Lenny?” He raised his eyes to Toya’s steady gaze. “Can the nanites fix me?”

Lenny fought the battle inside of him, the one side that wanted to give his sister this. The other side knew just how very different the brain was from an organ. You could replace an organ, but you couldn’t replace a brain.

“Give me a little while to figure that out, Sis, okay?” The look of disappointment on her face hurt him. It twisted his guts around. “Brains aren’t like organs, not really, so this is a good first step.”

“Okay.” Her voice was sad, and Lenny fought a wave of guilt. He couldn’t just inject a bunch of machines into his sister, no matter how much he wanted to make her better. He had months of research ahead of him. Somehow, he would figure it out; somehow, he would make his sister better.

Watching the goat slowly stand up and walk away from them an hour later was still a highlight. With Jack’s research, and his own tweaks, Lenny knew he could make a difference and, soon, in Toya’s brain. Those damaged areas...he could teach the nanites to re-lay synapses and create new connections, he was sure of it. And when he completed his research, Toya could finally return to the brilliance that was her birthright. And right now, that kind of brilliance was exactly what they all needed.

Dragon Boat

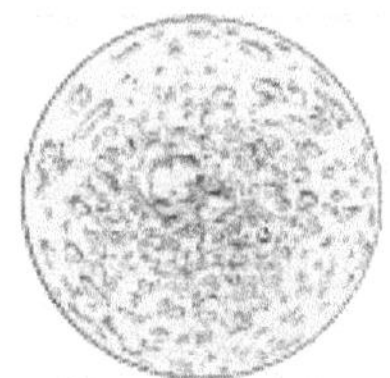

Mars Year 15, Week 02, Day 012
(Earth Date: 07.02.2100)

Liu awoke to Huan banging a pipe on the floor. At age 300 days, approximately eight Earth months, Huan was already on the verge of taking his first steps. Perhaps it was the lower gravity of Mars that sped up the walking process, or simply that Huan was advanced; Liu wasn't sure which. Nevertheless, it had caused a move back to a bunk room. Huan had a dangerous fascination with the pond in the garden Hab but lacked the common sense to stay out of it.

Liu swung his legs over the edge of the bunk and Huan turned and smiled, his tiny face lighting up as he burbled a greeting in Liu's direction. He dropped the pipe he had been holding and crawled over, his bare feet barely showing past the edge of the simple outfit Liu had sewn for him. The back of the outfit was wet, and Liu sighed. He would need to sew some more. Huan had grown dramatically in the past few months, and Liu struggled to keep up with the laundry and clothing needs of a now-ambulatory baby. The ever-present red dust had stained Huan's hands, knees, and even parts of his face. No matter how much Liu cleaned, it was there, on the floors, and, ultimately, on the baby.

It doesn't hurt him, so I should stop being so obsessive over it.

Liu picked his son up and kissed him, his fingers running along the baby's sides until Huan rewarded him with a host of chortles and squirms.

He smiled at Huan, avoided the wet seeping from his back end, and made a note to sew several onesies in the next few days. It was warm enough that Huan could go without for a while, but without the simple cloth covering his wrappings, he had taken everything off. The mess that resulted from that was enough to make a grown man cry. Liu had cried, multiple times, which seemed better somehow than retching and causing a worse mess.

It had taken a Mars week of silence from Mission Control, where each of his transmissions met with no response, before he had thought to look for the communications satellite in the sky. He had seen nothing. There was no familiar light passing overhead, and none of the queries he had made to the mainframe he expected to be orbiting 36,000 kilometers above him in space received any response.

Later, far later, he had thought to go back through the records. There had been a meteor shower shortly after Huan's birth. Sure enough, the electronic signal from the communications satellite had stopped, abruptly, at the height of that shower. Liu realized then that it wasn't unrest, or a coup, at Mission Control–no one was receiving his signal because the satellite he depended on as his sole means of communication was no longer there.

He couldn't reach Earth to tell them about the planet killer heading towards them. He couldn't warn his home world of the terrible danger they were in.

Mars didn't have the large number of satellites that Earth did, and the mission planners had failed miserably in anticipating the ability of a random meteor shower to take down a vital piece of equipment like the Tongxin satellite. Combine the lack of foresight from Mission Control to share technology with Huygens Outpost and it was a recipe for disaster.

Whatever the object had been, it had torn apart the small satellite, and with it, ripped away Liu's lifeline to Earth. How ironic was it that it had happened just days after Huan was born?

After he realized that there was no way to talk to Earth, he had fallen back into a haze of depression. It hadn't lasted long, not in the face of Huan's needs. His son showed him every day how necessary Liu was to his survival and how important it was that he snap out of it, give his little boy what he needed, and move forward.

As he peeled off the soaking-wet fabric, along with the layers of swaddling underneath, Liu thought about the future.

I need to figure out my next step.

Huan chortled and wiggled. A row of tiny teeth, shiny and white, brightened his smile. He had been cranky, so cranky, for the past ten days, as the teeth pushed their way through the gums. Now that they were all the way clear, Huan had returned to his normal, happy self.

Transitioning him to solid food had been challenging, and Liu was fascinated to see how clear Huan's likes, and dislikes, for certain foods were. He had assumed that babies were empty vessels, and that one's food preferences were based on what you were raised eating, rather than personal taste. Huan had disproved this theory, over and over.

After he cleaned and covered the baby, Liu set Huan down on the floor to crawl and explore while he began to wash the clothes in the small sink. The water stores, despite the high usage in the past few months, were still more than adequate.

One of the first tasks the first team had accomplished upon landing on Mars was to drill deep into the regolith. Just as the scans had shown, a large, semi-frozen lake was deep below the surface. It had been easy enough to insert warming coils that melted the clean, pure water enough to pipe up into the station. That same water also led to unlimited amounts of oxygen generation, thanks to simple electrolysis. They siphoned off the water, passed an electric current through it using the solar panels to generate the power, and the system was simple and, thanks to the massive underground lake, endless.

Despite this, he still felt as if he were doing something wrong. Water was possibly the single-most important resource on the planet, and Huan's needs for diapering caused a great deal of water usage. Any time that he thought about even attempting to travel to Huygens Outpost, three enormous obstacles stopped him short.

One, his and Huan's lack of exposure to the ESH virus. Anyone they came into contact with there at Huygens could spread the ESH virus to them and, as far as Liu knew, there still was not a cure.

Two, the act of simply getting there, of being able to convert and maintain a vehicle intended solely for short-range trips into one that could carry them safely, as well as have enough food and water stored inside to last them the full journey.

Three, figuring out how to care for an active, curious baby all day, every day, as he slowly made his way across over 5,400 kilometers to arrive at his destination.

The three questions swirled in his head, occupying a significant amount of his attention, every day, as it had for the past thirty Mars weeks. Interspersed with that was the simple act of living, with a small baby, no less. Huan took up nearly 100% of his focus. The baby was Liu's reason for waking up each morning, and the Huan's rhythmic breaths lulled him to sleep at night.

He had spent countless hours painting the halls of the Hab with murals–images of Chen and Fen, but also his parents, Fen's sister Shu, whose image he had found on Fen's tablet, her arms full of two smiling children.

He had food enough for at least seven more years with Fen gone and Huan not requiring the full calories of an adult. Without the fear of running out of food, and faced with limitless energy, oxygen, and water–Liu focused on caring for Huan. When he wasn't doing that, he was creating art and working on the bigger problems of travel and how to make the trip to Huygens Outpost.

He had to warn Earth. Even if it meant risking being infected with the ESH virus.

Each morning he ran checks from the Control Room, making sure all the systems were running as intended, that there were no major atmospheric leaks or degradation of the seals on the airlocks. Most of it remained automated, but he started there, stepping through the mini-airlock into the large room, reviewing the reports, and then moving through the station, examining each of the outer rooms and noting if there were any changes, discolorations, or cracks in the walls and windows.

It was all heavily lined, even the windows, with a transparent substance that served much as lead would, blocking the radiation from the sun where Mars' weak atmosphere did not. Without it, the astronauts would have received far higher doses of radiation than anyone, even the Chinese government, was comfortable with. With the lining in place, they were safer from radiation than people on Earth were when out for a walk on a sunny day.

He had followed the same path down the corridors, carried on the same routine for so long, that when his mind came up with a solution, he stopped in mid-stride, frozen between the hallway and the Control Room. His left hand was on Huan's back, where the baby hung against him in a sling. His right hand was on the inner half of the airlock. It was a smaller space, but not so small that a man in a full suit couldn't stand in between the two airlocks.

An airlock. We could take the entire Control Room, detach it from the science station, and load it with its double airlock on the skids built into the back of the larger rovers. I could operate the rover remotely inside of it. And I would have an airlock I could go in and out of if it was absolutely necessary to access the rover externally for any reason.

He gaped, his eyes locked on it, and Huan gabbled and kicked his bare legs as they stood there, unmoving. "Bah, bwah!"

"I know how we can go there, to the Outpost," Liu said, looking down at Huan. The baby smiled widely up at him in response. "I had been thinking about it all wrong. I kept trying to figure out how I would drive there with me in the front and you in the back."

"Bah, gwah!" Huan said, kicking again, as if in agreement.

"Instead, I just need to program it like NASA once did with the first automated rovers it sent down. Teach it to auto correct, avoid obstacles, and as long as we take it slowly, I can just operate the rover from inside of the Control Room."

Huan gurgled his agreement and kicked again, grunting a little now, a look of concentration on his face. Liu grimaced...that only meant one thing.

A few minutes later, he was proved right. As he changed the wraps that covered Huan's nether regions, the baby wiggled and kicked, cooing and gurgling proto-words. "Baba, baba."

Liu looked up from his calculations of how much space they would take up with the food stores and water. He beamed at his son. "Yes, Huan, I am your Baba!"

Losing Fen overshadowed the first days, even weeks, of Huan's life. Liu missed her in ways he didn't know were possible. In some ways, it had felt as if Huan had taken her from Liu, stolen her life in exchange for his own. Now that he had spent weeks upon weeks, three quarters of an Earth year, actually caring for Huan, Liu felt different. His mission, his reason for life, was in being the best father Huan could have. Nothing else in his life had compared to that.

Liu wished his parents could see him now. And that he could tell them how right they were. No wonder they had pushed him to marry! He missed

Fen, though, every day, in every way, and saw her features in Huan. In some ways it made him love Huan more, and other times, well, he wasn't perfect.

The important thing he needed to keep in mind was that he could make the journey with Huan. Once they arrived at the colony, Liu could connect into the Hab airlock if he wanted. International cooperation had insisted on standard sizes and equipment early on, a fact which he was quite thankful for now, in the middle of a Chinese civil war and worldwide catastrophe. If there were any survivors in Huygens, he would find them.

Over the next thirty days, Liu found his skills tested several times. He had only tinkered with remote control programming in secondary school, as an after-school hobby, and he had been on a team with several others. Here he was on his own. It took a while to program the various scenarios into the autopilot. What to do if there was an unexpected obstacle, a sudden decline or incline he hadn't expected when he plotted the journey back when Fen was pregnant? Liu also needed to anticipate the amount of water he would need to carry or collect along the way in order to survive, how much fuel he would need to power the rover, and how to produce enough oxygen using the MOXIE unit he scavenged from the shuttle. He would also need to figure out how to store enough food for the journey, along with basic living supplies. He estimated that they could travel approximately ten hours a day at a sedate 17 kilometers per hour. Between the solar panel contributions and the fuel provided by the MOXIE, they could trundle along all day before needing to stop. Otherwise, they wouldn't have enough power to supply heat as the temperatures plunged into the negative digits. The MOXIE unit would also allow them just enough oxygen that, unless he took up jogging in place, they would have more than enough to survive. At least, as long as there was enough water.

Enough water, that was the big unknown. Prior to setting up the base, there had been extensive scans for water sources by Beijing Mission Control. Gale Crater had proved to be an excellent source; the scans had shown that it was on the edge of a large, underground aquifer. The underground water sources on Mars were well known, having been scanned repeatedly over the past eighty years. However, it was one thing to know there was water there, and an entirely another to access it. He couldn't take the large machinery they had used to access the aquifer near Gale Crater, but he could take a smaller unit and had already figured it into his weight limits. However, there were limits in how deep it could drill, which led to further research on which of the scanned and verified water sources he could access and how long he would have to get to the next site before running into issues.

Liu pondered each additional problem in between caring for Huan and maintaining the station. Their very lives were at stake. One or two missteps would be survivable, but the reality that he was on a planet with no breathable atmosphere, one that was fatal with just one breath, one hole in his suit or a crack in the Hab walls, was never far from his mind. If only China had created a land rover that could handle long distances, like Huygens had, the circumstances would be different.

Liu shook his head. There was no point in dwelling on could have been–he had to deal with the hand he was dealt.

We could stay here; perhaps things will improve.

The thought would surface regularly, but he knew better. Without contact with Mission Control on Earth, and without being able to understand anyone on Huygens Outpost, he was alone. If he waited too long, then it would be too late to do anything at all. The small shuttle that could take them to the Mazu and ultimately back home operated at gees that he feared would hurt, if not kill, Huan. Not to mention that his son had developed here on Mars, at a fraction of Earth's gravity.

What would his life be like if we returned? Would Huan spend his days in a wheelchair or in pain? No, he was born here, and here he will stay.

He was washing the soiled wraps while Huan babbled at his feet, gumming a strip of cloth and playing with small fabric- and cardboard-edged mirror, when the solution to where to find the shallow water sources struck him.

The plants, I need to follow the plants. Why didn't I think of it before?

Twenty years before humans had set down on Mars, the Mars landers had begun the long and complicated process of terraforming Mars. They had begun with constructing the enormous mirrors in space. In another three, perhaps seven years, the mirrors would warm the poles enough to turn the ice to slush, and eventually the red planet would see water flow again through its valleys. Other automated devices had been in charge of the greening of Mars by seeding the regolith with plants found in the coldest regions of Earth, the artic tundra. Caribou moss, bearberry, tufted saxifrage, and eventually even Labrador tea and arctic moss, once the water was flowing. The Seeders had spent the past thirty-five years slowly traversing the equator, seeding it with billions of samples of several plants known to survive under the coldest of conditions. It had resulted in a patchy, green band of life, one that thrived on the heavy concentrations of CO2. The plants could serve as an excellent indicator of water stores near the surface of the soil. All Liu would have to do would be to follow the plants; they would help him find the water they so desperately required.

His shout of glee surprised Huan, and the baby dropped the mirror and stared up at him, eyes round. Liu reached down and picked the baby up, a smile on his face. "I've solved it, Little One, and I know just how we will make the journey!" Huan gurgled with delight as he placed his tiny hands against Liu's face and patted his father's cheeks gently.

Ten days later, the rover re-engineered with remote controls, extra parts, and equipment backed up slowly to the Hab and gently connected with the Control Center, lifting it and then sliding it onto the wide base. At some point, in the detailed planning that had gone into the Beijing Science Station, an engineer had made sure that this could be a possibility.

They couldn't have imagined such a long journey, however, or the additional weight requirements of the water, fuel, backup parts, and more, but the rover would serve the two of them well. Liu packed the food supplies in so they doubled as furniture in their small, yet efficient living space. The wide front window screen was now to the left, the only way the Hab would fit on the skids of the rover. It meant that Liu would have to depend on the outside cameras if he wanted to see where they were going. He had it fully automated, however, using the same technology as the autocars which had swept through the world, becoming the preferred manner of transport over the past two decades.

Liu's thoughts drifted to Chen, and Chen's poor, doomed wife and child, and he reminded himself that what had happened there was beyond the ability for the autocar, much less a human driver, to expect. Accidents still happened, and people still died, but the statistics since autocars showed a sharp decrease in vehicular deaths. He would be safest letting the rover operate under its own controls.

Once Liu mounted the control center with Huan safely inside, Liu set the radio transmitter to repeat his message at one-minute intervals. Right now, it might not be loud enough, but as they drew closer, he hoped someone on Huygens would answer and warn Earth. The sooner Earth knew, the better. It would take years for the asteroid to reach Earth, but it would also take years for them to prepare for such an event. He wanted to make sure they had all the time possible.

He walked through the main hallway, his suit on but his helmet open. He stared for a moment at Fen on the mural. In it, she was smiling, a tiny version of Huan cradled in her arms, the baby staring wide-eyed into her eyes. He preferred to visit her here, rather than her grave. It was here that she felt most alive to him, other than when he looked into Huan's face.

"Your son, our son, is growing, Fen," he said aloud to her image. "I wish that you could see him. He is walking now. And he is so very intelligent. Words will come soon." He paused, his eyes filling. "I will tell him all about you. And someday, someday we will return here, and he will come to see how beautiful his mother was." The serene expression on her face wavered, warped by his tears. Only silence greeted him. He could hear the low hum of the fans as they continued to work. The environmental controls would continue to maintain the temperature, the lighting, and more in his absence. Even the fish in the pond would survive and likely multiply. He could hear his voice echo through the empty hallway. This base was meant for more than just the three of them. They were supposed to have been the first of many. Now there would be no one. The place felt desolate and lifeless. Liu closed his helmet, took one last look at Fen's face, and headed out the airlock. Huan was waiting, and they had a long journey ahead of them.

Is There Anybody Out There?

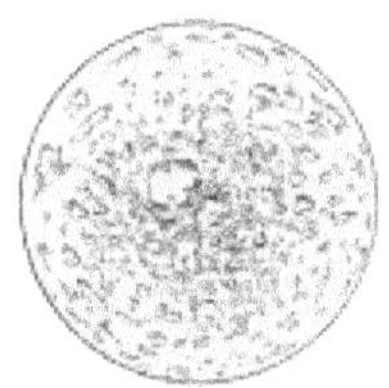

Mars Year 15, Week 05, Day 042
(Earth Date: 08.01.2100)

At night, the Hab was not silent. The fans cycled the air, a gentle hum that had long faded into the background and was only noticeable when they failed to turn on. There were a host of machines that ticked and clicked, all essential to their survival on the red planet. All of their noises were expected, and Toya, along with the others, had grown so used to hearing them, that she would have only noticed when they were absent.

But this sound was far different. It woke her from her deep sleep, a tinny crackle of a voice, and drew her down the hall. She pushed aside the covers and got up from her bed. Just a handful of steps took her out of the room into the living area of the Family Hab. Lenny was asleep at his desk in his room. His door was open and a small desk lamp still shining, but he didn't move. Burrito was nowhere to be seen, but then again, it was the middle of the night. She was likely exploring or causing havoc. Recently she had eaten most of a crop of strawberries and it had outraged Abdul. She didn't know what a strawberry soufflé tasted like, but after seeing the damage Burrito had done to the fruits, she wasn't going to enjoy it anytime soon.

What was it she had heard? Just as she was ready to dismiss it as a dream, it began again. The voice speaking words that were familiar, yet not. As if speaking to her from a distant memory. The voice issued from a small speaker in the living room, where another of a dozen of Lenny's half-finished projects lived. She sat down on the couch and listened to it again. "Hoohan Dee-cho. Shway nung ting wuh shwuh. Yo yee guh sheeow sing sing sheeow hung chow goo chowng ye deech yo."

The speaker was male, she could tell that much. But the rest? Toya felt frustration rising. Why must there always be the reminder she had been more? She *remembered* being more. The years had passed, but the feelings and the memories remained. It was as if the roads in her brain suddenly went from highways to dead-ends following The Event, as Mom had called it. The roads were all still there, paths that she could walk along, understanding something until, BAM, the road ended, and it left her with the overwhelming suspicion that if she just tried harder, the road would reappear and with it, her knowledge.

When she was younger, she would get so frustrated. She would end up crying, even screaming. It had been so hard. She had memories of understanding these things, the foreign words that tripped off of new colonists' tongues. She had known those words once. But now, they were all muddied up and confusing. In her dreams, she often swam in rivers that turned thick, muddy, once-clear water turning into sludge, difficult, if not impossible to make progress through.

She had described the dreams once to Mom, who had nodded and told her, "Dreams are a lot like reality, honey. Often they center on what we struggle with the most." She had hugged Toya to her. "Your dream of swimming through water that turns to mud, it's a lot like your struggles to learn. What you need to do is keep swimming, no matter how thick the mud gets. Keep swimming, baby, just keep swimming."

The voice stopped, and a moment later, it began again. "Hoohan Dee-cho. Shway nung ting wuh shwuh..." Toya tried focusing on the sounds. She had known so many languages before The Event, now any non-English word was simply an echo of a memory. Familiar, but elusive. Sometimes, when she sat and thought about it long enough, she would imagine that the damaged part of her brain was smooth, with no bumps or folds, a smooth blankness. Her understanding, her capability to understand, ironed flat in that place, and the path through it obscured.

She stood up and walked into Lenny's room and shook him. "Lenny, wake up, your radio is talking."

"Mmhm, okay," Lenny mumbled, burrowing deeper into the crook of his arm, away from the light.

"Lenny, wake up." She shook his shoulder more violently. "The radio!"

His head shot up and cracked against the cabinets overhead. "Ow, damn! Sheesh, Toya, what are you doing here, anyway?"

She had started the night out at Nix's, like most nights. "Petra showed up, got him all mad, and he told me to go back here." Toya's face flushed. "He says he doesn't like her like that anymore, but why did he send *me* away?"

Lenny groaned. "That woman is a nasty piece of work. Don't sweat it, Toya. Nix likes you and don't you forget it."

"I don't know why. I'm stupid compared to Petra."

Lenny hugged her. "There's more than just smart and stupid in the world, Toya. You've got something Petra will never have."

"What?"

"A heart. And that's why Nix wants you, not Petra."

The voice started again. "Hoohan Dee-cho..."

Lenny's head swiveled towards the living room. "What was that?"

"I told you, your radio is talking. But I can't understand the words."

Toya followed Lenny as he ran into the living room. "It sounds like words I used to know, but..." She shrugged. "But I can't seem to make sense of them."

Lenny listened intently until the end and then said, "It's Mandarin, I think. But that's the best I've got. I wonder why he's broadcasting."

Toya frowned. "Do you know him?"

"Well, no, but he's got to be from the Beijing Science Outpost. There's three of them there, according to the mission leader, Chen. I haven't heard a word from them in months, heck, longer than an Earth year." He frowned. "I don't even know what to say in response. Is this guy even broadcasting to us?"

Toya wasn't sure if Lenny was asking a question or just thinking out loud. He did plenty of thinking out loud, as he continued researching the nanite applications. Bessie had fully recovered thanks to the nanites, and they had walled off the oleander bush so it wouldn't happen again.

The voice repeated, "Hoohan Dee-cho. Shway..."

Lenny reached out and grabbed the transmitter, tapping his foot until the end of the transmission and then pressing the button down. "Hello, Beijing Science Outpost, are you reading me?"

Toya watched her brother as he tapped his foot impatiently, waiting for a response. A moment later, the voice sounded again, the same words, intonation, and Lenny snapped, "Damn it, it's got to be a recording. But why record it in Mandarin?" he asked aloud, staring at her. "Who is it for?"

"I studied Mandarin," Toya stated, but Lenny seemed to think it was a question.

"Yeah, that's what Mom said. You recognize any of the words?" he asked, his eyes brightening.

"Nope." Being stupid sucked. "I mean it sounds familiar, like something I used to know, but..." Toya's words dwindled away and they sat in silence until the recording began again. She watched her brother turn the volume down. "I hate being stupid."

"You aren't stupid, Toya," Lenny said. "You have brain damage."

Toya held back a scream of frustration. "So, fix it. Stick those nanites into me and tell them to fix me, Lenny!"

"I want to, but..."

She turned away. For months now, he had been giving her excuse after excuse and she was tired of it. "You don't. You keep saying you want to, but you don't, Lenny."

"Toya! That's not true!" She turned back and watched as he rubbed his eyes, his shoulders slumped. He sat down on the sofa. "I need to make sure I don't hurt you somehow, or make it worse."

Toya felt tears gathering in her eyes. "I'm willing to take a chance. Petra is right, I'm useless."

Lenny winced and shook his head. "See, that woman is just a jealous, mean bitch. It's no wonder Nix sent you back here. You don't need to hear anything she says, Sis. She hates you because Nix sees the real you, not some damaged lump." He ran his hands through his hair. "This isn't the time for this, but seriously, Nix loves you. I know you and me used to argue all the time, and yeah, you have had your moments–hell, so have I–but it doesn't matter how smart you are."

Toya sat down across from her brother and glared at him. "It's been almost two months, Lenny." She bit her lip. "I want to help. If my brain worked right, I'd be able to tell what he was saying, wouldn't I?"

Lenny's gaze slid away. "Yeah, probably. I just want to perform a couple more tests, and..."

"And what?" Toya asked, pressing. "Is it because I'm too stupid to understand, or that you're scared it won't work?"

"You're not..."

"Stupid. Right, you said that," Toya interrupted, tossing her hands in the air. "You can't do human trials on anyone else, Lenny. I'm the most useless person here, remember?"

"Stop it, Toya. Stop repeating the awful things that woman said to you."

Toya leaned forward. "I will, just as soon as you help me." She met his eyes. "What was it you said to the goat? 'Just a pinch'?" She shoved her sleeve up. "I want to be smart again, Lenny. You weren't there, but I *remember* it. I remember how it felt just like I know how I feel now. I think I'm getting it, understanding an idea, and then it's like a river of mud, walls instead of doors. I hate it." Tears were forming in her eyes.

She had been waiting, patiently. Why couldn't her brother see that? All of this time, waiting for something to change, for him to turn to her and say he was ready. Instead, all she got were non-answers.

He was staring at his hands. "It's ready."

"What?"

"The program for the nanites. The one for you. It's ready," he said it again, louder, and looked up. "I didn't tell you because, well, because there's a risk and I'm scared, Toya. I'm scared of something going wrong and losing you, and I'm scared of what Nix would do if I did something that really hurt you."

Toya sucked in a deep breath. "Lenny, go get your nanites and your tablet and inject me now."

He blinked. "It's the middle of the night."

"Now, please." She was ready. Since he had first talked about the nanites, and as she had seen it work in the goat, she had known it had to work for her. It would. The waiting, all the waiting. "Now, Lenny. Please." She stared at him, torn between pleading with him and screaming.

Lenny nodded slowly and got up. "Okay, but I really think I should get Nix."

Toya grinned, and a fierce joy surged through her. "Let's surprise him."

Lenny stared at her. "He's going to kill me."

"I won't let him."

He called out, "NARA, lights please." The room lit up, and they both blinked in the brightness.

For all that he had been studying, all that these supposed miracles workers were, the vial was as small as the one he had brought to the goat. He set the syringe down next to it and turned on his tablet.

Toya gulped; she hated needles. Lenny caught the look on her face. "You sure you want to do this, Sis?"

"Yeah, even if it means a shot." She took a deep breath. "Go ahead."

"Okay." He loaded the syringe and checked his tablet. "I got thirty thousand nanites ready to do their jobs." He reached over and inserted the needle into her arm.

"Ow! Shit, Lenny! That hurt!" She rubbed the injection site. It felt cold, ice cold.

Her brother's eyes were fixed on her, watching her intently. "How do you feel?"

"How do I...oh wow." The sensation of cold had flashed through her entire body and now she felt nothing. "I felt cold and now I don't, but I can't shake the feeling that I have bugs crawling through me," she said, her skin prickling into goosebumps.

Lenny grinned. "Well, we always have creatures on us and in us. Without them, we wouldn't live. But I can understand how you feel." He glanced down at his tablet. "They're clustering in the cerebrum, near both the Broca's area and the Wernicke's." His voice petered off as he continued to stare at the readouts. He looked up again. "Still okay?"

Toya frowned; she felt strange. The room seemed to turn and warp. The fingers of her right hand curled, shaking, then jerking. She tried to stand and immediately fell back. "I, uh..." Words left her and the light in the room seemed to first dim and then extinguish, leaving an utter blackness in its wake. She was out before she hit the floor.

"Toya? Toya!"

Lenny watched in horror as his sister's hands and arms trembled and shook, the muscles of her hands, arms, legs, and even her toes twisting and contorting. She fell to the floor, her head banging against the carpet and the side of the chair.

"NARA, issue a Code Blue and wake everyone up. I need help!" Lenny cried out and rushed to Toya's side. Even the tendons in her neck were standing out as her entire body continued to flail and convulse. Nix was first through the door, although it felt like an eternity as Lenny fought to put something soft under Toya's skull. James, with Abdul close behind, was next, and finally Petra slunk in, her eyes red, her face full of resentment.

"What the hell is going on?" Nix asked. "Has she ever had a seizure before?" Lenny couldn't force the words out of his mouth. He had slipped a cushion under her head and Toya continued to shudder, her body twisting in unnatural ways. Nix's eyes fell on the syringe and the familiar vial and tablet. "Lenny, what did you do?"

Lenny could see the fear in Nix's eyes. "She begged me, Nix. She said she was willing to take the chance." He faltered, words deserting him.

Nix pushed him away from Toya and pulled her against him. "So help me, Lenny, if anything happens to her, if she doesn't come out of this, I'm holding you responsible."

"At least she was good for digging and planting, even cleaning," Petra muttered. "Now she'll probably end up as a vegetable. Congratulations, you made her completely useless, as if she weren't already a burden."

Nix turned his wrath in her direction. "You, Petra, this is your fault," he growled, fury distorting his face.

Petra's eyebrows shot up. "Me?" She laughed. "Exactly how do you think I'm to blame?"

"You tell her she's stupid, that she's worthless," he snarled. "How small of a person do you have to be to treat her like that?"

Petra's face paled, and her jaw worked, the muscles tightening. "I just..."

"You're just a pathetic woman who drove away your lover and likes to spread your insecurities on young, susceptible women," came a quiet voice behind her. Abdul stood there, staring at her dispassionately, while James moved into the room and knelt beside Nix.

Petra stepped away, closer to the door. "Well, I know when I'm not wanted," she said, tight-lipped. She turned and disappeared from sight.

James put a gentle hand on Toya's wrist. "NARA, vitals on Antonia Antes, please."

NARA's gentle tone issued over the room's speakers. "Blood pressure, elevated. Pulse, elevated. Patient is experiencing a grand mal seizure. I advise admittance to the nearest health care facility."

"Yeah," Nix growled, "No shit." He leveled a stare at Lenny that made the teen's blood run cold. "What in the hell, Lenny?"

Lenny's voice shook. "I'm sorry, Nix. She heard a transmission from the group at Gale Crater. It's, it's..."

"Can you two work this out later," James interrupted. "We need to get Toya to the infirmary."

Lenny shut his mouth and found tears forming in his eyes. Toya was still convulsing, not as bad as before, but still.

What if the nanites have damaged her? What if I can't get them back out?

He looked down to see that his hands were shaking. James and Nix gently picked Toya up. The seizure was ending but her eyes remained shut, her body limp. They moved through the room, gingerly negotiating the door, and began down the hallway. Lenny followed, then turned back to grab the tablet. He looked up and Abdul reached out a warm, comforting hand. His hair was a bird's nest of curls and his eyes were still blinking away sleep.

"Don't worry, Lenny, she will be okay," he whispered, and Lenny's tears spilled over, tracking down his cheeks.

"She wanted it so bad, Abdul. How could I tell her no?"

Abdul shook his head. "There is no time for that now, Lenny. Focus on what's important, yes? Those nanites you put in, what are they doing right now?" He pointed to the tablet. "What's done is done. Now focus on what comes next."

The man's brown eyes were kind, and Lenny felt hope bloom again. The seizure didn't mean that something had gone wrong. He nodded, eyes on the tablet and the data that was streaming through it from the nanites, and followed as Abdul led the way to the infirmary. By the time they had arrived, Toya was already in one of the beds, an IV in her arm. A small monitor in one corner beeped, monitoring her vitals. She looked so pale and small. The extra pounds she held had melted away, her figure slim and fit thanks to Nix's attention and influence. But all that Lenny saw was a pale, unconscious version of his sister and, despite the readouts on the tablet, he found himself suffused with guilt once again.

"The nanites are clustered in her brain and making progress..." His voice died away as Nix advanced towards him, menacing in his fury.

"The goddamn nanites caused her to have a grand mal seizure, and she's still unconscious, Lenny!" He grabbed Lenny's shirt and pulled him up in the air. If Lenny hadn't grown 5 centimeters in the past six months, he would have been dangling in the air. As it was, his toes barely scraped the ground.

"Nix! Stop!" James warned him, "Put the boy down. He's as scared as you are."

Nix released his hold on Lenny's shirt, and Lenny lifted the tablet up. "I'm so sorry, Nix. I should have waited for you. I should have. But the nanites are working. Look."

His fingers danced on the screen and linked to the large monitor on the wall. It blinked, then incorporated both the data from the monitors they had hooked up with the information the nanites were sending from Toya's brain.

The three of them stared at the data streaming in, silent for the moment. Nix was the first one to speak. "I can't make heads or tails out of that shit." He glared at Lenny, his hands clenching, the knuckles white.

Lenny looked over at James, who shrugged. "Sorry, I can tell you the inner secrets of creating a self-sustaining city on a dusty, inhospitable planet, but I'm not much better off than Nix here."

Abdul stood in front of one of the readouts, his eyes focused on a parade of numbers.

"Okay," Lenny sighed, "Fair enough. Here's what it's telling me. The nanites found the damage, and..."

"Why did she have a seizure then?" Nix interrupted. He clenched his teeth, his face still red. "Do you even know, Lenny? I thought you said you weren't ready, that the nanites could cause damage if not programmed properly. Did you just shove your damn machines into your sister without a care in the world?"

Lenny's face flushed, and his tone was defensive, "I care. Of course, I care! Toya, hell, the stories I heard growing up, I wanted that Toya. For that matter, *Toya* wanted her old self back..."

"And you would do anything to get it, wouldn't you?" Nix growled. "As if there wasn't a price to pay to play God and fuck with her brain!"

"You said you wanted it too!" Lenny cried, confused by Nix's reaction. Hadn't he stood there in Durham's Hab and said as much?

James raised his hands placatingly. "Both of you, this isn't helping. The nanites are there now; let them do their work."

Abdul leaned close to the screen, ignoring everyone else, his brow furrowing as his eyes focused on the screen. He reached over and highlighted one reading, gasping in shock.

Lenny and Nix didn't notice thanks to Nix's continuing fury. "She's not a farm animal, Lenny, she's a human being!"

Abdul's gasp and whisper caught James' attention. His head jerked up, his eyes wide, as Abdul pointed to the results on the screen.

Lenny was about to snap back at Nix when Abdul laid a hand on his arm and pointed to the screen. Lenny's eyes widened. A drumbeat of fear started in his stomach and spread throughout him as he gaped at the information on the vid screen.

"Oh, shit," Lenny said.

"What the hell is happening now?" Nix asked, panic creeping into his voice.

"Toya is pregnant."

Nix's face changed first to fear and shock, before it morphed into a fury that Lenny had never seen before. Nix reached for him, picking him up off of his feet like a rag doll, a roar of rage issuing from his mouth.

Lenny dangled in Nix's grasp, more afraid than he had been since the ESH virus broke out and everyone had gone nuts. He could see Abdul hanging onto Nix's arm, likely hoping to convince Nix to put him down. The breath whooshed out of Lenny as Nix slammed him into the nearest wall, and his vision narrowed as Nix's hold on his collar tightened.

It was the flash of the syringe in James' hand that saved him, a swift plunge into Nix's arm and seconds later the man had released his hold on Lenny and was slumping to the infirmary floor.

"Christ, Leonard," James said, shaking his head at him, his eyes focused on Nix's slow descent into unconsciousness, "if you could have screwed that up worse, I don't know how." He turned to Abdul and said, "You get his feet. I think I can handle his head and shoulders. Let's see if we can't get him onto the other bed there."

When Lenny stepped forward to help, James held up a hand. "Honestly, I think you've helped enough."

Lenny felt shame spreading through him, along with a healthy dose of anxiety. A baby. Toya was pregnant!

Once they had levered Nix onto a nearby bed, they both returned to stand next to Lenny. Abdul spoke first. "There is a strong chance of miscarriage. One report from Earth stated that survivors have showed high rates of miscarriage and/or infant mortality."

Lenny continued to stare at the readout showing there was a second heartbeat. "Nix is going to kill me if something happens to that baby, or to Toya."

"Let's take one day at a time," James advised calmly, "shall we?"

Abdul laid a hand on Lenny's sleeve. "Why don't you head for Sydney Hab, and give us some time to deal with Nix? You can monitor her progress from there, can't you?"

Lenny nodded, not trusting his voice not to crack or the tears not to come. *What have I done? And what if she doesn't wake up?*

He went to the Hab that he and Toya had shared and gathered a few belongings. His tablet continued to show a livestream of data as Lenny fled through the link in Eden Hab towards Sydney Hab. The first rays of the sun were showing on the horizon. Lenny felt the tears track down his cheeks as he entered Jack Durham's Hab and sat down to watch the progress of the nanites as they flowed through Toya's brain.

Please let it work. Please, Toya, come back to us.

My Fair Lady

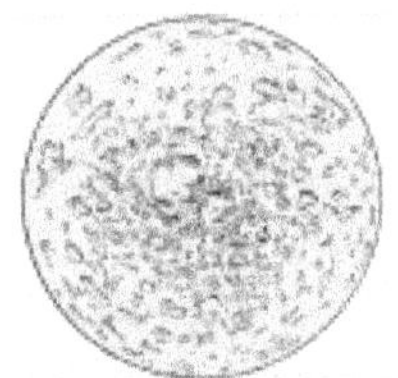

Mars Year 15, Week 07, Day 062
(Earth Date: 08.21.2100)

It was the notification that woke Lenny from a fragmented sleep, one filled with nightmares. Toya had figured prominently in them, just as she had for the past twenty days.

"NARA, do I have notifications?"

"You have one new notification and twenty-five blocked notifications," NARA answered. "Would you like to hear them all?"

"Just the new notification, please."

The blocked notifications were from Nix, and Lenny already knew what they contained. To say that Nix was angry was an understatement. When Nix had come to in the infirmary after being sedated by James, he'd been pissed. According to Abdul, Nix was so ready to bust heads, that James had sedated him again. They had loaded him onto a gurney, returned him to his own Hab, and then locked him inside. It had been a tense twenty-one days, and Nix hadn't spent it well. According to the video reports from NARA, he had trashed the inside of the Hab and dented the door before giving up. Early on, Abdul had quietly unlocked and delivered enough MREs to last Nix for thirty days or more while he was showering one morning. Ever since, Nix had inundated Lenny, James, and Abdul with messages. Lenny sighed; he must have deleted at least fifty of them yesterday alone.

"The program, My Fair Lady, completed successfully at 0300 hours and evacuation has begun."

Lenny jumped from his position on the couch with a whoop of joy. "NARA! Lights!"

Each day, for the past two Mars weeks, Lenny had stared at the screen of his tablet and watched the repairs slowly inch along. Most of the nanites had stayed clustered in the Broca's and Wernicke's–both centers of language development and control–while a handful of others had moved about Toya's body. He wasn't sure if they were scouts, or stragglers, or what, but it appeared they were all heading into the digestive tract now, according to the scan.

He had chewed every fingernail he had down to the quick and worn a track in the carpet of Durham's living room from walking back and forth, obsessing over the nanites' slow progress. He had lost count of the number of times he had been ready to shut the program down in the past few days. Anything so that Toya would wake up.

Something had stopped him, though. Perhaps it was hope, or fear even. What if 87% wasn't enough? What if the nanites simply needed more time? He had gone back and forth with it, even voiced his concerns to James and Abdul. It was James who had said, "Give it a few more days. She's stable, the baby is doing fine, and Nix might be pissed as hell but he's not going anywhere."

And so, they had waited, watching the progress inch forward, a percentage point or two per day.

Until now.

He grabbed the tablet, turned it on, and stared at the numbers. The bright lights were momentarily dazzling, but when they cleared, Lenny could see that the number had changed. "Holy Toledo! It's at 99%!" he crowed.

He ran out of Jack's Durham's Hab, the door hung open behind him as he tore down Sydney's empty hallway towards the airlock and passageway that would take Lenny through Eden and into Philly.

He was out of breath when he arrived at the infirmary. "NARA, lights!" The room brightened instantly, and he skidded to a stop next to Toya's bed. Her eyes were still closed. Here, surrounded by white walls and floors and covered with a white sheet, she looked paler than usual, and he could see the small baby bulge that tented the sheets over her stomach. It had terrified him that the nanites would somehow interfere with the pregnancy, but so far, everything seemed fine, and despite the grim odds and reports of miscarriages from Earth, Toya's pregnancy seemed to develop normally. Beside her, Burrito nestled against Toya's hair. The creature woke at Lenny's abrupt entrance, blinking in the bright light, and growled at Lenny.

"Lenny?" James walked in, rubbing his eyes and yawning. "What are you doing here in the middle of the night?"

"It's done. The nanites, they, they finished, James! They finished!"

"You didn't change the parameters?" the older man asked, staring at the overhead monitor.

"No! NARA woke me as the program finished. It completed repairs to the damaged cells!"

James opened his mouth to respond, but for Toya's voice, which sounded sleepy. "What are you two going on about?" She sat up in bed, resting on her elbows, and looked around. "What am I doing in here?"

Lenny stood there, immobile, waiting for a sign. Had it worked? Really worked? And what would happen next? Would the things she had learned still be there? Or would she know what she had before? He had so many questions.

Burrito sat up with a grumble and a hiss and dropped to the ground, waddling out of the door. She was likely looking for somewhere more peaceful, and less crowded, to sleep. Burrito had stayed there, curled against Toya, for most of the past twenty days. James and Abdul had said she only left Toya's side for a few minutes at a time.

James spoke first. "What do you remember, Toya?"

She blinked. "Dreams, mostly. Detailed ones. A radio transmission that was warning Earth of some large asteroid on a collision course, Nix threatening Lenny, you and Abdul being all lovey dovey to each other." She shook her head as if clearing the fog out of it. "And a really nasty one of Petra telling me I'd be a vegetable forever and she would get Nix." She frowned. "That one really sucked."

James looked grim. "I caught her in here a week ago. I told her to get out and not come back, and I haven't seen her since. Neither has Abdul. I think she's lying low in London Hab."

"Wait," Lenny said, Toya's words turning over in his head, "What did you say about the radio transmission?"

"The one in Mandarin?" Toya frowned again, looking confused. "Wait, was that a dream? Or.... Lenny, what am I doing here?"

"Event amnesia," James commented. "Although you obviously remember some events that led up to it and during it. Very interesting."

Toya stared at him and, before Lenny could speak, her face changed expression to one of excitement. "You put the nanites in me, didn't you?!"

Lenny nodded, wordless, overwhelmed with emotion.

"And they worked, didn't they? They did! They worked!" Toya gasped with shock. "I remember now. There was a radio transmission in the Hab, and a man's voice." She closed her eyes, wrinkling her face in concentration.

Lenny felt a pang of guilt. He had forgotten all about the transmission. He hadn't even checked it or responded to it.

"It started out, 'Hoohan Dee-cho,' which I think means asking, no, calling, Earth." She shook her head and opened her eyes. "I don't remember the rest."

James patted her arm reassuringly. "Don't worry about it; I'm sure you can listen to it another time."

Toya's frown deepened, and she ignored James. "NARA, please play the radio transmission from the Antes/Snelling Family Hab."

"Accessing," came NARA's smooth reply. "One moment." There was a pause, and then the man's voice issued through the speakers. "Hoohan Dee-cho. Shway nung ting wuh shwuh. Yo yee guh sheeow sing sing sheeow hung chow goo chowng ye deech yo."

Toya scrunched her face in concentration as she translated, "Calling Earth. Will, no, no, *can* anyone listen me? No, that has to be 'hear.' 'Can anyone hear me?' That's it."

"So, it's just that? Noth..." Lenny stopped short as Toya raised a finger, silencing him.

"He's saying something else, give me a moment." She stared into the distance. "NARA, put it on repeat, please."

They all listened intently as the words began again. "Hoohan Dee-cho..." Toya nodded slightly, her lips forming the sounds silently. Once, twice, and finally on the third time, Toya gasped, her eyes flying open in shock.

"Well, don't keep us hanging here, Sis," Lenny begged.

Toya's shock had turned to something far grimmer, her lips compressed and thin. "He's saying, 'Calling Earth. Can anyone hear me? An asteroid is on a collision course with Earth.'"

No one spoke.

"Well," James said in the stunned silence, "Shit."

Off Road

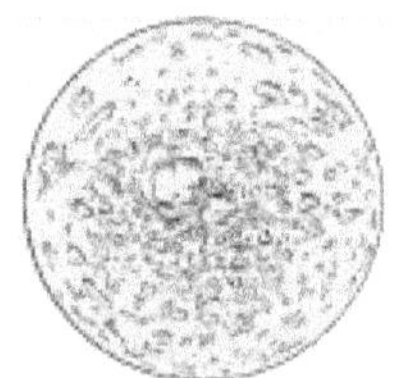

Mars Year 15, Week 07, Day 064
(Earth Date: 08.23.2100)

Liu closed his eyes, defeat crashing in a wave over him. In his arms, Huan whined, a tiny fist striking out, his sharp nails scratching at Liu's cheek. Liu couldn't find the words to speak; he couldn't trust himself to.

My fault, my fault, my fault.

Huan wiggled, wanting down, and Liu set him on the floor. His mouth held the bitter taste of failure. It burned like stomach acid, and Liu pictured his teeth dissolving into it, the disappointment was so bitter. All the planning, all the problems he had expected. It hadn't been enough. He had failed.

It should have worked. If Fen or Chen had been here, it would have. But there was just me, and I am the weakest point of this. I didn't consider the terrain and equipment failures and now, now we are going to die.

Huan toddled over to the small bench where Liu had created a small space for the baby to play. In its former life, it had held boots and safety equipment. Now it housed a few pitiful artifacts that could be considered toys, cobbled together from belts, unused transmitters, and more–Huan chortled with glee as if seeing them for the first time.

Liu's spirits sunk lower than ever at the sound of his son's laughter.

Fifty-two days, and now what do we do? We are going to die out here, slowly. I must watch my son die in front of my eyes.

It had been three days of immobility, locked in place. They weren't far from the edge of Millochau crater, nearly two-thirds of the way to their destination, and mercifully within drilling range of a plentiful subterranean ice sheet. It would keep them in water and oxygen for far longer than they would have food.

Liu tried to push past the despair, to think of something, anything, that would help. He had come so far, over 4,500 kilometers, by his estimation. The way had not been straight, nor as simple as he had hoped it would be. In following the sporadic plant life, thus ensuring they would have enough water to survive on and power the MOXIE, he had added nearly 1,000 extra kilometers to their trip. That wouldn't have been a problem if it hadn't been for the miscalculations in what weights the rover could pull and at what speed. Liu should have known better than to trust the listed specifications. While well within the weight limitations, the rover hadn't performed as expected, not even close. Where he had conservatively estimated it could run at 17 kilometers per hour and at least ten hours per day, with an expected 170 kilometers per day of progress, it had little better than half of that. The rover had needed longer to charge, and if he didn't want to run out of oxygen, the longest he could drive the rover each day was typically eight hours. The speed wasn't what it should be. He found the sweet spot was right around 100 kilometers. And for thirty days, it had been the same, day in, day out.

Disaster had struck on the thirty-first day, as they edged out of Hesperia Planum and slowly declined into the edges of Tyrrhena Terra. The sandstorm had appeared out of nowhere, cutting visibility, and their progress, to zero. Liu didn't dare continue as sand and regolith pummeled the vehicle, turning day to night.

Thankfully, it had happened when the rover was at full charge, and Liu could extend the drill rig into the regolith and find water shortly after the vehicle rocked to a stop. Water powered MOXIE, and MOXIE, along with the solar cells, kept them alive. He spent the five days holding and playing with an ever-increasingly fussy Huan, who sensed there was trouble and cried as the scratching from the sandstorm outside abraded the vehicle.

Once the sandstorm moved on, Liu had managed an EVA outside in his suit to clear off the solar panels and brush the dust from the viewing window. They moved on. But something was wrong. The rover moved slower now, and with an extra growl of discontent, eking out 80 kilometers a day where once they had managed a hundred.

Liu was endlessly thankful that he had taken more than twice the food stores he believed would be necessary. If he hadn't, they would have run out shortly after the sandstorm. He watched the odometer with ever-growing concern as they limped their way through Tyrrhena Terra, following the infrequent and dwindling line of plant life through what was a rather dry section of Mars, hoping to get to the next ice sheet before the rover ran out of juice and powered down.

Whatever was wrong, it had grown significantly worse, and by the time they reached the Millochau crater, Liu felt the despair creeping through him as if Death itself had moved into the rover with them. He could imagine Death sitting there, perched near the airlock, waiting for the next failure, the next error to come forward and take them.

And then, three days ago, there had been a terrible groan and the rover ground to a halt. Liu had fought panic as he suited up for the EVA, his fingers trembling, thankful that Huan was sleeping at the moment, his tiny, round face serene as he lay on his side on the narrow bunk that they shared, swaddled in a pile of blankets.

He had spent an hour out there, perhaps more, until the sound of Huan first stirring, then sitting up and crying for him, had issued over the radio feed in his suit. Whatever the problem was, it was deep inside of the rover and far beyond Liu's abilities to fix while encased in a pressure suit. He had closed his eyes, leaned the edge of his helmet against the hard metal of the rover, and held back from screaming in despair, before returning to his son.

The next two days, he had exhausted every option, chased each wire down to its origin, and reached as far into the guts of the rover as he dared, trying to solve the problem. Each time, Huan had slipped off to sleep, Liu had suited up, retrieved the tools stored in the rover's cab, and tried to work on the problem.

They had never intended the rover for outdoor excursions during sandstorms. The red Mars dust was prevalent enough, but the sandstorms were deadly for the machinery. They had spelled the doom of many of the early automated rovers, and Mission Control had underestimated the need for the rover to be accessible when in an EVA situation, rather than a climate and temperature-controlled construction hangar. What he would need to do to fix the problem was impossible in this situation.

My fault, my fault, my fault. The rover intended only for short-range missions–a few hundred klicks, not 6,000 kilometers through a sandstorm!

Liu heard a small sound over the radio. He was directly below the viewing window and he looked up to see Huan's tiny body pressed against the thick, tempered plastiglass. His tiny hands flexed, and his little mouth opened up in a shout of happiness when he spied Liu. It crackled over the radio and Liu felt his heart thump in pain, fear, and guilt. He had sworn to love him and care for him–even if Fen hadn't been alive to hear it. He had promised, and now he was going to fail. They would die here, and it was all his fault.

Liu slowly stood. He had tried to anticipate every possible scenario. Liu couldn't have imagined the time to get to Huygens Outpost would double, but still he had planned for it. He had thought he could fix anything that could go wrong, and he had certainly been wrong about that. But he had done one thing before he left. It was a last-ditch choice, one that sent chills and horror creeping up and down his body. But he had it. If there was nothing left, if there were no other option, he would have it there. He tucked it away, deep under their narrow bunk, waiting. If all hope evaporated, he had a way to make sure that Huan would not suffer. He didn't care about himself so much as he did about Huan. He couldn't bear the thought of the child he had grown to love slowly starving to death.

Liu walked to the end of the Hab and climbed into the outer airlock. There he pressed the buttons and waited for the outer door to seal, pressurize, and the inner seal to unlock. Huan squealed with glee as Liu pulled off the bulky helmet.

"Baba! Baba!"

The baby's hair was greasy, as was Liu's. He wrinkled his nose briefly as the stench within the tiny Hab, with over fifty-two days of living and no baths, wafted around him. He slid out of the pressure suit as Huan toddled over to him. Liu picked up the boy and hugged him, Huan's little hands grasping the lank lengths of Liu's hair.

Later, as Huan breathed low and slow, his tiny body curled beneath a blanket, a stuffed mouse that Liu had sewed for him out of scraps of cloth grasped tight in his hand, Liu tallied the food stores once more. With the MOXIE in place, the solar panels on the roof of the Hab, and the drill unit accessing what appeared to be a decent reservoir of icy water beneath the surface, they had virtually unlimited stores of heat, oxygen, and power. What they didn't have was unlimited food. Liu had already reduced his intake to just two meals per day, and if he went down to one meal a day, they had ten, possibly twelve days of food left.

Liu turned off the last light and quietly climbed into the narrow bunk, curling his body around his son. Huan's breathing remained steady, and his tiny body was warm against Liu's chest as he pulled the baby to him. Holding Huan close was both comforting and painful.

I've failed you, Fen. I have failed to keep Huan safe. Please forgive me.

The box was just beneath him. Just within reach. If he had to, he would, but what Liu couldn't do was let go of some small hope, some tiny, desperate, insane hope that someone at Huygens was still alive and that they could hear him. That they would hear his message and respond.

If they just answer, I could tell them where I am. They are close enough to help.

Liu didn't want to open that small box. He didn't want to look at the needles inside filled with a compound that would take his life, Huan's life, and send their souls soaring into the void.

Liu wanted to live. He wanted Huan to grow up, to learn of his mother, to live a full and long life. Even a life here, in this barren place, had to be better than death. It had to be.

Liu fell into an uneasy sleep, filled with dreams of needles and death and Huan's cries following him into the afterlife. As he slept, his eyes moving beneath their lids, his body occasionally twitching in REM sleep, Liu fought inside his dreams to protect the child wrapped in his arms. He fought with every part of him, conscious, dream state, and more.

Somehow, I must save him.

The radio crackled at the far end of the Hab and a young woman's voice roused him from his sleep. He jerked awake, then held still, shocked. Someone at Huygens spoke Mandarin? Why hadn't they responded before? As the voice stumbled over the words, twisting sounds, the emphasis on several incorrect, it was confusing, and difficult to understand the entire meaning of the transmission.

Liu sat up, gingerly, and Huan sighed and kicked once before his body returned to its rhythmic breathing and heavy sleep state. The message stopped, and the silence felt deafening. He wanted to reach out and take this woman in his arms and hug her. Despite her accent and mispronunciations, she was the first voice he had heard in close to a year, other than Huan's babble.

Just as he thought he had imagined it, that it had all been a dream, it began again. It was on a loop, just as his had been! He reached out and turned the volume up.

"Wènhòu běijīng kēxué shàosuǒ. Huì gèng sī zài zhèlǐ. Liù gè xìngcún zhě jūn chéng bìngdú yángxìng. Nín guānyú Ultima Thule de chuánshū yǐ shōu dào bìng zhuǎnfā. Nín mùqián de zhuàngtài shì shénme?"

Liu shook, his entire body vibrating. He was close. They would hear him, and they had the means to rescue the two of them. He knew it. His body bowed, and the tears came then. Huan would survive. Liu could forget the box under the bunk. He would never have to see the needle slide into Huan's tiny arm, nor his own.

The message he had set to repeat when they left Beijing Science Station...Huygens had heard it. They had understood it. The tears flowed freely. The thought of others, even if he had to speak to them through glass or breathe separate air, others who had survived and could help him. He could barely move from his position of prayer at the console. With a shaking hand, he reached for the speaker, pressed the record button, and spoke, his voice thick with emotion.

"Wènhòu huì gèng sī. SOS, wǒ zàishuō yībiàn,SOS. Zuòluò zài Millochau huǒshān kǒu de xī biānyuán, jù nín de wèizhì yuē 1600 gōnglǐ. Liúdòng zhàn yǐ tíngzhǐ yùnxíng. Qǐng xiézhù. Chuánshàng yǒu liǎng míng xìngcún zhě. Hái shèng wǔ tiān de kǒuliáng."

Huan stirred and Liu pressed Send as the horizon slowly lit up, the sun rising on a brand-new day. He walked back to the bunk and picked up his sleepy son and hugged him tightly until the boy squeaked in discomfort. "We are safe now, my son. They will help us and you will soon run and play in a brand-new place."

The survivors of Huygens could help them. And for the first time in several days, Liu felt hope rush through him.

Message from Toya: Greetings Beijing Science Outpost. Huygens here. Six survivors, all positive for virus. Your transmission regarding Ultima Thule received and relayed. What is your current status?

Message from Liu: Greetings Huygens. SOS, I repeat, SOS. Stranded on west edge of Millochau crater some 1,600 kilometers from your position. Rover has ceased to function. Please assist. Two survivors on board. Five days rations left.

Sixth Mass

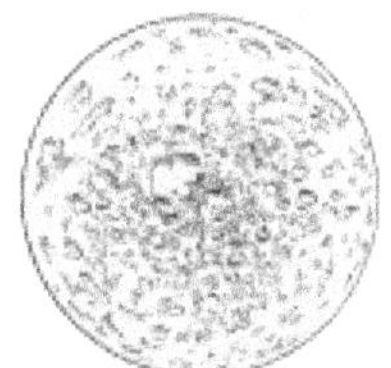

Mars Year 15, Week 07, Day 070
(Earth Date: 08.28.2100)

"Well?" James asked, eyebrows raised. The four of them sat at their usual table in the Mess Hall, their plates still filled with food that sat cooling, untouched. Everyone looked at Lenny and Toya expectantly.

Toya spoke first. "It isn't good. According to Liu's data, which we have spent the last week confirming, the asteroid that was Arrokoth 486958, or better known as Ultima Thule, fractured after an impact in the Kuiper Belt. The asteroid was a distorted eight shape, with the bottom chunk far larger than the top one. It looks as if the impact separated the head from the body, sending the larger piece, some 14 kilometers in diameter, on a collision course with Earth."

"Likely it will fly by," James interjected then, "that's what usually happens, right? They record thousands upon thousands of near misses each year."

Toya stared at him; her left eyebrow raised. "I did the math, James."

She said nothing more past that, and James reddened, his ears turning pink.

Well, of course she had. He'd read the colony's history surrounding the oxygen deprivation incident that had injured Toya. Hell, it could have been *his* design that had failed. He had checked on her each day that she lay there in a coma, wondering if she would wake up. And if she did, would she be the person she had been before the oxygen deprivation? He had *seen* the deep well of intelligence return to her eyes when she woke up.

Still, he persisted.

"Yes, but are you sure? I mean the calculations are..."

"I'm sure. I ran the numbers multiple times, following the procedural verification system set in place by Lazinsky in 2041 after the LaFevre incident."

The LaFevre incident, where incorrect calculations led to a panicked announcement that a Near-Earth Object over 10 kilometers in size had a 93% chance of impacting Earth, had been a black eye for astronomers everywhere. The resulting panic had led to riots, traffic jams, and thousands of suicides across the planet. In the aftermath, a top astronomer, Maxwell Lazinsky, had prepared a protocol to avoid panics happening again in the future.

Thanks to his program, over one hundred Near-Earth Objects had been updated with data that verified the accuracy of the scientist's calculations well before a near miss.

"Okay, so what are we looking at?" Abdul asked, likely hoping to move the subject along without further embarrassing James.

Lenny added, "They have just over two and a half years to prepare for what is likely to be an extinction-level event."

There was silence in the room. James thought of what it would be like, the enormous rock creating a firestorm in the atmosphere and on land as it hit with devastating force, destroying anything in its path.

Abdul's hands reached up and covered his face, and James could hear him murmuring a prayer. Nix looked ill as he stared at his meal rapidly cooling on its plate. He had barely spoken in the seven days since they had released him from his Hab. Nix had charged out of the door like a bull, looking for a fight. He had calmed immediately upon seeing Toya's face, stopped in his tracks, his eyes fixed on hers, and then swept her up into his arms.

Nix had yet to say anything at all to Lenny, from what James had seen. He wouldn't even look at the kid. Despite what was, rather indisputably, a happy ending to the first human trial of the nanites, it would take a while for everything to go back to normal. Nix still harbored resentment towards Lenny, as well as Abdul and James for sedating and imprisoning him.

"We have to warn Earth," James said, the image of a fireball consuming Earth filling his mind.

"Already done," Lenny answered, a glum look on his face. "They seem to think that the Asteroid Defense System will protect them."

Toya scowled. "They will likely waste another week, possibly longer, refiguring the math like we did, and who knows how long until they realize reality. The chances of breaking up something that large will result in a hail of asteroids the size of several small towns hitting the Earth in multiple locations."

"And this is worse?" James asked.

Lenny chimed in as he shrugged, "Honestly? It's a crapshoot either way. Lots of people are going to die, and those that don't had better have food stored up for at least seven to ten years until the skies clear and temperatures return to normal."

"Seven to ten *years*?" James' voice betrayed his doubt. "Are you sure you aren't overreacting?"

Toya quirked an eyebrow. "April 10th, 1815, the Tambora volcanic eruption changed the world climate by merely 1 degree overall, but it plunged Europe into a crisis that had women committing infanticide rather than watch their children slowly starve to death."

"But that was..." Abdul recovered enough to object.

Toya continued as if he had not spoken, "Thera, estimated to have erupted sometime between 1645 and 1500 BC, was so powerful that it caused tsunamis estimated at over 45 meters in height, wiping out the Minoan culture in its entirety and spawning the very real myth of Atlantis. I remember being obsessed with the 2062 discovery of the lost continent and several significant archaeological treasures when I was four. Fascinating stuff." She tapped her fingers on the table. "I mention volcanoes, because they have the same effect as an impact from an asteroid would, only on a far smaller scale." She leaned back in her chair. "This asteroid is 14 kilometers in diameter. The one that killed the dinosaurs was estimated to be approximately 11 kilometers in diameter. Think about that. When the remains of Ultima Thule impact Earth, we are looking at an extinction-level event worse than what killed the dinosaurs. We can't pinpoint where it will impact yet. More importantly, we can't calculate the vector of approach, which could mean the difference between an extinction-level event or something closer to the Tunguska event of 1908. We won't know until very late in the asteroid's approach. Trying to break it up might simply cause more projectiles to pummel the Earth, not unlike the Shoemaker-Levy comet that hit Jupiter in 1994. It changed the face of Jupiter for years! If Earth underestimates this thing, humanity might very well go extinct. Earth's skies will be dark for up to a decade. It might plunge the planet into an ice age. This could be the end of the human race on our home planet. This changes everything for us. At present, we don't have any way of creating a new species on Mars even if the artificial wombs worked, and we need to increase the solar array by twentyfold if we hope to offer shelter to more than a few hundred refugees."

James looked at the food on his plate and pushed it away. His appetite had vanished. "What are you suggesting?"

"Considering that Earth is facing its sixth mass extinction-level event, and that humans will likely be an endangered species, we need to convince them to send us as many colonists as humanly possible," Toya answered. "And we need to find Petra, because if we are going to expand in the way I'm hoping that we can, we are going to need her expertise, desperately."

Nix growled, "No way, anyone but her. We are better off without her."

Toya turned her gaze towards Nix. "Actually, Michael, we have never needed her more than we do right now. I read over the plan she was pushing for one hundred years in Cryo, and it's brilliant. With a few changes, it is absolutely doable, and in a century, we could wake up to a world we could actually live and breathe in."

She smiled then. The beauty of it struck James. He'd never seen how pretty Toya was, not until now. With her eyes bright, and a little pink in her cheeks as she leaned forward, her excitement over Petra's plan for Cryo so clear on her face, James suddenly saw what had drawn Nix to her. He'd seen what most could not in Toya. Something more than just intelligence, something deeper and richer.

"In order to survive, we need to put the terraforming of this planet into overdrive, at the same time as we figure out how to house thousands, if not tens of thousands, in Cryo until this planet is habitable. And we need to do it *now*.

"Two and a half years will go by faster than you can even imagine. And when that asteroid hits Earth, everyone better be underground or on a spaceship heading for Mars or Zarmina's World because Earth will probably plunge into another ice age. A seven-year estimate on the world returning to normal temperatures is the best scenario we can hope for. Reality may be far more dismal than any of us care to contemplate."

Toya said it matter-of-factly, pulling no punches as she outlined exactly what would happen to Earth when the asteroid struck. This was possibly more terrifying to James, and from what he could see, everyone else as well. He knew from Nix that Toya had been pulling all-nighters as she analyzed the data they had received from Liu.

The act of retrieving him and the baby, Huan, from the edge of the Millochau Crater had actually gone rather swimmingly. Toya had woken them all up five days ago with the news that the Chinese rover had broken down and that the two only had a few days' worth of food left. Compared to the Beijing Science Station, Huygens was massive, and their resources were as well. Whereas the Chinese had only had the Mazu, which they used for the long journey to and from Earth, Huygens had several mid-range shuttles and even a long-range shuttle available for use. Nix had cross-trained on them, and while he had made Abdul green around the gills as his passenger in it, they had arrived at Millochau three days ago without incident, carrying a special, baby-sized, and thoroughly sanitized, suit for Huan.

They had moved Liu and Huan onto the shuttle, with the baby howling his distress the entire time. It had made the flight miserable until the last thirty minutes, when the child ceased wailing and fell asleep in Liu's arms.

Once they had returned, and through Toya acting as an interpreter, they had learned of the Chinese commander's suicide and the lone female member of their crew dying in childbirth. Liu was still recovering from the 6,000-kilometer journey. He had settled into a fully decontaminated section of the Philly Hab that they had prepared with every level of care. They had sectioned off the environmental unit so that Liu and little Huan breathed air completely separate from the rest of the Hab. The closest that James or any of the others could get to Liu and Huan were conversations over a speaker with a thick glass partition installed in the hallway between them. They could not share the same air or touch them. For now, the ESH virus remained infectious and deadly to any Unaffected Persons like Liu and Huan.

If it hadn't been for the clear and present danger of the planet-killer heading toward Earth, James knew that Toya would be hard at work with Lenny attempting to figure out if the nanites could fix the ESH virus as well.

The kid had kept his nose to the grindstone over that project for days now, stopping only to help cross-check Toya's math on trajectories and the impact study she had prepared.

And as for Petra Salinger, James turned that over in his head.

Toya is right. Petra is difficult to work with, but she has the knowledge necessary to multiply the atmo generators and help fine-tune the warheads that we need to detonate on the far side of the planet.

The woman was devious, petty, and unpleasant, but they needed her. They needed to come together and plan for what they could do to help Earth.

Their plan had to include massive power generation, likely from a small nuclear reactor, in order to hold thousands of people in Cryo for the ten years or more it would take for Earth to return to normal.

They also had years, if not decades, ahead of them to build cities far bigger than the current Huygens Outpost.

Toya's review of Petra's plan, that of pushing the planet into an accelerated greenhouse effect, was another fire that needed stoking. They had avoided it before, but Toya had a point–they needed to accelerate the process if they had any hope of offering a second home for humanity within the solar system.

Toya stood up. "I think I should talk to Petra myself," she said, and her poise struck James. The old Toya had been fidgety and prone to ill temper, likely from frustration over her brain damage. Her memories of how she had been before the oxygen deprivation incident had figured far more prominently in her day-to-day life than anyone, except perhaps Lenny, had realized.

How frustrating it must have been for her to remember being smarter and to feel stunted, to feel stupid every day over things she remembered being able to do. And now, with her brain's functionality apparently completely restored, it was obvious how intelligent she had been, and was now again.

"Absolutely not," Nix interjected, shaking his head. "You will not talk to that woman."

Toya blinked at him in surprise, an incredulous smile tugging at her lips. "I beg your pardon?" She said it gently, but James could sense the steel that stood behind it. Toya was no longer willing to be told what to do or be protected from herself or others. Of that, he was sure.

Nix grimaced and he sounded irritated and defensive. "She's bad news. The way she talked to you, to any of us, it was unacceptable."

Toya reached out and took his hand in hers, her voice calm. "Michael, I wasn't asking, I was informing you. I will speak to Petra, and we will come to a truce, arrangement, meeting of the minds, or otherwise fortunate happenstance." She smiled at him gently, likely to lessen the sting of her words, and then turned to Lenny. "Why don't you tell everyone about your progress with the nanites, Lenny."

Nix's face reddened, his jaw tightened, but he said nothing. He just gave a curt nod of the head that James hoped was agreement as he ground his teeth, clearly unhappy with Toya's decision.

James wondered if they would stay together. They had founded their relationship on a different dynamic from the one that they now found themselves in. Toya's brain, now healed by the nanites, could lead to a completely different relationship than what they had just four weeks ago. It wasn't his business, but he still wondered about it. The idea of Toya talking to Petra instead of Nix or himself was rather brilliant. He couldn't help wishing he could be a fly on the wall when she faced the bitter woman as a peer. Petra wouldn't like it, not one bit. Her only advantage over Toya, that of her intelligence, was now lost. The two women were on equal footing, with Toya now in charge of all of her faculties. How would Petra react to that?

James realized suddenly that Lenny was talking, and that he'd missed whatever he had been saying.

"For now, there doesn't seem to be a workaround. It might be a programming error; I just don't know."

"So why couldn't we try it on a live subject?" Abdul asked, as he folded his hands in front of him as if in prayer.

"We...we can't," Lenny stammered. "I mean, if we try it on Liu, and he dies or becomes incapacitated as Toya was, and in a coma, there would be no one to care for the baby. And we can't try this on a *baby*. Who knows what could happen?"

"But that's what you did, Lenny." Nix's response was low, furious. "You tried it on a baby. Toya's and my baby. Or have you forgotten already?"

Lenny paled, suddenly quite aware of what he had threatened with his experiment, no matter whether Toya had been willing. His mouth opened, but no words came out.

Toya stood up abruptly. "And we're done here. Michael, if you wouldn't mind, we need to talk." She turned and walked out without another glance at anyone in the room. Nix sat there for a moment, still glaring at Lenny, and then silently stood up and followed Toya out.

There was silence in the room and Lenny stood up as well, silently gathering his tablet and his plate. "I'm uh, I'm going to head back over to Sydney Hab. Let me know if you need me."

James watched him go and turned back to Abdul. "That's a kettle of worms I don't want to touch."

Abdul traced the edge of his plate with one fingernail and tucked his dark hair behind an ear. James could see it was time for another haircut. He was getting better at it. Good enough that Nix and Lenny had also come to him and asked for a trim at different times last week. Abdul's hair was the softest he'd ever felt, though. Soft as rabbit's fur. James resisted the temptation to reach over and touch it.

"They will work it out. They have to. Our survival depends on it." Abdul paused and stared at the tablet showing several different scenarios of the asteroid's impact on Earth. "As does the future of humanity."

Arrival

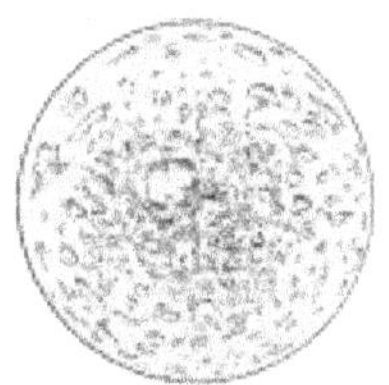

Mars Year 16, Week 7, Day 066
(Earth Date: 07.04.2102)

"Life Ship Mars Hope, initiate landing gear and reverse thrusters to slow your descent." Abdul's voice sounded measured, with no sign of concern, although the ship with five thousand refugees from Earth was coming in at 30% more power than necessary.

"Roger that, Huygens, reversing thrusters," came an equally measured response.

They were still coming in too fast. Abdul felt his heart rate ratchet up a notch, his hands clammy. Despite this being the smallest of the string of ships from Earth, it was the first.

By the time the Esperanza appears next week, with eighteen thousand refugees, I'll be a pro at this.

He jerked slightly when James put a hand on him. "They're coming in hot."

Abdul nodded. "Hope, increase reverse thrust by 20%. You're coming in hotter than we'd like."

"Roger that, Huygens, increasing reverse thrust by 20%."

Abdul focused on the readouts, his body relaxing as the indicators moved to green.

"You're doing great, Hope, initialize landing gear and prepare for landing."

The ship appeared now, breaking through the haze from the last sandstorm, the thrusters firing four columns of fire beneath them as the enormous ship fell the rest of the way towards the surface. It seemed impossibly fast, but at the last moment, slowed, and then, with a great deep roar, the flames vanished, and the entire ship landed in an enormous cloud of dust. Abdul swore he could feel the ground shake as it touched down. The debris cloud engulfed it, the finer particulate reaching up the sides of the massive ship and covering it in red dust. It looked, Abdul thought, like a wayward child who had been caught playing in mud.

Mars Hope was more than twice the size of the now long-scuttled Juniper Supply Ship. And inside of its bowels were five thousand refugees, gently snoozing in Cryo, blissfully unaware that they had arrived. And if all went as planned, they would stay that way. Except for the skeleton crew of one hundred engineers who were committed to staying on Mars, the rest of those in Cryo would stay asleep. They would be woken in fifteen more years, long after the asteroid strikes and the decade-long wait for Mother Earth to recover from the onslaught.

The skeleton crew would remain awake for the time it would take to build a new city on the opposite edge of Huygens Crater. They would construct it and then have the choice of joining Mars or returning home to Earth.

In exactly one Earth year, the fragments of Ultima Thule would begin their bombardment. It had taken time for the leaders on Earth to accept this reality and far longer for them to begin the planning necessary to save as many people as possible. Toya had been right in her assessment that they would try to break up the largest of the pieces. The crew on that mission had all died, caught in the blast by a rock twice the size of their ship. Seeing the footage that the Batair had transmitted of their last moments had been horrifying. In the space of ten minutes, they had watched their doom hurtle toward them and had been helpless to escape.

Abdul wasn't surprised at the reports of a quintupling of suicides following that doomed mission. Earth had suffered so much in the past few years, losing over 99.6% of its population, and now an extinction-level event was rolling through the deepness of space, inevitable and deadly.

James squeezed his shoulder, leaned close, and whispered in his ear, "You did it. I told you that things would go well."

Abdul sighed, relief rushing through him. "You were right." The night before, he had tossed and turned in their shared bed, until James had wrapped his legs and arms around him, effectively pinning him, and gave him a stern lecture on believing in himself more. That had led to more energetic acts, which had tired him enough to slip into sleep spooned tightly against James.

The overhead screen switched to a different camera, one that was on the side of the Philly Hab. The ship had landed far from Huygens Outpost. There was no need for them to be close by. The ship held everything they needed to create the short-term shelter they required to construct the future city–the first of its kind on Mars that would not require pressurized domes. The windows would not need to be foot-thick plastiglass, and the homes, while without character or charm, would have thick insulation against the hot and cold extremes that they would still see here on the red planet for several centuries to come.

A slight click behind him and Abdul turned to see Toya had entered the room. Toya's arms were full of one struggling toddler. Both of them looked determined to get their way, and Abdul was betting Toya had met her match.

Selena Michaela Nix had been born after a short four hours of labor, over one Earth year ago. By the age of nine months, she could speak in full sentences. By eleven months, she was reading philosophy.

She had shown the same ease in mastery for languages that her mother did. Now, at just fifteen Earth months, Selena was quickly becoming fluent in Spanish, having already mastered her native English, then Mandarin and Arabic.

"I want down!" Selena whined, her tiny mouth frowning as she noted the gigantic ship on the viewscreens. "We missed it, Mommy! We missed it!"

Toya sat the child down with an exasperated sigh. "Well, we wouldn't have if you hadn't reprogrammed the door codes on the Food Storage!" She looked up at Abdul and James. "So much for the Fibonacci sequence for the win; it took her less than two days to figure it out."

James choked back a laugh, blinking rapidly as he fought to keep a smile off of his face. Selena's mouth and hands still held traces of what could only be Choco-Snax.

Toya's eyes flashed to James. "Oh yeah, go ahead and laugh, Uncle James, you know this is your fault, right?"

James roared with laughter then, his hands up in the air. "For the record, I had no idea I was unleashing her inner chocolate demon!"

Toya stared at him, fighting her own smile, and shook her head. "Selena's been a tad obsessed since you gave her that bite and told her where they were." She smiled down at her daughter with no small amount of satisfaction. "But Daddy has fixed that problem, hasn't he, Selena?" She looked at Abdul. "We instituted a biometric system on the door. Michael will ping you later about adding your own access to the Food Storage. Every adult will have one."

"Uncle Lenny isn't an adult yet," Selena said, as she clambered up onto a stool in the Control Room with James' help.

Toya sighed again and bit her lip before grumbling, "Keep it up, and you'll be an only child."

James laughed again. "Maybe Abdul and I can get you to donate an egg and be a surrogate. I think I'd like a go at a handful like this."

Abdul gaped at his partner in shock. "What?"

James simply laughed again before leaning down to Selena's level and pointing at the screen. "I recorded it for you; would you like to see?" The little girl nodded in response.

Toya turned to Abdul. "Will Liu be joining Michael at the launch pad?"

He nodded. "That's the plan. Huan will probably nap for another hour and NARA will notify me when he wakes. I'm on babysitting duty now that the ship is on the ground."

He had been happy to babysit Huan. The little boy was a treasure and had already picked up plenty of English words, soaking up the second language like a sponge. He wasn't quite to the level of fluent, but he was a fast study. In another Martian year, he would be fluent. Liu was making progress as well, but it was a halting, laborious process.

It had taken time, and plenty of testing, before they had created a successful vaccine to the ESH virus.

Despite all of Earth's efforts towards finding a cure when it had first broken out there in China, and later in the Midwestern city of Kansas City, Missouri, it had been the one-two punch of the nanites Lenny developed that had helped create a foundation for a cure. When Lenny had injected Toya with the nanites, the tiny machines had moved quickly, first clustering in the areas of the brain damaged by the oxygen-deprivation event. There they had not just rebuilt, but also, as Lenny explained it, re-imaged the cells as one would a computer, preparing them to process data efficiently once again.

After he had finished, they had then targeted the ESH virus and rendered it inert inside of her. Lenny had been the first to realize that Toya and her unborn child held what was essentially a disarmed virus inside them thanks to the nanites. He had pored over the reports once the nanites were collected and debriefed.

Together with Toya and Abdul, Lenny had then harvested the inert virus and cultivated it. After additional testing, they had created a vaccine. They had administered it first to Liu and then, after two full months of observation, into Huan. Despite their successes, and open sharing with Earth, the vaccine was not in production there yet.

The concerted efforts to get as much of the population underground or off-Earth delayed testing and production. Many refugees were in Cryo on Mars, others at the space stations. They had even sent some to the Ptolemy Lunar Colony and a fleet of Unaffected Persons were on three separate life ships headed for the G581 system to join the colony there. There was, after all, just one Earth year left until impact.

"They came in too fast," Selena said, studying the replay. Abdul winced.

I should have had Toya or Lenny handle it. They can do the calculations in their heads. Even Selena could have managed it better.

"Yes, the life ship captain was a little lax on the reverse thrusters." James paused as the replay of Abdul's voice came over the speaker, advising them to increase reverse thrust. "But as you can see, Uncle Abdul handled it perfectly." His hand was on Selena's tiny shoulder, and he turned, smiled, and winked at Abdul. "Do you want to meet them?"

His gaze traveled to Toya, who shrugged and spread her hands. "By all means. If it gives me a moment's peace from the incursions in Food Storage, it's worth it."

The recording had ended, and the screen returned to the live view, which showed a long tube extending from the large dome, the original settlement before Huygens Outpost was built, to the life ship. It was nearly in place. Another twenty minutes to allow for pressurization and heat and they could open the airlock. The crew could then walk through the pressurized tunnel to their new home. Their home in the dome was temporary. If all went well, in less than five years' time the first city on Mars would be ready. Then, aside for groups of ten crewmembers in shifts of five-year stints, everyone would be in Cryo. There they would wait as the accelerated terraforming of Mars continued for the next one hundred years.

They had already detonated the nukes stored on Phobos on the far side of the planet. The results had been encouraging, and the readings were well within the expected range. Creating a greenhouse effect on a planetary level took time, but far less time than before, thanks to Petra's plan. She and Toya and Nix were still wary around each other, but it was obvious to Abdul that they were all trying to make a go of it and watching what they said or did, in order to keep the peace.

It had been a surprise to everyone when Petra had shown an interest in Selena. At first, Nix had been quite protective, but as the baby developed at an astonishing rate, Petra had been the first to step in and suggest learning opportunities that none of them had thought of. She had also been the first to note that, daughter of a child prodigy aside, Selena's progress was beyond what any of them had expected. It had led to the question of whether the nanites were somehow involved. It had been a sobering thought and one that continued to be on everyone's minds as Selena quickly passed Huan intellectually. Liu's son was now nearing three Earth years in age. Any hopes that Liu, Toya, or Nix had for the two children being able to play together were quickly disabused as Selena sped past the elder Huan in both ability and interest.

"Yes, yes, let's go now!" Selena half climbed, half slid off of the stool and reached up to tug on James' fingers. It was quite a feat, because of her small stature and his lanky frame.

"Of course, Princess." James saluted her and then swept her up in his arms. "Your chariot awaits!"

"Pressure suits, if you please, James," Toya called out after them. "Selena needs the practice."

"I hate pressure suits!" Selena yodeled in return, her head peeking over James' shoulder.

"Don't care!" Toya called back. Her shoulders drooped once the two were out of sight. "She's exhausting. I don't think she slept over four hours before she was up working on the damned lock to Food Storage. She wouldn't even touch her eggs this morning she was so full of chocolate!"

Abdul stifled a grin and Toya glared at him as he let loose a belly laugh. "Michael tells me this is my payback for being a righteous pain in the ass when we first met. Maybe he's right."

Her glance strayed to the viewscreen. It switched every few seconds to a different camera. Currently, it was one of the closer cameras. They both watched the puff of dust rise as the tube connected with the exterior hatch of the spaceship.

"It's going to be different now," she said, in an almost wistful tone. "The halls will be filled again."

"Well, not as many as before. At least, not for a while," Abdul noted, although he felt it too.

It would be nice to see more than a handful of familiar faces, Abdul thought. To not know every person's history, what they had eaten last, or who they were sleeping with.

It had taken time for them to find a sense of peace, of community, and they still had their twists and turns. They had come so far from the broken, haunted survivors they had been to the odd family unit they were now. Liu and Huan, as well, had become an integral part of that.

Even Petra, who had been such a thorn in Nix's side, and openly hostile to everyone, had made amends with Toya. Abdul had always wondered what Toya had said to Petra to make such a difference, but she had remained closed-lipped about it. She had marched out of Philly Hab, and then taken a full day to resurface, facing down a frantic Nix the following morning and saying only, "We have worked it out."

The day after that, Petra had been there at breakfast in the morning. She had calmly announced that there would be another meeting regarding the plan for Cryo.

The next day, Petra and Toya had presented a two-prong plan for welcoming over half a million refugees from Earth as well as a one-hundred-year plan for the greening of Mars.

"I am detecting an ascent to wakefulness for Shih-Fong, Huan," NARA announced over the comm.

"Thank you, NARA." Abdul stood up. "Join me?"

Toya smiled. "How about I take Huan and you make some of those fried pancakes? Michael and Liu will bring the group straight over here after they run the power cables in and make sure the Cryo units are stable. I'll bet you they would love them."

They both glanced up at the cameras. In the distance on the plain behind the spaceship, the shine of solar panels stretched as far as the eye could see. It had been backbreaking work installing them, but they were ready to power the Cryo units aboard the spaceship for years, even decades if need be.

Abdul grinned. The recipe that Liu had shared with him for pinyin, fried scallion pancakes, was addictive. "Will do."

Toya smiled in return, her eyes lighting up. "Fantastic! I've been craving them!" She turned to leave, her hand on the door handle, before she stopped and turned back. "Hey, don't forget, we are putting names into the pot for what to call the new city." She winked. "Don't forget to add any you come up with!"

Moments later, hands deep in flour and a pile of diced fresh green onions ready to go, Abdul thought again about how far they had come. More than that, he daydreamed of a green Mars. It was within their reach. The teams from Earth shared that dream with the Huygens Outpost survivors. Abdul thought back to those dark days when James had first found him, starving, alone, in the Cairo Hab. His hands worked the scallions into the mix, smoothing, working until it was elastic, ready to roll out and fry.

He had survived losing Gerard, his light, his love. He had found a new love in James. Where Gerard's and his love had burned hot, James had come to him slow, cool. Sometimes it felt like the complete opposite of what he had with Gerard. Despite this, he was content. He tore off a small chunk from the enormous ball of dough and rolled it flat. The thinner the better, Liu had told him in his halting English.

Abdul thought of the thousands more sleeping in Cryo, packed in tightly as they silently moved through space towards Mars, fleeing the coming cataclysm. It wasn't enough. They couldn't save them all, but he prayed each morning and night that the people of Earth would survive. Petra had once said that prayer wouldn't change anything, but Abdul refused to believe that. During his darkest moments, alone and in mourning there in Cairo Hab, he had prayed to Allah for help and James had appeared. Each day that Toya was in her coma, he had prayed as well. Even if his prayers did not make better outcomes happen, they made him feel better.

The oil popped in the pan, showing it was at temperature. They were on the precipice of a new beginning. Abdul smiled as he set the first pancake to sizzling. Food was love. He would fill their new friends and neighbors full of it.

She Dreams of Mars

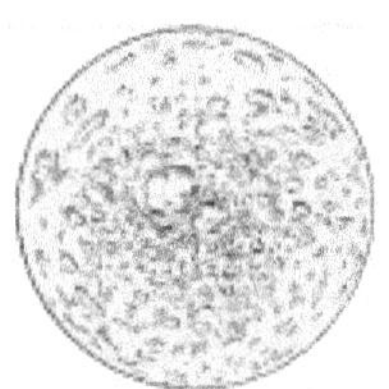

Mars Year 16, Week 44, Day 432
(Earth Date: 07.04.2103)

"Huan! Stop touching it!" Selena's small face contorted in anger. She slapped at Huan, who laughed at her and feinted to the left. At nearly four Earth years of age, he was deep in what Nix had recently referred to as the "asshole stage" of childhood.

Toya suppressed a smirk at the memory of Nix's rant.

"Seriously, Toya, boys that age are assholes. And they stay that way for at least ten to twenty years longer," he had said to her when she told him she was pregnant with their son.

"Yeah, well, I think it lasted longer than twenty years for you," she had retorted, grinning at him to lessen the sting. He had laughed then and pulled her closer.

"So, no Cryo for us then?"

Although the risk of permanent damage to the neural pathways was small, they only recommended Cryo for children aged three Earth years and up. They had long planned to put Selena into Cryo shortly after her second Mars birthday and join her there.

"Not for another two and a half cycles." She frowned. "Do you think we should put Selena in after her second birthday as we originally planned or just wait?"

"What, and give her the advantage over Michael Junior? Hell no, let's toss her into Cryo and give the boy a few years to catch up. He's going to need it."

"Michael Junior?" Toya rolled her eyes at Nix. "Oh no, we're naming this baby Stanley Isaac Nix. And yes, we should totally toss our girl in Cryo;

otherwise, we'll spend the rest of her childhood just trying to keep her from blowing us all up."

The elongated, "Mooommm!" jolted Toya out of her memory.

Selena's tiny voice turned into a shriek of rage. "Huan touched the controls again!"

"Okay, okay." Liu swooped in and wrapped his arms around his son, neatly avoiding Selena's tiny fists swinging in the air. "Huan, you not good to Sleena, you need listen more." He shrugged apologetically at Toya as she strode into the fray as well.

"Selena Michaela Nix, you do...not...hit." She picked the girl up and gave her a small shake. "We've talked about this." Despite being arguably the smartest person in the room, Selena was still a tiny child. She was prone to fits of anger like any other child her age. At three and one-half Earth years, she was precocious and brilliant, but she still took the occasional nap. And considering her mercurial mood swings, Toya wondered if perhaps her daughter was overdue for one.

"Mom, I had the telescope dialed in just at the right settings and *that boy* ruined it. Twice!" Tears were brimming in her eyes.

"That boy has a name and we do not hit, Selena."

The child's lip trembled in anger. An errant tear spilled over and ran down her left cheek. Selena turned away and glared at Huan.

If looks could kill, Huan would bleed out right now. Or suffer acute decompression sickness.

"Should we go?" Liu asked in his halting English, concerned as Huan did his best to escape his captor.

"No," replied Toya as Selena hissed, "Yes."

"Stop it." Toya gave her another small shake. "You are acting your age again, Selena." It was likely the worst thing she could say to her daughter, and Selena's tears increased exponentially.

"He wou-wou-wouldn't stop touching the buttons." The child hiccuped the words out. "I hate him."

"Well, you liked him fine yesterday when he shared his Choco-Snax with you."

"Well, I don't like him now!"

Nix arrived then, a bemused smile on his face. With as much noise as their daughter was making, he had likely heard her from all the way down the hall. He reached out and took her in his arms as she continued to wail, "Daddy, Mom unlawfully detained me!"

Behind Toya, Liu let out a small snort and Toya looked back to see him desperately hiding a smile. He plastered a stern look on his face before snapping off a string of words in Mandarin.

"Nǐ bìxū shǒu guījǔ. Qǐng wù chùmō bō pán! Fǒuzé, nín xiànzài yào shuìjiàole!"

Toya, now fluent in Mandarin and Cantonese, translated it instantly in her head.

"You must behave. No touching the dials! Or else you are going to bed right now!"

This gave her an idea, and she turned to Selena. "The same goes for you, young lady."

Selena gasped in horror. Mandarin had been the second language she learned, and she knew it well. The threat of being put to bed and not getting to see the first pieces of what remained of Ultima Thule hit the atmosphere of Earth was likely too much to bear. She shot another dark look at Huan, who had also quieted, and then one of reproach in Toya's direction before settling in her father's arms.

A moment passed before she asked in a small, yet dignified voice, "Father, please put me down. I need to correct the latitude on the telescope."

Nix nodded. "Of course," he said, and set her down until her tiny feet touched the floor. She straightened her clothing, shot Huan one last scathing glare, and walked over to the controls. The Heinlein telescope was the largest on Mars and it was in the perfect position to view the bombardment.

They had prepared for a staggering amount of people. Five hundred thousand men, women, and children currently slept in their individual Cryo units. The Gan De space station had another fifty thousand, the Lunar Colony, wiped clean by the ESH virus, were able to power one hundred thousand Cryo units, and there were a fleet of ships on their way to Zarmina's World with nearly two hundred thousand Unaffected Persons aboard four ships. It had been the only place to send them where they could truly be safe.

As for the rest of the more than twelve million people left behind, there had only been a few underground bunkers and caves available to put to use. Despite the ESH virus devastating the world's population, less than one in thirteen survivors had a chance of surviving the incoming asteroid.

Toya tried to remind herself that she had done everything she could. Hell, they all had. Ironically, it was Petra who had reminded her of that two days ago.

"I'd like for you to put me in Cryo now, Toya," she had said.

"What, now?"

"Yes."

"But the bombardment will be in less than two days."

"I know. It will only make me sad. And I know that we have done everything we could to help Earth," Petra had said. "You especially."

"Me?" Toya had asked, wondering what the punch line was. When would the old Petra rear her ugly head and rip her a new one?

"What with the changes in storage and fuel usage you recommended, yes. You increased the ship's, all the ships', ability to hold more Cryo units by re-engineering the Cryo units themselves. That made them easier and quicker to manufacture, took less energy to operate, and you figured out how to add additional units where the older engines took up too much space." She smiled then, and Toya blinked, trying to hide her surprise. Petra was pretty when she smiled. "I ran the numbers, Toya. Your changes alone saved over one hundred thousand additional lives on Mars alone."

Toya had known that too. But she hadn't really thought of it as *her* changes. Lenny had been part of it as well, focusing on the engines mostly, but it had been her that came up with the design changes to the Cryo units which made them less bulky and more energy-efficient.

Petra continued, "I don't want to see it. The bombardment, that is. And you don't need me for at least ten years. I'll take a five-year shift then if needed."

Toya nodded. "I get it. I really do. Cryo it is, then."

They had begun the process that evening. The series of injections and, as Petra had laid there, unmoving, her eyes half-closed, she had reached up and taken Toya by the wrist.

"You remember what I said. You did everything you could to save as many as you could." She'd smiled then as her eyes slipped shut. "See you when Mars is green, Toya."

Toya leaned close to the woman who had once been her enemy and said, "Dream of Mars, Petra." And then pressed the buttons to close the Cryo unit around her, watching as the automatic processes took over and Petra's Cryo unit wheeled away on its track.

She slept now, along with hundreds of thousands of others now, oblivious to the horrifying level of destruction that Earth would soon be experiencing.

The room was filling up. Not just Nix and Liu, James and Abdul, but the Tennysons, a wife-wife duo who had revolutionized the solar cell fields that now blanketed much of the southeastern quadrant of Arabia Terra and produced enough energy to run five large cities. For now, most of that energy was taken up with the needs of the half million Cryo units. In addition, there were several new multi-acre factories that belched enough chlorofluorocarbons into the atmosphere to help push the goal of a greenhouse effect that would warm the planet and provide them a breathable habitat to live in. Mars would never be as warm as Earth–it would average around 1.7 degrees Celsius instead of Earth's balmy 14.8 degrees Celsius–but the equator would be far warmer than the planet average.

"Like Finland, or Norway," Petra had said, and Toya had shrugged. Those places were just names; they didn't really mean anything to her. Her memories of Earth were of claustrophobic cities and smog that choked out the sun. The only thing that mattered was that they could grow crops, breathe the air, and not freeze to death. And after living most of her life in the domes of Huygens Outpost, those grandiose goals were more than enough.

It was standing room only now, and the enormous viewscreen was now on, showing Earth hanging there, a beautiful blue marble in the darkness of space. The last ships had left weeks ago, scattering themselves among the system and the stars, determined to never again put the fate of humanity in one place.

Earth had learned its lesson in the wake of the ESH virus. Given more time, they could have saved hundreds of thousands more. But with just two-and-a-half years' notice, it hadn't been enough, not nearly enough.

You did everything you could.

"It's beginning," someone shouted, and Toya looked up. A bright ball of fire was streaking down through Earth's atmosphere, then another, and another. They continued to fall, and at first, there was nothing, nothing at all to show that the onslaught damaged the cradle of humanity. Mother Earth was fine, would be fine. A glimmer of hope ran through Toya, hope for a world she had barely known, and had no real ties to any longer.

And then a pinprick of darkness, as if a small pimple had appeared on the face of the mother of them all, spreading slowly, so slowly, then faster, gaining speed. With it appeared red, orange, but mostly an ominous ever-expanding circle of black. The fiery projectiles continued to hammer, to burn, and to make more pimples, more darkness that then gave way to gray clouds that no telescope could penetrate.

One by one, the satellite chatter fell silent. The satellites themselves falling, struck by the shower of rocks of unimaginable size, winking out, becoming bright spots of fire as they entered the atmosphere and burned their way down to the roiling clouds and fire below.

They all stood there, silent, watching it happen. They watched the world they had come from, the cradle of humanity, burn. The dark clouds obscured the surface. The blue of the oceans slowly disappeared beneath it. Eaten, perhaps, and obscured.

The broadcasts from Earth ceased entirely, and the world itself looked alien, unrecognizable. Toya watched in horror with the others as the largest fiery missile, a rock that was at least four kilometers in diameter, burned its way through the roiling clouds and disappeared beneath them.

The silence was complete. Mother Earth, disfigured, said nothing more.

Note to Reader

Wow! You made it! Thanks for reading G581: Mars and rest assured, there's more, lots more. Another two books in fact.

I hope you enjoyed Mars and that you will stick around for G581: Earth. In a moment, I'll share the first chapter with you, but I would like to ask you a favor first.

I'd like to ask you to please review this book.

Simply put, reviews provide proof that someone has read this book and liked it or hated it enough to write a review of it. Social proof is a powerful thing. I'm not asking you to rank it five stars and tell everyone it's better than *Cats*. Though by all means, five-star away, I won't complain at all!

My job is to write stories – ones that pull at your heartstrings, make you mad as hell, depressed, elated, and more. I want to spend the rest of my life writing books, crafting universes filled with interesting characters and clever conversation. Your review helps make that happen. It keeps me going in the short-term, and it steers others towards a book that they might not have read otherwise. So, write a review. Copy and paste it to Bookbub and Goodreads, along with your favorite bookselling platform.

This starving writer would much appreciate the boost.

Acknowledgments

This might be a part you skip over, but to me it is essential. Because, just as it takes a village to raise a child, it often takes a village (or at least a good group of friends/readers on Facebook) to write a book.

#1 on my list? My husband Dave, who once said, "I look forward to growing old, stinky, and slow with you." It's important to have someone at your back who loves you and supports you, no matter how many crazy requests you throw his way. (P.S. Thanks for the "secret doors," my darling, I love them.)

To Emily, who despite delving into the fractious teen years, has done it with all her heart and kindness intact. Emily, my sweet girl, you continue to inspire me to be a better human being each and every day.

To Little Miss, who I hope to someday call my daughter. You may not share our blood, but you definitely share our hearts.

To Owen, my sweet boy, you are the son I never knew I needed. I miss you so very much. Every day, in every way.

To Rocky, sweet girl, live free and wild and, if possible, I hope you will remember us.

To James Blevins, for finding a way for me to calculate distances using the handy, dandy, latitude/longitude distance calculator over at the National Hurricane Center. You were a lifesaver!

To Suzanne Rebecchi, for kindly helping with fraction conversions when my writer's brain was rejecting math. And kudos to Rebecca Liberty for showing the math.

For Dani, who likes every single one of my posts. I couldn't have a better fan and friend.

For Kerrie, for your proofreading and supportive words.

Thanks to all of you. I couldn't have done it without you!

Secret of Survival

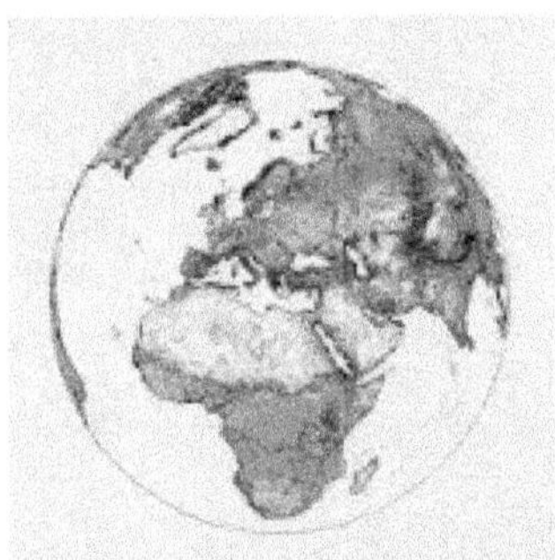

Earth, China's Ghizhou Province
02.08.2099

Before Dawn

In the pre-dawn darkness, Jia could hear sounds emanating from the tiny, cramped kitchen. Mama had always hated it, that kitchen, and it had surprised Jia that she hadn't wanted to move to Auntie's after she passed. Cheng had told them both that they could have it, and Jia couldn't understand why they had stayed in their tiny house. Cheng's house had been nearly twice as big, something that Xiao Wang had long coveted and envied her younger sister for having.

Jia had asked Mama and received no genuine answer. The older woman had simply muttered something about spirits and continued stuffing her face with greasy Chow Fun. She had forbidden any further discussion on the matter.

A sound of glass breaking blasted through the quiet and Jia jumped up. Mama had been acting weird, well, weirder than normal. Jia's phone lit up as she fumbled for it. It was earlier than she had initially thought, just after three in the morning. What was Mama doing up?

She slipped on her house shoes and reached for the wall to help guide her in the gloom. A light would be too bright, and she was far too tired to have it shining in her eyes. She hadn't fallen asleep until after one, anyway, what with the craziness that was going on outside and all around them. Her neighbors, people she had seen every day of her life for the past sixteen years, were acting as if possessed. There was a desperate hunger in their eyes as they devoured anything they could lay their hands on or fit into their mouths. It was like something out of a horror movie.

Seeing their next-door neighbor eating a rat, raw, had been the last straw for both Jia and Xiao. They had closed the doors and windows to the house, preferring the fetid, greasy air to that of the insanity beyond the house walls. Mama had locked the door, then insisted on moving the couch against it.

"Everyone has gone mad," she muttered, and then headed toward the kitchen to polish off the Xiao Long Bao that Jia had made for her the day before.

The recipe, doubled on Mama's request, should have lasted them for days. The large pot had been full to the brim of the tasty dumpling soup, enough to feed a family of five with leftovers. Instead, it had quickly disappeared; the bowls filling the tiny sink and then spilling onto the counter. Jia shook her head at the thought. Mama was eating like the neighbors, like the rest of Guiyang, as if it were a compulsion. Their cupboards were looking bare, and Jia dreaded having to shop later in the morning. She inched her way down the hallway, and rustling noises continued to guide her way.

Xiao Wang sat on the cracked and peeling linoleum floor, the refrigerator door wide open, lighting the small, dingy kitchen in a weak, yellow light. The sound of breaking glass had come from the jar of fish sauce on the door. It was now on the floor, shining, sharp shards mixed with the dark-brown liquid that had spread across the floor. Xiao looked up then, her eyes shiny and desperate. Food dribbled down her chin, her hands covered with fish sauce. She paused in mid-lick, her mouth working on swallowing the salty mess, throat convulsively swallowing.

"I'm so hungry, Jia, so hungry."

And with that, she reached into the puddle and pulled out a piece of glass covered in sauce. Jia screamed and ran forward to stop Mama, but she was too late. Into her mouth went the sharp glass shard. Blood sprayed from Xiao's mouth, and Jia looked at the few pieces of glass remaining, realizing with horror that it was far from the first piece her mother had swallowed.

Jia screamed.

The Road Out

Jia peered out of the window, her stomach rumbling, aching. It had been four days now and the world around her was silent. She had nearly fled her house hours after her mother died, a pool of blood slowly spreading from her mouth, her eyes sightless and staring. It had been mere minutes after the last piece of glass disappeared down Mama's throat. Xiao's hands had been remarkably strong as Jia had tried to pry a piece of jagged and sharp glass from her hand. Her blood had mingled with her mother's and she had screamed over and over as Xiao's body convulsed, her back arcing. Seconds later, the sound of her head slamming against the cracked and dirty floor had terrified Jia into a numbed silence. It had taken seconds, but each one had felt like an hour.

Jia had sat there by her mother's side, until the sun had risen and Xiao's blood had congealed, her body cold and rubbery to the touch. Outside, the bright morning sun had been at odds with the horrifying sights visible from the smudged glass window in the front door. Jia had kept the curtains drawn, and the door locked and blocked by the couch. On the first day after Mama's death, the door had shaken and cracked under the pounding of feet and hands. The heavy wooden couch in front of it, however, had held it closed. Whoever was on the other side eventually gave up and tried another house.

It happened repeatedly the first day, and the second. By the third day, as Jia sat in the gloomy living room, her stomach growling with hunger, there had only been one person who had tried to get in, a neighbor, one she knew slightly, a friend of Mama's. He had scrabbled at the door, called for Xiao, and cried. She had almost opened the door. She had stood up and grabbed the side of the couch to hoist it out of the way, when she heard his next words, "I'm just so hungry. So hungry."

Jia was hungry too. But it wasn't the same, and she knew it. Why did the virus not touch her? Before the newsvids had stopped transmitting live, the newscaster had described the virus in excruciating detail. The city outside was in a frenzy of consumption, desperate to put food into their hungry bellies, and finally, when the food was all gone, anything else that could fit into their mouths.

She had watched numbly as the newsvids showed Guiyang residents eating vegetation, small animals, even non-food objects, glass and metal, even chemicals. It made what Mama had done seem almost tame. She had sat there hunched in a chair, watching the newsvids until a stark black-and-white viral contagion symbol replaced them. Beneath the symbol, there were orders instructing everyone to stay inside.

She had stayed. The smell of Mama's corpse had grown, and the streets had been quiet, eerily so, for over twenty-four hours now.

Jia had slept poorly, there in the living room, unwilling to go into the kitchen and look for any scraps left from Mama's rummaging through the cupboards. The flies–how they had found their way inside a closed house was beyond her–were thick and buzzing. Jia could barely stand the smell. Her stomach roiled now, not just with hunger, but with nausea. She had to leave, had to find a way to food, to other survivors. If there were any. The silence was deafening. She had never felt more alone.

It was difficult to move the couch. She panted, straining to move it. Just days ago, with Mama helping her, of course, it had been easy. It was more than it being just her moving it, and Jia knew that.

If I don't get food soon, I'll die.

And despite her fear and terror at the thought of stepping into a city empty of inhabitants and life, the urge to survive took hold, and she heaved at the couch again, felt one leg catch on the worn wood floor and gouge a deep scratch in it. Mama would kill me if she saw that. And then she laughed. It was small, dry, and sounded as if it were someone else, someone unfamiliar. A bark of sound in the silence. Jia shook her head, and the movement caused the world to dance and spots of light to appear before her eyes. She strained, pushing again at the couch, and it moved away from the front door enough for her to slide behind it, unlock the locks, and open it. Jia pushed one last time, and the couch gave way, giving her enough space to slide through the opening and into the bright sunshine overhead.

She blinked, shading her eyes, and weaving slightly as she stood upright on the doorstep. The street was empty, preternaturally so. The small trees that dotted the tiny front lawns were devoid of leaves. Not a single leaf remained from the ground to over six feet in height. They looked odd, as if a mad landscaper had stripped them bare. A new aesthetic, perhaps, and Jia held back a hysterical laugh at the thought.

There was no sound, not a voice, not the twittering of birds, the sound of traffic, nothing. It was as if they had emptied the city of its inhabitants, but worse, stripped it of every animal and plant as well. She walked down her block, past another, the sickly-sweet smell of rot the only constant. She saw bodies then, scattered, lying where they had fallen, eyes staring. Jia swallowed down nausea, sick at the sight of death at every turn. It took an hour for her to reach Hequn Road and when she did, she wished she had gone some other way. The road was littered with bodies, the open-air market where she had loved to share a bowl of Hot Pot with Cheng before he had left for Hong Kong or where she and Mama would shop for the week's meals in tatters and bodies lay among destroyed stalls, pots, and thick clouds of flies.

It was here, however, that she found other survivors. Hollow-eyed and unsmiling, she joined them as they left the city, stumbling as they moved away from the city and into the countryside. In the countryside, there was little food to be found. The fields were stripped bare. As day faded to night, Jia and a group of other survivors captured, cooked, and ate a goat from the remains of a farm. She felt slightly guilty as she sat by the fire and crammed down bites of the poorly cooked meat.

The family that had worked this land were dead, their corpses swollen and rotting in a field 200 meters away.

As her hunger pangs subsided, Jia and the others watched jets streaking across the sky. They stared as each of the aircraft dropped their deadly cargo and enormous explosions lit up the sky. Beside her, a young man stared at the fire blooming in a column in the sky.

"They're too late to stop it. Everyone is dead."

"We're not," Jia said, softly.

"We might as well be. They will shoot us on sight, I think." He shook his head. "They're too late. Far too late. All that's left are the dead."

Two Years Later

"Just a pinch, now, Jia." The technician's face was round, kind. "Folks tell me I'm the best at this." She slid the needle into Jia's skin and released the flexible tubing.

Jia watched as the blood filled the ampules with a thick red froth. "What do you hope to find?" She said it haltingly. English was still new, and she had been struggling to learn the language for nearly eight months now, ever since she had arrived with other ESH survivors to the new city of New Athens.

The woman smiled at her. "You are a rarity, Jia. And we are just doing some genetic testing to find out your profile and see why you, and not any of your other family, survived the virus. AB negative blood in the Asian population is incredibly rare, less than one in one thousand have it."

She filled a second and the third ampule. "We will do a full profile and you can pick up the results tomorrow if you like."

Jia nodded, smiling tentatively in return. "Yes, thank you."

The next day she returned, struggling to remember the words in English to describe what she needed. "I ah, I pick up, um, the..." The woman manning the front desk stared at her and Jia felt embarrassed.

"Ah, Jia! I see you returned for your lab results." It was the kind technician, the one who had taken such care the day before. She had been right; she was one of the best the med center had. The blood draw hadn't hurt a bit. "Come in, come in!"

Jia heaved a sigh of relief and followed her into a small office.

The woman pointed at a chair. "Sit, please. I want to talk with you a moment." She waited until Jia sat down and then sat in the chair opposite and handed Jia several sheets of paper. "What can you tell me about your father?"

"My father? He died five, no, six years ago now. We were not close." Jia toed her chair rung. "I am sorry, I should not say that."

The woman nodded thoughtfully. "You noted here that your parents were both full-blooded Chinese."

Jia nodded, confused. "Yes, of course. Why?"

"Well, according to these results, Jia, your father was not Chinese. He was of European descent, probably from Germany or possibly Austria." She tapped the bottom of the first page. "Those genetic markers right there are quite clear. You are only half-Chinese, which means the secret to your survival was in your genetic heritage. I'm sure your father was an AB blood type, and if so, he may have survived the virus. Have you logged into the Survivor Network yet?"

Jia blinked at her, at a loss for what to say. Bao Wang was not her father? How was this possible? She opened her mouth, then closed it. The words in her head were all in Mandarin, not English. She had no idea what to say.

The woman looked concerned. "I am so sorry, Jia. I didn't think about how shocking this would be for you!" She put a hand on Jia's shoulder and squeezed it lightly. "Look, if you need anything, the Survivor Network can help. Not only is it a way to reconnect with family, but it also provides counseling and support groups for people who are still struggling with our new reality. I hope you will consider signing up and taking advantage of the services. Who knows, you might even find him."

"Find...him?" Jia's voice sounded hesitant, stretched.

"Your father." She smiled. "After all this, wouldn't that be a miracle?"

Jia walked from the Med Center in a scattered fog, her mind replaying moments of her childhood on a fast loop of memories. Her mother and father fighting, his staring at her with something akin to hatred, and him never, ever holding her or loving her. She had seen other fathers with their daughters. Her friends had loved their fathers, and their fathers had obviously loved them in return. But hers? She had never understood it and, even now she felt traitorous and unworthy even thinking it, it had been a relief when he had passed. His absence from their home had allowed it to feel less like living in an enemy camp and more like a home, even if Mama did not understand her or her dreams.

She stared at the papers in her hand, shocked at her new reality. Her father wasn't her father. Her father, the only one she had known, the one who lay in a casket in the ground thousands of miles away, wasn't her biological father. So... what? Mama had an affair? Just imagining it was mind-boggling.

She walked back to the comfortable suite of rooms assigned to her in the large apartment block on the west end of New Athens. Here she was alone, free to decorate the walls in a way she saw fit, and eat and live how she wanted. It was such a far cry from living with Mama in Guiyang or in the internment camps that she had found herself in. Around her, China had dissolved into civil war, slowly tearing the corpse of what had been the largest nation on Earth into tiny, worn, and tattered pieces.

It had taken over eighteen months before she had qualified to go to the Reformed United States of America.

She sat down on the couch and poured herself some tea as she stared at the papers the woman had given her. There was the website too, scribbled in the margin. A few taps on her tablet and she had pulled up the Survivor Network.

She blinked as the screen splashed a message of welcome and prompted her to enter her information. She typed it in and clicked the Search button.

Jia held her breath, hoping for it to match her with someone just as much as she hoped it wouldn't.

A moment later, it chimed softly with a match. Her genetic profile, listed in a standard identifier on the papers the technician had given her, had found a match in the system and it displayed a photo next to the details. He lived in New Munich, the report listed, and he had allowed his genetic profile and contact info to be shared with any potential genetic matches. Did that mean he had been looking for her? Possibly? Probably. She sucked in a breath and let it out slowly.

A question appeared on the screen: "Notify Genetic Match?" She could log out now, walk away, and never have to talk to him, never meet him. Her finger hovered over the button, hesitating.

Jia clicked it. He was, after all, the secret of her survival.

I hope you enjoyed the first chapter of G581: Earth. I hope to release this book in late summer, early fall of 2021.

About the Author

Fueled by homemade coffee ice cream, a lifelong love of words, and armed with strong female (and male) characters I cross genres like the Ghostbusters crossed the streams in pursuit of the question.

"What is the question?" you ask.

The question is simple. It asks, "What would you do, if..."

What would you do if you were fifteen years old and the world as you knew it fell apart? Would you run? Would you fight? Would you survive? – Meet Jess and her brother Chris in War's End[1].

What would you do if you had a chance to live your life over? Not just once, but twice? – Meet Dean Edmonds in Fate's Highway[2].

What would you do if everyone you loved was lost to a terrible virus and you faced the real possibility of the extinction of the human race in the dark void of space? – Meet Daniel Medry in G581: The Departure[3]

What would you do if hitmen were after you and you had no idea why? – Meet Lila and Shane in Hired Gun[4]

If I don't keep you turning pages late into the night, desperate to know what happens next, then I have failed at my job. I'm a Taurus and born in Missouri. That makes me bull-headed and stubborn to boot. I don't believe in failure or mistakes, only learning opportunities and clever conversation. There's not much I won't do to make you burn the midnight oil reading my words while you suffer sleep-deprivation the following day. It's my secret superpower.

Born in flyover country, I've also lived in Arizona and northern California. I am an eclectic mix of snark and oddball humor. My colorful metaphors would make a fishwife blush. I'm an incompetent gardener, a dreamer and doer, in love with old houses and shooting pool, and chief organizer of all thing's household and financial. Feed me tiramisu and I'm yours forever.

---

1. https://books2read.com/u/bwYNpY
2. https://books2read.com/u/bPJG5Y
3. https://books2read.com/u/4jDgPl
4. https://books2read.com/u/bP0dOj

Join my Facebook group at General Malcontent's Grumbles and Scribbles: http://bit.ly/3jo0MVU

You can also find the latest updates on my writing adventures at: http://christineshuck.com

Sign up for my newsletter at: https://mailchi.mp/c05ceb84e66a/subscribe-me

Follow me at:

Twitter: @christineshuck

Facebook: Christine.D.Shuck

Instagram: christinedshuck

All Published Works

Christine writes cross-genre and her books can be found in e-book and in paperback through most book distributors.

Non-Fiction:

Get Organized, Stay Organized – 2008

The War on Drugs: An Old Wives Tale – 2012

Fiction Series:

War's End

The Storm

A Brave New World

Tales of the Collapse

Gliese 581g

G581: The Departure

G581: Mars

G581: Earth (Summer 2021)

G581: Zarmina's World (Spring 2022)

Chronicles of Liv Rowan

Fate's Highway a.k.a. Schicksal Turnpike

Benton Security Services

Hired Gun

Smoke and Steel (Spring 2021)

Broken Code (Fall 2021)

Don't miss out!

Visit the website below and you can sign up to receive emails whenever Christine D. Shuck publishes a new book. There's no charge and no obligation.

https://books2read.com/r/B-A-BOLF-FTHLB

BOOKS 2 READ

Connecting independent readers to independent writers.

www.ingramcontent.com/pod-product-compliance
Lightning Source LLC
Chambersburg PA
CBHW070635310726
48982CB00001B/284

* 9 7 8 0 9 8 2 0 0 5 1 7 0 *